CLAYTON COUNTY LIBRARY
865 Battlecreek Road
Jonesboro, Ga 30236

THE HEROIN FACTOR

by

JAMES MCEACHIN

The Rharl Publishing Group
PMB 550, 16161 Ventura Boulevard, Encino, CA 91436-2523
rharlpub@aol.com

Rharl and Colophon
are registered trademarks of
the Rharl Publishing Group

Printed and bound in the United States of America
Library of Congress Catalog Card Number: 98-68156

1 3 5 7 9 10 8 6 4 2

ISBN 0-9656661-4-X
CIP data available

This book is a work of fiction. Names, characters, and
incidents are the product of the author's imagination or
used fictitiously. Any resemblance to actual events,
or persons, living or dead, is coincidental.

Printed on acid-free paper

"Ater you take that first hit, you don't care what you're doing. You take a second, and God himself doesn't care. After that, both your will and your mind are gone. The monkey is on your back, and nobody but nobody knows what an addict will do."

Wyatt W. McKnight

Acknowledgments:

My family,
and especially my daughter, Felecia.

Charles Blackwell
David B. Charnay
Dennis & Molly Fredrickson
Bob Garon
Dean Hargrove
Robert Juran
Bill Link
Bart Ryan
Russ Sarno
William Spillard

I am indebted to
Johanna Morrison

*Not poppy, nor mandragora, nor all the drowsy
syrups of the world shall ever medicine thee to
that sweet sleep which thou owedst yesterday.*

William Shakespeare
Othello, Act 3, Scene 3.

1

He stood there in the rain trying to puff on the butt of a soaked cigarette with shaking hands. His memory had been shattered, and swirling around a bankrupt mind was the phrase: *Please don't die.*

It was shortly before 4:30 a.m., and downtown Los Angeles had not done a very good job of tucking itself away for the night. Because of the fish and produce markets only a few blocks away, traffic still rumbled by and the homeless still wandered around aimlessly. Those who had concern about the rain found shelter in alleys and doorways or snaked inside soggy cardboard boxes they had fashioned into mini-quarters. Diagonally across the street from where he was standing there was a giant Buddha that towered in the yard of a Korean church. From his room on the third floor there in a drug rehabilitation facility that was racked by neglect, the few times when he was able to think clearly he used to gaze down at the Buddha.

Last night the Buddha had gazed back. It was made of stone.

The two detectives parked at curbside continued their wait. When he first shuffled out from the building, Devro, the chunky black one, rolled the vehicle's window down and hollered, "Hey, we're over here, Lieutenant."

Seeing that he wasn't going to move, Devro started to holler out again.

From behind the wheel, Kiesner, his German companion motioned for him not to. From the way the man looked he thought they would have to get out and escort him to the car. "And don't forget, Devro," Kiesner said, "he's a captain now."

It was a very sick man they were talking about.

Mentally he was in and out. When he was in, he was troubled. When he was out, he was a wreck. He suffered emotional turmoil, delusion, and confusion. A police psychiatrist described his condition as a type of schizophrenia. Its subtitle: Brief Psychotic Disorder. An episode lasted a day; the longest was a month.

He had been that way for a year.

His fall had been long and hard, and for that year he had carried his illness from the hospital to various rehabilitation facilities and back again. He showed no signs of full recovery. The question remained: Would he ever come back? His two subordinates waiting in the car believed he would. The department didn't know. Moreover, the department wasn't concerned.

The Los Angeles Police Department had its reasons.

Long before his fall, he was not a well-liked policeman. He was not known for keeping his views to himself. Most of the whites in his division considered him a racist. Most of the blacks thought he was aloof. He was neither. He was a veteran of the dark streets of Los Angeles, and he was therefore angry.

He had been in the department twenty-eight years; a lieutenant for nine. Before his illness he had passed the test for the rank of captain, coming in first on the list. He was not interested in the rank.

He was dark; six feet, two inches; smoked too much, not a specimen of good health, didn't watch his diet, and worked out only occasionally. He had been working in narcotics eight years. He worked alone. He preferred it that way.

It was exactly a year ago, on the night of June 25, when he had been summoned to the chief of detectives' home. It was Friday; the weather typical. The call came in at nine. At eleven he was still thinking about it. He wasn't feeling well to begin with, and now his captain was pulling him off a job and he didn't like it. The captain didn't like him. Equality was working. He didn't like the captain.

Midnight, and the detective was on his way to the captain's house. It was a bland little cookie-cutter nestled in the heart of Northridge. Northridge was suburbia at work. Chartered in the '40s, raised in the '50s, and spanked by a 6.7 earthquake in the '90s, it was located in the northwest section of the San Fernando Valley. On a fast drive it was twenty-two minutes from the hustle and bustle of downtown Los Angeles. The distance made for good neighbors. The blacks were at arm's length, the Mexicans hadn't invaded, and the median income topped the fifty-thousand mark.

The captain saw the car when it drove up. He should have. He had been planted in the window for over an hour, his already fierce eyes steaming. Herman Ault was his name. He was a short, bald, uncouth man with no racial tolerance. Once while relieving himself in the Whitehurst division john he referred to the urinal as an NAACP blood bank. There were no blacks in the department around when he said it. Had they heard it, they would not have taken the matter upstairs. They would have provided their own discipline. One in particular would have come close to killing him. He was the one the captain was waiting on. His name was McKnight, Wyatt W.

The stumpy man, who had a face that looked as if it had been molded in concrete, waited for the graying black man to walk up the walkway. When he threw away a cigarette he had been puffing on and granted a reluctant foot permission to touch the first step, the captain withdrew from the curtains where he had been waiting. He would choose not to ask why it had taken over two hours for his subordinate to show up. Instead, he tightened his bathrobe and stepped out the door, saying, "The wife just had the carpets cleaned."

The black man knew it was a lie. The white man didn't want him in his house. It was fine with the black man. Being in the company of a bigot was bad; being in his home was puke-inducing.

Captain Ault was swift and really wasn't concerned about an answer. He leveled an eye. "What about the Dinaldi operation?"

"I've got tabs on everything."

"What's that supposed to mean?"

"It means I know who's pushing where, distribution points and pickups." McKnight started to reach for his handkerchief. He stopped.

The captain caught it. Suspicions growing, he said, "And?"

"The stuff is coming in through an import/export furniture dealership on Figueroa. The owners and operators are the Fortmullers, Gail and Matt, a good couple gone wrong. I can give you more details, but I'm sure that's not why I'm here."

"You're here because you were told to be here."

"You snatched me off a job."

"I know that."

There was nothing said for a moment. The reason why nothing was said was that the captain was still hard-eyeing. And he was burning inside. The tension was obvious. The stumpy man finally spoke. "They scraped LeCoultre's body from a ditch. He was murdered. I received word at 8:17, a few minutes after it happened. Looks like he was pumped through the car window and chewed up by a dog."

"Sounds rough."

"Murder always is. A cop's is even worse. Double it if it's one of mine."

"Was the dog in the car?"

"How should I know? I wasn't there."

"Where'd they find him?"

"In the Valley?"

"Whereabouts in the Valley, Captain?"

"Encino."

"That narrows it down to how many square miles?"

Suppressing the urge to order the man off the property, the captain said, "He was in a hotshot car near that Park & Ride thing on Hayvenhurst. Near the Sepulveda Dam."

"Where was his partner?"

"If you'd read the board, you'd know LeCoultre was on the second week of a three-week vacation." Ault shoved a piece of paper into the black man's hand. It read: "His last words: *Can harm.*"

McKnight scanned it. "I don't get it."

"Neither did the Highway Patrolman who found him."

The detective looked closer at the small, notebook-size paper. The writing was scribbled. "What is this 'his last words'?"

"Can't you read? Or hear? I just said they were his last words. The Highway Patrolman wrote Sergeant Verneau B. LeCoultre's last words down on paper. Notebook paper. Presumably with a pen. A ballpoint pen. The words were: *Can harm.* According to him, that's what he *thought* the idiot said before he died. And to make matters worse, again, according to the Highway Patrolman, it looked as though he hadn't crapped, shaved or bathed in a month of Sundays. Your job is to find out why."

"Check it, Captain. Murder is homicide's job. I'm in narcotics."

"I'm chief of detectives, I know what you're in. Or maybe I should say, what you're into. But if you're telling me you're not going to accept an assignment, I'll hang you out to dry."

"Put it on ice, Captain. You know I've only got thirteen days before I hang it up. Try reading my disability report. It's on your desk. It's on your desk because you are chief of detectives. As chief of detectives, you make the assignments."

"That's what a chief is paid to do."

"Well, let's go back and check the records to see what your pay has led you to do to me."

"You're a W10. Your assignments have been as good as anybody else's. If not better."

"Somebody on this porch has a defective memory. From day one, under your command, I've been mired in the ghetto, chasing junkies, pushers, hopheads and assorted crud, all while the more privileged under you weren't doing much more than waiting for the change of seasons."

"That's your version."

"It's not a version. It's fact. Now, let me finish. Because I happen to remember one night in particular. I needed a backup, and I needed him in a hurry. And who did you send? This same peanut-brain who not only needed a road map to find South Central, but wouldn't get out of the car when he got there. And the results? I got the left one shot off. But don't you or the department worry about it, I have the remains. Home. Pickled in a jar. Thirteen days, Captain. And the clock is running."

"First of all, you're talking about something that happened years ago. And if you're still bent out of shape because your testicle was hurt and your night life shortened, that's your problem. Not mine. LeCoultre was a cop, just like you. If he arrived late and didn't get the job done, you should have taken it up with the chief. Not me. Now, I don't have time to stand out here in the middle of the night, arguing about something you're still boiling over. I know you're going out, and to be frank about it, I'll be glad when you do. You're a pain. But you ought to cool your heels long enough to consider something. I can arrange it so that you can go out with full pay. How? Don't ask. You just handle the case. Leave the rest to me."

"You can't make that deal."

"City Hall can."

"I don't trust City Hall."

"I do."

"I don't trust *you*."

"I'll put it in writing."

"Witnessed and on my desk by 9 a.m.?"

"Six p.m. The end of the working day."

"And no later."

"And no later," the captain confirmed. "Now, who do you want with you? And don't say nobody."

"Then I'll take the next person to it. Devro."

"He's in robbery."

"From the looks of this place, so are you."

"Wyatt William, you're a goddamn cynic. And it's that same cynical attitude that keeps me hoping you never make captain."

"Herman," McKnight said, not appreciating being called by his middle name, "I'm sure it's not my cynicism alone. Now, who do you want on the case with me?"

"Whatsisname. The German. That kraut who's over here under the pretense of *method-learning* and *international goodwill,* whatever the hell that is. He's probably a goddamn Commie, selling secrets to the Russians."

"The Russians are no longer a threat, in case you haven't heard."

"I don't need you to tell me that," huffed Ault.

McKnight maintained his composure. "What's the story behind the case?"

"LeCoultre had a problem. The Highway Patrolman who found him said there were enough tracks on his arms to run a train."

"If he was on *horse,* he was a *junkie.*"

"I don't need you to tell me that either. And besides, no one but a relic uses the word horse. Or junkie. That kind of talk went out with high-button shoes."

"I'm glad I'm following suit."

"I can't wait. The sooner the better," the captain flatly agreed, then muttered through tightened jaws, "Imagine, a goddamn addict in the police department, as if we didn't have enough problems."

"I don't see why you're surprised. This is the LAPD. You've got every other kind of loser in here."

"You need to be in counseling, you know that, Lieutenant?" the captain responded harshly, for the first time calling him by rank. He came back to LeCoultre. "And keep this thing hush-hush. A case like this could give the department a bad name."

"Give the LAPD a bad name? You're a funny man, Captain."

"Don't get cute, McKnight."

The detective opened his mouth to respond, and didn't. He started to reach for his handkerchef, changed up, and patted for a cigarette. He thought better of it, and said, "I'm still a little confused about something. A cop's been shot. A detective sergeant. It's been a couple of hours ago. Why isn't there a team assigned to it? And how're you going to keep it hush-hush with all the media around?"

"We've held off the hounds before. We can do it again. As to a team, it'll be done. After you do the prelims."

"Why not assign it to homicide now? If word gets out that a cop was murdered and you've only assigned a single…"

Ault wouldn't let him finish. "Don't you ever *think*? Verneau LeCoultre was on *horse*; he was a *junkie*. Your words. He became a 'junkie' on 'horse,' if you can say such a thing, by using narcotics. LeCoultre was also a policeman. A detective sergeant. Common sense should tell you that if a detective sergeant was a hophead on the job, somebody else on the department could be involved. The last thing we need after the heat we've been taking from that so-called trial-of-the-century fiasco is the public coming down on the department again."

"We've had a couple of trials of the century. Which one are you referring to?"

"That modern-day version of the Scopes Monkey Trial, with that nip on the bench."

"You'd better watch your mouth, Captain."

"You threatening me, Lieutenant?"

"I'm advising you, Captain."

Ault turned to go back into the house. "Get on it, and get back to me as soon as possible." He stopped. "Oh. And notify the son of a bitch's wife."

"You make me glad I've never married."

"You were," answered the captain. "To the department. When you used to be good."

"You're blowing smoke again, Captain. It makes me think it might not be a bad idea for you to call the chief while I'm here and tell him what the deal is."

"C'mon. The man's way over in Hawaii at the police chiefs' convention. And he's staying over there for a couple of extra days."

"The area code for the Ili Kai is 848."

"What's that supposed to mean?"

"It means that the Ili Kai is a hotel in Hawaii with a telephone. The chief is in that hotel in Hawaii with a telephone. You can call the chief on the telephone at that hotel in Hawaii. Again."

"What do you mean 'again'?"

"I'm sure you called him before to tell him of the demise of one of his officers."

Ault bit on it for a moment. "How would you know what the area code for Hawaii is?"

"Maybe I'm part Hawaiian."

The captain simply did not like the man or his black skin. He glared at him for a long moment, and went back inside to make the call.

The weary detective had been standing on the first step for the better part of the conversation. Handkerchief out, he moved up and held by the door. He could hear the captain as he dialed the numbers. The voice was deliberate; gruffly obvious. "Area code 1-848. Telephone number 603 da-da-da-da. ....Chief Verler of the LAPD's suite. ....Chief...? Captain Ault. Sorry to wake you. Listen, Chief, I've got Lieutenant McKnight here. He's been looking a little hollow and burned-out lately — and that tells me something, but I'm assigning him the LeCoultre case.... I'm glad you agree, sir. Now, as you know, Mac has less than two weeks to go before that disability. ...What was that, Chief? ...Right, he is a damned good man, and we'll all be sorry when he goes. It'll be a helluva loss. You'll be glad to hear I've just worked out a deal with him, since he's our primo man in narcotics. Now the way I see it, LeCoultre probably burned somebody in the ghetto and was popped in the Valley. I promised Mac that if he'd get on it and wrap it up as quickly and quietly as possible... Huh? ...And that's exactly what I told him: We gotta play it close to the vest. And if he does that, I told him we'd see to it that he goes out with full pay. And with lots of honors. ...You do agree? Right. And as you say, it is the least we can do for a man who has dedicated his life to law enforcement. Thank you, Chief. ...I'll pass that along. ....Bring some of that good Hawaiian sunshine with you when you get back." Apparently the chief said something that amused the captain. He guffawed and hung up.

He came back outside to the lieutenant. "You heard the call. It's all set. And I hope you noticed I went out of my way to praise you."

"That's fine, Captain," said McKnight. "But the next time you dial Hawaii, try using the correct area code. I suddenly remember: It's 808. Not 848."

From the molded-looking, carbon-copy homes in Northridge to the Park & Ride lot on Hayvenhurst near Magnolia in Encino it was less than a sixteen-minute drive. Despite the captain's assertion of wanting to keep the case on a low-profile note, there was still a fair amount of activity when McKnight arrived. The stringers had been kept away, and the tow truck was just pulling out with the vehicle LeCoultre had been driving. McKnight didn't get a good look at it as it slowly pulled away from a street lamp, but it was easy to tell that the car had rolled over once. It was new: A Jag, XJS; wine-red. It had no license plates.

The Highway Patrolman who had originally scratched out the wording on the notebook paper Ault had given McKnight was still there. He was talking with a photographer and two men from the mop-up detail when McKnight came over and introduced himself, flashing his badge. With monotone efficiency, the Highway Patrolman explained that LeCoultre had been shot, and that he had been in the car alone. The car, traveling in a southerly direction, had jumped the curb, crashed through the chain-link fence and veered over in what amounted to a catch basin. He had not been wearing a seatbelt, and the body had been thrown from the car. The policeman went on to explain that, judging from the heat of the engine at the time he had arrived, LeCoultre had either been driving for a long period of time or had been driving at an excessive speed.

In answer to the question as to how he had happened upon the scene, the patrolman said he had been flagged by a motorist who saw the car as it was going over. It had been seconds earlier.

McKnight noticed a syringe that had apparently been dropped as the body was being dragged from the car. Using his hankerchief, he picked the syringe up, gave it a quick look, and in reference to the note, asked, "Where'd you come up with: ....*Can harm?*"

"I didn't have time to write anything officially," answered the patrolman. "When I saw the car from the roadway there, I was afraid it was about to go up in flames, so I dragged the body as far away from the car as I could. In the process, he started muttering something. I quickly grabbed my notebook and started scribbling. I thought whatever he said might be significant." McKnight then asked him if there were any cars around when he first came on the scene. "No," replied the Highway Patrolman. He went on to repeat that the only car he had encountered in the area was the one whose driver had flagged him. It was driven by a woman who continued north on Hayvenhurst.

McKnight digested all that was said, then looked at the paper again. "*Can harm*," he repeated thoughtfully. "Lemme hear how he said it again?"

"Well, that's just it. I'm not positive he said *can harm*. Could've been something else."

"Okay, start it from the top again."

"Well, as I said, he'd been tossed out of the car..."

"Holding on to the stash, you said."

"Right. And a needle. Same as you got there. He was holdin' on to it as tight as he could. I had his wallet which showed a badge. I removed his I.D, and asked him to verify his name and that he was a cop by blinking the eyes. He did. I started to move away and he kinda said something like: *"Can harm."*

"Again."

"Can harm."

"One more time," said McKnight, pocketing the syringe and positioning his ear close to the Highway Patrolman's mouth. "Say it the exact way he did."

"H-annnn haarmmmz."

"Are you using a 'z' or an 's' on the end of that?"

"No, sir."

McKnight didn't appreciate the idea of having to make the notification of death to LeCoultre's wife. First, it was not policy; next, if the captain wanted it done, he should have done it himself. Of course, knowing Eve LeCoultre, no matter who told her, it was not going to have much of an effect. She was not expected to play the role of the grieving widow. There would be no tears.

McKnight had met the woman before. Several times. As with her husband, they had never hit it off from the start. The last time he had seen her was at another of those long-winded, rah-rah, gung-ho police functions that he loathed to attend. That night, like the few others, he should have stayed at home. After the speeches and drinks, the cops started acting as juvenile as ever.

Vern and Eve had missed the speeches, but they came in fighting drunk, made up, stood on the chairs, danced on the tables, drank more, got mad again, and were still stumbling and cursing each other long after the affair was over. On the road home they were stopped because Eve, supposedly the soberest of the two, was operating the vehicle as though it had been manufactured by the maker of M-27 tanks. She hit more vehicles than the troops did in Beirut. Fortunately, she was stopped. Stopped, but not arrested. A drunken LeCoultre waved his badge at his brother-in-arms, and that was it — for the moment. Pulling away, Eve managed to uproot a fire hydrant.

Despite an intriguing name, wasted because neither of the two were French, Eve and Vern had been stuck with perennially sad, droopy faces. Born in nearby Pasadena, they looked more like brother and sister than husband and wife. Both of them sounded, acted, and looked as though they had been conceived during a hurricane.

Vern was redneck-ugly, and Eve was a skinny, caustic-mouthed, bottle-haired blonde with discolored roots and legs that gave silk stockings a hard time. She spent her off-hours in a squatty little Burbank bar called the Peanut House. For work, she masqueraded as a receptionist at one of the sedate downtown stock-brokerage houses. With her profane mouth and lack of responsibility and/or respectability, McKnight had often wondered how she got the job.

On her knees, somebody said.

Although he knew better, the detective thought he would try her at home before going to the bar.

It was 1:12 a.m. when he arrived. Dabney, the 12-year-old son who should have been in bed hours ago, was anything but a clean-cut youngster. He was wasting time in the second-floor window. Because of the nearby street light, he saw McKnight when he climbed out of the vehicle and headed to the door. He waited until the visitor was close enough to knock, took a final snort of coke from a wrapper, rolled it up and tossed it down. McKnight saw the tiny ball as it landed near his feet, but he ignored it. He looked up. "Is your mother in?"

"Is yours?"

The detective didn't say anything. He simply looked at the boy and tried to decide which of the two did he remind him of: The mother or the father. He was a nice-looking kid, and didn't look like either. Passing on the thought that wasn't his business, he asked: "Where's your mother, kid?"

"Out."

"Out *where*?"

"Probably in th' back seat of a car. Takin' care of business, if you get my drift."

It was sad to hear a kid talk like that, but having been raised under the influence of Eve and Vern, it was not surprising. Nothing he could say or do; the detective turned to head back to his car. The boy called back down, and said with challenge: "You know what was in that wrapper?"

"The end of your life, if you don't stop using it," McKnight answered as he continued to walk away without turning.

"Hey, cop. You here about my dad?"

McKnight wouldn't respond.

"Betcha are. Otherwise you wouldn't be here," said the kid. "What'd somebody do, stick a blade through his ribs?"

This was a boy talking about his father. The policeman winced inside. He couldn't help it. It stung him again. This was a *young kid*, talking about his own father. But again, the lieutenant didn't say anything.

"Figgers," said the boy. "Sooner or later all creeps get what they deserve. Includin' you."

The Peanut House was on Alameda, down from scrawny-looking NBC Studios, and about an eleven-minute drive from Eve's house. It was an out-and-out dive. Multi-colored neon lights flickered through tiered shelves and winked through smoke-covered glasses, and settled on two large barrels of roasted peanuts. Trash receptacles were nowhere to be found. The floor was the depository. It was thick with slippery crushed peanut shells, and, even at that hour, the hard-hat crowd was still going strong.

When the detective entered, he made an attempt to bypass two inconveniently placed pool tables that did everything but make a smooth entrance possible.

At one of the tables, one of the players, a giant of a man with a metal, claw-like hook serving as a hand, threw an eye on the black man, downed a Coors, and said to the others, "I see they bussin' 'em into bars now."

It got the desired response from the crowd. They laughed and snickered.

McKnight was unruffled. He eased into the big man's face. "Is that your best shot?"

"You just came in. You haven't seen me shootin' anything."

"I was referring to your sense of humor."

"Well, in that case, it wasn't my best. Would you like to see my best?"

"Don't cheat yourself."

"I'll try not to," said the one-armed man. He manufactured a sneeze that deliberately sprayed the black man's face. "S'cuse me," he grinned.

McKnight didn't move. Coolly, he reached for his handkerchief and dabbed at his face. "Let me advise you. They say I'm a cop with an attitude. I'm not up to snuff; I'm carrying a .44 Magnum. The nearest morgue is 2.6 miles away. You might have a cold, but try that again and you might be refrigerated."

The hook called his bluff by sneezing again. The spray was thicker. McKnight did nothing. The hook, as if to prove a point, took his time and rubbed the metal claw against the black man's spit-pitted face. "Look at this," he laughed. "Even with spit the color don't rub off."

There was still no action from the detective. With the patrons looking on more intently and a few set for action, McKnight gave the man a final look and quietly moved over to the bar where Eve LeCoultre was sitting. The crowd was disappointed. A few even called out some choice words. All were racially derogatory.

Eve, tilting a glass to her lips, had witnessed the action, or lack of action, and turned her back to him, facing the bar. Despite the new anti-smoking law, her ashtray was running over. Feeling his presence, and before McKnight could open his mouth, she lit a non-filtered Camel from the butt of another and said huskily, "I hope I never need a cop when you're around. Or a man. What a joke. I've never seen anybody like you. Somebody spits in your face, and you walk away. And you're supposed to be a lieutenant? God help us all. You're an embarrassment."

"May I see you for a moment?"

"Anything you have to say to me can be said right here."

McKnight leaned in. "I think it'd be better in private."

"If you've got anything to say to me, say it here or keep it to yourself. I'm not going anywhere with you. I'm embarrassed enough just sitting here with you in my face."

With a cue under his arm, the hook came over. He was crushing a peanut with his claw. "Is he botherin' you, Shugga?"

For the first time, she turned. "You ever know a nigga who didn' bother somebody?" The bottle-haired blonde with the bad roots and worse legs coughed again. "But I can handle 'im."

The hook laughed and moved away. "Holler if you need help."

"'K," said Eve. She made the already bad habit of smoking seem even worse by taking another puff. She tried to keep the smoke and another cough in her lungs by capping them with a drink.

McKnight promised himself he'd quit the obscene habit of smoking in a week. "I don't want you to 'go' anywhere, Eve. I merely want to tell you something in private."

"Say it here, or sy-yo-nara."

"It's about your husband."

"My *estranged* husband," she corrected with a cough.

"Okay, your *estranged* husband," McKnight said. He was still hoping for a change in attitude.

"And what about 'im?"

"He's dead."

"You ain't just whistlin' Dixie he's dead. I used to sleep with the sonofabitch. I know how dead he is."

"Eve, tonight Vern was killed."

"Was he killed in the line of duty?"

"Honorably."

"You lyin' ass," said Eve. "He didn't have no honor."

"Doesn't make any difference now, does it? He's dead."

"Pardon me while I brush away a tear."

"I was hoping you'd be at home, so I went by the house to make the notification."

"Hope you didn't scare the neighbors when you showed up."

"I tried not to," McKnight said tolerantly. "Your son told me you'd be here."

"I'm surprised he was home."

"Strange, a lot of children are home and are asleep at that hour," answered McKnight. "It was, after all, after 1 a.m."

"Big deal," Eve said dismissively. She took another drink. "Did you keep pokin' your nose in my business and tell 'im that his dad was dead?"

"No, I didn't. I felt I should leave that to his very sensitive and caring mother."

She was angered by the remark. "You'd better get the hell out of here while the gettin' is good."

"Which means you don't care to talk about your husband?"

"Which means I don't 'care' to talk to you about nothin'."

"Then consider the notification made," the detective said. He prepared to leave. "Before I go, Eve, a word about your son…"

She stopped him. "The only thing you can say to me about *my* son is that he is *my* son. An' I don't need a you-know-who to tell me a damned thing about him. An' notice I didn't say *nigga.* I'm a lady."

"And all class," concluded McKnight.

Cold. He left her. On the way out he stopped at a wall socket that was just to the right of the sputtering Coors beer sign. With care he unholstered his .44 Magnum, took the butt of the gun and tapped on the once-yellow plastic plate, browned by smoke and grit. He tapped lightly on it until the wires were exposed. With his keys, he unloosened one of the wires and pulled it out even further. With everyone's attention on him, he re-holstered the weapon and strolled over to the man with the hook. He looked him over. The hook glared back. That was his second mistake. Before he knew what was happening, the detective had him by the arm, and, like a dance, spun him around and sent the man's big back slamming against the wall. The metal hand shot up, then, sliding downward against the wall, the metal points of the clawlike hook touched the exposed wires, killing the lights and flooring him. He was out.

The detective's departure was wearily casual. He was sweating a bit. Diarrhea was a problem, and small abdominal cramps nibbled at his insides. He had all the symptoms of the flu. The trouble was, he had never contracted the bug.

The lieutenant stood under the bar's light for a moment, thinking about the man inside. What he had done to him was sufficient. But had he been his old self, he would have done more

He lit a cigarette and called the paramedics from his car. He knew the man wasn't dead. He also knew that it was one white man who would never spit in a black man's face again.

2

Morning. Los Angeles was throbbing. The freeways were crowded, and in the air, pollution was on the rise. On the airwaves, even though it was almost three years after the conclusion of the trial that his captain had referred to, the pollution was just as bad.

The "verdict" was still burning and dividing. It was no longer a matter of the just vs. the unjust. It was the lunacy of race. As with past nights of late, McKnight had not enjoyed a good night's sleep, and listening to the morning talk-shows at home, and later on his car radio, only made matters worse. He wondered why he bothered to listen, then he wondered if the talk would ever end. No, he concluded. For the first time in recorded history a black had gotten away with the murder of a white man and a white woman. Not paying the price for killing a white man was woeful; not paying it for killing the white woman was enough to make one want to alter the Constitution and change the rules of evidence.

The "verdict" was certain to create outrage for the next millennium.

He wondered what the victorious attorneys *really* felt. Bottom line: was *anybody's* conscience working?

After going back out to the Valley to see if he had overlooked anything at the crime scene, the lieutenant arrived at the morgue at 6:16
a.m. He had called Nicki Aladanti, the head examiner, at 5:40 at her
home. She didn't appreciate being awakened that early, but since it
was McKnight, she submerged her feelings. She agreed to meet the
lieutenant at 6:45. She was half an hour late.

McKnight was already downstairs waiting in the colder-than-most
building. He had gone upstairs, used the john, tried to make one call,
come back down and tried to spend the minutes thinking about the
case. He spent most of the time staring at the ceiling rather than
through the wired window where an all-night bootie-and-mask-wear-
ing technician was nonchalantly draining blood from the body of a
young woman. He had been in the building many times but he never
relished being there, and the thoroughness of the ghoul-bent techni-
cians on the other side of the glass only made it worse. Just thinking
about having to go into the sterile room, packed with so many dead
bodies that they were ready to spill out into the corridor, was enough
to ruin a good day. He did think the city was missing a good bet,
however. With every result of human mayhem wrapped in plastic
and sheets, he thought the coroner's office should have been a mandatory pit stop for every young person in the city bent on crime. Particularly the gang-bangers.

Somebody would get the message.

When Nicki, the examiner, finally did show up, McKnight strongly
hinted at conducting the questioning elsewhere. The examiner
wouldn't hear of it. Surrendering, McKnight balked inwardly and
mentally prepared for the job at hand.

In another room, Nicki slid the tray out from the refrigerated unit.
The detective was quick to notice how badly LeCoultre's torso had
been bitten. He was even more surprised at how obvious the spike
marks were, meaning LeCoultre's addiction was much more severe
than he had originally believed. How could that have been? he wondered. The mental figuring lasted for a protracted period, then he nodded for the lady, whom he had known for years, to shove the body

tray back into the refrigerated unit. Taking note of the many units, he wondered about all the dead. Who were they, what were they, and where were they now? He felt queasy for a moment, rescued himself, and resumed thinking about the case.

In the meantime, Nicki, the medical examiner, said something to the worker who had already thrown the sheet back over the body of the once beautiful young redhead, stretched on the stainless steel table the next row over. The worker, who was not a doctor and had not performed an autopsy, lifted the sheet. Nicki gave the face a closer look, withdrew, went to the sink and washed her hands. McKnight, who had not touched anything, joined her in washing his hands. He also gave his face a quick splash. Nicki gave him a bemused look, then led him back to her office. It was down the gurney-filled corridor and up two flights of stairs. The sleep-starved detective would have preferred using the elevator. The medical examiner preferred to walk.

Nicki Aladanti was a swift-walking, short brunette with a sunny disposition. She didn't look like a medical examiner. She looked like a school teacher, a McKnight favorite. Before becoming a cop, he had thought about becoming one. In fact, he had already selected a school.

"So, how long had he been on the stuff, Miss Nicki?"

"There's a great deal of concentration there, Wyatt. From his condition, it's hard to tell."

"Ballpark."

"It's a tough call. What makes it rough is that the punctures weren't all that old. I'd say one to two weeks at best."

"So, then, being on the horse was relatively new to him?"

"I hear it's hip to say: *On the Harry.* They don't call it horse any more."

"After eight years as a narc and seeing what it does to people, maybe they shouldn't. Maybe it should be called what it is: *Death's door.* But the question remains, Miss Nicki, would you say the stuff was relatively new to him?"

"From what I've been able to determine thus far, yes."

"But, then again, being new, his arm…"

"Arms."

"All right, *arms*," McKnight said, as they made the swing to the second landing. "But if he was all that new to shooting up, the arms couldn't possibly have been in that condition."

"You saw them for yourself."

"True. But as a cop even LeCoultre couldn't have been that dumb. He didn't exactly dazzle with brightness, but no way would he have tracked his arms up like that. And if he really had the monkey on his back…"

"'*Monkey on his back*'?" Nicki interrupted. "Another oldie."

"You ought to team up with Ault."

"Never."

"Sure. Then check the books and learn the history of this stuff. Then hit the streets. Might do you two some good," said the detective. "Anyway, if LeCoultre was on the stuff that strong, he would've shot up between the toes, under the nails, on the butt, around the penis, under the armpits, anywhere to avoid exposure, as long as he could get it."

"You don't miss anything, do you?"

"I'm paid to be thorough. But wouldn't we see evidence of that?" McKnight asked.

"In a lot of cases. But he could've gotten hold of something different, mixed it with heroin and the combo sent him through the roof."

"Is that possible?"

"Now it's you who should check the books," she said. "In this day and age, anything's possible. Go on the Internet, find out for yourself. Hey, if kids can make their own pipe bombs, adults sure as hell can make their own dope. And, again, you saw his arms. They alone should tell you something." She made the turn to go into her office. "And may I remind you, again, that the punctures weren't all that old. When DNA and the results of all the exams come back, we'll know more."

Inside the office, generously decorated with photos of a happy young home life, McKnight sat on the edge of the desk. The woman continued to the connecting room.

He called out: "The Highway Patrolman said he was carrying. What happened to the merchandise?"

"Coffee?" she called back, standing in front of the urn.

"No, thanks."

"You're not into caffeine?"

"Coffee is not good for the complexion," said the detective. "Besides, I'm not into anything addicting."

"You smoke."

"Quitting. End of the week."

"Good for you. I'd hate to see you downstairs prematurely."

"If I stay on this job, anywhere I land won't be prematurely."

She chuckled. Her voice arose again. "Hey, does it bother you that we're talking about a cop who was a stone addict?"

"This is the LAPD. Nothing bothers or surprises me."

"Wyatt, has anyone ever accused you of being a cynic? Or being just plain ol' antisocial?"

"Never."

"Well, if they do, and need references, give 'em my number."

The cop cracked a brief smile. His mind went back to the case. "What happened to the merch LeCoultre was carrying?"

Nicki emerged with the cup. "Upstairs, set to go to the lab to be tested."

"Why so? Can't you tell what it is already?"

"Of course. I've already said it's heroin. But we don't get to see that kind any too often. It was pure and uncut. And I'm thinking one of the syringes could have had something even newer in it."

McKnight perked up: "Something newer?"

"Possibly. Like it was from a different kind of poppy."

"And you say the regular stuff, the kind we don't see too often, was pure and uncut?"

"Right."

"That is really odd."

"Tell me about it. This was none of that 30/70 or 40/60 stuff. This was the best of the best. And were you told about the ribbon and paper?"

"Ribbon and paper?"

"As in gift wrap. Maybe the Highway Patrolman didn't see it, or didn't think it was important. But ribbon-tied paper was in the envelope forwarded for analysis. It was found in the Jag, along with a few more syringes."

"Are you trying to say that someone was giving a cop new, uncut heroin as a gift?"

"I'd say so. I should have some more info by late this afternoon. I'll give you a buzz."

"Please do," said McKnight. "Could he have been giving the narcotics to someone?"

"Not likely. I'm betting prints'll prove LeCoultre was the receiver, still it'll be a judgment call. The paper was torn, as if somebody was in a hurry. The package wasn't opened. It was ravaged, if you can say such a thing about a package."

"It paints a picture," said McKnight. "Any trace of designer drugs?"

"None."

"Crystal, amyl, or oxides?"

"No."

"Crack, smack, or rock?"

"Negative."

"Peyote, mescaline, or LSD?

"Nada."

"Meth?"

"No signs."

"Tar?"

"Nope."

"BC Bud, the Canadian connection?"

"No traces."

"Toad licking?"

"How would you know about toad licking?" Nicki asked.

"I got a complaint from a frog," quipped the detective.

"That's a real juicy way of getting high, you know."

"Listen, I couldn't help but notice one of your cohorts had been carving up on a young redhead down there. What was her story?"

"She's a Jane Doe."

"No prints or anything on record?"

"That's why she's a Jane, Wy. She's here because free-basing led to an epileptic seizure, and she choked to death. But she was going down anyway."

"Why so?"

"Coke had eaten everything in her nose but the hole."

"You're so gentle, Ms. Nicki," McKnight said, tossing another wry look her way. "How long has the body been here?"

"Here, not too long. But she's been dead forty-eight hours."

"Age?"

"Mid-twenties or so."

"Where'd the body come from?"

"Hotel downtown. The Virage."

McKnight thumped a cigarette from his pack. Nicki pointed to the *No Smoking* sign. "Makes sense," he said, putting the pack away. "Certainly don't want to corrupt the lungs of the dead."

"Or the lungs of those who work around the dead."

"Touché," said the detective.

"And I don't mind saying, Wyatt, you're already looking a little beat around the eyes. Are you well?"

"It's the hours and stress of the job, Miss Nicki." He quickly shifted subjects. "On LeCoultre. You're sure there were no signs of skag or chasing the dragon?"

"The nostrils looked relatively undisturbed. No burnouts or anything." She tossed him a small bottle. "He had more of those in his pockets. The Jane Doe had some in her purse."

"You say that as if they knew each other."

"There's a connection."

"How do you know?"

"Check the label."

"What are they?" McKnight asked, studying the bottle.

"Plain old no-kick placebos. They don't do zilch. And notice the dated label?"

"Connection?"

"Purchased in England. Where would LeCoultre or the redhead get pills from an English pharmacy?"

"An addict will steal, Madam Coroner."

"True," Nicki said, agreeably. "Meaning he, or she, could have lifted them from a new arrival. Or tourist?"

"Something like that. And I don't think either one of them could have gotten pills from one of the stores the Brits run. Now, Nicki, on the phone this morning you said you had a preliminary from Forensic?"

"Uh-huh. It appears that your cop was hit with an automatic .380 PPKS Walther, with a silencer, no less. Oh, and I should mention the slugs were TKWs. You ought to go next door and get the report."

"Obviously I intend to. But the slugs were bronze and Teflon-coated?"

"Yep."

"I didn't know they made those things any more."

"They're not supposed to," said Nicki. "It's illegal. People aren't supposed to rob banks, but they do. But that's what he was hit with. Now, I'm gonna go out on a limb and say this, so don't nail me to the wall with it: I figure that because of the embedded glass, one of the hits came while driving, the vehicle spun out and crashed."

"The Highway Patrolman mentioned something about a dog. LeCoultre's shoulders and forearms were severely bitten. Where would the dog come in?"

"Through the door."

"Cute."

"Just kidding. Where's your sense of humor, Wyatt? Oh, that's right, your name is McKnight. You never had one."

"Particularly as an antisocial cynic, and particularly at this hour of the morning. And particularly in an overcrowded morgue."

"You don't like morgues?"

"I don't like the inhabitants. I have trouble with people when you can't tell what they're thinking. Now, about the dog?"

"How he figures into this thing I can't say for certain. But LeCoultre was attacked by the dog before he was hit. Obviously."

"How do you know that?"

"Had to be. It's even in the Highway Patrolman's report. But even if it weren't, he was there shortly after the car rolled over. When would LeCoultre and a dog have time to fight? Now, judging from the bites, scrapes and rips on the hands and shoulder, I'd say he'd been through the mill, and ended up trying to escape from something."

"Sure. The dog."

"Ah, but the dog didn't shoot him."

"You're bright, Ms. Nicki. You belong in a morgue."

The lady chuckled. "Say, how come the boys up in Homicide are not on this?"

"Madam Coroner, the man is dead. Isn't that punishment enough?"

To get to work from the coroner's office was a fourteen-minute drive if the downtown traffic was light. This morning it was fifty-fifty. It was 8:08 when McKnight arrived in the parking lot of the Whitehurst station. On the corner, just east of the Spanish-inspired building that had been his on-and-off home for a third of his time on the department, there was a diminutive, broken-down nun in a wheelchair. Her habit was frayed, she wore a smile, her voice was strong and saintly. What she was saying could not be heard, but she was enthusiastic in waving her Bible at the heavy foot traffic.

On the concrete bench directly in front of the building, which had been set for demolition two years ago, sat Heinrich Kiesner. From

Germany, he was in this country on special assignment, as Ault had said. The quiet-speaking, handsome young man had just completed a stint at Parker Center and was winding up his tour at Whitehurst. This morning he was having difficulty reading the sports section. American box scores confused him. His head was buried in the newspaper. It would have stayed that way had not McKnight brushed by.

"*Guten morgen*, Mr. Kiesner. Do you make it a habit to get your news in front of the police department?"

He lowered the paper and leaped up, revealing a freckled face. "Oh, Lieutenant. I was just catching up on the baseball scores."

McKnight moved on.

Kiesner folded his paper and caught up with him. "From what I've heard about you, I figured you would be getting an early start. I have already moved my things into your office."

The loner didn't like it, but said nothing. Not only was the young man unneeded company, but he was also presumptuous. The lieutenant continued to move briskly inside the building. Passing the desk, he tossed a quick wave at Rusty, the female desk sergeant who, for some reason, was just coming on duty. Kiesner, having been at Whitehurst for only a short while and not really knowing the woman, did likewise and moved abreast of the fast-walking senior, who slowed for a moment only because Rusty had called after him.

"Mac, I understand you're on the one that happened last night?"

McKnight nodded affirmatively and moved on.

"I am going to congratulate you, Lieutenant, because I have learned you are soon going to be a captain," Kiesner said. "And I am going to love working with you for the month more I am here in the United States. I am glad you requested me."

"*Danke schon*, Mr. Kiesner," McKnight said curtly. "But I didn't request you. My request was denied. Not a wise choice by any stretch, but Devro is his name."

"He is here at Whitehurst, working?"

"Let's just say he's here. After six years on the department, Devro's work ethic has yet to be established. And for your information, Mr. K, the advent of captaincy doesn't interest me. The game is this: Last night, at approximately 8:17, one Detective Sergeant Verneau LeCoultre was shot and killed on the outskirts of town. It was in the Valley, the community of Encino. His death was drug-related. The gun used was a 9mm, 380 PPKS Walther. A silencer was attached. The slug was an outlawed TKW." He handed the young German the Highway Patrolman's note. "This is our only clue. We're looking for a nut that's new to the game."

"The time of death was 8:17 p.m.?"

"20:17. Approximately."

Slouching down the corridor and up the stairs to the detective bureau was the man of whom McKnight had spoken. Roland Devro. He was with his partner, Elliot Washington. They were a black Mutt-and-Jeff combo, raised in the streets, and not a duo one would have classed as hard workers. They were just coming in, but they were dragging and climbing the stairs as though they were getting off from the midnight shift.

It was easy to see that the lieutenant didn't request working with Devro because of his brainpower. Always jive-talking, and, to McKnight's way of thinking, on the job by default, McKnight thought he would have done better tap-dancing his way through a black sitcom.

The plump one grinned at McKnight and spun a look to the quiet-appearing Kiesner. They were about the same age. "I hear you goin' back 'cross the pond, my good German bro. When you gets there, send me a Mercedes. Make it a pink one. Tee, hee, hee."

Why McKnight liked him, and had gone so far as to request him, was a mystery. Maybe it was because he was so blissfully *colored*. Maybe it was because his head had that recessed look, and his forehead was forward and heavy, and he walked funny — like his arms didn't go to and fro, they swung from side to side, giving the body a sort of tilt-forward look, and, like his short, thick thighs and stubby legs, they were kind of curved, like they could mount a tree and swing from branch to branch with primordial ease. *And frightening familiarity.*

Inside his office, McKnight sat, and, as he did just about every morning, slid open the bottom desk drawer, removed a bottle of liquid shoe polish and began quickly dabbing at his shoes. He did it neatly. But as he bent over he was feeling a bit dizzy. He stopped, mopped his brow and his nose, and continued. Kiesner watched him for a bit, thought about the case, and asked, "How do you know so fast that it was a 'nut' who killed Sergeant LeCoultre?"

"The manner of death, the type of weapon used. And only somebody two slices short of a full loaf would leave pure, uncut heroin on a dead man." The phone rang.

Trying to show efficiency, Kiesner answered. It was the officer LeCoultre had been working with before he went on vacation. It was he whom McKnight had tried calling during his wait at the morgue. "It is Eddie Palmer," the young German said, handing over the phone. "It is going to be good working with you, Lieutenant."

"You've already said that. My question is, why?"

"I was a student in sociology. *All* people interest me." His tone indicated that he was anxious to talk to the veteran lieutenant about race in America. He had heard that the man was not one to hold back.

Still working with the polish, McKnight pushed the man's interest to the back of the brain and secured the phone to his ear with his shoulder. "Palmer? McKnight."

"You called earlier, sir?"

"I wanted to find out what was going on with you and LeCoultre."

"I'm sorry about what happened, sir."

"It's a national tragedy. The flags are at half-staff; we've alerted all the ships at sea. Now, what were you guys working on?"

"Nothing."

"Nothing? We've got thousands of unsolved murders on the books, there's almost an epidemic of crime in the streets; there are so many dead bodies in the morgue that the coroner can hardly keep 'em all on ice, and two detectives working the night shift didn't have anything on the fire?"

"I thought that's why I got the assignment, sir. But for the three weeks I worked with the sergeant, nothing went down."

"What'd you do during your shift?"

"Nothing. Just rode around."

"'Rode around' doing *what*?"

"Nothing. He and I just drove around the city."

"Hold on, Palmer," McKnight said, putting the bottle down and capping his hand over the phone. "What part of Germany, Mr. Kiesner?"

"Stuttgart. Capital of Baden-Wurttemberg."

"By the by, let me congratulate you on how well you speak the English language."

"Thank you, sir. I have been learning it for a long time."

"You've done well. Now, the drug problem in Stuttgart?"

"Growing. That's why my department wanted me to come here so badly, to study some of your techniques. I would really like to find some solutions. Do you have any ideas, Lieutenant?"

"Yes. But in this country they appear to be too complicated for endorsement," McKnight said, not straying from that cynical tone.

"I would like to hear one of them."

"I'm happy to oblige," said the lieutenant. "I advocate busting the kingpin, and putting the money where it's needed: In schools — like they are *supposed* to be doing with the lottery money. But it seems to me that if the dealer is properly ensconced in a place where he cannot get *to* the dope, he cannot *sell* the dope. If the user is in a position where he cannot *buy* the dope, he cannot *take* the dope."

"It is very logical."

"With that kind of thinking, you'd never make it in public office, Mr. K," McKnight said. He grabbed a tissue, and swiftly returned to the phone. "Palmer, did LeCoultre ever say anything about a case, or what you were *supposed* to be working on?"

"No, sir. Never said nothing."

"Did he ever stop and talk to anybody, mention any names, go into any joints?"

"Nothing while I was with him, sir."

"He didn't bitch about his wife, gripe about the job, pick his nose while trying to get a freebie from a hooker, or do anything nasty like cops are known to do?"

"No, sir," answered the young man.

"All right, you'd come on at midnight, your lunch hour should have been somewhere around 3:30 a.m. Where would you have it?"

"He'd drop me off at home, and I assumed he went home, too. Or maybe he could have stopped at one of the all-nighters."

Stuck, McKnight muttered to himself: That damn LeCoultre was about as slippery as a politician in heat. "So there's nothing you can tell me, Palmer?"

"Can't think of anything, sir."

"If you think of anything, holler." The lieutenant hung up, drummed his fingers on the desk and thought about firing up a cigarette. Thoughts of Eve LeCoultre stopped him. "Check out Mr. LeCoultre's desk, Mr. Kiesner. See what you can find."

"I have already done so, sir. It is as clean as a pot on the stove."

He was trying to be hip. The lieutenant forgave him. "No phone numbers, notes or anything?"

"No, sir. Not even a pad of paper to write notes on."

"What about in records? Did you check his activity report?"

"Every evening has been the same. Mileage, but no contact," Kiesner said, handing over a sheet of paper that contained a list of numbers. "But I did track down his last known addresses."

"'Addresses?'" McKnight said, emphasizing the plural. He didn't know the cop had had more than one address. He quickly glanced over the list. "'From his house...to Chinatown...to the barrio?' Doesn't figure."

"And another strange thing, Lieutenant. I ran a check on that Jaguar he was driving. It belonged to him, but it had been registered for less than thirty days."

It was another surprise. "I saw the car, it didn't have any plates or tags on it. At least not in the rear," the lieutenant said, more to himself. "Now that I think about it, it didn't even have a new-car registration in the window." He wondered if he had missed it. He had been slipping lately.

"The car was registered," Kiesner said, double-checking. "*And*, according to the dealer, it was paid for by a cashier's check."

"Then it must have been a gift. LeCoultre couldn't afford to buy cheese for a churchmouse, let alone an XJS." McKnight stopped drumming and sent his mind fishing. "Make a note to track that cashier's check." He came back to the note. "Can harm.' *Can harm.*" He then tried duplicating the sound the Highway Patrolman had made. "'....*H-annnn Harmmmz.* ....*Can harmz.*' What th' hell does that mean?"

"Maybe he was, to use an American term, 'fooling around on his wife,' felt guilty and wanted to let it out. You know, like it was harming her."

"Have you ever met Mrs. LeCoultre, Mr. Kiesner?"

"No, sir, I haven't."

"Well, I can assure you yours is an incorrect observation. Eve LeCoultre couldn't be harmed by a Scud missile."

"Are you sure he said *Can harmz*, Lieutenant?"

"There was no 'z' on the end of it. But I'm not sure of anything. Neither was the Highway Patrolman. On the note he wrote down what he *thought* LeCoultre said."

Kiesner was leafing through a batch of old reports. Surprised, he asked, "Are there two LeCoultres assigned here at Whitehurst, Lieutenant?"

"No. Why?"

"Here are some old reports that are signed by a *Lieutenant* LeCoultre."

"Detective Sergeant LeCoultre was busted for alcoholism two years ago."

"Really?"

"He should've been kicked off the department entirely," said McKnight.

"You think so?"

"I know so."

"So *Sergeant* LeCoultre was a *Lieutenant* LeCoultre once, and he was not a good man."

"He was worthless."

"And he was an alcoholic?"

"And he had plenty of company."

"Oh, my," said Kiesner. "Did you know him very well, Lieutenant?"

"Apparently not well enough. He ended up being an addict. And a thief. And probably a hundred other things."

"An addict," mused Kiesner, finding it difficult to understand. "I wonder if he realized what he was doing."

"After you take that first hit, you don't care what you're doing. You take a second and God himself doesn't care. After that, both your will and your mind are gone. The monkey is on your back, and nobody but nobody knows what an addict will do." It was said strangely.

Kiesner thought about it. He also wondered why the lieutenant had said it in that manner. "How long did you know him, sir?"

"We came on the department at about the same time. A week after he was on the job he pistol-whipped a young street black into submission."

"What did the young black do?"

"He was breathing."

"My, oh-my. So, what was LeCoultre's punishment?"

"He was rewarded. The incident was conveniently exorcised from his record."

"Wow," said Kiesner. He gave it another thought. "So, he was a lieutenant at one time. And he is now a sergeant."

"*Was* a sergeant. He is now dead. Taking the wrong fork in the road will do that to you, Mr. K."

"So, he came down, and you are going up."

"Don't bet on it."

"Why do you say that?"

"I won't be here long enough to go *up*. If I hung on for the next millennium, I still wouldn't go *up*."

"I am told you cannot be stopped, if you have passed all the tests.

And you have all the qualifications, they say."

"This is the LAPD, Mr. Kiesner. Gremlins work here," McKnight said, ending that part of the conversation. "Say *can harm* like you were out of gas."

"Huh?"

"You're a dying man, Mr. Kiesner. You've had a fight with a dog. A fierce one. You fought hard and you won. You've made it to your car. You're hurt. You're sweating. You're driving along, and suddenly you've been shot. You crash. You've just been dragged from your overturned vehicle, which left no skid marks. You want to leave a message. You've got dope in your hands, and death at your door. Say the words: 'Can harm.'"

Kiesner, finally understanding, tried it. *"Kannn harmmmz."*

McKnight encouraged him to say it several more ways, including dropping the "z." Nothing worked. "Too much movement of the mouth," he advised. "The Highway Patrolman didn't do that."

"Do you think Sergeant LeCoultre could have been talking about the error of his ways?"

"He didn't live that long."

"But it could be that he was about ready to stop doing what he was doing. Get cleaned up. Maybe confess. Maybe even talk to a priest."

"He was too busy walking on thin ice for a priest, Mr. K."

"I fail to understand, Lieutenant."

"Detective Sergeant LeCoultre was an atheist," McKnight said, putting the polish away. He did the same with the syringe. Feeling victorious, he sprang to his feet. "Let's get to the game, Mr. K."

The city was fully alive. Traffic was bumper-to-bumper, and the pedestrians were scurrying around like homeless ants wondering where the sand went. To get away from the soon-to-be-beaming sun, the pale, weak nun in the wheelchair had moved to another corner.

But she was still at Whitehurst; still on a corner, still waving her Bible for glory.

A fidgeting, anxious young woman stopped by. "Can I refer you to the Good Book?" asked the nun.

"Chapter 10, verse 2," responded the young woman knowledgeably, and looking as though she needed a lot more than her soul saved. McKnight, apparently accustomed to whatever was taking place, continued walking purposefully to the undercover car.

"So, all people interest you, Mr. K."

"Yes, sir."

"Reason?"

"It came from my father. In the war he was in the White Rose."

"What was the White Rose?"

"It was a group of young Germans against the government."

"Germans against the government in Hitler's Germany?"

"Yes, sir. When he came to power."

"And your father lived?"

"For a time."

McKnight gave it some thought and dismissed what he was thinking. It wasn't the time to go into it, and he didn't feel like driving. "Are you licensed?"

"Yes, sir."

"First stop, the cleaners," the lieutenant said, tossing him the keys.

Eleven minutes later the rust-colored car was being bathed in suds on West Olympic. McKnight, having again forgotten about Eve LeCoultre's smoking habits, lit a cigarette and wandered off to do some thinking. His new partner didn't move with him. His eyes were glued to the car. He wouldn't allow his eyes to move, because McKnight had told him that in America thievery at some car washes was more common than the soap and water they used.

When the lieutenant wandered back, his stomach was bothering him. The problem was nothing new. Still not taking his eyes off the car, Kiesner asked, "Did you grow up in the streets, Lieutenant?"

"Black cop growing up in the streets is a cliché, Mr. K. Where I came from, quiet dirt roads were the order of the day."

"Where was that?"

"The Mississippi Delta."

"I have heard of that place. It is a poor part of the USA?"

"A very poor part."

"I bet you were glad when you got out of there and found civilization."

"I'll be motoring back to that pure and honest part of the country in twelve days, six hours, and forty-four minutes, Herr Kiesner," McKnight said, putting the German ill at ease. "I've already purchased a motorhome for that purpose. I'm to take delivery any minute now."

When a car-wash worker waved a rag, signaling that the car was ready, the first thing McKnight did when he got to the car was to remove his gun from his belt and lock it in the glove compartment. It was done, of course, after checking to see if anything had been swiped. Removing the gun and locking it in the glove compartment surprised all hell out of Kiesner. It led to another question or two and ended with the German asking, "But what if you have to get to the gun and shoot somebody in a hurry?"

"Although tempted as late as last night, I am no longer interested in shooting anyone. And besides, a cop polices; a jury convicts. Or at least they are supposed to. But this is Los Angeles. We have our own sense of justice." It was a statement that, for the first time, had the detective thinking about the punishment for LeCoultre's killer.

There was no question that the perpetrator would be caught. He would probably get life, and be out in twenty. On second thought: Murder? Los Angeles? White? Make that fifteen. Seven, with good behavior. Less with influence.

Again the lieutenant was thinking racially. Again he wished he didn't have to. He grew up waiting for the *One nation under God* concept to kick in. It never would. People were not people. They were colors, quotas, and categories.

Although the captain had voiced the opinion that the crime had been ghetto-related, McKnight thought that the assessment was nothing short of characteristic stupidity. He had tossed the idea out of his mind the moment the white man had said it. It was beyond asininity, he continued to think. Why in hell would a ghetto black go all the way over from his territory to the doldrums of the San Fernando Valley to kill an idiotic, strung-out cop and leave the stash on him? And, too, he reasoned, if there had been a chase that had lasted all the way from the south side of L.A., a clear thirty-minute drive at best, and on a warm night such as last night's was, the engine would have been burning, not just hot, as the Highway Patrolman had said. Clearly, LeCoultre had been dusted by someone not all that far from the area where the car had spun out. And, it had to be considered, the patrolman was on the scene within seconds. With the assessment, however, it didn't stop the cop from starting his investigation in downtown Los Angeles. His reason was that, according to the information Kiesner had come up with, LeCoultre had lived in Chinatown, which in itself was strange. LeCoultre was an equal-opportunity bigot.˙He hated all minorities. Not just blacks. He hated everybody. He was a lot like the captain in that regard. Anyone a shade beneath cartoon-white made him nervous. For him to have lived among the Chinese *and* the Mexicans, he had to have gone off the deep end.

The detective and his German partner started and concluded their Chinatown investigation with speed. Within the hour they had moved to the area known as Chavez Ravine, the Mexican enclave near Dodger Stadium, and then, just to check something out, they drove to the upscale Los Feliz district.

McKnight knew a connection there, a heroin dealer. Kiesner remained in the car while the lieutenant went inside to an apartment. Apparently changing his mind, the lieutenant immediately came back out to the car. He was cramping and sweating just a bit.

In the meantime, back at the Whitehurst station, Sgt. Rusty Halloran, the plump and rosy-cheeked female desk sergeant, had received a call. The voice on the other end had been English. To Rusty it sounded close to English royalty. It was proper, and whoever the woman was, as nutty as she ended up being, the voice was still distended with breeding.

"Good morning, good morning, good morning," the voice had said with unmatched cheer, and doing much to further the artificial note of culture. And then, suddenly, it changed from poise and musical brightness to a note of glumness. It was still elegant, but it had switched to gloom. It was now almost whispering: "Who am I speaking with?"

"Sergeant Rusty Halloran."

"And you are?"

"The desk sergeant," Rusty said, always showing patience.

"You are a sergeant?"

"Yes."

"In the Army?"

"No. I'm a policewoman. You called the LAPD. I'm the sergeant of the desk at Whitehurst."

"And are you actually at a desk?"

"Sitting."

"How lovely," the voice said, obscurely, and now without the whispering effect.

"Thank you."

"I'm standing."

"Wonderful," said Rusty.

"I'm standing, overlooking my pond."

"How fortunate you are."

"And your name again?"

"Rusty Halloran, Sergeant."

"Do you mind if I call you Rusty?"

"Please do."

"I like Rusty better than Halloran."

"So do I. Now, may I help you?"

"Is that Irish? Rusty Halloran?"

"I'm told it is. But to me, more American than anything else. At least I am."

"It's a wonderful country, America is, isn't it?"

"It's lovely. But, now, may I be of help to you?"

"It's truly freeing."

"Yes, it is. But may I help you, ma'am?"

"Yes," said the voice. Then it stopped.

"Hello?" Rusty said, and waited. "Hello, are you still there?"

"Rusty, I'm so distraught."

"Well, why don't you take a deep breath, and start at the very beginning. I'm here to help. First tell me where you're calling from."

"My home."

"Located where, dear?"

"In Encino."

"So you're located in the Valley."

"It sounds like a song, doesn't it, Rusty?"

"Very much so," said Rusty, insincerely. "Now, may I have your street address?"

"It's very painful, you know," the woman said, switching the subject.

"I understand. Take your time."

"Thank you, Rusty," the voice said, and then lapsed into another silence.

"I'm waiting," Rusty said, kindly.

"It's very hard, you know."

"I understand."

The voice quickly whispered, "I don't know why he did it."

"Did what, ma'am?"

The voice dropped almost below a whisper: "Why he killed him."

"Suppose we start at the top, ma'am."

"At the top?"

"Yes. The beginning. And could you keep the voice up some, ma'am?"

"Thank you, Rusty."

"Glad to be of service. Now, you were saying?"

"I was saying something, wasn't I?"

"Yes. You were saying someone had killed somebody."

"Oh. Well, last night...." she broke it off and glumly started again. "You're going to find this hard to believe."

"I can believe anything, dear. This is the Whitehurst station. You won't believe some of the calls. You can say anything to me that you'd like."

"Thank you, Rusty. You're very dear."

"And so are you. Now, what's the problem?"

"I don't have a problem."

"Obviously someone does. So why don't you tell me what you started to say earlier."

"About what?"

This is a rough one, thought Rusty for the second time. "Why don't you start with your name first, then tell me about the someone who was going to kill somebody. You can start with either one."

"I can?"

"Yes. Give me your name, keep the voice up and tell me about the killing and perhaps I can connect you to someone who can be of help."

"I hope so. Because, Rusty, last night my clown went berserk and escaped from his trunk. ...No, he was not in the trunk. He was in his sitting area. And I overheard him and my dog talk about killing one of your policemen. And they actually went off and did it."

"The dog and the clown went off and killed a policeman?"

"Yes," whispered the voice.

"Was that a 'yes'?"

"Yes."

"I can hardly make out what you're saying, dear, so please try to keep the voice up. Now, you said your clown and your dog killed a policeman?"

"Yes."

"Do you have any idea who the policeman was?"

"Yes."

"Who was he, dear?"

"His name was LeCoultre."

Rusty held the phone tighter to her ear. "Did you say *LeCoultre?*"

"Yes," she whispered.

It's a good thing the name had been confirmed, because Rusty, as kind and patient as she was, was either going to pull the plug or patch her in to someplace else. Now, very interested, she asked, "And where is the dog now, ma'am?"

"Dead and buried. When they came back, the clown dug a hole in the yard and pushed him in it."

"And where's the clown now?"

"Sitting out front," whispered the voice.

"In front of your house in Encino?"

"Yes," she whispered. "He's back in his sitting area waiting for me to drive him back to the Savoy, like he's always done since we've been here."

"And the Savoy is located where, ma'am?"

"London, England."

"Lemme get this straight," Rusty said, knowing the woman had to be treated delicately. "You said that a clown killed a dog, and the clown is now waiting for you to drive him back to London, *England?*"

"Yes," said the woman. "That's why I'm whispering. He eavesdrops, you know."

"I understand. Now, ma'am, exactly what kind of clown are we talking about? The type we see at the circus, or is he a play-clown? Like a toy?"

"He used to be a play-clown, then after we left the Savoy in London, he changed. Now he has a mind all his own. Like he's supposed to stay in his trunk. But he refuses to do it."

"I see. Now, if I heard you correctly, you say the clown and the dog…" Rusty stopped herself. "By the way, was the dog real? I mean, he was not a play-toy, like the clown used to be?"

"Oh, no. He was a big dog. A Rottweiler, I think."

Rusty reconfirmed, "And the play-clown… er, *former* play-clown and the Rottweiler conspired to kill who, ma'am?"

"This policeman named LeCoultre," the voice said, as if having witnessed a conspiracy. "They said they were going to do it. And they actually succeeded in killing him."

She definitely knew something. And Rusty knew the woman wanted to talk. If there had not been any legitimacy to the call, she wouldn't have known the name of LeCoultre, or that a dog had been involved.

There was silence on the other end of the line, and Rusty asked another question: LeCoultre's first name. Getting no response, she asked the question again, to no avail. She tried it once more and, knowing the woman was still on the phone, and without trying for a trace, advised: "Ma'am, the officer I think you should be speaking with is a Lieutenant Wyatt McKnight. He's in charge of the case. He's very easy to talk to. You'll like him. And your name is, dear?"

The voice was back to normal volume. "Dotty Rochester. Metro Press."

"Okay, Dotty, you just hang on for a sec. I'll try to connect you with Lieutenant McKnight. If he doesn't answer, someone else will pick up. May I get your number first, in case we're disconnected?"

There was a click on the line. "Dotty" had hung up.

Rusty was a tad miffed. She couldn't do it there, but had she been at home she could have traced the call by dialing star-69.

Thinking of the number sixty-nine had Rusty wondering about the age of the caller.

She was in her middle years, and she was a case history in bizarreness. She was from England, as she said, but there was more to the story. She had left England a year ago, heading for Japan. But instead of getting on JAL, she had hopped on a United Airlines flight.

When she arrived in Los Angeles she was accompanied by an equally mentally-impoverished real-estate agent. She was going to introduce the Englishwoman to the Emperor of Japan.

"Nee ga yang h'lows shee yung." The elderly Chinese woman

was unable to speak English. It didn't bother McKnight. He knew her language.

Having followed a lead, the two detectives had returned to Chinatown and were standing on the steps of the rundown apartment. Kiesner had just shown the woman a picture of LeCoultre.

"All right. One more time," McKnight said. "Hie mie nee ga yang?" His diction was good.

"Nie-la. Nee ga yang, hinee doe. Ho noy," answered the woman, pointing up to a third-floor window.

McKnight looked up. No more questions were needed. "Do'or ja'air. Bahj-mo," he said, courteously, leaving.

Kiesner couldn't wait until they were back inside the car before saying, "Now, that was really something. I've never heard of that: A *black* speaking Chinese. Do you ever get tongue-tied, Lieutenant?"

"Not quite as much as talking with an airhead, Mr. Kiesner."

"Airhead?"

"A mental cripple, sir."

The German got the point and apologetically switched the subject. "Did Sergeant LeCoultre ever live there?"

"No."

"But she was pointing upstairs to the third-floor window."

"That's why we're leaving. She should've been pointing to the morgue."

The next stop was at the Virage Hotel, where the body of the young Jane Doe had been discovered. They spent about an hour there, then it was back to Alvarado.

The Mexican landlord had been rude and testy. He shouldn't have been blamed. Because McKnight had a badge and spoke the language with fluency, he thought he was from INS, the immigration cops.

"No hay una persona como LeCoultre aqui. Nunca estuvo aqui. No se de lo que hablas," concluded the man.

"Esta seguro?"

"Si."

McKnight tossed a look to Kiesner, who was dizzy because the black man had spoken yet another language. "I think the gentleman is lying, Mr. K."

"I think so, too."

The German didn't know. He was trying to make a contribution.

From the neighborhood stores to the post office the two men went, trying to pick up whatever little tidbits they could find about the cop who had moved from the Valley, leaving wife and son, had become an addict, and had been slain.

By noon the results of the investigation remained skimpy. They had learned from the postal worker who covered the route that three weeks ago LeCoultre, although comparatively new to the area, had put a hold on his mail and that he had no forwarding address. The two men pushed on.

From a bar on Temple, they learned that LeCoultre had been in several times with a young redhead who, assumed McKnight, had been the one he had seen in the morgue. The connection came because of the placebo route, and it reminded him to get the name and number of the pharmacy off the bottle and put in a call to England. Because of the eight or nine hours' difference in time, it would have to be early in the morning. As Nicki had said, the label was dated and so there really was no hurry. He doubted that the bottle would lead to anything significant, but being the stickler that he was, it was worth checking into.

Three other downtown bartenders also told the detectives that LeCoultre had said he wasn't drinking any more. They all said it had been three weeks ago.

In checking the branch of the Bank of America close to the area, the three-week theme came up again. That was when LeCoultre had closed out his anemic account. There was no record of his having written a cashier's check. Added to that, when he was seen on the streets, he had no car.

Continuing to grind it out the old-fashioned way, McKnight and his partner busied themselves checking everything and every place imaginable. The assumption was that if, at the time, LeCoultre wasn't drinking any more, he had to be doing something. McKnight knew the man. On the question of getting help, he would check, but it was for certain he wouldn't have done anything as sensible as getting in touch with something like Alcoholics Anonymous. That was out of the question. And the detective knew the man was too far gone to have quit drinking altogether without having replaced it with something. LeCoultre was the type who couldn't function without being on the streets and ingesting something that could corrupt the body's system. He had never been the stay-at-home type, and since his separation from Eve he was apt to be doing anything. The Highway Patrolman, of course, had found narcotics; there were obvious tracks on his arms. But still something else bugged McKnight, who had an old-fashioned bulldog tenacity when working on a case. It was probably the Jag. The fact that it had been paid for with a cashier's check didn't help. Could LeCoultre have been dealing? It was doubtful. Users weren't dealers. At least heavy users weren't. And, according to what he had seen and had been verified by Nicki, the medical examiner, LeCoultre was a two-track user. But then again, as he had reasoned earlier, if the cop, neither a snorter nor a snifter, was that hard a user, he would have tracked up in different places.

Strange.

It was the detective's intention to go back out to the Valley's holding yard to give the Jag a thorough going-over, then check with DMV to find out the name of the Jaguar dealership. But he was hit with another idea. It took them to several stores that dotted the downtown jewelry district. They got lucky on the sixth try.

Bunny Workman was a thief. Except in the presence of the police, he made no bones about it. He had a pudgy face that didn't sit well with the cold-black hair that he wore in a ponytail. His major assets were accomplished fingers.

He was at a jewelry display case at the Kahazani section of the jewelry mart on Fifth, and was about to again put his art into practice when McKnight brushed past several customers and armed the choppy-faced little man to the rear of the store.

"Okay, Bunny, you're going to tell me something, or I'll have you thrown under the jail. I don't like the way your eyes were moving."

"Eyes are s'posed to move. What am I, a corpse?"

"Keep on looking with thievery in your eyes, and you might become one."

"I'm supposed to be looking! I'm an entrepreneur!" Bunny protested. "I'm an entrepreneur, an' I was observin'!"

"You're a thief. You're a thief making the rounds, and you were preparing to steal that man blind, just as you've done with a dozen others. Now come off of it."

"Hey, you got me wrong."

"If I turned you upside down, you'd drop more jewelry than a hock shop."

"Why're you pushin' me so hard, Mac?"

"Understand this, little man. First of all, it's *Lieutenant* McKnight. Wyatt W. Next, I've got a cop who's dead. He was murdered, and he was using. You knew him."

"Who? You said all that an' never said *who*?"

"How many cops do you know who are users?"

"Th' whole damn department could be on the Harry, as far as I know."

"Well, let's talk about one in particular. LeCoultre, Verneau B. The walking wounded. You knew him."

"So?"

"Quit gassin', little man. Talk."

"I knew him only because we'd grab a drink at the same place sometimes."

"So you did know him?"

"Of course I knew him. Down here, who didn't? But with me, it was always clean an' sociable."

"And you socialized at?"

"A place called Forte's."

"Keep talking, Ace."

"Forte's is a bar in Encino. On Ventura and Balboa."

"It doesn't fit. Why would you go way out to the Valley to socialize?"

"A change of atmosphere."

"You can do that by going to your neighborhood church. Now, why were you out there?"

"We just like it. They don't do nothin' in there, honest."

"Just as you aren't telling me nothing. You're skirting, Mr. Snitch. I want to know what you know. And I want to know it now. If you don't start talkin', I'm going to hang a number on you."

"You ain't got no cause. Go ahead, check me out."

"In that case, let's get serious. You're holding."

"Holding!? Whaddaya talkin' about! Go ahead. Check me out. Check my pockets."

Without saying anything further, McKnight asked Kiesner for the car keys and instructed his bewildered assistant to hold the man in place. Quickly he weaved his way out of the mart and onto the street where the car was parked. He returned just as quickly. "Now, as I was saying, little man, you're holding."

"What are you, nuts? I told'ja, I ain't holdin'! I'm legit!"

McKnight reached into his pocket and, and as though checking, planted an unseen packet and a book of matches in the man's shirt pocket. "You're a blood-sucking barracuda who'd sell his grandmother at a swap meet. And, Bunny, you are holding."

"I ain't holdin'!"

"Check your left breast pocket."

"You just checked it!"

McKnight didn't say anything. He simply stared.

Finally, the little man sent his hand up and felt his pocket. He removed the small plastic wrapper and book of matches. He stared at the cop.

"What's that in your hand, Ace? Looks like coke to me. Or is that powdered heroin? A spoon must be around some place, because I see you have your matches. Planning on a normal high, Ace, or are we planning on spending the afternoon chasing the dragon?"

"C'mon, Mac…"

"What's that stuff look like to you, Mr. K?"

"I'm not sure, sir," Kiesner said, not exactly certain of what it was.

"Well, you'd better be sure Mr. K, because you're going to have to testify at the trial." He turned his attention back to the snitch. "By my count it'll be your third time going before the man. Not nice. Under mandatory sentencing that should net you…fifteen-to-twenty? Maybe a few years off for good behavior?"

"I'm clean. And I know my rights."

"To repeat, you're holding, little man. And let me remind you of your rights and our system of justice. You know the drill. I start out by booking you at Parker Center. It's bad enough there, but at some point you're chained and waltzed over to the county jail. Thick with minorities, it's run by the Sheriff's Department. Some of the deputies are not human. They're goons. To show you who's in charge, they start off by calling you every name in the book, and saint or sinner, they don't mind calling your mother a whore. The cells are crammed; they're hot, stinking, and the crust on the stainless-steel toilets is bumpier than the road to Burma. Your mind is gloomy, and your future is bleak. Some sixteen hours later, you're still being cursed, insulted and processed into the system, and you'd better not mention sleep or your rights as a human being. Guilty or not, felon or miscreant, you're in the L.A. County jail system and that's all that counts. You're a 7-digit number, and you'd better be ready for the fun that follows. Utter one complaint and you're on your way to Siberia. That's the hole. Take it from me, God, country, the rats, and the roaches on patrol, that's one place you don't want to be. Shall I continue, Mr. Snitch?"

The system hadn't changed; he didn't want to be a part of it — again. Bunny surrendered: "You sure you want to hear it? The man was a cop."

"We know that better than you. Now, spill it."

"The word is, your guy was strung out over some chick who was givin' away free stuff, an'…"

"A chick who was giving away free heroin? C'mon, get real, little man. You're still doing a number, and I don't like it."

"I ain't doin' a number on you, Mac. Your guy was on the pony. That's what the word is."

"Who is this 'chick'?"

"Nobody knows."

"Support your fairytale, Snitch, or I'll hand you your head. We're talking about Horse. Harry. Smack. Diacetylmorphine. $C^{21}H^{23}N^{05}$. Whatever you want to call it, it's still the heroin factor. And I want some answers."

"I ain't got no answers, and I ain't lying."

McKnight looked to the eye-wandering German visitor and said, "Get involved, Mr. Kiesner. Ask the little man a question."

Kiesner, attempting to make up for the earlier faux pas and match the street-wise McKnight, asked, "What did this 'chick' look like?"

"Don't nobody know."

McKnight fired back. "Don't nobody know what she looks like, where she works, where she's from, where she scores her connections. Come off it, Mr. Snitch."

"Wy, honest to God."

"You've got until 5:45 to find me and God some answers."

"5:45? I can't do it by then!"

"The clock is running, Mr. Workman."

The little man scrambled away. Kiesner watched him as he disappeared amid the shoppers, and searched for something to say. Finally, he asked: "Where to?"

The lieutenant brushed away a small cramp. "Back to headquarters to run a make on every female who was, and is, dealing."

Threading their way back to the car, the young man from Germany, troubled by the American's procedure, released a question. "Lieutenant, I noticed you didn't exactly handle that by the book."

"The last book I read said that in some parts of ancient Rome, rats were looked upon as a delicacy. Would you suggest that I keep on reading?"

Kiesner was still pondering the question when they reached the car. He switched to another question. "Are you in favor of your mandatory sentencing laws, Lieutenant?"

"Ten years for a first-time offender because he has a rock, weed, or a bit of dust in his pocket? It's hysterical, excessive, and political. It's a snow-job. This is supposed to be a democracy, not a tyranny."

Kiesner cranked up, and nosed the vehicle into the thick traffic. "This morning, Lieutenant, you said you would not make captain."

"The department would promote Captain Kangaroo before me. Maybe even you, and you're not even a citizen."

"So why did you take the test?"

"Some people are into heavy metal. Me? I'm into masochism," said McKnight. "But even if they did make the mistake of even *thinking* about promotion in my case, I say to you again, and anybody else who cares to listen, I won't be here to accept it. Get it in your mind: I'm out of here."

"For good?"

"Forever."

"Then how do you like this as your farewell case?"

"Actually, I prefer the one that's pending. That's when I've taken my last earthly breath, and I'm planted a solid six feet under. There, after resting up a bit, I intend to rise up and put a bug in God's ear, and ask Him to introduce me to the devil. When we meet, I hope he's wearing designer jeans. The tighter the better, and preferably the kind with a chic label on the hip pocket. It's good for accuracy. Assuming the devil is of average height and weight, 22.86 centimeters to the left and exactly thirty-seven stitches down from the heart of the label is the area in which I intend to propel my foot. Because anybody who creates this much hell on Earth ought to have his posterior kicked from here to the shy side of Venus. And that goes for whether we're talking about a he, she, or it." Hardly stopping for the words to sink in, he asked, "I'm still curious about your father. Whatever happened to him?"

"He was killed the month I was born. The sympathizers did it."

"What are you? Thirty...?"

"Thirty-three."

"Thirty-three," mulled McKnight. "I know there are meatheads and sheet-wearers all over the world, but you're not telling me that serious Nazism was still around over there in the Fifties?"

"It was there. It is still there. Like it is here. It will never die."

"I find that hard to swallow."

"Lieutenant, not long ago a German magazine took a poll. Thirty-eight percent of the people polled said that if it had not been for the war and the Holocaust, Hitler would have made a great statesman."

"And not a great Pope? Disappointing."

"I'm serious. Forty-four percent said Germany should remain racially pure. That is why I like talking to you about race in America."

"I gather that happy-talk is not part of your makeup."

"As long as I am learning something, it is all right."

"Your father had to have been a teenager during the war. Was he considered that much of a threat?"

"Worse. He was like somebody I am beginning to know."

"How so?"

"He spoke his mind."

When McKnight and Kiesner arrived back at Whitehurst, Rusty was still on the desk. She caught them en route to the stairs heading up to the office.

"Hey, Wyatt, some guy just called, saying something about your RV was in. And a lady by the name of Dotty Rochester from Metro

Press was tryin' to reach you earlier. She said it was about the LeCoultre case. I tried to patch her in, but we got a disconnect. But you were out, anyway. She was *veddy, veddy* British. And weird."

"I don't believe we have a 'Metro Press' in L.A."

"That's the point. And I gotta tell you, her conversation was so nutty I won't even try to repeat it. But she knew something."

"How so?"

"She mentioned LeCoultre."

It registered.

"Write it up and lay it on my desk," McKnight said to Rusty. "ASAP."

"Will do."

Moving off, Kiesner said: "I thought your captain said this case was supposed to be hush-hush, Lieutenant."

"If, at any time, you believe my captain, Mr. K, I have a little property on the moon I'd like to talk to you about. Stop in I.D. See if there's anything new on druggies, female, white."

Kiesner peeled off. Catching up to McKnight were Devro and Washington, who, working in robbery and with the day half gone, still hadn't gotten started with their workload. Devro grinned, "If I'd been workin' on that case, I'da had it solved by now."

"So would Charlie Chan," McKnight said as he swung into his office.

Devro laughed and winked at the approaching Robecca, a black policewoman who worked inside and had been blessed with hall-of-fame legs. She was a nice one, but she suffered the plague of sisterhood. Young; together; trying. Too good for the garden of the damned.

Inside his office, McKnight sat for a moment, thinking of why he had returned to the office rather than remaining on the road. He looked at the center desk drawer, shifted his attention and went to his Rolodex. He could still hear Devro's voice. "Hey, Becky," he was saying, "Is it true you carry a straight razor in yo' holster?"

"Get lost," she said.

McKnight was on the telephone when Robecca poked a head inside: "How're you feeling, Lieutenant?"

McKnight cupped his hand over the mouthpiece: "I've felt better."

"You look a little beat, sir. Can I get you a sandwich? Or maybe a soda or something?"

"No, thank you, Robecca. And, Robecca, tell Devro if he continues to treat you like you're from the jungle, I'm going to find a pot, pretend I'm a pygmy, and have him for dinner."

She laughed. "I'll be glad to."

On the phone: "City desk? Jake Chamness. McKnight calling."

The editor was a jolly, rotund man who couldn't utter the word *hello* without making it racist. He was another who added to McKnight's crust.

"Wyatt, you ol' hamhock. I didn't know they let Negroes use phones."

"Jake, editor or not, at least you're consistent."

"Howz that?"

"You'll always be a horse's ass."

The fat man laughed: "Wyatt, you're a riot." He stopped, gave his rhyme a thought. "Hey, I like that! *Wyatt, you're a riot.*"

"It's brilliant, Jake," the detective said, lighting a cigarette, "With your 'Hee-Haw' brand of humor, you should be writing for television. Better yet, make it the movies. Help 'em raise the bar with 'Dumb and Dumber, Part Two.'"

"I might give 'em a call," he laughed. "Hey, what's this I hear about you going around checking up on one of your own men?"

"Routine. The guy's due for a promotion and the brass wanna make sure he deserves it."

"What about a promotion for yourself?"

"This is the LAPD. They've got a thing against promoting a certain kind of colored folk over here."

"Don't feel bad, Wyatt. We got a thing about promoting *any* of 'em over here."

"Jake, somewhere there must be an old Caucasian proverb that says you cannot promote what you do not hire."

Jake laughed. "And I'm gonna keep it that way."

"You and the rest of the nation."

"Hey, what else do you people want? You've got a black chief over there."

"Most of the tribes in Africa have black chiefs, Jake. They weren't the ones who brought apartheid to its knees."

"Hey, that's a good one," Jake laughed again. "Speaking of knees, did you hear the one about..."

"I'm going to cut you off at the pass, Mr. Jake, because I know where you're going. I don't listen to jokes about women. Life's too short, and they're too important. It's a stretch, but ten-to-one your mother was a woman," the detective said, curtly. "Now, do you have a woman on your staff by the name of Dotty Rochester?"

"Unh-unh."

"Ever heard of her?"

"Nope. Anything up?"

"No. Just somebody playing games. Ever hear of anything called Metro Press?"

"Nada. Why? Wha'sup?"

"Now, now, now, Jake, don't get newsy. Talk to you later."

"Hey, don't hang up. What about getting together for a drink sometime?"

"Can't."

"Why not? You got something against being out with white people?"

"Keep it a secret, Mr. Editor, but what I've got against whites could very easily raise the dead and give sight to the blind."

"Trouble with you and your people, Mac, you want everything to be perfect."

"The man in pain under another man's foot is not seeking perfection, Jakey-poo. Relief will do just nicely, thank you. And what's this I hear? You, an honorary member of the Klan?"

"Now, don't tell me you'd let a little thing like that bother you?"

"Not ordinarily Jakey-jerk, but you're getting carried away. At the last meeting, I heard that in addition to your pastel sheet, your hood was fashioned out of a lampshade with little fringes on the bottom. And *that* bothers me."

On the hangup, Kiesner came in with a box of cassettes and several books containing female suspects. "Devro was just telling me he knows about half of these ladies intimately."

"Devro will also tell you he once saw Ray Charles teaching Stevie Wonder how to drive."

"They both are blind."

"No," said McKnight. "They can't see. Devro is blind."

Robecca poked a head back in. "I told him, Lieutenant."

"Good."

"What about a Coke? You really don't look well, sir."

"Coke is not good for the teeth, Robecca."

She laughed and left. McKnight directed his attention back to the photos while Kiesner headed for the bathroom. When he returned, he joined McKnight in the mug search. The young German was somewhat surprised at the number of females on file. He commented on it once or twice, then after a while, and feeling that they were not getting anywhere, asked, "After we finish going over the photos, Lieutenant, what do we do?"

"Take it back to the streets. No. Let's hit Century City first. We'll check out the upscale users. They aren't into needles, but bags are just as bad."

Kiesner leaned back in his chair thoughtfully and finally came up with the question that had been bugging him since morning. "Lieutenant, you are on this case because of the narcotics angle."

"I'm on this case because of politics, and knowing Ault, I'm sure he has something wicked up his sleeve. But your question, Mr. K?"

"You have a war on drugs, a cop has been killed, but we have not been in the black neighborhood; we have not talked to one black, yet your captain insists some of your people were involved."

"First, try to understand I'm too old, black and ugly to give less than a kitty's tit about what a brain-dead captain thinks, or anybody else for that matter, and you, he, and all interested parties should try splitting a Valium; get some crack, back it with freebase, meth yourself down, and with plenty of coke, relax, light up a joint, sniff a little glue, drop a few Quaaludes in some PCP, and be reminded dope is not a byproduct of blackness."

"But narcotics *is* in the neighborhood. And blacks have been known to use narcotics."

"Blacks have been *known* to love chicken, but the Colonel owns the store. Blacks have been *known* to love watermelon, but guess who owns the farm? What you're doing is extending the myth, Mr. Kiesner. That's dangerous. But what counts is this: Your basic black was not responsible for the death of Detective Sergeant Verneau B. LeCoultre."

"How did you so quickly come to the conclusion?"

"The man was killed with a Walther, was he not?"

"You said he was."

"Now, go back a few years and consider possible CIA involvement with narcotics. Next, consider the interest of the power structure. Now your banks. Then factor in your users. We're talking about an illegal U.S. industry that even our government says rakes in billions. That's billions with a "B." Now tour your ghettos. What do you see? A pair of Nikies here, a ghetto-blaster there, and wanna-be hipsters wearing baggies so loose they could almost hide the national debt. But where are the billions? *Show me the money.* Something's wrong with the picture. Statistics show that seven out of ten drug abusers have jobs. There haven't been that many black people working since the Amistad docked. The arithmetic ain't right. It's not going to *be* right until the con jobs stop and somebody starts zeroing in on the truth. The truth starts from the top down, not the bottom up. At a cost of twenty-five billion dollars, from Columbia alone, we import a ton of cocaine a day. Every year, one point one million drug-related arrests are made. I can tell you who is in jail, but I'll be damned if I can find the money. Now it seems to me, we don't have a war on drugs in this country, we have a war on people," he stopped for a moment, reached for a tissue, and continued. "To get back to the case — and keep in mind, please, that the upper-level ghetto dopers, not in command of one ship, plane, or train, don't import a damn thing into this country, and are too ignorantly busy participating in genocide and/or self-annihilation by killing and ripping each other off — for peanuts. But when was the last time you or the captain heard of one dusting anybody with a Walther, particularly a 9mm, 380 PPKS Walther — with a silencer and an outlawed TKW slug which is almost strong enough to penetrate a tank, travel to the San Fernando Valley's creampuff Encino to use it, and then end up leaving the stash on the man? And let me remind you, he even had some newer stuff on him." He quickly switched to something else that was on his mind. "Call upstairs and see if the captain will be working until six."

Kiesner slid the telephone closer to him and dialed Ault's extention. Ruth, the captain's loyal secretary answered. "Hello, Miss Ruthie. It is Heinrich Kiesner. Yes, I am doing fine. Thank you for asking. Miss Ruthie, I am working with Lieutenant McKnight. He would like to know if the captain will be working at six."

"He has nothing on his calendar, but I believe he'll be here," Ruth responded. "Would the lieutenant like to schedule something?"

Kiesner cupped his hand over the mouthpiece: "He should be here at six, Lieutenant, she says. She would like to know if you would like to schedule anything?"

His stomach grumbling, McKnight leaned over and grabbed the phone. "Ruth, I'm already scheduled. I just want to make sure he's here." Without waiting for a response, he hung up.

"So, Lieutenant," Kiesner picked up, "our suspect is unusual?"

"Our suspect is bizarre." The lieutenant answered as he headed for the bathroom.

Upon his return, Kiesner asked, "This I am going to ask only because I want to learn, Lieutenant. I would love to hear what you have to say."

"I would love to accommodate you, Mr. K, but we have a homicide on our hands. We've got to get to it while I'm still up to speed."

He hadn't intended to say it. McKnight was never one to admit that he wasn't up to par. He was slipping. His face reflected it. It caused Kiesner to ask about his apparent cold. It was a question that had been simmering all morning long.

The response was negative.

"Can you refer me to Verse 20, of the good Chapter 100?"

The nun on the corner opened her Bible, and sent her fingers working. Kiesner took note of her as the car pulled out.

On Fifth Street, the nun's dexterous fingers were still on his mind. "That old nun works hard at saving souls. She's on that corner every day." If he was expecting a response from the lieutenant, he didn't get any. Kiesner changed the subject. "So, we're looking for a suspect who fired a .338 Walther."

"The gun came from Mr. LeCoultre. He either swiped it or shook somebody down and took it, more than likely from a collector."

"What do you think of legalizing drugs, like they are thinking about in some parts of Europe? Keep the profits from bad hands."

"God help us all if legalization ever happens."

"Why?"

"A society simply cannot give up because it appears evil is winning. It's my understanding that almost three million people have used heroin in their lifetime. And let's not mention the sixty-five mil who've smoked pot — and the millions more hooked on other things. What is it they say, traces of cocaine can be found on one out of every four U.S. dollars in circulation?"

"But with legalization, you eliminate the profit motive."

"Rape doesn't have a profit motive, and we've not been able to stop it. Should it then be legalized?"

After Century City, and, for good measure, checking out

Westwood, and neighboring Brentwood, the two found themselves stepping off the elevator on the twenty-second floor of the Plaza building, downtown Los Angeles. The towering building was a smoke-colored, upright glass coffin. No bricks, no steel, no style. Eve LeCoultre was a receptionist at one of the larger stock-brokerage houses with strong credentials. She was not the least bit pleased at the sight of McKnight. Without allowing him to get to her desk, she stood and promptly marched across the lobby. It was a parade. She looked like Yaser Arafat with a dress on.

Inside the glass-encased conference room, she slammed the door and exploded. "What the hell are you doing here?!"

"Working."

"You don't work here!"

"When it comes to trying to find a policeman's murderer, I work everywhere."

"So what do you want from me?!"

"I want to know *when* Vern left you. I want to know *why* Vern left you. And I want to know *who* Vern was seeing after he left you."

"I don't think that's any of your goddamn business."

"It may not be, but the man is dead. My job is to find out who killed him."

"Do I look like his killer?"

"No one is making that assumption," McKnight responded, and swung a look to the daydreaming Kiesner. "*Stay* involved, Mr. K. Get with the game. Ask the bereaved widow a question."

"Er… you see, ma'am, our line of thinking is that if you could tell us something about the separation of your marriage, perhaps it could lead to something."

Eve evaluated the German accent and pushed McKnight: "Who is this drip?"

McKnight stepped back in. "Was the breakup over another woman, Eve?"

"Why don't you ask me if it was another man?"

Outside, walking swiftly back to the car, Kiesner, still smarting over being called a drip, said, "Boy, that woman was really something."

"But not without reason. After all, she was married to LeCoultre."

"Why do you think she said that 'other man' thing? You don't think Sgt. LeCoultre was gay?"

"She'd say anything at this point. If Mr. LeCoultre found it in his pants to take off with, or because of, another man, her reaction would be shame, indignation, hurt. Hate would be the last on the list."

The lieutenant thought it over. "Check that. Eve LeCoultre can't be shamed, isn't familiar with indignation, and thinks hate is an ally. Let's just say LeCoultre left, and let it go at that."

"Where to?"

Hoping he could eat, he said, "We grab a bite, then hit the Valley."

They stopped at the Valley Inn on Sherman Oaks. Kiesner lunched heartily, McKnight nitpicked over a salad, and they were off again.

The wrecked Jag was in an Encino impound yard. Along with the crime unit, the two went over the car with a fine-toothed comb. Except for bits of wrapping paper, along with more ribbon, and two more syringes that were tucked under the front seat, they found nothing useful. In truth, McKnight should have discovered the syringes when he went over the car earlier, but he hadn't. He knew he was wrong. He spent a moment silently criticizing himself, then directed his partner back to the heart of the city. En route, they checked with DMV.

After the DMV visit, and picking up speed in the investigation, McKnight led Kiesner back into a few outlying pool halls and gambling dens, then out to Hollywood Park. Not finding any information at the racetrack, they came back to the downtown area and went in and out of bars and restaurants, and double-checked the morgue. Just in case, they toured the Melrose area, checking West Hollywood's gay area. They found nothing. Back downtown they went, and on a downtown street, realizing he wasn't getting anywhere, McKnight leaned on a parking meter and lit a cigarette. He was showing fatigue. It was becoming more evident that Vern LeCoultre wasn't his only problem.

With awareness Kiesner asked, "Problems, Lieutenant?"

"A ton of 'em," McKnight said, resisting a nose-wiping urge. He was almost talking to himself, as if he hadn't been thinking clearly. Nothing fit. "What did the murderer want? Gift-wrapped heroin was found on the man. Syringes were still in the car. Again, that eliminates your everyday doper. The body evidenced dog bites, which could have happened anywhere. He was shot in a remote area; he was filthy. And the dope was the 'best of the best.' Nothing figures."

"Maybe he was shot because a deal went sour."

"Possible. But I doubt it."

"Why the doubt?"

"LeCoultre had the dope on him. I say again, not too many people dealing in dope would leave pure, uncut heroin on a dead man. And they surely wouldn't leave even newer heroin on him."

"Maybe it is a simple case of a drive-by shooting."

"I would doubt that, too, Mr. K," McKnight said, freeing himself from the meter.

"So what do we do now?"

"Head for home."

On the way back to Whitehurst, McKnight was still immersed in thought. Kiesner knew it. To get him off the subject, he asked, "If you hadn't become a policeman, Lieutenant, what would you be?"

"I'd be someplace making a serious contribution."

"Doing what?"

"Working as a Playboy Bunny."

"They are long out of date here."

"And I am grateful to say, Mr. K, so am I."

"I take it you are bothered by the way this country is headed?"

"Oh, are we headed someplace?"

"The old American expression is, I believe, you are doing your thing. From the top down."

"I suppose, Mr. K, that's why from the bottom up there's a burglary every ten seconds, a rape every eight minutes, a murder every twenty-seven, and last year the poor remained hungry while 214,796 hogs were slaughtered."

"Lieutenant, sometimes you've got to look on the other side of the coin."

"All right, let's do that. Skirts are up, pants are down, and the people can't wait for film at eleven."

"This America is really something."

"But with all the potential of being second only to heaven," McKnight said, confounding the man all the more. "Can we say the same about the Federal Republic of Germany, Mr. K?"

On route to the station, they made three stops. One had been at County General Hospital, where nothing new was learned about the young redhead, the next had been at a stationery store where McKnight had gone in and purchased gift-wrapping items. The last stop had taken them all the way out to Irvine in Orange County, to check on the present the retiring cop had made to himself.

Irvine was not quite an hour's drive in light traffic. With its spotty and squatty look, it was not exactly a place where one would take an out-of-town tourist, but it was the place to purchase an RV.

McKnight had placed his order several weeks ago. It was being serviced when the two arrived.

Direct from the factory, McKnight's motorhome was a 37-footer, pewter on top, satin on the bottom. It was called the Spectrum 2010, and it was a honey. It was so advanced that it looked like one had to have a pilot's license to crank it up. McKnight loved it. He immediately dubbed it the *Big Bad Boy,* and couldn't wait to set it on the road. Kiesner was thrilled. McKnight almost had to drag him from behind the wheel to get him back to the car. Even at that, the enthusiastic German spent the trip back to the station talking about the wonders of the Spectrum 2010.

When the auto pulled into the Whitehurst parking lot, the senior

●

detective was back to the troubled silence.

Kiesner got out of the vehicle and waited. Finally he asked, "Coming, Lieutenant?"

McKnight stepped out of the vehicle with the store-bought ribbon and paper, as well as the recent ribbon and paper they had found in the Jag. He also had the other syringes they had found in the car.

He was still deep in thought.

"Same problem, Lieutenant?"

Again he settled on the case. "I can't figure the angle. And it bugs me. LeCoultre was a new-to-the-game idiot. Why would someone want to kill him?"

"If he was an idiot to you, maybe he could have been an idiot to somebody else, Lieutenant."

"Apparently he was. But that doesn't tell me anything. Nor is idiocy ample reason for murder."

"But we are looking for a nut that is new to the game. Your words."

"Add 'interesting' nut."

Kiesner thought about it, looked at the lieutenant and said: "I think you could use someone a little interesting in your life."

Kiesner had correctly assumed that the lieutenant wasn't married, but the comment was a little too personal for a man who believed in distance, and whose personal life was never discussed. "We'll pick it up early in the a.m. And we've got to check out that placebo bottle with England sometime in the morning. In case I need you for tonight, where'll you be?"

"Taking my wife to the movies. Maybe we will have a late dinner. We will do the same tomorrow night."

"You and the wife go to the movies every night?"

"Why not. It is free. Just whip out the badge, and you go in. Same with eating in restaurants."

"Cops. They're the same all over."

"Don't you ever take advantage of any of the freebies, sir?"

"Freeloading is not what the city pays me for. And I hope that when you return to Germany, yours won't either. By the way, Mr. K, what is your rank in the Stuttgart Polizei?"

"Soon to be an inspector. That is why I am here, to learn everything I can. I paid for the trip myself."

McKnight ended it. "Before you take off, go across the street and pick up the phony, broken-down nun. Book her, and that phony, cut-out Bible."

"For what, sir? She has been referring people to the Good Book. You need more people like that. That is what is wrong with the world. Not enough people doing good things."

"Say the word *refer*, Mr. Kiesner."

"Refer."

"Accent the first syllable, Mr. K."

"Ree-fr."

"Round it out, Mr. K."

"Re-ferrr."

"Think about it, Mr. K."

Kiesner gave it serious thought and came up with nothing. McKnight asked him to think about it some more. It took time.

More time was taken. Kiesner was about to give up. Finally he exclaimed: "Re-ferrrr. *Ree*-fer!"

McKnight nodded agreeably.

"That sweet old lady? She has been selling marijuana over there?"

"The verse is the amount; the chapter, the cost," answered McKnight. "Have a good evening, my friend."

Kiesner couldn't get over the nun's ingenuity. He stood looking across the street. It took time, but he finally reacted to the "my friend." It was unusual for the lieutenant to use the term. "What is our first stop in the morning, sir?"

"First we have to call that pharmacy in England about those pills." He changed his mind, "Let's see, nine hours difference. Four or five a.m. I'll be up."

"You are up that early in the morning, Lieutenant?"

Again he was slipping. He shouldn't have said it. "I meant to say I'll set my alarm for four or five. If I do, I don't know what our first stop will be, but I certainly can tell you about the second and third. At ten my motorhome will be ready. You'll drive me out to Irvine. I'll pick that baby up, and you'll follow me back to my apartment. We'll take off from there."

"What a thrill that is going to be, getting that RV. I'm telling you, Lieutenant, that is the prettiest thing I have ever seen. I would love for my wife to see it."

"Let me see what I can arrange. Maybe you can take her for a spin this weekend. Take her to the mountains."

"You would let me do that?"

"Of course. I might even stock it, and fill it with gas for you."

"You would do that?? And you would let me and my wife use it and you have not even had it on the road??"

"Your wife has to be a nice young lady. She deserves it."

"Wow! You are really a great guy, Lieutenant."

He couldn't accept the compliment. "I'm really not that good," he said strangely. "Maybe I used to be. But no longer."

He gave his young partner a look, thanked him, and went inside. Kiesner simply stood there, smiling. He admired the man.

When the lieutenant arrived back at his desk, after having made another pit stop, his phone was ringing. On it was Nicki.

"Wy, we're in luck," said the medical examiner. "The new mixture in the heroin we spoke about? Guess where it comes from?"

"China or Afghanistan."

"Wrong. Right here in California. And did you know the California state flower is a poppy?"

"I'm from Mississippi, Ms. Nicki. All I know, and all I long for, are those sweet-smelling magnolias."

"Nice. But you live here, and your state flower is a poppy. It's called: The genus *Eschscholtzia californica*. Cut it, and mix it with something like phenylcyclohexylamine and you're ready to float beyond the moon. LeCoultre had traces of it in his system. Anything more than a trace, and he wouldn't have made it to the car. He would've already been dead. 'Bye."

Even before she hung up, the detective was carefully digesting everything that was said. He absently returned the phone to its base. Thinking long and hard, he went into his pocket and extracted the two fully loaded syringes and carefully placed them in the center drawer of his desk. They were with the ones he had found under the car seat-- the ones he hadn't procedurally turned in to the property room. He looked at them for a long while before closing the drawer, then he picked up the report Rusty had placed on his desk. He found it interesting. So interesting, in fact, that he read it twice. Normally one reading of a telephone conversation would have done it, but not this time.

The best of the best, he said to himself.

The woman, whoever she was, was definitely involved. But there was something about her that was pulling him in another direction. From the same drawer where he had placed the syringes, he slid the drawer back out and pulled out a few small items and began wrapping them in various ways for study. He was interrupted by the telephone. On the other end was Bunny Workman.

"Wy? Bunny. I got a li'l bit more on that chick your cop was foolin' around with. Know what she looked like?"

"She looked like a human being. A tall, good-looking redhead with a problem. And the problem is, she's a corpse. And a corpse with no prints anywhere. Tell me something I don't know, Mr. Snitch."

"Did you know she worked at some private club? The hoity-toity kind. Know what I mean?"

"I'm not on my game, Mr. Snitch. I've had a bad day. I want a name. A first and last."

"I'm gettin' it. I'm just callin' in now to beat the clock. Buzz you back in a couple. Where'll you be?"

"You said it earlier. In the Valley, at Forte's. I want to live like my dead cop lived."

It didn't seem so at first, but what Bunny had said added to the mystery. If the redhead had worked at a private club, it meant that she was used to the high rollers. LeCoultre couldn't have been a high roller. Why and how would she have tied in with him? And why would a good-looking young lady quit a job over a broke, cloddish, Clem Kadiddlehopper-looking hick who was easily thirty years her senior?

No sooner had McKnight posed those questions to himself than he heard Devro's voice. With the day shift clearing for the day, he was in the corridor, loud-talking his way to the lieutenant's office. Spotting Robecca, standing on a stool pinning a note on the bulletin board just down from the office, Devro, with his arms swinging from side to side like an ape-in-waiting, looked her up and down, and wolfed, "Hey, Becky, they say never stick your pen in comp'ny ink, but legs like yours make me wanna change comp'ny policy."

"Sit on it, Devro."

Devro laughed and moved his dangling arms inside to McKnight's office. He took a double look at the crowded desk.

"Ribbon, bows, presents? What's this, brother-man? You gonna be moonlightin' with somebody?"

"Just trying to see how and why somebody would be gift-wrapping heroin."

"Oh," Devro said. He reached in his pocket for his wallet and slapped a ten-dollar bill on the desk. At the same time, McKnight's telephone started ringing. Devro picked it up and announced himself. Hearing no voice on the other end, he hung up. "Ten to one you can't run it down to me."

McKnight knew what he was referring to. He picked up the ten and put it in his pocket. He rattled, "Although out of his league, your Mr. LeCoultre was light housekeeping with a dizzy. She's rich, bored, and off-the-wall. A basket case, add interesting. Why interesting? She's nuts, but not dumb. Male companionship was, and is, needed on a temporary basis. Enter the clod LeCoultre. Enter games. On drugs, Mr. LeCoultre conned the dizzy out of a fancy auto; got it, left her, and tied in with an employee, a yuppified redhead with flea-market values. Your Mr. LeCoultre ruined her, came back to the dizzy, robbed her of the dope, and got blown away for his troubles."

McKnight had a few facts wrong, but voicing what he was thinking helped. Had his mind not been somewhat beclouded, he knew he would have been even better. It didn't make any difference; Devro overdid his response. "Oooweee, you was jammin', Jack. You got the game down, Homes."

"Devro, Buckwheat is dead. Stepin Fetchit is gone, and Messrs. Amos 'n' Andy are no longer with us. Wouldn't it be wonderful to pay homage to their cultural contributions by allowing them to rest in peace?" There was no point in waiting for an answer.

The lieutenant grabbed a tissue, mopped at his forehead and nose, and flipped a cigarette into his mouth. He lit it, leaned back in the chair and crossed his legs on the desk. "Listen, Mr. Black, I've been working with the young German all day."

"Nice dude, ain't he."

"Nice and bright," answered McKnight. "Give or take a year or two, you two are about the same age. Now, I pretty much know what his goals are. What are yours?"

"To get under as many skirts as I can. And as quick as I can."

"Doesn't the world situation concern you; the problems in this country; the fact that as a people, we're losing it — that there *could* be something behind this genocidal talk; that over half of the black families have no fathers at home; that, young and old, drugs are killing us; that the number one cause of death among young black males is homicide — committed by the hands of his black brother; that there are more blacks in prison than in college — sent there by the white man; that our young women are nine times more likely to suffer with the AIDS virus than anyone else, that as a young black male…"

"Black an' proud."

"All right, black and proud…"

"Hey," interrupted Devro, not the slightest bit concerned with what McKnight was driving at. "Guess who I got lined up for tonight?"

"Back up. What are you proud of, Devro?"

"Can't at the moment," tossed the fun-loving chubby one. "But y'know who the broad is?"

It was useless. "May I assume you are going out with your lovely but long-suffering wife?"

"Man, you better get outta here and bring me somethin' serious. I mean somethin' *real* serious, Jack. I ain't about to waste this good night an' these good looks on nothin' that even looks like no wife."

"Sorry for thinking logically."

"You're entitled to be wrong once in a while," said Devro. "Y'remember that lady faith healer I busted for assault, pickpocketing, grand theft auto, and larceny?"

"You don't want to talk about what you're proud of, but yet you want me to comment on somebody you're trying to nail?"

"Whip it on me, Main Brother."

"For the umpteenth time, Devro, I am *not* your 'Blood,' 'Homeboy,' 'Main Brother,' 'Jack,' or anything else. My mother was literate enough to give me a name. I'd appreciate your using it."

"But we still homies. Bloods. Even the captain said that."

"Great," said McKnight. "Here's a man so crippled with bigotry he could qualify for handicapped parking, and you're listening to him."

"Why not? He's cool," said Devro.

"It is precisely that kind of logic that's got black people headed for the endangered-species list."

The telephone rang again. Devro picked it up. Again, there was no one on the line. He hung up. "We ain't goin' nowhere, list or no list. An' if the man knows, he knows."

"Mr. Negro, are you ever going to wake up?" said McKnight.

"I ain't 'sleep," Devro whined.

"If you think the man truly knows, you're right. You're not asleep. You're in a coma."

Devro stood to leave. "Mac, you gotta get into harmony."

"When I want harmony, I'll go to a symphony. The name of the game is respect. Slaves got off the boat in harmony. Where'n hell did it get them?"

Devro slouched away. "You gotta lighten up, Jack. You can't keep pushin' on that ol' envelope."

McKnight's telephone rang again. He picked it up. "McKnight. Detectives."

The voice on the other end was English and calm. "I want to see you."

It was just that brief.

As he placed the telephone back on the receiver, he ran the case over in his mind again, and thought about the call Rusty had received. Concluding that it was the same voice, he dug for the trooper's note and looked at the *Can harm* wording. It took longer than it should have, but now he thought he had a fairly good idea about what LeCoultre had been trying to say. He was aware that it took him practically the entire day to figure out something that the McKnight of old would have figured out in a fraction of the time. Wanting to tie something together, he was about to call Jake Chamness' office at the newspaper again when Robecca came in. She had manufactured an excuse for being there by carrying a memo from Captain Ault.

"Services for Sergeant LeCoultre will be on Monday. The captain would like for you to be there. Oh, and here's a copy of his 'ghetto' assignments he thinks you should have. Funny. I didn't know the sergeant ever worked in the ghetto, did you?"

McKnight didn't respond. He watched her as she placed the memo on the desk, and said a quiet "Thank you."

Hesitating, Robecca tossed an inviting look, and said, "Y'know, there's a nice little soul-food restaurant down on Crenshaw."

"I'm on a diet, Robecca," the lieutenant said, keeping his distance. She was a nice young woman, and a very nice-looking woman. She deserved a hell of a lot more than she was after. He was far too removed, and far too old. She needed something solid. He also thought about the word "deceptive." Young black women did not deserve to be deceived. There was already too much of that in a race that was shackled by deceit and self-destruction.

Without going farther the lieutenant rested his case, thinking that if he hadn't been so removed he could have had a daughter her age.

The young policewoman started to move away, but came up with something else. This time she was more serious. "Y'know, Lieutenant, something's been bothering me. You know, Dr. Martin Luther King's birthday?"

"Date of birth: 15 January, 1929."

She leaned over the lieutenant's desk as if revealing a secret: "I never wanted to say anything about it before, but it's been on my mind because I'm scared. I'm just plain scared. An' then I think of all the problems we're having, an' our kids rappin' an' fallin' apart at the seams with nobody to turn to. I mean, like we don't have a leader or nobody to turn to. That's why I was thinkin' of Dr. King. An' then I thought about his birthday, and how we're supposed to celebrate it. I know you didn't, but did you ever hear any of them nasty jokes that goes around on his birthday? I mean, even from the captain upstairs. *And* including that black Uncle Tom who moved upstairs next to him."

"I don't think the good Reverend is worried."

"Lieutenant, I'm serious."

"We both are," he said. "Robecca, let me ask you: If you were God, and two men stood before you in judgment, and one said: 'Ma'am, in the year 1776 I was a holder of slaves, but I fostered a cause and fathered a nation and today, as I stand before you, I am proud to say my work is done, for that nation is the greatest nation on Earth.'

"And if the other man standing before you were to say: 'Ma'am: Two hundred years later, in the shadows of this man's monument, in the city that bears his name, I too fostered a cause. I am not without sin, but I spoke of freedom and dedicated my life to justice, and I tried to raise that great nation's conscience. But today, as I stand before you, ma'am, I am sad to say, my work is yet undone'. Now, if you were God, Robecca — and it is altogether possible womankind serves in ways yet unknown to man — but if you were God, which man would you invite to sit beside you?"

She thought about it. She thought about it some more. She appreciated it, but still there was a problem. "I know what you're saying. But, Lieutenant, Dr. King was not perfect."

"None of us are, Robecca. And he was not supposed to be. Perfection suggests completeness, and only God is complete."

That did it for her. Eyes bright, the young black policewoman walked around the desk, planted a kiss on the lieutenant's cheek and departed. She was feeling great.

McKnight watched her leave, checked his watch and dialed the captain's office.

"Ruth? Tell the captain the time is 18:01 and change. I don't see anything inspirational on my desk."

"Oh, er, Lieutenant. Will you hold for a moment, please?"

"Certainly," responded McKnight, sounding as though he were waiting for the other shoe to drop.

It did. Ruth came back, "I'm sorry, Lieutenant, but the captain is not at his desk."

"Oh, he's not? Then I gather he's on his way down to mine?"

"Er, no. But he did leave word that he would be getting back to you first thing in the morning."

"'First thing in the morning?' Thank you, Ruth."

McKnight hung up, and, knowing the woman was lying, dug into the lower desk drawer, pulled out the bottle of liquid shoe polish along with a brush and some rags and tossed them into the wastebasket. He topped it with the ribbons and wrapping paper. He then pocketed a cigarette lighter, grabbed the basket, circled the room, and finished filling it with anything he found suitable. Topping it all off, he emptied a box of bullets into the basket, carried it upstairs and sat it directly in front of the captain's door. He pulled the lighter out of his pocket, lit it, and dropped it into the wastebasket. He casually walked down the stairs, went outside and waited under the Captain Ault's window.

It didn't take long for the desired effect. Sounds of exploding bullets and a terrified scream filled the air. Seconds later the flaming basket came crashing through the window, landing almost at McKnight's waiting feet. The captain jammed a furious head through the broken window. The zinging bullets had him thinking about jumping. He looked down and saw McKnight waiting.

Ault almost stabbed his thick neck with a shard of glass. "Goddamn you, you hophead bastard!"

An unruffled McKnight looked up. "Sorry, Captain. I didn't know you were in." He lit a cigarette and walked away.

There were times when smoking was just too good to think about quitting.

Ault didn't say it loud enough for the black man to hear, but he said it: "Why Lincoln ever freed you sonsabitches, I'll never know."

3

As one could have gleaned from her call to Rusty earlier that morning, the Englishwoman, Leslie Van Horn, was not only bizarre, she was a certifiable psychotic. Somewhere between 8 and 8:20 the previous night she had shot and killed a man, and had been casual enough to indicate to a cruising Highway Patrolman that she had just passed an accident. Twenty minutes later she was humming merrily in her shower with a clear conscience. If she had been asked what she had been doing half an hour earlier, she would have been stuck for an answer. She didn't realize she had been out of the house.

Leslie's home could have been described as a Japanese villa. Protected by a healthy Doberman Pinscher, it was in the secluded area of Encino, a community that fought hard to be the Beverly Hills of the San Fernando Valley. It didn't succeed. Though given roots and early-day glitter by the likes of Al Jolson, Bogart, Clark Gable, John Wayne, Bud Abbott, Encino had the houses, big and sprawling, but it had no Rodeo Drive, no Canon Drive, no Beverly Drive, and not quite the dazzle of the Beverly Hills streets. It had the residential hills, but not the sizzle. Anyone interested in "drop-dead" shopping was out of luck. Encino, in the main, had only the car-jammed thoroughfare of Ventura Boulevard which beckoned for the big dollars. With no shortage of dog-nasty dotting the streets leading to the hills, Encino, to its credit, was heavy with banks, eateries, an array of shops, and it was the place for good sedate living without glitzy pretentiousness.

Leslie's villa was less than a mile from Ventura Boulevard. It was set at the deepest curve of a cul-de-sac, and was also only a few minutes drive from the Sepulveda Dam, where LeCoultre's body had been discovered by the Highway Patrolman. The house, inspired by the nearby Japanese Gardens, was backed by a stunningly beautiful guest house, and styled as though it could have been a contemplative Oriental retreat. It was one-story, and was tucked behind a thick, seven-foot-high wall. There were no other houses around.

Leading to the two and a half acres of dense verdancy, there was a split gate made of deeply carved wood. It was centered with a huge bright red Oriental figure that connected and formed a design when the gates were closed. The design spelled the word *hope*. Behind the gate was a pond, a small red-and-black bridge, and numerous bonsai trees. In the midst of everything was the Chisen-Kaiyushike, a Japanese garden that harmonized with the edifice itself. It was calm and restful. Back from there was a mid-size Buddha. At night it benefited from a small spotlight.

Contradicting the setting, however, there was a strange, occasional knocking and rhythmic squeaking that came from a small swing-like seating area just outside the front of the house. It was the swing that created the squeaking.

Creating the other sound was a toy the woman's father had given her when she was four. It was a four-foot, toe-tapping, male, toy clown with a lazy, slothful, indolent look. With one leg draped over the side, enabling his wooden foot to touch the ground, he was leisurely reclining on a small swing-bench. He was next to a settee, and his foot would start dragging or tapping at the slightest hint of a breeze. He was dressed in bright, multi-colored clothes; he was chalky-white with bright orange hair that fell from underneath a pea-green chapeau. When upright he was controlled by strings and had a constant, irritating grin on his face.

Leslie had been deathly afraid of the clown when her father gave it to her; she was even more frightened of it now. But as frightened as she was, from childhood on she always kept it in view. And when she had fled England almost a year earlier, the clown was the first thing she had packed.

Leslie Van Horn's arrival in the United States had been a strange one. How she managed to find the villa was even stranger.

Encino, the supposed crown of the Valley jewel, was also the home of Alyne Condon, a Valley real-estate agent who was as batty as she was. Although Leslie was on the wrong plane, and Alyne made her dippy contribution by thinking they were on a boat and even went so far as to traverse the aisles looking for life rafts, the two happened to sit together. The conversation that ensued after the initial hellos would have sent Sigmund Freud digging for his flask.

Alyne was a non-stop talking machine. No subject under the sun was safe. By flight's end, Leslie, unable to handle the onslaught, had taken a handful of pills — placebos — and had fallen asleep. It didn't stop Alyne. After explaining the inner workings of the Greater San Fernando Valley Real Estate Association, Inc. and its tie-in to the CIA, an organization she had been tapped to head because of her well-rounded knowledge of the Internet (meaning Interpol), she explained why she was on the boat returning from an undercover mission to Guam, then launched into some of the great houses that were available in Encino, California. The best one, she said, happened to be the one she was staying in. She would be moving out of it shortly, thanks to her "two good buds," John Wayne and Bobby Whatsisface, the Emperor of Japan. Leaving bag and baggage behind, the three were off on a lifelong round-the-world safari. It was an idea they had come up with while quail hunting in Balboa Park — a park most sane people would say couldn't support the feeding habits of a sparrow.

When Leslie awoke, the plane was making its final approach to

LAX. Alyne was still talking. When the plane landed she launched back on Encino, and talked all the way through Customs. But the Encino connection apparently worked, and by the time the cab arrived at the villa Leslie was hooked. There was a lock-box on the front door and their entrance had to be made through a broken rear window. Save for a few personal items that included a straw mat, a pair of woolen unmentionables, two burned-out candles, some empty cans and a discarded earthquake emergency kit, the place was empty. It didn't bother Leslie. It was the American way, she thought.

She was thinking the same when, the very next morning, Alyne was armed away by a birdlike woman who was backed by two strait-jacket-carrying attendants who had arrived in a barred van and looked suspiciously like they were from the nearest asylum. It was the British consulate that had tipped them off. From out of the blue, Alyne had called the embassy, leaving a message saying *Hold the boat.* There was another person joining her, the Duke and Bobby Whatsisface on safari. Fortunately, Leslie declined the offer.

The Alyne Condon episodes did work to Leslie's advantage, however. The real property owner, an understanding woman named Jean Zambello-Sincere, there when Alyne was armed away, saw how interested the Englishwoman was in the place and offered it to her on an option/purchase plan. Leslie preferred ownership, and although helped by lawyers, and, belatedly, by the British consulate, the wire transfer of funds, the closing of escrow and other matters proved too taxing for her, and so she settled on a lease.

Leslie could have bought the villa. She was anything but a poor woman. She had a strong inheritance from her grandparents, of which her father, Dr. Bernard Van Horn, was in charge. The doctor, a peculiar but well-off surgeon in Bath, England, always saw to it that she had everything she needed. It was strange, because he knew Leslie had a problem. He knew, too, that she was apt to end up anywhere on the planet. But he never questioned what she was doing or why. There were times when she needed extraordinary amounts of money, but still he wire-transferred whatever was required without question.

When she returned home, as he knew she would, the only thing that was of apparent concern to him was whether or not she had regained the ability to remember her childhood years.

She never did.

One of the first things Leslie did after optioning the property was to convert the guest house into a laboratory. When her mind was in reasonable order, and as she had started doing before leaving England, she started dabbling in floriculture. Leslie loved the freeing jollity of nursing the little splendidly-colored but short-lived plants from the Northern Hemisphere that were referred to as poppies, and, later when the petals fell, the tubelike stems would expose seed pods that, when slit, would ooze with a milky sap that would eventually darken and be the source of opium, morphine, codeine, and heroin.

Now that she was in the USA, and when she wasn't consumed by fear of the clown, she had her eyes on the genus Eschscholtzia californica, the state flower of California. In her mind it was a convenient, happiness-giving, beautiful little poppy with seeds so rich and versatile that, according to the books, they were used as bird seed, and in baking and cooking. And they had such all-around versatility that they were used in making soap, paint, and varnishes. There was no question about it, the little poppy with the unripened, oval-shaped seed pods that was selected to be the state flower in 1890 was about as useful as any plant could be.

What Leslie did not know was that Eschscholtzia californica was a poppy with herbal properties so strong that it could kill a person. Even the tiniest dose, injected or ingested, wreaked havoc with the brain. In some cases, two doses could kill the brain. Soon she would grow them and would be experimenting with them. And she never lost sight of the objective. Somewhere she had read that the Sumerians called the poppy *Hul Gil* — the flower of joy.

She thought it was all so charming.

But optioning the villa and setting up her poppy shop wasn't Leslie's only large expenditure. Six months after settling in, she was talked into acquiring a nightclub. It was downtown, tiny, but exquisitely beautiful. It was closed when she got it, and it should have remained that way.

Leslie acquired the club — already named the b.c. — to spread joy. It didn't work. Leslie didn't know if it worked or not, because she never went there. But, then again, neither did any customers.

Angie, the young woman in the morgue, had run the one-person operation, but one would never have known it. She had been at Leslie's house in the Valley; in fact, she had stayed at the house several times after having gotten the job on the strength of the previous owner's recommendation. But night after night she would sit alone in the club, alternately doing her nails and painting imaginary pictures on the wall. After the pictures started moving and the walls started talking, she would coke up, call Leslie and say that the crowd was thinning and that it was time to close shop. Leslie would agree, never asking how things went, or anything of the sort. She would merely say, brightly, "Have a nice night," sneak a peek at the clown, and continue with her experiments.

Not that Angie was interested in drinking, but she would collect a few bottles along with a few other items and leave, stopping on the streets only to negotiate a coke deal. The very attractive young woman was off to see her new boyfriend. A lot older than she, normally he would be either in his room or at a den just off Sixth and Flower Streets. Wherever he was, the lanky, square-jawed, redneck-looking man would already be on the road to a drug-induced stupor.

His name was LeCoultre.

4

Months later, it seemed everything was working smoothly at the villa.

With the big, fierce-looking Doberman at her side on the night of the murder, Leslie Van Horn was — on the surface — the epitome of the serene, picture-perfect, contemplative woman. The Japanese influence was in full effect. Dressed in a stylish kimono, she was sitting on a tatami mat in a silhouetted silence, quietly overlooking the pond in front of the house, all the while LeCoultre was rifling the back of the house. She had to have heard him. As dope-driven and clumsy as he had been in his search, he was anything but careful. He didn't have cause to search the house, however. Had he been thinking at all, he would have known that all he had to do was go to the lab. There he would have found stacks of neatly wrapped little packets all set to be distributed to the poor. He knew heroin was there. It had been the prime reason he had landed there in the first place. In striking up the relationship with Angie on their first coke-happy night three weeks earlier, he was told that the lady was a nut and that she had found a way to manufacture and process heroin. Angie knew because she worked for the lady, and on top of that, she had been asked to drive to a few of the more undesirable areas of town and donate the little gift-wrapped packets to the needy. The needy, however, never benefited from the gesture. Angie would drive downtown and sell the packets — an act that accounted for any number of illnesses.

When LeCoultre made inquiry as to why she didn't keep any for herself, the young redhead pointed out with pride that she was not into heroin. She was a casual coke user, she said. The fact that her nostrils were seared beyond repair didn't seem to register.

Leslie Van Horn favored the poor. When she and Angie first met, she thought Angie was poor, which was one of the reasons she was hired. In a way Angie *was* poor, having sold everything she had ever owned to support her habit. But it was something Leslie didn't know. She also didn't know anything about chemical addiction, substance abusers or any of the other terms and conditions that could afflict a user. She didn't know that the narcotized mind could become about as confused as hers. She was on the other side of the street when it came to such matters. It was the lack of knowledge, naiveté, really, that caused her to hire the young redhead in the first place. When times became even tougher for the redhead, it was the same lack of knowledge, or naiveté, that allowed her to stay at the villa off and on, which accounted for LeCoultre's first visit.

Having been told by Angie that her employer was into drugs, and mistakenly thinking she was a normal dealer, the next time LeCoultre came he brought a present with him. It was a 9mm .380 PPKS Walther, a gun he had improperly taken in a shakedown months before going on vacation. On the second visit he spent the afternoon attempting to teach her how to use the gun. Probably out of fear, Leslie never got the hang of it. She was buying a second car at the time, but in appreciation for the gun, she allowed the two the use of the car. It was the wine-red XJS — which was supposed to be in her name but LeCoultre, with the help of the dealer, pulled a fast one on both women and it ended up in *his* name.

But after Leslie got to know the two, she didn't like them. They were slobs. They were not clean, they were not to be trusted, and the cop, whenever he came by the villa, had always managed to say something racially disparaging about blacks and drugs. It led him, of course, to a haranguing about a cop called McKnight in his division at Whitehurst. The opinionated, hard-charging black cop was a fixation with him. Race and rank fueled jealousy and left the man who had been reduced in rank embittered to the core.

LeCoultre despised McKnight. The animosity had been long-standing, but it was not a one-way street. McKnight hadn't liked him from the start. It stemmed from a gut feeling, and not because LeCoultre had done anything overtly at the time.

McKnight, born in the Mississippi Delta and victimized by racism in his youth, had grown up with the notion that it was in his best interest to keep his racial antennae ever high and always sharp, particularly around people like LeCoultre.

Although the lieutenant was four or five years LeCoultre's senior, they both had come to the department at the same time, had graduated the academy at the same time, and many times they had worked out of the same division. But despite his instinctual feeling, feelings that were soon supported by vile jokes and "accidentally" stated racial comments, McKnight didn't allow himself to touch the depths of hatred as had LeCoultre, and one time he had even gone so far as to make an attempt at civility.

It was at the Christmas party in '82. As it turned out, the two men had been promoted to the rank of sergeant a few months earlier. McKnight, working out of South Central at the time, had taken it upon himself to drive to Whitehurst to extend a congratulatory hand to LeCoultre and a few others he knew. When he got around to LeCoultre, the white cop from Pasadena accepted the hand. But then he made a show of taking out his handkerchief and wiping his hand clean.

McKnight could have killed him.

LeCoultre's fixation with McKnight became a fixation of Leslie's as well, but hers was rooted differently. It started as a curiosity. But the more McKnight was vilified, the more interested she became in him. The curiosity mushroomed into a fantasy. It got to the point where she decided that if LeCoultre said another negative word about this man called Wyatt McKnight, she was either going to run him off the property or unleash the dog on him.

She presumed the clown would help.

But before Angie, before LeCoultre and his castigation of McKnight, before even opening the club, the woman was always alone in her thoughts. And, as it had been in England, her thoughts were frequently morose. There were times when, back home, she involuntarily wanted — indeed tried — to stretch out; to break free; to have fun with the mind. But always she was denied; always there was something to stop her. Everything was framed in gloom and melancholy, and it was so deep-down disturbing that even trying to lose herself in the classics, art, poetry, and books on travel failed.

With effort she could, at times, mask her inner disturbance by pretending to be cheerfully upbeat, but the opportunities were few and buoyancy could never be sustained.

Everything failed Leslie. Even the freeing United States failed her at first. For the first few months she was still shrouded and beclouded by God-knows-what, and then she was becoming even more confused; even more fragmented and disjointed. It bothered her immensely, so much so that after leasing the house, she fell into an even deeper depression. She was unable or unwilling to eat, and, in the beginning, spent the earlier part of her evenings circling what amounted to her living room. Then there were times when she would slap at the air and, almost like in penitence or self-flagellation, she would flail herself. As the evening wore on, and not able to sleep, she would lie on her mat, always face up, and, as in a state of catatonia, do nothing but stare at a darkened ceiling. By morning she was seized by guilt.

The bright, bold California sun heightened the uniqueness of the villa, but it also created another dilemma. Even though Leslie believed she couldn't fully enjoy the grounds because everywhere she went the clown trailed her, she would slide the rice-paper doors back and do nothing but sit and vacantly stare at the pond.

The problem now was that the poor had nothing, while she was living in opulence. And so, for the most part, she remained inside and once the staring was over, she sought to lose herself watching television. Like many other things, for an unsettled mind it was not the best thing she could have done. She was bombarded by screaming newscasts, and disheartening tabloid and talk shows, something she was not accustomed to. In England she had never had a television set.

With the day gone and the fearful night approaching, Leslie would become even more depressed. If she didn't circle the room, and sometimes after she had made a series of circles, slaps, and mild acts of penitence, she would sit there alone, night after night, hearing virtually the same things over and over. Always there would be something about the poor, the sick, the disadvantaged.

It didn't come quickly, but she eventually drew the conclusion that the only way to truly help the downtrodden was to make them feel good. Struck with the idea that Americans had a fixation with sedating, she began eating again and spent the next month in the library, studying the manufacture of heroin. It led to her converting the guest house into a laboratory. It was the perfect place. It was situated at the end of a path and was off from the pond, which was discreetly tucked behind the row of bonsai trees. Off from there was the stylishly small hothouse where she grew her poppies.

Angie hadn't been seen for two weeks. Leslie probably wasn't thinking of her or LeCoultre the night the cop sneaked back to the house with robbery on his mind. The young woman, in her final stages, had overdosed on cocaine in a downtown hotel. The cop had spent almost two days traveling his haunts without heroin. He was in bad shape. Even getting to the Valley and breaking into the house presented its problems.

But Leslie didn't react to any of the noise the burglar was making.

She simply maintained an aloof quiet while he was in the back, stuffing his pockets with the little packets she had already prepared for distribution. Near the end, LeCoultre was panting, searching, and dropping things, and giving every indication that he was not worried about being heard. Still Leslie gave no reaction. It was only after the house became quiet, when she felt whoever it was had cleared the house and had gotten as far as his car, that she decided to do anything. Even at that the move was quiet and subtle. She quietly nodded to the Doberman Pinscher to take care of matters for her.

When the dog zipped outside, LeCoultre was braced alongside the fence, preparing to inject himself. He was almost crazed at that point, and any living thing that tried to stop him from injecting himself with heroin was in for trouble.

Leslie had heard the initial stages of the fight between man and dog, and, assuming the dog was winning, she was about to resort back to that seemingly contemplative state when the clown popped into her mind. Checking on him, she discovered that not only had the dog lost the fight and was obviously dead, but also that the man had staggered to the Jag and was backing it through the gate.

Maintaining her composure, and now knowing who the burglar was, the woman got her keys from the drawer, found the gun that he had given her, and went for her car. A minute and a half later the two vehicles were almost neck and neck on Hayvenhurst Avenue. Because it did not run straight through, Hayvenhurst was not a well-traveled street. But it would have made little difference. LeCoultre was hoping to make it to Ventura Boulevard, head east, and eventually catch the I-405 freeway that paralleled Sepulveda Boulevard.

With beads of sweat dripping from his head and with him trying to negotiate the vehicle while trying to inject himself, the woman pulled her vehicle alongside his, pressed her window button down and leveled the gun. She inhaled deeply, turned her head away from the direction she was pointing, and fired. The first shot very easily could have knocked out a street light; it had been that high. The next shot was lower. It punctured a bus-stop sign. The third hit the curb. With both cars going from side to side and virtually X-ing the street, Leslie got the idea that she was not supposed to turn her head while firing and that despite the powerful kick from the gun, she had to aim and fire at the prey. While she did not aim properly — and had it not been for the thought of crashing she would have closed her eyes — she nonetheless did what she had to do. The next bullet hit the target, sending both man and car careening into the basin.

She came to a stop, made a U-turn and headed back home. On the way back, she flagged a passing Highway Patrolman, indicated that she had just passed an accident and drove on. Four blocks away, she slammed on the brakes and started screaming. She was terrified at the sight of the gun on the front seat. She didn't know how it got there; she was afraid to touch it.

In the shower minutes after the murder, Leslie Van Horn spent several moments trying to recall the clown's activities. Suspicious that it was he who had placed the gun in the car, she tiptoed out of the shower and went into the room to sneak a peek at the swing where the clown was seated. She didn't like what she saw. The clown was looking ominous in the dark. She thought he looked as though he had just murdered someone. Badly frightened, she crept back to the bathroom and locked the door. She spent the night huddled in the corner of the shower.

Creeping out at daylight, she took another fearful peek at the clown, tiptoed back to the shower and remained there another two hours before crawling out. It was then that she decided to call the police, getting Rusty, the desk sergeant. After their talk, she buried the dog, cleaned up and sneaked out to her car. The weapon was still on the front seat. She shrieked when she saw it, then settling, she got it and tossed it as far over the wall as she could. She mentally shifted gears, popped back into the car and drove off as though she didn't have a care in the world.

Leslie went on an early-morning shopping spree in Beverly Hills. She followed up by touring the streets, looking for a detective whom she didn't know, and couldn't describe.

5

Forte's was dead. The bar was a step up from most of the Valley's watering holes, but the Happy Hour crowd hadn't yet arrived and the hors d'oeuvres weren't out. McKnight wouldn't be there when the body-rubbers arrived, but he knew that within an hour or so the walls would be jammed. Mostly happy acts would be decorating the place, but not to be discounted were the hide 'n' seekers — the square pegs in the round holes, begging for company yet wanting to be alone in a world that failed to understand the plight of the lonely.

Sitting four stools down from where McKnight had seated himself was a striking young blonde named Gena. She was sipping on a milk-colored drink and had her body positioned so that her tanned, trimmed legs would grab the black man's attention.

Cy, the bartender, had wavy hair and an easy smile. Until the phone buzzed, he had been wiping the same glass for minutes, apparently wanting to see if anything was going to happen before the expected crowd arrived, and between the only two customers in the place.

He picked up the phone, listened to the caller, then held it up.

"Hey, Sport; you McKnight?"

"Yes," answered the detective as he pushed a cramp and crushed out a cigarette. "And I smoke too much to be into sports."

The bartender handed over the phone, and emptied the ashtray. "Whatever floats your boat."

On the phone was Bunny. "Hey, Mac-Wacky, I got some…"

"Hold it, germ. The name is McKnight, and don't forget it."

"Big deal," retorted Bunny. "Listen, I got that info for you. Th' broad's name was Angie."

"Angie *what*, little man?"

"I dunno. But she used to work at some joint called the b.c. She met your guy and dropped out of sight."

"Anything else?"

"What do you want for nothin'?"

"It's not for nothing, Mr. Snitch. I caught you holding, remember?"

McKnight offered the phone back to the bartender. Now that he'd seen the place and had received the call, he thought he'd pop into Paoli's or the Sugar Mill, since he was already in the Valley. Both were lively spots he remembered from about a year ago. The owners were nice, if a bit fuzzy, and the music was tolerable. Monty's on Topanga Canyon Boulevard would work, too, he thought. But, tired of people, he decided he would go home.

Gena, having caught his eye, indicated she was leaving, and held up her tab.

"It's on the house, Babe," waved Cy.

She left a tip and slid lithely off the stool. In doing so she displayed more thigh to the disinterested detective. She held the position for a moment to see if she would get a reaction. Disappointed over the lack of interest, she gave him another look and departed. Cy, short for Cyril, slid down to pick up the tip.

"You're a hard nut to crack."

McKnight lit another cigarette and sent a spiral of smoke from his mouth. He didn't say anything.

"She had eyes," Cy persisted. "She told me that when you first came in. Comes in here to catch the atmosphere. Can't get this kind at the club where she works. Her name is Gena. Works at the b.c. It's new; a beautiful little spot. I'm told a broad named Leslie Van Horn owns it. Nice. Action. Mucho bucks. Conscience money, they say. Comes from England."

It was all just a little too easy for the thinking man, but something clicked. Rusty, describing the woman as a nut, had told the English-woman that it was he who was working on the case. Subsequent to that, the woman had called several times. There was no doubt that it was she who had called and hung up during his conversation with Devro. Earlier, he figured, she had done the same while he was talk-ing with Kiesner. It was amateurish and silly, but still there were a few questions that had to be answered. Nevertheless, things were falling into place.

It was obvious to him that the young woman, Gena, was a plant, sent there by the Englishwoman. Since only Bunny Workman knew where he would be at that hour, he had to be the connection. As to the talkative Cy's involvement, it was probably negligible, as was Bunny's, really. He was only a hustler and would do anything for a quick buck. Nine times out of ten, Gena, receiving instructions from her employer, the Englishwoman, was told where to go, and was told to be enticing. She came into Forte's, reasoned the detective, slipped Cy, the bartender, a quick twenty or so, and told him what to say. It was just that simple. It was almost to the point of being amusing. And now so were the words: *Can harmz.* The only thing was that LeCoultre, in the state he had been in, never intended to say *Can harmz.* What he was trying to say was the woman's name, the one Cy had just mentioned.

The detective silently repeated the name several times. He was satisfied. There was no question about it, the trooper had definitely made a mistake. If you didn't use the voice or lips, and if you let the sound come from the back of the throat, it comes out *Hannn Hornnnn. Van* Horn.

"Cy, exactly where is Miss Van Horn's club located?"

"Downtown. 'Round Third and Spring. I'm told it's classy and hip; private. It's for people with plenty of scratch; you know, the kind who don't deal with the 'common' folk. S'matter of fact, I hear it's so hi-falootin' that you gotta have on a tux just to get through the front door. And tonight is really gonna be a big night. The place will be loaded with women. And some of 'em won't mind crossin' over, if you get my drift. An' if you can get in, which I'm sure you can. You really ought to check it out. Make sure you got on that tux, though."

"You're overselling again, Cy. Any reason?"

"You look like a regular guy. The kind who deserves a night out."

"Looks can be deceiving," said McKnight.

"But not yours."

McKnight finished up. He stiffly stood. "How much do I owe you?"

"Club soda? It's on the house."

"You keep giving away the store, and you won't be able to keep your doors open."

"It's an investment."

McKnight laid down a five. "I'll check your club out one of these days."

"'One of these days?'" the bartender echoed. "I know how you black cats are when it comes to something like that."

McKnight leaned into his face: "How are we, friend?"

"Sorry," said the bartender.

The detective knew he was lying.

McKnight lived just south of Wilshire, not far from Doheny Drive. It was one of the better sections of the city, the kind that blacks had had trouble moving into not so very long ago. It was racially mixed now, but prompted by thoughts of people in the department like Ault and LeCoultre, or maybe because of the little, thought-to-be-harmless racial clichés uttered by someone as simple-minded as Cy, the bartender, often his mind would drift back to the days when the whites had tried to keep them out — not only from that area, but from the areas close to it, even going so far as to try to kick the velvety-voiced Nat "King" Cole out of the house he had bought to raise his family in. It was like that all over California then, even in liberal San Francisco, when the whites didn't want the great ballplayer Willie Mays moving into a white area.

But Los Angeles, being what it was, gave Mr. Cole fair warning of the whites' displeasure. They poisoned the family dog and called the IRS on him.

It was an interesting time then. The whites didn't want the blacks moving in, but the blacks wanted, indeed *fought* for, integration. Yet when the successful blacks tried to move into the white enclaves, they were not always supported by other blacks. They thought they should have remained with their own people.

Maybe it was because he was fatigued and had only a week or two to go before cranking up the Spectrum 2010 and heading south, or maybe he was fighting hard to keep from thinking about the syringes he had purposely left in his desk drawer, but the early-day dilemma faced by the blacks pushed his mind onto a related thought: The influx of foreigners and the ease with which they could now settle. They could live anywhere in the city. But he wondered how many of them realized the debt they owed to the blacks. Not that the debt would be paid, or even acknowledged, for that matter — but he wondered how many of them knew what it had taken to get them there. How many of them had had to resort to civil revolt, or had ever marched or had a cross burned on their lawns? He wondered, too, who would have been there had they been asked to join the struggle. Not many, he concluded. The Chicanos, more than likely. Few others.

Maybe the rest didn't have to. They had assimilated and had joined the oppressor.

There was nothing special about the long-time policeman's apartment. If you hadn't known the man, you wouldn't have gotten to know him by way of what was exposed in the three-bedroom place.

It was depersonalized. You wouldn't have gotten to know whether he loved music or silence; if he loved art, cared for books, was able to cook, or was satisfied leading a solitary life. In his defense, though, most of the personal items had been packed and stored in the second bedroom, waiting to be moved out. Other than the investigation, the only thing on his mind was getting the Spectrum 2010 home and setting that Big Bad Baby on the road, exploring, all the while heading for the uncluttered life in the Mississippi Delta.

When the man entered his apartment he had a rented tuxedo over his shoulder. He had been quietly cramping and sweating, and so he went directly to the bathroom. He got undressed and immediately took a cold shower. He hadn't had one since morning and he had been aching for another one for hours. When that was done, he threw on his robe, looked at the tux and came back out to the living room.

With at least an hour or so before taking another shower and getting ready to go to the club Cy, the bartender, had spoken of, it was time to try to relax. He had given up alcohol and it was clear he craved something else, but he poured a drink, kicked his slippers off, slid down into his favorite chair and lit a cigarette.

Before his change, or, as he termed it, before unanswerably surrendering to a bitter disappointment that he promised God he would overcome one day, he used to love to sit in the old thick-armed Naugahyde chair and do nothing but think.

He had had the chair for over eighteen years. It had been given to him by a Jewish merchant whose life he had saved during a burglary attempt by a trio of addicts. He used to stop by to see the old man, just to keep an eye out for him. One day he stopped by, and he was met by a crew from Nicki Aladanti's office.

The addicts had returned and had turned into killers. McKnight vowed he would get them. He did.

It took him less than three days.

The lieutenant was feeling fairly good, or as good as he could feel about having solved the *Can harmz* puzzlement. Soft instrumental music, or maybe a Dinah Washington oldie or an Erroll Garner classic, would have added to the moment. But like the rest of his things, the old eight-track tapes, albums, and the more recent CDs had already been packed. Maybe he should have kept one of them out, he thought. But which one? The Otis Redding standard *I've Been Loving You Too Long to Stop Now* popped into his mind. Lately it had been a frequent occurrence when he was relaxing at home. Each time he tried to dismissed it, but the title hung with him. It was a love song, but he couldn't go along with it. Taking it literally, he felt that no one but no one could love anyone that much. He certainly hadn't.

But then there was a line in the song that said something like *You've become a habit to me.* So then, maybe the song didn't have to be restricted to a person. Maybe it could embrace a *thing.* As he had done before, he looked at the cigarette, thought about the unmerciful struggle of quitting, refocused on the word *habit*, and thought about the awesome power of heroin. Interestingly, that thought merged with other thoughts, all having to do with the love of a woman. That, too, was power.

Lately, he had begun to wonder which was stronger. He didn't have a woman in his life, but he was generous enough to give the female gender the benefit of the doubt and almost concluded that the love of a woman conquered all. But then again, something told him, the reason why people became addicted in the first place was that they had so often underestimated the hard, addictive power of narcotics.

Heroin was unbeatable. He, of all people didn't need the reminder. As if to prove the point, he thought about his career and the hundreds of addicts he had known and arrested over the years. He knew — he positively *knew* — that there wasn't an addict in the world who didn't live and die by the code: *I've Been Loving You Too Long to Stop Now.* But, there again, there wasn't a lover in the world who wouldn't say the same. And so the addict and the lover would keep on living and dying because of a euphoria. But the question remained: Which of the two loves was stronger?

Drifting on, two opposing forces entered into his mind. One, oddly, was born out by something LeCoultre's twelve-year-old, coke-sniffing son had said: *"Sooner or later all creeps get what they deserve. Includin' you."* It was the statement that he had in mind when he couldn't accept Kiesner's compliment about being a great guy.

Nicki Aladanti had given birth to the second force: *Your state flower is a poppy. Cut it, and mix it with something like phenylcyclohexylamine and you're ready to float beyond the moon.*

The thoughts weren't as jumbled as they appeared.

The tired detective took a few leisurely sips from the glass and allowed his mind to slip back to the Spectrum 2010. It was relieving. He thought about what he would have to load the Big Bad Boy up with; what kind of snacks and traveling items he might need. That started him to wonder about where his first stop would be on the road. Shoot up to Vegas, maybe? Drop a few at the tables there, and take the I-40 across? Nope. Las Vegas was too glitzy for an old cop who had just about seen it all and done it all, and who was just leaving another city bent on artificiality and crassness. It'd be better to take the I-5 to the I-10, cut across New Mexico, and maybe pick up the I-20 through Texas. That should be a pretty good drive. And, since it was all over, and there was nothing to rush to, he could pull the Big Bad Boy to a stop just about any place he wanted, and maybe do a little reflecting; think about a career that had been long and interesting. And if there was a lake around, all the better. Whatever, reflecting was always good for the soul — and warding off demons. And cramps.

"Lieutenant, how many arrests have you made in your career?"

"Beg pardon?"

"You were raised in the Delta and you're on your way back to the Delta. But you came to Los Angeles to attend UCLA. You dropped out in your second year. Your interest was in social studies, you gave thought to becoming a school teacher. But you ended up as a cop. It was a fair question. How many arrests have you made in your career?"

"I'm a little too tired to go into that now. I'm getting ready to go out and possibly arrest a woman for murder. She has a severe mental problem. I've gotta be on my game. I have to prepare. After all, this is not the McKnight of old."

"Are you sorry about that? Not being the person you used to be?"

"Very, very much so. I'd give anything I've ever owned to go back even seven months. A year and seven would be even better."

"Back to the question. How many arrests have you made in your career?"

"Hundreds, I'd say."

"How many were guilty?"

"Ninety-nine point nine percent."

"Any regrets?"

"A few."

"How many fights have you been involved in?"

"Lots."

"How many shots have you fired?"

"Loads."

"How many people have you killed?"

"Oh, God, what a question. *How many people have I killed?* What a question."

"And?"

"I'd rather not say. I'm well over average, I believe."

"How many people have you shot and killed, Lieutenant? I want a number."

"Four."

"Were you in the right?"

"According to the law, I was."

"What about the higher law?"

"What higher law?"

"You know."

"I think I'd better pass on that one."

"Afraid to think about it?"

"Could be."

"Why?'

"I don't like to think about things like that."

"Afraid you'll see the people you've killed again?"

"No. But what a strange thing to ask."

"Perhaps. But why fear answering the question?"

"Okay. I'll answer: Somehow, somewhere, someday, I feel the shoe will be on the other foot."

"So. The question wasn't so strange after all. You, apparently, believe in a form of reincarnation?"

"I believe there is a reason why the Earth is round."

"And?"

"It's trite, but I believe that 'what goes around, comes around'."

"And that includes people."

"If you say so."

"Did you have to kill those four people?"

"Probably."

"Did you have to kill those four people, Lieutenant?"

"I don't know. I really don't."

"Could you have handled matters in any other way?"

"Looking back, I suppose so."

"But you're not certain?"

"I'm not sure of anything."

"Can you remember the people you've killed?"

"I try not to."

"Why is it that you try not to remember them?"

"I don't know. I can't explain it."

"How does it feel when you kill someone?"

"Oh, boy. Here we go. I'll tell you. It's an incredibly strange sensation. Maybe not when the person is first hit, because you're caught up in the passion of the moment and you're protected by a certain immunity. If he were a real bad guy, say like a murderer or somebody who was going to inflict serious bodily harm on a child or the helpless, and you stop him with a bullet, you feel good. Damn good."

"How long does the feeling last?"

"For about two days."

"Then what?"

"Then you start paying the price."

"How so?"

"This is not for publication, is it?"

"Why do you ask?"

"Because killing is such a personal thing. No one likes to admit they're bothered by it. Same with people who've killed in war. It's something no one likes to talk about. I know guys who've shot people and have been married for twenty or thirty years and have never said anything to their wives about it. You couldn't pry the story out of them with a crowbar."

"Why not? Is it because it's buried too deeply in them?"

"On the contrary, it's not deep at all. Seeing a person fall is never far from the surface of the mind. That instant, that moment, that time is never erased. It's always there. And so is the person, for that matter. They're gone, but not forgotten. You killed. Do you have any idea what it means when you say that? When you've actually done it? The person you've killed really won't let you forget. They're always there. Always. I don't care if it's in a nightmare, a simple dream, while you're out shopping, in the shower, or on your way to church, or boozing it up in a bar, or in the bank, or taking a dump or taking a stroll, it's there. There is always something to remind you of that day, that person, that time, that instant. Why? I don't know. Maybe it's because human life has this thing called sanctity attached to it. You know? *The sanctity of life.* Maybe there's something behind this thing that we'll never know, until it's too late to tell anybody. But the human being you've killed is always there. Not so with anything else. The farmer never sees the pigs he's slaughtered; the matador never sees the bull. I don't know. You tell me. I suppose that's why I've never really worried about Joe Slick, the lawyer, getting Joe Slayer, the murderer, off through trickery. He may have gotten him off, but he never freed him. The smile may be bright in daylight, but the midnight hour holds the truth. The dead don't die. They're always behind the eyelids; always on call from the mind."

"Who were the people you killed?"

"A couple were murderers, two were in a drug shootout, another involved a kidnapping, and another involved a burglary, and there was one...."

"Why did you kill them?"

"I just said what they were."

"Yes, but you have also lost count. You said there were four. But you were numbering more than four. And it appeared you had even forgotten another."

"Yes. But I didn't say I had forgotten them."

"Why did you kill them?"

"It was kill or be killed."

"And so they were all armed? And they were all firing or pointing a weapon at you? Your life was in jeopardy?"

"I can't say that."

"Then why did you kill them, Lieutenant?"

"It was in the line of duty."

"Why did you kill those people, Lieutenant?"

"You want me to say something like impulsive authority. Don't you?"

"I want you to say why those people are dead."

"All right. I'm gonna go along with that impulsive-authority thing. Wanna know why?"

"I want to know why you killed those people."

"Lemme say this. Maybe it'll help. Now, I certainly don't recommend this to any cop, as many know — maybe even you, for that matter — but for the last year or so I haven't carried a gun on me. It's close by. But I don't carry it. I gotta tell you, making that decision was one of the hardest things I've ever had to do. I'm home, right? We're having a chat. I don't have a gun on me. I don't mind saying, pal, I feel naked as all hell."

"You feel a loss of power and authority?"

"In a way, yes."

"And so in not having the gun, you can no longer react quite so impulsively."

"Something like that. Impulsive authority has been reduced to a slow crawl."

"Going back to the people you've killed — if you had it to do all over again, would they be dead?"

"If I had it to do all over again, I wouldn't be a policeman."

"So the answer is 'no'?"

"The answer is 'no.'"

"You'd be the school teacher you once thought about becoming?"

"With kids the way they are today? I'm sorry, friend. But I can't think of a more thankless job. Kudos to all those who are doing it, by the way. Can you imagine where we'd be without teachers?"

"Why would you not be a policeman again?"

"Because when all is said and done, when you take the oath and pick up the badge and strap on the gun, you work for the people, but you live for the evil that people create."

"Well said."

"Thank you. By the way, who are you?"

"You don't know by now, Mr. McKnight?"

The graying detective sat there a while longer and emptied his glass in thought. The *I've Been Loving You Too Long to Stop Now* refrain popped into his mind again. The word *habit* was stronger. This time he toyed with the melody and asked himself: Loving *who* too long? Loving *what* too long?

Certainly not in my case, he said. *I've never had a choice.*

The case re-entered his mind. He thought about LeCoultre and how he had bottomed out. He was a cop; he was a redneck-looking slob of a human being and had never dealt from the top of the deck, but he was still a cop and at some point he must have been at a crossroads, or at the fork in the road, and he wondered why would he have allowed himself to go that far. Couldn't he tell what was happening? Couldn't he maintain control? Was he so weak he couldn't stop? Didn't he want to?

The lieutenant got up and poured himself another drink. He had been drinking vodka, but he switched to brandy. Neither would get the job done. Deep down, he was craving something else. He brought the telephone back to the chair with him, took a moment and gave the Englishwoman a thought. Strangely, while dialing, he wished he could have been placing the call to her. Thinking that bizarrely, he mused, it was definitely time for him and the Big Bad Boy to be hitting the road.

With phone in hand he hesitated for a second, believing he was now able to answer his queries about the song and its title. In a life devoid of romance, he concluded, the question could never be *who* do you love and when did you start; rather, it had to be *what* do you love and when did you start loving it.

He was uncomfortable with the thought.

On the other end of the line was Frankie. She was a dark-skinned, classy, Dahomey-looking lady who placed one squarely in mind of the former ambassador from Uganda. In fact, that's just who she was. When her term was over, Frankie Mobassa had resisted the call to return home, departed Washington and settled in Los Angeles.

"Hi, Frankie, how are ya?"

"Fine, Wyatt. And you?"

"Okay."

He lit a cigarette, and said nothing else.

"Well," said the lady with the long, elegant fingers and nice accent, "why are you calling? On your way to Uganda, or some other place of African intrigue? Even though you sound a tad fatigued."

"No, I'm staying right here in the good ol' U.S. of A. Why would you ask something like that?"

"With your views, I thought you'd want to go back to the mother country."

"Second time I've heard the term today," he mistakenly said. "Somebody must be trying to tell me something. But, no, m'lady, I'm not. Close, but no cigar."

"Well?"

"Believe it or not, I'm calling to see if you'd like to go out tonight?"

"That's interesting," she responded, "particularly since I haven't heard from you in seven and a half months. Is that a custom of black men in America? Steam 'em up and disappear?"

"Actually, we don't have a custom. We're too busy shadow-boxing in the dark."

"I can certainly believe that."

"But, Madam Ambassador, I have been thinking about you."

"It's been so long you've forgotten, Mr. McKnight. It's 'former' Madam Ambassador. But thank you for the thought. Are you still working?"

"Meaning have I turned in my badge?"

"And gun. And cynicism. And anger. And all the other things that make a woman securely uncomfortable."

"'Securely' uncomfortable? That's a new one."

"It shouldn't be. The average man has the ability to make a woman uncomfortable. You manage to take it one step farther. Thus the term 'securely.'"

"And so the more distance between the two, the more secure?"

"The more distance from the man with the gun, cynicism, and anger, the more secure."

"And with those things gone, happiness abounds?"

"It'd be a pretty good start. It could make for a happy ending."

"You didn't read the book, Miss Frankie," McKnight said, taking a sip. "Uppity blacks are not entitled to a happy ending to a sad story."

"You're admitting yours is a sad one?"

"You don't mind if I plead the Fifth?"

"Please do."

"Thank you. But to answer you, no; I haven't gotten around to turning anything in yet. But soon."

"And then what?"

"For a month or so, I'm aiming to tour the veins of the nation.

Then I go back home. Home to Bigfoot country, where I hope the old dirt roads remember me as well as I remember them."

"And after that?"

"After that, I'm going to sit on a crumbling front porch, and maybe, on a good and distant Sunday morning I'll catch an old Baptist preacher whooping it up in church, take a final tour or two in my Spec 2010; come back, park that Big Bad Baby where I can keep an eye on her, ease into my old rocker, and slowly rock away the years."

"It sounds provincial enough. But I thought you were a native Angeleno. You seemed to have had that Los Angeles flair."

"Now I *know* it's time for this Wyatt to get out of Dodge."

"And so where is home, Wyatt?"

"I don't think you'd go for it, Frankie."

"From the way you sound, I don't think I'd go for it, either."

"Don't want this to sound like a committment, but maybe you and I can get together before I go. Work some things out."

"You're so romantic."

"I'm trying."

"I'm not convinced."

He said nothing.

Frankie spoke. "So, the policeman is going out tonight?"

"Even rented a tux for the occasion."

"But tux or not, you're a policeman to the bone, Wyatt. And if the policeman-to-the-bone is going out, he's going out on a case?"

"I used to be a policeman-to-the-bone, Frankie. But no more. I've slipped a little, I'm sorry to say. You are right, though. I am going out on a case. And I have a feeling it is going to be a most interesting one. I might even have to be saved from myself."

"Have a nice night."

"You don't care to go with?"

"Forget it, Wyatt," Frankie responded, hanging up. "You don't want a woman. You want a condition."

Ouch.

That was the stinging, tight-shouldered reaction the man gave.

He hung up and re-dialed.

"Metro," the policeman on the other end of the line said. He was the desk sergeant for the evening shift. "Santiago here."

In part Spanish, McKnight said, "Mike; McKnight. Listen, have whoever is in charge of detectives tonight get in touch with Scotland Yard, or maybe Interpol, in re a Leslie Van Horn. Call Kiesner at his hotel with the results." He added lightly: "Tell detectives to tell the Yard or Interpol that the woman might not be a woman. She might be a condition."

The moment he hung up, his phone rang.

"McKnight."

The voice was delayed. "It is not necessary to identify yourself. I know who you are."

Another delay, and she hung up.

It was an English voice. It belonged to the troubled woman with the inner pain.

If she had his home number, he wondered what else she knew about him. He was becoming intrigued. Now he was glad Frankie had declined the offer. There was something about the woman caller; something in her voice; something pulling — a closeness.

Did she sound anything like he had imagined? No. She sounded better. Hurt, but better. And on top of that, he had detected a tinge of playfulness in her voice. Mind games, perhaps?

Whatever, it definitely was going to be a most peculiar night. The hurt-but-better woman who wanted to play had killed a cop.

It was time to get ready. To be fully ready, though, he would, at last, relent and stop by his office first. A little pick-me-up was needed. Frankie said he sounded *a tad fatigued*. Nicki and Robecca had said something similar.

He certainly didn't want fatigue to become a factor.

"One question before you go, Lieutenant. I forgot to ask. You've spent years pursuing the narcotics offender. Have you ever been tempted?"

There was no response.

6

It was 9:20 when the detective drove from Whitehurst to Third and Spring. He was feeling better, but his shoulders were feeling a little tight in the tux. He hadn't worn one since he had attended the affair where Eve and Vern LeCoultre had put on another demonstration of their affection for each other. He recalled that it was a formal ceremony, paying tribute to slain officers. Eve and Vern were late again. When they arrived a soloist was singing. Higher than two kites in a windstorm, the duo took it upon themselves to join in. They did not send the dead away in peace. They sounded like two drunks at a karaoke audition.

Now LeCoultre himself would be numbered among the next group of the departed.

McKnight was glad that he and the Big Bad Boy would be long gone by then.

The club was not exactly what he had imagined. Probably from the way the bartender at Forte's had said it, McKnight thought it would be a stand-alone building. But then nothing the bartender had said could be trusted. He was only passing along the information Gena had given him.

The b.c. was located on the second floor, which was really the main floor of the spiffy-looking Marquis Hotel. The first floor was where all the stores were located.

When McKnight went upstairs and found the club, nicely marked with tiny gold *b.c.* lettering, it didn't have a club-looking front, there were no people about, and it appeared there never would be any. Checking further, he found nothing was stirring. Oddly, the door was locked. Peering through the glass door, it was easy to see a delicate desk in the tiny reception area. Gowned and striking a lonely pose behind the desk was Gena. Puzzled, McKnight faked a turn as if leaving. Gena saw him through the door. She quickly rose, unlocked the door, and, without saying anything, held the door open for him to enter. Gone were the overly friendly, thigh-and-higher gestures that she had used at Forte's.

Once inside, and past the reception area and what now amounted to Gena's anteroom, he was struck by the outright classiness of the place. It was dainty; a showplace for lovers of etched and beveled glass. The lighting was indirect and warm. It spilled over handsome tables with double-layered tablecloths that draped to an expensive, patterned carpet. Dominating the back of the bar was a large hand-painted picture of a chess board with a purposely overturned knight at the foot of the queen. It was a meaningful work, one of exceptional artistry.

Gena spoke for the first time. "And you are?"

The tiredness and fatigue gone, he was up for the occasion. He was on his game.

"I'm the same person you saw in Forte's earlier, the one you had eyes 'n' thighs for? Remember Forte's? The bar in Encino?"

She didn't respond.

"Maybe it's the tux that's throwing you."

Without comment, Gena led him into the bar area. It, too, bespoke elegance.

Going behind the bar, she asked, "May I offer you a drink?"

"So, what do you think about the tux? A little too tight in the shoulders, maybe?"

"May I offer you a drink, sir?"

"Why don't I have the same as you were drinking earlier, Miss...???"

Not answering, she poured a glass of milk from an etched pitcher, placed it on a napkin and left. McKnight gave her and the situation a thought. He was about to concentrate on the chess painting when he heard a voice coming forward.

At the rear of the club, behind the beveled and floral-etched glass that served as a partition, opposite where Gena had departed, came the woman: Leslie Van Horn. She was tall, with chestnut hair and large hazel eyes. She was certainly more attractive than he had imagined. Dressed in a refined off-white evening gown, she was sauntering in his direction. She was busy concentrating, talking to herself as she moved. Her steps were measured, the voice unmistakable. It was low and rich with culture. The years had been many but good.

Taking into account her telephone calls and what Rusty had said about her, the detective had expected her to be out there. She didn't disappoint. She was south of the planet Pluto.

It didn't matter. He was ready.

She went behind the bar, stood just beneath the painting and planted her eyes on the only other person in the room. Without moving her eyes left or right, she used an intercom to reach Gena at the tiny reception desk out front.

"Gena, you may leave now."

She waited until she heard Gena departing through the front door, and began preparing two cocktails.

"Olives, onions, or lemon?"

McKnight, who had been looking on with an expression that ranged between a mellowed amusement and charity, looked around, acting as though someone else had entered the club. Seeing no one, he asked, "Are you talking to me this time, ma'am?"

She was upbeat. "Yes. And is this your first visit to the club?"

He lit a cigarette. "Actually, I was trying to get in last night. But the line was too long."

"Really?"

"Yes. Wall-to-wall people. Almost as many as you have in here tonight. Let me congratulate you on doing a bang-up business."

"It does get hectic."

"Frenzied, from what I can see. Tell me, if I'd been able to fight my way through the crowd last night as I did tonight, would I have found you here?"

She overlooked the question and smiled as she turned for two cocktail glasses. "Olives, onions, or lemon?"

"Onions, if you don't mind," McKnight said. "I've been told that onion pits are good for the complexion."

"Well, you look just peachy."

"I owe it all to the pits."

"Oh, how clever. And what a charming response."

"Thank you," he said. He watched her drink-preparing routine and was glad he wasn't a cocktail drinker. "Since we haven't been introduced, may I ask, do the initials b.c. stand for anything I would be familiar with?"

"Where did you get the initials from?"

"I somehow thought it was the name of the club I'm sitting in. It does say something like b.c. on the door. Small 'b', smaller 'c'."

"Oh."

"And?"

"'And' what?"

"The b.c. stands for?"

She smiled. "Bright and cheerful."

"I guess I should have stayed home."

"You know, you have an interesting name."

"Thank you," the detective said. "But I've never really cared for it."

"You don't like Wyatt?"

"No. It makes me think of Wyatt Earp; like I should be out on the plains, gunning for somebody."

"What kind of a name would you like?" Leslie asked pleasantly.

"Since I'm basically a low-key guy, I could do with something a bit more sophisticated. I applied for Hootie and the Blowfish, but it was already taken. Isn't it interesting, though. You and I know each other's names and we've yet to be introduced."

She smiled, finished preparing the drinks, placed two napkins on the bar and handed him one of the glasses. She gave him another smile and elevated her glass for the toast. *"To us."*

McKnight held his up for the touch. *"And all the ships at sea."*

She took a delicate but fumbling sip. Clearly, she was not a drinker. "Picking up from where we left off last night, this is your first visit?"

"Yes," McKnight said. "And I was just thinking, how strange. Last night I was led to believe tonight would be another high-actioner here. Lo and behold, I get here and the door is locked. No worry, though. The people look happy."

She took a stab at taking another drink and overrode the response. "You look like the kind of a person my grandmother would have married."

"Now I know why the door was locked."

"You tango wonderfully, she said."

"Your grandmother said that?"

"Yes."

"Well," McKnight said, "now that I think about it, she wasn't so bad herself. Tell her I miss those wild and wonderful nights we shared."

"She's dead," said Leslie.

"I stepped on her foot once," McKnight said. "I hope that didn't contribute to the cause of death."

"She wasn't doing anything at the time."

"Just forgot to take that next breath, huh?"

"She died of natural causes."

"You don't know how sorry I am to hear it," said the detective.

"The way she used to move, I thought her end would come on the dance floor."

"I'll be sure to pass along your concern."

"I hope you don't encounter too much difficulty in doing it, being that she's dead."

"It shouldn't be difficult at all," said Leslie. "She's very understanding. And she speaks foreign languages well."

"I imagine being planted six feet under allows one to get involved with a lot of different hobbies."

"Have you ever been planted six feet under, Mr. McKnight?"

"If I recall, that's where I stepped on your grandfather's foot. Of course I was wrong for doing it. But, as he said, being planted under all that dirt sorta took the sting out of it. Now, tell me something. I only ask because I'm new to this planet…"

"Oh, are you really?" she said with bright-eyed liveliness. "But you have qualities I have long admired."

"Such as?"

"As I was saying to you last week at dinner, I have always been mesmerized by your thoughtful and quick-witted responses. I like your earthiness, your sureness, your depth, your sound observations; your keen sense of 'with-it-ness.' You have both feet planted firmly close to the ground. I like that."

"*Close* to the ground, but not *on* the ground," McKnight said agreeably. "You have no idea how good that makes my feet feel. Anything else?"

"I like your humor."

"And I'm beginning to like yours."

Her eyes twinkled. "Do you, really???"

"By all means," he said, continuing to match her buoyancy and functioning like the McKnight of old. "Let me tell you why I'm beginning to like your humor. And you. Off-the-wall fun and games has always had me on the floor. Show me a good game and I howl. I'm on the floor. Rolling. Now, I don't quite get all your humor, such as the locked door, the girl that was up front, my being here alone with you; your tracking me, apparently; calling me at home and on the job; doing the tango with your dear old grandmother — that is, after she passed away. But any and all of the above gets me."

She moved to the other end of the bar to pluck from a bowl of cashew nuts. "Peanut?"

"Thank you," McKnight said, accepting the single, curved nut that was offered.

She bounced from nowhere: "Father is a past chess master."

"Well, isn't that the cat's meow," McKnight said, munching on the cashew and sliding down the bar to get more. "I happen to be rather swift with Chinese checkers."

"Oh, good. Because when Father was alive I despised playing with him."

"Why?"

"He cheated."

"At Chinese checkers, chess, or life?"

He had touched a nerve. She wouldn't respond. There was a change in her attitude. It was like she was leaving buoyancy behind and was taking an involuntarily trip elsewhere. He tried to recapture her attention. "Helloooo…?"

She was staring off into space.

"Helloooo…? Anybody home?"

Her large hazel eyes blinked rapidly. "You called?"

"I tried to, but the phone was busy. My psychiatrist is on it. He's just received word that his canary won the lottery, and he's calling the Canary Islands to double-check the numbers."

She reclaimed her position. "What a lucky girl."

"Guy," McKnight corrected. "Now, here's one for you: Let's say I'm a cop; I know that you know I'm a cop. And let's say you've got a pretty good act going for yourself. In fact, it's great. It holds my interest, and it's been said I'm a hard nut to crack. Now, with that great act sugar-coating a problem or two, let's say you want me to think you're a space cadet and you've just landed your spaceship on planet Earth, and I do. I go along with it. Then I bring up the name

Dotty Rochester. Would you be familiar with it?"

"Should I be?"

"Now, now, now, Miss Space Lady. Not nice. Rule Number One: there are over 3,000 languages spoken on planet Earth. In none of them do we answer a question with a question. One more time, the name: Dotty Rochester? Familiar with it?"

"Doesn't ring anything upstairs."

"Maybe there's nobody home."

"That's because I sent them all back to England. On a subway."

"A subway from L.A. to England? Great. Where'd you find it?"

"The same place you found your spaceship," said the woman. "Another peanut?"

She had problems all right, serious problems. There was no doubt about it. *She was nuts, but not dumb.* She was also clever. She was ingratiating, clever, and sick. Not a bad combo for a murderess who manufactured the "best of the best" of heroin, thought the detective.

But then again, he wondered, was he jumping to a convenient conclusion? Was she really that clever? Or could it be that he was making the mistake of not understanding the twisting, labyrinthine corridors of a troubled mind; a case where the logical was trying to apply the same set of standards to the illogical; the rational expecting the irrational to do as the rational expected? If so, he wondered, what was it that was feeding her?

He was candid enough to admit to himself that he was on neither a legal nor a firm foundation when it came to dissecting the brain, and that her mental condition shouldn't have been his concern. She had, though not proven at the moment, had committed a crime — and was responsible for a narcotic, sprinkled with something he had never heard of — but that should have been that. He wanted to go deeper.

Why?

"Another peanut?" she asked, again holding up a single cashew.

"No, thank you. I can't afford to have the senses dulled." He pulled out another cigarette and lit it. "Why don't we try another name: Angie. I believe she worked for you here at the club. I'm sure you'll remember her. She was a beautiful redhead, a little older than your other young lady whom you've just dismissed."

"You mean Gena?"

"Yes. But Angie, the redhead, I'm sorry to say, is no longer able to entice anyone to go anywhere. I had the distasteful chore of viewing her coke-abused body in the morgue this morning."

"What a pity. Is he still in my employ?"

"The lips, ma'am, it helps when you watch them. Angie was a *she*. I say *was* because *she* is in the morgue. *She* is dead in the morgue. *She* is dead in the morgue because *she* died of an overdose; a drug overdose."

"Then *she* won't be returning."

"*Remarkable*. So, then, I can assume you knew her?"

"Who?"

The detective moved to the other end of the bar. "Listen, I imagine a lot of people would enjoy playing ring-around-the-roses with you. Maybe I would, too, but I'm the nervous type. I'm uncomfortable in crowds. So I hope you don't mind, but I'm going to have to get serious and cut to the chase on this thing. Now, I don't know why you have this setup, or anything else that you're doing. For kicks, maybe? Obviously you're not in the club business. But that's not my immediate concern. It seems…"

"Excuse me. May I interrupt and ask what is your immediate concern?"

"Apprehending a policeman's murderer."

"And you need my assistance?"

"Only if you'd like to fill me in, then stick your wrists out so I can cuff 'em and waltz you down to the police station."

"Kinky, aren't you?"

"Not really."

"You just like strange things?"

"No."

"Then don't be revolting."

"Sorry I introduced the subject," McKnight said. "What I should've been describing with the cuffs is the procedure we use when arresting the perpetrator of a crime. Particularly murderers."

"Do you like talking about crime?"

"Do you like committing them?"

"You're answering a question with a question. Not nice," Leslie said smartly. "Rule Number Two. If you continue with that kind of talk, I'm going to get seriously angry."

"Pardon me while I run for cover," said McKnight. "Because I imagine that when you get seriously angry, you do serious things. I wouldn't be surprised if it didn't include shooting a cop."

She wouldn't respond.

Out went the cigarette. "Is it your normal tendency to want to murder when you get seriously angry, Miss Van Horn?"

Still she didn't say anything. She couldn't. Her facial expression was molded in puzzlement. It was as if she wanted to say: What are you talking about?

"Miss Van Horn, do you have a dog?"

She looked away. The face fell into despair. She removed a handkerchief from her purse and dabbed at her eyes. "I had a dog."

"'Had?'"

"Yes."

"What kind of dog was it?"

"She was a poodle."

He knew better. But she had undergone a change, and so had he. He was patient. "Miss Van Horn, did you know a Detective Sergeant Verneau LeCoultre?"

"No."

"Ever heard of him?"

"No."

When she spoke, she sounded quiet and truthful.

"To go back a bit. You said you *had* a dog. A poodle. What happened to it?"

At first she couldn't think. Then she said, "The clown killed her."

"The clown killed the dog?"

"Yes. And then he tried to go back and hide in his trunk."

"Am I to understand that this is not a real clown, that he's not a rent-a-clown or something that escaped from a circus? In other words, he's a toy clown?"

"No. He used to be a toy. Now he's real."

"How long has he been real?"

"I can't remember."

"Do you know why the clown killed the dog?"

"Anger. He's always angry. It was wrong of him to do it, wasn't it?"

The detective remained quiet.

"And I told him that."

"Did the clown say anything when you told him?"

"He barked."

"The clown barked?"

"Yes. He was mimicking the dog, making fun of him. Then the dog barked. And then they started barking at each other. They were really angry."

"And the clown became angry enough to do something about it?"

She answered with a tear in her voice. "He told him he was going to shoot her, then he went off and did it."

"And this happened when?"

"Last week."

"How did the clown kill the poodle?"

"With a gun," she sobbed. "He tried to get away, and the clown caught up with him. They were in their cars, driving side by side, then the clown turned his head and pulled the....the....that thing."

"You mean a trigger?"

She nodded.

"The trigger of a gun?"

"Yes."

"Where did it happen?"

"Near my home."

"In Encino? On Hayvenhurst in Encino?"

"I think so. But I'm not certain."

"Were you in the car when the clown pulled the trigger?"

"No."

"Then how would you know that the two cars were driving side by side?"

She couldn't answer. His questions remained quiet. "Let me ask you this, ma'am. Could the killing have taken place last night?"

"I don't know. I wasn't here. Or there."

"If you weren't here nor there, where were you?"

"Home."

"Was anyone home with you?"

"The clown...after he came back."

"Came back from where, ma'am?"

"From doing whatever he was doing."

"Do you have any idea what the clown was doing?"

"I don't know," she said wearily. "I'm so confused."

"That's all right," said the detective with compassion. "Take your time." Although his fingers were toying with his glass, his eyes never left her. "Is it possible, Miss Van Horn, that the clown could have been in the form of a person? That it's nothing more than something like a *deus ex machina*? Something that provides a twist or an unexpected solution to a problem, but something that is not real."

"But the clown is real," she said. "I know he's real."

"And you don't think he could be a person you know? A person such as yourself, even? Maybe you in a different frame of mind; maybe you — trying to protect yourself against a policeman who knew you kept narcotics in your home? And knowing that, he burglarized your place and you went after him?"

She heard none of it. She was lost. She moved to one of the tables and sat down. She got up and went back behind the bar for a glass of water, came back and found the bottle of pills that was in her purse.

McKnight allowed her a moment to herself, then came over and sat next to her. He was sitting close because he wanted to see the bottle's label. Unable to see it, he asked, "What kind of pills do you take, ma'am?"

"Something for my health."

"Do they have a name?"

She couldn't remember. He waited and asked if he could see the bottle. She allowed him to look at it. It matched the bottle Nicki Aladanti had shown him in the morgue. The label was just as old.

"Miss Van Horn, do you have any obvious ailments?"

"No."

"But you're taking pills. And the label doesn't say they're aspirins."

"I take them for my health."

"Would you say you're in good health or bad?"

"Both."

"You're in good and bad health," repeated the detective. "You're from England, is that correct?"

"Yes."

"Whereabouts in England?"

"The Cotswolds."

"Is that anywhere near London?"

"When I'm in London I stay at the Savoy."

"That wasn't what I asked, but okay. So when you run out of pills, how do you re-supply?"

"I don't."

"I take it, then, after these are gone you won't be taking any more?"

"I'll only be taking those I've already taken."

Unwilling to push, he mentally registered the date and handed the bottle back to her. "I noticed that the date on the bottle is rather old. A year and a half, at least. If you're taking them for your health, how do you manage to make them last for so long?"

"I try not to swallow them," she said, weakly.

"Now, to go back a bit, ma'am, how did the clown kill the dog?"

"He shot him."

"You said *him*. Earlier you referred to the dog as a *she* — three times. Which is it?"

She didn't answer the question, and her eyes started brimming with more tears. "He shot him while he was driving the car. The dog was trying to escape in his car. A new car that I had just bought."

"Which you bought with a cashier's check?"

"It was with some kind of paper, I don't know."

"And why was the poodle trying to escape?"

Still downcast, she said, "He had taken something that didn't belong to him."

"From your house?"

"Yes."

"Could the 'something' have been narcotics? Heroin, for instance?"

"No."

"Then what was it?"

"Why do you ask?"

McKnight was thrown for a fraction of an instant. "A cop was killed, ma'am. It's my job to ask relevant questions. What was it that was taken from your house?"

"Medicine for the poor."

"You're sure it wasn't heroin?" the detective asked with uncommon interest. "A special kind of heroin?"

"I know heroin is a narcotic. I would never have it in my house. It is not a good thing. My mother is proof of that. Any narcotic is bad."

"Does your mother live with you?"

"I live alone. She lives at the Savoy."

"I suppose you mean in London," said McKnight. "Okay, this 'medicine' that you had in your house, where did it come from?"

"I made it. Do you remember if I made it in my laboratory at home?" she asked, confused. "Could I have made it someplace else?"

He eyed the crestfallen woman longer, stood, and from out of the blue, came up with something he thought was novel. It was far-out; *way-out*. But so were the circumstances. Taking the *deus ex machina* route, he backed off and casually said, "That clown is an animal."

She was shocked. *"Is he???"*

It wasn't exactly psyc 101, but it was working. "Yes, something is definately wrong with that clown."

"Oh, good, good, good! I'm so glad someone agrees with me."

"I have to," McKnight said. "Clowns are weird. Yours is disgusting."

She stood and shouted. "Yes!"

"Your clown is beyond contempt."

"Yes!!!"

"He's evil."

"Oh, yes, yes, yes, yes, yes, yes, yes, YESSSS!"

"Sick!"

"Y-y-y-yes!"

"Without redemption!"

"Y-y-y-yesssss!"

"Incorrigible!"

"Yes!!!"

"He reminds me of a lot of people I know! Does he do the same to you, Leslie Van Horn!?"

"Yesssssss! Yesssssss! Yessssssss!!!"

"He reminds you of people like *who*, Leslie Van Horn!?"

She started holding her head. "I can't remember!"

"Yes, you can, Miss Van Horn. Say it! Yes, you can! Now say it!"

"I can't remember," she said, holding her head and then her ears, as if fighting off a ringing noise. "I can't remember!!"

"Yes, you can! Let it out! The clown reminds you of people like *who*?!! "

"*LeCoultre!!*"

"Yes!" McKnight fired quickly. "*LeCoultre!* Now we're talking disgust. We're talking base. Low!!"

"Lolololololololo!!!"

"*Why*?!"

"He didn't like you, insulted my mother, and killed my dog!"

"*Who* did that?!"

"LeCoultre!"

"And he bugged you, and irritated you, and like screeching fingernails on a blackboard when you were a little girl in school, he got under your skin and made your flesh crawl!"

"YES!"

"Hear it?! Screech-screech-screech-screech-screech!!!"

"Yesssss! It's driving me *insane*!!!"

"*Who* did that?!!!"

"LeCoultre!!!"

"Say it again!!"

"*LeCoultre!!!*"

"Again!!"

"*LeCoultre!!! LeCoultre!!! LeCoultre!!!*"

"This thief, this jerk, this clown who got under your skin and screeched and screeched and screeched those fingernails on the blackboard to such an extent that the only thing you could do, you *did* do! And *that* was *to*...???!!!"

She lashed out and exploded: "*KILLLLLLL HIMMMMM!!!*"

The room fell silent; McKnight was unmoving.

Leslie had said *Kill him* with every ounce of strength she could muster, but she had absolutely *no* idea of the implications. Too exhausted to continue, she moved from around the bar and almost collapsed at the table. She was spread-eagled; limp. She held in that position for a few minutes, then chuckled to herself and tilted her head back in satisfaction.

McKnight kept his eyes straight on her. She said something about being *too pooped to pop*, and slouched down farther.

McKnight, continuing to watch her like a hawk, said nothing.

"Aaaaahhh," she said, after resting up a bit and moving her head slightly from side to side. "*That* was fun. Stunning. You really gave my brain a workout. What an experience. I really needed that. *Whew-ooowee.*"

"Miss Van Horn," the detective said, slowly and seriously, "I would like to get down to the specifics of Mr. LeCoultre's murder."

"I'm too whacked to even think of another game."

"The game is over, ma'am."

"I know. But, oh, what fun. You're really uplifting. What we are able to do together is simply amazing. I didn't know two people could ever get along like this. What we have going is simply *w-w-wonnnderfulll.* It's pure magic!"

"Miss Van Horn," he said quietly, "we have nothing going but the issue of a man's murder."

From the corners of her large eyes she looked at him. "What issue? What murder?"

"...Miss Van Horn; it is *Miss*, isn't it?"

"Yes, it's *Miss* Van Horn. I'm not married. And neither are you. You sound as if it's news to you."

McKnight pulled out his badge and came close to her table. "I hope you forgive me for tricking you into making the admission. As a policeman I still have a job to do, that is, I still have to get substantiating evidence. But for the moment..."

"Excuse me," she interrupted. "What is that you're holding? That thing you've just removed from the pocket of your tuxedo?"

"A cop's badge."

"Is it yours?"

"I believe it is. It identifies me as a lieutenant with the Los Angeles Police Department. Now, as to your admission..."

"Admission?"

"The *admission* of murder. A murder you've just admitted to."

"You're sure you aren't taking your part of the game too far?"

He said nothing.

She looked at him. "You're dragging a bit. Have a seat. Enjoy. Rest up. If you insist, maybe we'll try another game a little later on."

"I'll give it some thought, but at the moment I have a job to do."

"Go and do it, and hurry back. I'll wait." She stood and volunteered, "Maybe we can do it together. What kind of work do you do?"

"I should have told you, I suffer from something called 'attention deficit disorder.' I think it's catching. To repeat: I'm a lieutenant with the LAPD."

"Oh, then that should make it fun."

"Miss Van Horn, why did you kill Detective Sergeant LeCoultre?"

"Hey, frankly, I'm getting just a little bit worried about you. No; I'm getting *seriously* worried about you. You don't know when to stop playing. You seem to have this fixation with murder."

"To repeat: Why did you kill the policeman?"

"That was your very last cocktail." Her gown flowing, she retrieved his drink and moved back to the bar. "In your condition you're going to hurt somebody. Most likely yourself."

"Miss Van Horn, I think it's time to read you your rights for the crime of murder."

"There you go again. That's all you could talk about before. That's all you can talk about now. Murder. Murder. Murder. It was only a game, Wyatt. Let it go. We took a little trip, had a little fun. But it's over. Do you realize you're back talking about the same thing you were talking about before we left? *Murder, murder, murder.* Are you trying to tell me something?"

"Y'know," McKnight said, his voice maintaining composure, "earlier, when you were going through your mental gymnastics, I said to myself: "Now, here's a woman who didn't get to be this way from singing too loud in the choir. You killed a man, Miss Van Horn. You killed a policeman in cold blood, Detective Sergeant Verneau B. LeCoultre. The gun you used is either at your house, in your car, or you ditched it. But I know you killed him, and there you stand, acting as though I'm here to investigate nothing more serious than the proper shade of lipstick. True, the detective was an addict; a sleaze; an embarrassment to my chosen profession, and, if I might add a more personal note, a bigot of the worst kind. True, Mr. LeCoultre burglarized your home, taking narcotics and paraphernalia, but I believe that was a game to you. You didn't have to kill him. Save for the art of the game, you didn't know the man that well. Did you? What did he do? Come by your house a few times because he knew you had narcotics there? He and the redhead, Angie? Did the Jaguar XJS do it for you? I don't think so. You wouldn't murder for that. I can tell by the extravagance of this place that money had little or nothing to do with it. So a moment ago I found myself asking, why would someone with as much as you have do such a thing? Then something came to mind.

"There have been others making headlines recently, but I was reminded of a case some years ago where a young girl got a gun and shot up a school for no stated reason other than she was bored with one of the days of the week. Irrational, yes; tragic even more — and one is forced to wonder what course of action this poor little girl with an overtaxed mind would have taken as an adult. But as a child, I'd bet, the whole thing started off as fun and games, then she got caught up in her own insanity. And couldn't stop shooting."

Leslie eyed him for a long while, stood as if to say something, then stopped. She started quivering, and sat again, this time pulling and nibbling at the corner of her handkerchief. She downed a glass of water, followed up with several pills, and looked up at him with imploring eyes. "Help me."

The change had been sudden and sincere.

It caused a change in the detective. And though he was now certain she had committed murder, again he was prepared to be patient.

But there again, the question was: *Why?*

Going along with her, he knelt down and spoke in a comforting manner. "I'll help you if you start with the truth. Talk to me. Talk to me about LeCoultre. Addicts like to return to the source. But I know you aren't a dealer, you aren't a user. Heroin comes from evil people. You're not evil. In fact, I don't think you hardly realize what the stuff is. But talk to me about the narcotics LeCoultre was using. It wasn't normal. It was pure and uncut — and also new. Where did you get it? Where do you keep it?"

"I don't know," she sniffed.

He relented. "Okay, then, tell me what happened last night."

"I don't know anything about last night. Only what I told you."

"But there has to be more," he said, but set to move away from the narcotics question. "If it helps, let me tell you this: Even if I were to charge out and collect a mountain of evidence proving you killed

LeCoultre, it's not the end of the world. You can be helped."

Her eyes dampened as she asked, "And nobody will confuse my witnessing a murder with being the murderer?"

"Leslie, *you* committed the murder. There's no doubt about it."

"No, Wyatt. I didn't. The clown did it. I swear it. And he's still at the house."

"I don't buy it, Leslie. Neither will a jury."

"But it's the truth, Wyatt. It's the God's honest truth," she said earnestly. "Honest. I had the clown bagged in the trunk for six months. Then one day he started banging and knocking his head against the sides and said that he was suffocating. So I let him out. Then he starts doing the same as he did in England."

"And he did what in England?"

"He started raving and scaring me. He's evil. He does rotten things."

"Where is the clown now?"

"Still at the house, sitting outside on his bench-swing. Just like he was last night. He's made the swing his home. That's where he stays. But, Wyatt, he's at the house. I know he is. I left him there, and he isn't going to leave. He'll never leave. Ever."

"If the clown is such a bad person — or thing — why do you still have him? Why didn't you get rid of him?"

"I've tried to. Many times. I even tried to get rid of him at the Savoy in London when I was coming here, but they didn't want him. He found out what I'd done, and threatened to destroy me. He's supposed to be my protector. But he's never done it. And he never listens to me. He's mean, and unruly. He's a terror. And he frightens me. He likes to scare me. He does it all the time."

She believed what she was saying. She was in trouble. The detective was even softer in his approach. "Leslie, you need help. Look at it this way: You'll never see the gas chamber…or be lethally injected…"

"You're going to kill him?" She was visibly hurt. "Oh, please, no, no, no. Killing is wrong. It's horrid. Oh, please — please — please…"

"Leslie, settle and just listen. You're being delusional. The clown can't be hurt. And the clown couldn't kill anyone. Such a thing can't be. The clown is *not* real."

"I used to think that, too," she sobbed. "But he's real. How can you know he's not?"

"For starters, you said you kept him in a trunk. A person can't live in a trunk for six months. And there's a ton of other things that *don't* hang together. They *can't*. But at the moment they're not important. The clown *couldn't* kill LeCoultre; he *can't* hurt you. He's *not* real. The entire thing is a figment of your imagination. Except for the dog — and it had to've been a *big* dog — nothing you've said is real. You killed LeCoultre. But it's not the end of the world. You'll never see the gas chamber; never do time, or have to go through anything of that sort. A little hospitalization, yes. But never time. They don't convict people like you. In all my years of being a cop, neither I nor anyone else has ever seen or heard of a person in your condition being convicted and sentenced to do even hard time, let alone anything else. But even if you're given a jail sentence, you won't have to serve it. And you've got something else going in your favor. I hate to say it, but you're not the underclass. A well-bred and good-looking person like you? In our judicial system? Then throw in your problems, honey, you..."

She interrupted: "You called me 'Honey.'"

"Yes."

"Which means you like me?"

"And the courts will like you. A jury will like you. The judge will love you. That is if it gets that far, which I doubt. But it doesn't matter that you've killed someone, you've got it made. You walk into any court in America, you'll get a spank on the behind, a little outpatient care, and you're home free. Even the man in the morgue could have told you that."

She tossed the words over in her mind. They were beginning to sound good to her. Very good. Very, very good. *With my problems.*

She stood, then sat again. *With my problems,* she repeated. She cleared her eyes, crossed her legs under that long elegant gown, folded her arms and leaned back comfortably: "Good point. Okay. What man? What morgue?"

The detective noticed how quickly she had changed again. Gone were the tears, shakes and insecurities. He smiled within, and withdrew. "You know something, lady? When you go to trial? Put on a football helmet, and charge admission."

"I beg your pardon?"

"When you go to court, have somebody outside selling tickets."

"What are you talking about?"

"You in court, Miss Van Horn. You, popping placebos and putting on an act. Charge 'em for it. Make some dollars. Big ones. We're talking show biz here. Hollywood. Boffo boxoffice. Here's how you sell it: 'Woman. English. White. Fresh off the boat. Zip code unknown. She gives the word 'psycho' new meaning. This one is a certifiable, fruit-of-the-loom candidate. She's got about as much stability in that brilliant but warped mind of hers as a 20.2 earthquake. She's charged with murder, but the clown did it after discussing it with a gun-totin' poodle. But the woman is the key. She's a nut of nuts; needs more than help. She walks into court like no other nut in the world. She uses an act, when she needs a net." He stopped. "Wait. Hold on. Where's your phone, honey, I gotta get you an agent. This is too hip for any sleaze merchant to pass up. This is world-shaking stuff. Let's get 'E.T.' and all the other air-waggers cranked up to do the PR. And don't forget the talk shows. You might even get lucky and get to kiss the ring of the High Priestess of Talk."

She sprang to her feet. "Now, just you wait one cotton-picking moment. I resent that! And I resent *you!* Just because I decided to have a little fun at my own expense does *not* mean I don't know what I'm doing *when* I'm doing it! Nor does it mean I am ever — *ever* — without *full* control and faculty! I do *what* I want, *when* I want! And get this through that thick skull of yours: I don't have a problem! *You* do! And I resent your inviting yourself here, toying with my mind; a most healthy, vital and agile mind, I might add, and insulting it, and badgering *me* with all your half-baked, cockamamie, Freudian nonsense! And most of all, I resent, in the strongest of all terms, your blatantly false and patently ridiculous accusations! I *witnessed* a murder. You are a policeman. I risked my life bagging your cop-criminal, and I get blamed for the crime. I even went looking for you to report it. And let me set you straight on something else: I can understand your overlooking my contributions to the happiness of the poor. But for you to accuse me of destroying a poor, defenseless little schoolgirl by a blackboard, and having her body end up in a warm morgue on a cold day, particularly after all I've gone through, and as much as I empathize with *all* troubled little schoolgirls, for you to do that surpasses disgust and goes beyond the boulevards of normal insanity! It is grotesque. And I don't like it! And, what's more, I don't like *you*!" She moved to the door. "I order you to get out of here. *Now!*"

McKnight walked over and calmly closed the door. "Question: Were you and the dog having fun killing Detective Sergeant LeCoultre?"

"There you go again!" she blistered, moving away from the door.

"That does not answer the question. But then again, I suppose I didn't ask it while strolling up your little boulevard of 'normal' insanity."

"*I am not insane!*" raged the woman. "And you have no right to say I am insane! And if you <u>think</u> it — *prove it!*"

"My job is to prove murder."

"But you keep harping on insanity!"

"Like you, lady, I get a little weird when normal. I shower in the clothes dryer and dry off in the washer. I breakfast on oven-warm ice cubes, and spend my daily eight driving in circles, trying to rack up frequent-flyer miles on my ATM card. I cap my day wondering if black-eyed peas ever sleep, and if ears of corn can really hear. My evenings? I spend them e-mailing the World Wide Web. I do that by sitting in the bottom of the pool, yodeling. For exercise, I graze — on concrete; and I don't even *think* happy until after midnight, that's when I know its time to catch the six o'clock news on my microwave oven. Mind you, that's only when I'm normal. When I get stressed? *Bingo!*

Even aspirins run for cover. Sound familiar to you?"

"I get <u>stressed</u> occasionally! Insane? Never! Prove I don't know what I am now saying! *Prove* I am not *now* in full and absolute control!"

"Oh, I'll grant you *can* have full and absolute control. For a moment or two. Surely no longer. I've just seen your act, lady."

She fired back. *"Prove insanity!"*

"I'm a policeman, not a psychiatrist."

"<u>You</u> made the charge! *Prove insanity!!!*"

"I don't have to prove it, but I will say this: And I'll say it in terms I *hope* you understand: You, lady, don't always come to a full stop at a red light. In fact, in times like these, you can't come to a stop, period. But I'm going to give you the benefit of the doubt, because in zigzagging down your own private highway, you do shift gears. How? I don't know. But you like to put it to the test; to take it to the limit. You and you alone murdered Detective Sergeant LeCoultre. Blame it on whomever or whatever you want, but *you* did it. *You* pulled the trigger. *You* committed the murder. There is *no* doubt about it."

"PROVE INSANITY!"

"I'll do you one better. What if I let *you* do it? What if I let you prove you're in control of that, quote, *most healthy, vital and agile mind* of yours? You say you are; I say you are not. If I'm proven wrong, I'm out of here. Case closed. It's closed, and you can continue zigzagging down that private highway without interference from me. It'll be another game, Miss Van Horn. A test, really. Win it, and you're on your own. Lose it, and you're in cuffs. Are you game for a test, Miss Van Horn?"

"You have the floor."

"That didn't answer the question."

"Do what you have to do, and leave."

"I leave if you pass the test. Flunk it, and we leave together."

She stood there, looking at him in silence.

He took the silence to mean acceptance. "All right, since no one knows a hell of a lot about this case but me, and possibly a young man who'll soon be on his way back to Germany, here's what we've got: I'm willing to let you get away with murder, a *cop's* murder, Miss Van Horn. In fact, I'll go so far as to provide you with an alibi if — *if* — you can pass a quick and simple test…"

"I am not dumb, Mr. McKnight. You have already said it's a test. How many times must you repeat yourself?!"

"All right. The objective: You're proving that you're able to control that 'most healthy and vital and agile mind' of yours. I say you can't even control your mind long enough to pass a test. Or even *complete* a test, for that matter."

"Will you get on with it!"

"I say again; for your freedom, are you game, Miss Van Horn?"

"You're stalling because you're trying to trick me."

"No tricks. My word of honor."

It was a standoff. She stood there, arms folded, chin firm, rapidly patting a foot in high agitation. Finally she gave in. "Before you start, I want you to understand this: I'm playing your silly little game as long as you understand I didn't kill anyone. Go ahead. Shoot your best shot."

"All right. Set yourself. Win, you go free; lose, and you leave in cuffs. Are you ready?"

"WILL YOU GET ON WITH IT!!!"

"….Quickly, Miss Van Horn! …as fast as you can: you're counting backwards — from 100 to 1. ….*GO!*"

"100, 92, 89, 76, 31, 57, 15, 47, 8, 10, ZERO! Which is why I <u>don't</u> belong in hospital. Now, would you like to hear the alphabet backwards?"

She was rapid-fire fast. He was not. Said the detective quietly: "From 'Z' to 'A', ma'am."

"That is *not* the way the alphabet goes."

"Then, Miss Van Horn," the detective said, maintaining a quiet demeanor, "why don't you take a moment and tell me how the alphabet does go. Backwards, or forward."

She sat stoically. She thought and thought. Her hands became fidgety. She tried wringing them. It didn't work. Nervously, she dug into her purse and nursed more pills between her long, groomed fingers. No solution there. She let the pills drop to the bottom of the purse, stared at the empty glass and tried to drink from it. Unable to swallow, she withdrew a hankie from her purse and gnawed on the four corners. There were no solutions anywhere.

He had not smoked for a while. He reached inside his pocket, got his cigarettes, lit two of them, and offered her one. She was not a smoker, but she took it, then didn't know what to do with it. He removed it from her fingers, and put it out.

Sobbing and looking away, quietly and haltingly, she asked, "M-m-may I...M-m-may I...May I call you a cab, Mr. McKnight?"

He had won, but he wouldn't take the advantage.

"I have wheels, Miss Van Horn."

Downcast, again she stumbled over her words, "Th-th-thank you for helping me," she said. "Is-is-is there anything I can do for you?"

She was pitiful; he was in sympathy. "No," he said quietly observing her.

"N-n-no one has ever helped me before. You did. You and you alone cared. D-d-d-do you have any idea what that means to me? W-w-what it means in my life?"

"I believe I do."

Inaudibly, she asked: "Will I...will I ever be seeing you again?"

"Yes," he said. "If you give me your address, my partner and I will be out to see you in the morning."

"F-f-for what reason?"

"For the arrest."

"I knew this would happen one day," she said, staring at her lap. "Do you think you will keep him in prison for the rest of his life?"

"The arrest won't be for the clown, Leslie. But if you wish for it to be the clown, then we'll make it the clown. Also."

"And you won't arrest him t-t-tonight?"

"No. There's no rush. I think it's best to let you two get your things in order, call an attorney, and do anything else you might think useful."

"Yes, I'll get him attorney," she unintelligibly mumbled. Almost in a daze, she asked, "…Y-y-you really care for me, don't you?"

He took time with his answer. "Yes."

"A lot?"

"…A lot."

She was pleased to hear the answers. They were simple and direct. She sat longer, sometimes looking away, sometimes looking at him. He remained quiet. Swallowed in a world of thoughts, she looked away again, and then back at him. It was a long, intensely involved look that was so strong in delivery that it almost seemed to have changed her appearance. Finally she extended her hand for him to help her up.

The detective responded as a gentleman, and she went to the counter. She scratched out her address and offered to verify it by producing her driver's license. It wasn't necessary, he indicated. She left, then returned with her fur coat and gloves. She looked at him quietly and asked again, "Y-y-you really d-d-do care for m-m-me?"

He couldn't hide it. The woman had gotten to him. He would have preferred lying, but he didn't. "I really do, Miss Van Horn."

There was a strange and tender deepness on both sides.

This time she cried.

When the tear-dabbing woman exited the building, the parking-lot attendant had her car ready. She climbed in and departed in a hurry. She was too emotional to do anything but keep the car on the road. Had she checked the rear-view mirror closely, she would have seen the detective's headlights trailing at a distance.

The strange and deep tenderness carried, and after a swift but erratic 30-minute drive, they arrived at Leslie's home in Encino. She fumbled for the gate opener, found it, and drove in. McKnight, who had fallen back to a safe, undetectable distance, slowed his vehicle at the corner and watched as the taillights before him made the turn, disappearing behind the closing gate that promoted the Chinese wording for *hope*.

Remembering that the lanky LeCoultre had been attacked by a ferocious dog, and not knowing that the dog had been killed, he removed his pistol from the glove compartment and tucked it into his trousers. He didn't think he would need it, and he wasn't keen on the idea of having to shoot an animal, ferocious or not. But to be on the safe side, he double-checked the weapon, backed the car farther out of possible view, got out and walked the rest of the way to the cul-de-sac.

Attempting to be thorough, he spent a long time studying the wall and street, trying to re-create in his mind what had happened to LeCoultre. He got as far as figuring that the XJS, the car the cop had been driving when he was killed, had to have been on the other side of the wall, and that LeCoultre had obviously fought with the dog on the inside of the compound while trying to make it to the vehicle. But that was only part of the scenario. There were many more questions; he needed many more answers — ostensibly. Everything that was needed was on the other side of the wall.

As the detective moved in closer, his foot accidentally stepped on something. It was a gun. He picked it up and, in the dark, determined that it was a 9mm .380 PPKS Walther. It was the gun she had tossed over the wall the night before; it was obviously the gun that had been used to kill LeCoultre. He started to take it back to the car, but decided against it. Instead, he separated the gun from the silencer, stuck both parts into his pocket, and struggled up the wall.

He stopped on top, allowing one leg to dangle on the inside of the compound. It was his hope to catch his breath while trying to see if anything could be seen in the dark. He knew what he wanted to find, but that would take time. Surveying in the dark, his eyes wandered to a row of small lights that ran along the foot of the wall, connected with the small light that emanated from the foot of the Buddha, and ran alongside more vegetation.

The detective was about to make the drop to go fully over the wall when it came.

At first it felt innocent enough, almost like a mosquito bite. But then it became more stinging. By the time he withdrew his look from the Buddha and looked down at his ankle — and at her — it was just about all over. But there was still time for a reaction.

The contents of the syringe that had jabbed him were almost as deadly as any bullet. It was heroin, but it also contained traces of the coma-inducing phenylcyclohexylamine along with a pinch from the California state poppy.

McKnight didn't respond.

It was startling in a way. It was but an instant — and he still had time — but he didn't do anything. Nothing. He didn't even *try* to fend for himself. He didn't kick at her, he didn't reach to free the needle, he didn't say *what the hell are you doing?* — nothing. He said nothing; he did nothing. And the veteran narcotics lieutenant *knew* it was heroin, and the fact that he knew that this amateur, this poor, unskilled, mentally unstable, schizophrenic, woman didn't know what she was doing was all the more telling.

But then again, going back and taking a closer look at *everything* he had done that day — and the *reasons* behind what he had done — maybe it shouldn't have been telling at all. And even more troubling, as that vanishing moment of clarity was being replaced by a slow-coming, ethereal opalescence, never once did he question the feeling.

And never did Wyatt McKnight look down again.

Dreamlike, he was fading away. He was at peace. A blessed peace. The Buddha was the last thing he saw.

The cold, slant, all-knowing eyes were gazing at him

below the upper torso, it was well over an hour before she was able to make a move. Then in a daze, with tears streaming, she finally arose and walked slowly around to the front of the house to look at the one thing that had ruined her world. What he had done to the other man could, in a way, be accepted. But what he had done to the man for whom she cared so deeply was an altogether different matter.

The clown had to pay.

She had decided she wouldn't lose control; she wouldn't be impulsive; she wouldn't act with rage. Restraint was the key. She would be like Wyatt had been in dealing with her; at first figuring out things logically, without emotion, standing always on a firm foundation, and then coming up with the solution.

Moving fluidly and easily, she went back into the house, and, spending more time in the kitchen than she had done before McKnight was injected, she got a plastic bag and returned to the bench-swing where the clown was seated.

She spoke quietly.

"Clown, I have known you all my life. I have allowed you to manipulate me, spy on me, terrify me, and destroy in my name. I have protected you since the day Father brought you into my life. Father said you were to be my friend, my protector. You were not my friend, you have never been my protector. You are not capable of being either. Even in coming over here from England, you preferred sleeping in the trunk and, if you remember, you demanded that the trunk be placed in the baggage compartment of whatever that thing was we were on. You did that rather than sit with me as protector or friend. And even when that fellow you shot — and you'll be just thrilled to know he was a policeman, which means you're on your way out anyway — but even when he and that young lady were here, sponging, thieving and taking advantage of me, you stayed out here, doing nothing, choosing not to get involved. And then when he told me about this other man, the man he hated, and a man whom I knew I would instinctively, for the first time in my life, possibly fall in love with, you wouldn't even help arrange a meeting. I had to do it all myself. But that's okay, Buster, he's here. Mr. Everything is here. He and I *will* be together."

She unfolded the plastic bag and leisurely continued, "Since you've killed someone — and the police are not going to let you get away with it — I suggest you take this plastic bag and put it over your head and walk over to the pond, and jump in. You'll find it's a lot more humane to end your life that way rather than hang around, waiting to be gassed. Wyatt said that's what happens to people like you.

"And when you get out there in the middle of the pond, don't bother to say goodbye. Just go. I never could stand the sound of that whining voice of yours."

Arms folded, she walked away.

When Leslie Van Horn returned to the unconscious McKnight, her sense of rationale was no better. She was equally confounding. Drifting back to what had taken place at the last stages in the club, and caring nothing about the beautiful gown she was wearing, she sat on the ground, and tearfully stroking him, began counting backwards. As he had requested in the club, from one hundred down to one she went. She did it with ease and perfection. With equal ease and perfection, she recited the alphabet backwards. As if to awaken him, she repeated them both, then, continuing to be savantlike, she did them interchangeably.

The woman was astonishing.

Throughout the entire period there was no response from McKnight. Sinking deeper in torment, she lowered her head gently to his chest and started ruminating. She started off by saying that the clown, deep in dementia, had injected him because he no longer had the gun. Now dead, he could no longer harm either of them. He had hanged himself. It was good riddance to a bad omen. Now she was free for the release, free to dig down deep and talk about things she had always wanted to talk about, things that had always troubled her.

She began with her childhood, which led her to speak of a blurred and obfuscated period that should have been the wonderful, defining time of her life. She took time talking about her parents, explaining that her father had been lost in the shadows. The shadows of what, she didn't know. She said that, except for the clown, she had always been alone and frightened. The clown was given to her, she said, to be company — a companion, really — and was there to fight fear, and to ward off this recurring thing that seemed to paralyze and warp her mind. It caused pureness and cleanliness to vanish.

The family was dysfunctional.

Continuing to speak softly, she stayed on the pureness theme for quite a period, talking about it as thought it had been the major thing that had escaped her. Constantly she came back to the word *fear*, and along with it, she injected the word *shame* with a disturbing frequency. As well as it could be understood, she had had other toys in her youth, and it sounded as if there could have been a story behind each one, but she wouldn't elaborate. Always, though, they would end up broken, and the story would end abruptly. Never once would she talk about normal toys, and when she returned to talking about her parents, the mother was always in the background; the father in the foreground, consistently faceless. He was not faceless when he was far away. He was faceless when he came close, when he was close enough to embrace his little girl.

During the latter part of the long talk, McKnight's body had made a few imperceptible moves. But he was not a well man. His heart was beating rapidly and he was drooling. She talked and stroked him longer. With his condition not improving, she went back to the house, came back and gave him another shot of something she had prepared. It was his second. Now his breathing became even more abnormal. There was no question, he needed hospitalization. He needed it in a hurry.

Her mind panicked with a sharp suddenness.

"What do I do? Where do I go?"

"Call the police."

"But what if they ask what happened?"

"Tell the truth."

"And they won't think I did harm to him?"

"Tell the truth. Point to the clown. He was the one who did it. Again."

"He deserves to be punished for what he did, doesn't he?"

"Yes. And he will be."

She started to race for the house, then stopped. Waiflike, she called back in a burst of tears: "I can't call the police and tell them the clown did it, because he's at the bottom of the pond!"

She came back to McKnight and slumped down. In anguish, she pleaded, "Wyatt…please help me. Please, please, help me…"

It was a long while, but slowly his eyes opened. They became slitted. For a moment they saw something. Dimly they saw the form leaning over him, the soft plea continuing. He started going out again, but in that moment of semi-consciousness the response to the form was deafening.

The shot from the .44 Magnum rang through the midnight air like a cannon. Her ears felt like they had exploded. Her face stiffened, then contorted.

"Ohmygod, ooohmygod, ooohmygod," she cried, her ears ringing so much that she tried covering them with her hands.

The blood that had started at the temple and had now seeped down the side of her face, cornered the mouth and stained the gown was running a little faster now. She knew she had been shot. But she wasn't worried about it. She was in a hurry to get her last words out. Surely the police would come. She didn't want them to hear her last words to the man she loved. Even more, she didn't want them to know that he had harmed her. Whatever he did, he didn't mean.

Fighting her ears, which had not stopped ringing, she took a moment and removed the gun from a hand that no longer had strength and flung it over the wall as far as she could. She came back to him, at first trying to whisper in his ear. But he was gone again. He was breathing, but not moving. With effort she tried dragging the body into the house. She was too weak, and she was barely able to make it herself.

But once she did, she went immediately into the bathroom and downed some pills. She was afraid to look at first, and for a time thought she had been hit in the ear. Both of them, in fact. Finally she summoned up her courage and looked in the mirror. She was wounded and bloody, but it didn't appear as bad as she had thought it would be. It was not good, and it was in the temple area, sliding all the way up to the hairline, but she felt it was not life-threatening. At least not immediately so. She and Wyatt could live with it for a while, and she would not have to call the hospital or the police. The two could be alone. And if only the head-splitting ringing would go away, she could nurse them both back to good health.

The first part of the long night was spent getting his body inside and tending to her wound. The pills did nothing to alleviate the pain. They couldn't. They were placebos.

Later the woman's ears were still splitting, but she ignored them as best she could. She spent the rest of the night alternately nodding off and trying to nurture him back into good health.

In daylight she tried to do the same. She was not successful. Although he had lapsed into and out of consciousness, his health was on a steady, drug-induced decline. He couldn't communicate, eat or do anything. It led her to believe that the only solution was to give him more morphine. It wasn't going to work, but she didn't know if it would work or not. She didn't know either, nor would anyone else ever know, just how telling her concoction would be.

Unlike last night and all she would come to know the next day, when she heard only the hard ringing in her ears, she herself had started feeling dizzy and her head started throbbing with pain again. She believed she was on the way out. But she was not.

Leslie Van Horn had metamorphosed. The transformation had been so seamlessly complete that even she didn't know it. The ringing gave way to a pulsating thud, which came almost with the bluntness she had experienced the instant she was shot. Only this time the thud was followed by a sense of ever-increasing clarity. She began seeing things. She had been stunted and she would not be able to remember things, but the forward thrust of her mind had been released.

She was able to focus. She was able to taste the inside of her mouth. Things were becoming rational; life offered stability, sanity. There was logic and comprehensibility to everything around her. It was if the dawn had broken through a mired darkness, lifted all curtains, shades, and shadows, and brightened paths she had never seen before. But the woman didn't revel in it. Throughout the entire ordeal not once did Leslie stop to think about what was happening to her. Normalcy, for the first time, had allowed her to feel balance, to see true colors, true forms, true life, but still she wouldn't stop. Tending to McKnight was the only thing on her mind.

By mid-afternoon the detective was on the verge of convulsing. The woman nursed him as much as she could, then, late that evening, she was forced to call the Whitehurst station.

It was 8:12. Mike Santiago, the sergeant whom McKnight had spoken to the previous evening regarding Scotland Yard and Interpol, was back on the desk when the call came in. Leslie told him who it was, and what she wanted. Lucidly she gave him both name and address and begged: *"Whatever you do, please, please, please don't let him die."*

Being a friend of the lieutenant, and familiar with the woman's name because of the call he had made the night before, Santiago acted with breakneck speed. He dispatched a ton of vehicles to the scene. She had given them the wrong address, but since the house was the only one in the cul-de-sac it didn't create a problem. They arrived within minutes, and there they found the woman slumped over the lieutenant. She was still breathing, and imploring him not to die. Even as they were taking her to the ambulance, she was murmuring over and over again: *Please don't die. Please, God, don't let him die.*

Maybe he heard her, maybe he hadn't. But for a solid year later he was saying what she had said. *Please don't die.* The trouble was, he couldn't remember who he was saying it about. His memory was gone.

8

Ault and most of the brass were not numbered among them, but for the few who cared at the Whitehurst station of the Los Angeles Police Department, there was much speculation as to what had happened that night at the Van Horn residence. A year had passed, and McKnight was still on medical leave of absence and had not returned to duty. A lot had happened during the intervening period. Aside from the rise in crime and a shakeup on the political front, one of the main things that had happened at the LAPD was that the long-talked-about promotions had come through. Even Captain Ault had moved up. He was now a commander, but he remained at Whitehurst.

McKnight's outpatient care was still going on. Not knowing whether he would ever be able to return to duty, he was still the subject of speculation. Most of the recent talk, however, centered on his having been promoted to the rank of captain. Everyone knew the promotion was not something that he had ever courted. The lieutenant had passed the test quite some time ago, but in light of others in the *bands* who hadn't scored as high as he in their effort to move up, it was decided he should be promoted as well. Promoted and then re-tired. It was obvious the department had serious concerns about his ever resuming his duties.

Well before the promotions, and under command of the then Cap-tain Ault, an investigation was conducted as to what had happened to the veteran policeman, but it was lacking in substance and thorough-ness.

Other than being shorthanded, the main reason for the investigation's slackness and indifference was that an embittered Ault was certain the promotion would be rescinded. After all, as he had repeatedly asserted, who ever heard of a promotion being granted to an officer who had been out as long as McKnight had been? Ault had also let it be known that McKnight had followed LeCoultre's path in furthering his addiction. He was certain of this, he said, because on the night of LeCoultre's murder he had summoned the lieutenant to his home to take a leading role in the initial investigation because he was a senior officer with expertise in narcotics. He was shocked and thoroughly disappointed, he said, because not only was the lieuten-ant hours late in showing up, but after reluctantly leaving the ghetto dopers he appeared glassy-eyed and listless, and acted as though he didn't fully understand what he was doing. Allowing him the benefit of the doubt, the captain said he brought the man inside his home and sat him down to go over some investigative points. Then, apparently, as though whatever he had in his system was wearing off, the lieuten-ant became obstreperous and insubordinate and started making out-rageous demands for his retirement.

McKnight's conduct had been so bad that night, averred the cap-tain, that, under threat, he was forced to call and awaken the chief, who was attending a convention in Hawaii, to enforce the demands, something neither man had any control over. But McKnight would not listen to reason, according to the captain. Asked why a lone and obviously troubled lieutenant was given the assignment of investi-gating a policeman's murder in the first place, the captain reminded everyone that, despite being shorthanded, other investigators were on tap, and McKnight, only minutes after the murder had occurred, had been tapped only to *start* the investigation.

But the larger issue, contended Ault, was that McKnight could have influenced others in his division. As an example, he said that the two longtime enemies, LeCoultre and McKnight, had secretly buried the hatchet and that, having always been suspicious of McKnight, it was his theory that the two had become "cohorts." In all likelihood, said Ault, it was McKnight who had introduced LeCoultre into the world of narcotics, which was no small feat for a man of LeCoultre's strength, a man who had shown much courage by winning the battle of the bottle some time ago. If a man with that much fortitude could be corrupted, reasoned the captain, there was no telling who else might fall on the lieutenant's sword. He concluded by saying that the McKnight assignment had boiled down to being a ruse. It was the only way to get all the facts. And there was never a cause to worry. He had Internal Affairs tracking the addicted lieutenant's every move.

As a commander, Ault was still saying the same thing one year later. He was, of course, grievously wrong, but, interestingly, he was not *one hundred percent* wrong. Yet there was no one to contest him. Wyatt McKnight was still disabled.

Little would anyone suspect that his commander had taken steps to help keep him that way.

9

The year had passed swiftly.

The radio call's instructions to Kiesner and Devro were to arrive at 4:30 a.m. at the rehabilitation facility and wait outside. Both of them knew why. Even in his still sorry state there was something that hung on, and the aging detective was still too proud to let anyone see him inside the place that had been one of his on-and-off homes for the better part of a year.

It was strange to see Kiesner behind the wheel of the car, as he should have returned to Germany months and months ago. Actually, he had returned, but through some machinations he was able to return to the LAPD. And he had returned to Whitehurst. Ault allowed him back because he thought the young man was reasonably harmless. Even had he not received permission from his department in Stuttgart, Kiesner would have found a way to return anyway. He had never stopped thinking about McKnight, and he always felt that he was partly responsible for what had happened to the man with the quick mind and fearless speech, a man who was not necessarily liked by the department, but a man whom, in the short period they had worked together, he had grown to greatly admire.

It was 4:12 a.m. when they answered the call. They were early. As the mounting beads of rain cleared down the windows and the wait stretched on, the young German said to Devro, "I still find this country strange. I mean, this is a hell of a place to put a rehab place, isn't it?"

A nodding Devro yawned. "If you know'd anything at all about this city, man, you'd know the rehab was here before that big ol' ugly thing over there was."

"Well, then, it's a hell of a place to put a Buddha."

"The Koreans like it. They own this part of town. We could'a had a taste of it, but like ol' Mac used to say, black people was too dumb to pool their money to get it. We ain't known for helping each other."

The radio broke the silence. "MW-9, did you respond to the 10?"

Devro threw a spiritless arm out for the mike and pressed for the transmission: "Waitin' on 'im."

Too lazy to place the instrument back in the receiver, he laid it on the seat and again yawned to Kiesner. "Ain't you due to go back home to Germany? I mean, this is your second trip, an' you done been here almost long enough to vote."

"Wednesday."

"Maybe that's why ol' Mac wanted us out here so early, so's he could talk about his promotion on th' way over to where we goin'. Maybe buy a couple of beers and wish you Owf-Wee De-same."

"The German word for goodbye is *aufwiedersehen*, Devro," Kiesner said. "And I highly doubt that's why he's called us."

"Wonder why the call came in through the fire department?" Devro said.

"I imagine he's done a lot of strange things since this thing happened."

They didn't talk for a while, and Devro, shifting to a more comfortable position, lifted a sleep-heavy eye through the raindrops and saw a figure.

"There he is," said Kiesner.

Devro rolled the window down and hollered, "Hey, we're over here, Lieutenant." Seeing that he wasn't going to move, Devro started to holler out again.

Kiesner motioned for him not to. From the way the man looked, he thought they would have to get out and escort him to the car. "And, Devro, don't forget, he's a captain now."

"He can still drown, can't he?" Devro said. "Hey, Mac! Over this way!"

He turned to the Buddha across the street in the yard of the Korean church for a final look. Unlike last night, the Buddha didn't gaze back.

The detective slowly got rid of the soggy cigarette butt and ambled to the car. He climbed into the back seat and lit another cigarette.

Just to see him move on his own was an achievement, thought Kiesner. Still, he was a long way from the McKnight of old. He was so distant from the McKnight of old that he had called the fire department to reach them. Kiesner was still wondering about it. What he didn't know was that, upstairs, alone in the room earlier, McKnight had suffered yet another relapse. He had been jolted by a thought and wanted the Whitehurst telephone number, which he had forgotten. It was the hallway's fire extinguisher and the apparatus on the wall next to it that caused him to think of the fire department. It said: *In Case of Emergency Break Glass.* This was an emergency. The gazing Buddha had told him so.

"Put your light on," he mumbled.

Devro got the dome-shaped red light, slapped it on top of the car's midnight-blue roof, and they were off. Kiesner was stepping on it. He knew that if the captain wanted the emergency light on, he must have wanted him to hurry.

No one said anything for the first few minutes. Only the radio calls that sporadically emanated from the speaker, and the slapping windshield wipers, came to life.

As the car pulled onto the freeway and headed east on the 101, both up-front men were aware of the captain's arm-rubbing, his sweatiness, his knee-shaking anxiety. They also noticed his runny nose, but they thought that it was from the rain.

After they rode for a while, to break the ice, Kiesner said: "Now that you've gotten your promotion, I guess that means no retirement now, sir."

The comment was directed to McKnight. It was the always street-talking Devro who answered. "Not now, Babycakes."

Devro swung his head around to take a look at the man who had recently been promoted. "Lieut... *Captain*, s'cusa me — with all you done been through, somebody should'a pulled some strings and made you a deputy. Fact, they ought'a made you chief. I ought'a be your deputy. Ha, ha, ha. *Deputy Chief Roland T. Devro*, chief of ALL detectives. Can you get with that, home-boy?"

Neither man paid any attention to what Devro was saying. Kiesner's mind had flashed back to the very first time he had seen McKnight after the Van Horn episode.

The mind that had once been alive with incisive and caustic observations was all but dead. So was the rest of the body. He lay there in the hospital room torpid-like, almost comatose. From his condition, the German could almost suspect what had happened. He recalled that McKnight had left word with the desk that if any information came through from Interpol in re a Leslie Van Horn, they were to leave word at the hotel where he and his wife were staying at the time. Interpol had nothing. The next morning when Lt. McKnight had not shown up for work and couldn't be found at his apartment, Kiesner had begun to worry. Knowing that if the lieutenant didn't get the chance to call England about the placebo pills as he said he might do, they certainly had to call when he got in. Equally important, they were due in Irvine to pickup the motorhome at ten. The clock had moved past eleven. He waited a few more minutes then took it upon himself to find the name of the dealership in Irvine and called there, thinking that maybe the lieutenant's anxiety over getting the "Big Bad

Boy" had gotten the best of him and that there had been a change in plans.

The original salesman was out to lunch, and so Kiesner was unable to come up with anything. He sat glumly at the desk for about twenty minutes longer. Something had to be wrong. The lieutenant was far too duty-bound and punctilious not to have at least called in, particularly on that morning. Hoping he was not jumping the gun, Kiesner made the decision to go to the captain. Ault couldn't have cared less. Disappointed, the German found his way back to the office. There he waited for another half-hour before making a stab at retracing the steps he and the lieutenant had made the day before. The trouble was, he didn't know the streets. Devro did, but he was out. If, Kiesner figured at the time, Devro and Washington were living up to the impression they had created the day before, they would not be giving the city a full day's work. Since it was lunch time, they would probably be languishing at a nearby eatery. Then again, the visiting cop suddenly remembered, earlier that morning Devro and Washington said they were going on special assignment. He checked with Rusty at the desk. She told him where they could be reached.

They were found at a pool hall. Both were as surprised as Kiesner had been when they learned that the lieutenant hadn't reported in. Acting swiftly for a change, Devro asked a few questions, got troubling answers, and jammed his pool stick back into the rack. He told Washington to hold the table until he got back.

In the car, Devro pushed more questions, ran with the answers and spun the car around to head for the jewelry mart on Fifth Street.

In no time flat they were there. Inside, at the Kahazani section, Bunny Workman, the snitch, was nowhere to be found.

Kiesner recalled that it was important to find Bunny, because he was supposed to get back to McKnight with the name of a female who had been dealing. Not finding Bunny, at Kiesner's insistence they went back to the department to confer with Captain Ault.

As usual, Ault was anything but pleasant. He had just returned from his second trip into McKnight's office. The two men stated their case, and three times Ault tried to end the conversation by implying that McKnight was a hophead — a user — and that he had walked. "And if you want to question me as to why I call him a hophead," blasted the captain, "ask yourselves this: Why would a man keep loaded syringes in his desk drawer?! We have a property room for that kind of nonsense!"

The two detectives were too embittered to respond to the allegation. The captain continued to talk heatedly. When he was able, each time Kiesner came back with: "But, sir, it is not logical that the lieutenant would just up and walk away."

"Ain't no way he'd walk or do nothin' like that, Cap," Devro added.

"He's not here, is he?! Have you seen him?! Did he call in?! He's gone and I hope like hell the sonofabitch *stays* gone. And if there's anything I can do to see that the sonofabitch stays gone, I'll do it!"

"But, sir," Kiesner tried to ask, "he was working on a case. Why would he leave at this time?"

"Because he was a maniac! And a criminal. He was an arrogant, race-baiting sonofabitch who couldn't play by the rules. Ever since I've known him, he's had to have his own way — and he thought nothing of this department," the captain fired. "And understand something: Wyatt William McKnight was *supposed* to be going out on disability! Even at that, he only had a short time before full retirement. But don't be too sure that would've happened, because he was heading for a fall. He knew it, and pulled a fast one. I say good riddance to a bad experience." To prove his point, he snatched at the phone and dialed a number. While dialing, he said to Devro, "And don't call me *Cap*. Do I look like a goddamn fedora to you?"

"Orange County Motorhomes, Lindencourt speaking," the voice responded to the speaker-phone.

"Mr. Lindencourt, this is Captain Ault again, LAPD. You're on the speaker. I've got one idiot standing before me who is about to be canned for insubordination, the other is about to be kicked out of the country on a U-boat. A certain colored detective is missing. These two think I've just rolled off a turnip truck and don't think I know what'n the hell's going on in my own goddamn division. Repeat what you told me earlier this morning, and what you've noted on the copy of a certain purchase order that I also found in the desk drawer of this same colored detective."

"Sure. I sold a Lieutenant Wyatt McKnight of your department a Spectrum 2010 RV last week. It was a 37-footer with a 12-foot slideout. He was supposed to come by and take delivery of it this morning. But I got a call from his lady friend late last night, saying that the lieutenant wouldn't be picking it up until later. No problem. She was a bit "eccentric," for the want of a better word. But as I told her, if he's unable to come in, we'll hold it 'til he's ready. Or we could even deliver it, if he wants. It's paid for. Nice man. Great to do business with."

"And why do you remember the caller so well, Mr. Lindencourt?"

"Next to being 'strange,' she had an English accent. Next, she…"

"Repeat that last bit, Mr. Lindencourt."

"The lady had a British accent."

Ault ended the telephone conversation without a thank-you. He ended the other one with fiery aggression. "Your lieutenant is shacking up with a fruitcake English woman. This self-righteous, slick sonofabitch who's always putting his foot in his mouth about race is shacking up with a *white* woman!" Ault steamed, as if he knew the woman's color. "Does that tell you two dipsticks anything?!"

"Yeah," said Devro, doing his bit for womanhood and civil rights. "It tells me that a good piece is a good piece."

Back on the streets, the two detectives spent the rest of the day looking for Bunny Workman, finally finding him at late that afternoon in a bail-bond office. Bunny wasn't in trouble but a friend of his was, and he didn't feel like talking. The cops again pushed him to talk. The little man tossed a mild profanity and said he saw no reason why he had to talk. His main man in trouble, Devro grabbed the snitch by the nape of the neck and rammed his head against the wall. "If you don't start talkin', I'm gonna ram it through."

"All right, all right, all right," Bunny gasped, "Whaddaya wanna know?"

"What was the name of the chick McKnight was lookin' for?"

"Angie."

"Did she have an accent?"

"No."

"What was her last name?"

"I dunno. I never got it."

"*What* was her last name?"

"I tol'ja I never got it. I'm tellin' you th' same thing I told Lieutenant McKnight."

"And you told him when?"

"Yesterday evenin'. He told me to call him at the bar."

"What bar?"

"Forte's. On Ventura Boulevard in Encino."

The drive had been quick. Forte's had picked up business; the hors d'oeuvres crowd was circling. Cy was behind the bar. Devro quickly I.D.'d him. Kiesner asked the questions.

"We are looking for a policeman who was in here yesterday around this time. His name was Lieutenant McKnight. Black, graying, about 6-foot in height. Do you recall seeing anyone like that?"

"Yeah. He was sitting right here in front of me. Said his name was McKnight. He got a phone call. The guy on the other end of the line asked for him by that name."

"Was he here alone?"

"You could say that. But he was awfully busy hitting on a fine white chick that was sitting here."

"Then that wasn't our McKnight," said Devro. "He wouldn'a been hittin' on one'a them skags."

"Easy, Devro," Kiesner said, and directed his attention back to the bartender. "Did this 'chick' have an English accent?"

"No."

"How long did she stay here?"

"Less than an hour. She left before he did. Got tired of him, I guess. I would've."

"He wouldn't have said where he was going after that, would he?"

"Didn't have to."

"How come he didn't 'have to,'" queried Devro.

Cy would no longer talk with him. He turned to the German. "Did you have a question, Officer?"

Kiesner asked, "Why is it you say he didn't have to tell you where he was going?"

"Because I had an idea where he was going at night."

Ignoring Devro, Cy loosely explained the conversation he had had with McKnight.

What the two detectives learned had them going to the club b.c. It was closed. The time was 8:15. Devro figured that if the club wasn't open at that hour, it wasn't going to open at all.

Promising they would get an early start in the morning, Kiesner drove back to Whitehurst. The two men separated for the evening.

The next thing they knew, McKnight was in the hospital.

10

"Where're we goin'?"

His diction was not good, and he had been wiping his nose with a soiled handkerchief, rubbing his arms, and scratching at his legs for the better part of the trip. They had been the first words the detective had spoken since ordering Devro to use the red light.

Devro shot Kiesner an "is he for real?" look, and said, "Where we goin'? We goin' to where you told us to go when we returned your call this mornin'. To where Leslie Van Horn lived."

Kiesner sensed that the senior detective was unable to remember. It was understandable, however. After all, he hadn't been on the streets in over a year. "Sir, do you remember anything at all about the case?"

McKnight didn't respond. He wanted the heater on, but he wouldn't ask.

Devro chipped in: "You remember th' broad who shot Detective Sergeant LeCoultre while he was drivin' a XJS? He had robbed her out of some dope?"

The captain resisted the urge to rub his arms and wipe his nose.

He lit another cigarette. Again he gave no response to the question.

Devro continued. "Captain…I mean *Commander* Ault assigned you to the case because it involved narcotics, and this jive-time woman got you strung out? She was from Cotswold, Paris?"

"*England*," Kiesner corrected, and added, "And the name of the area is *the* Cotswolds."

"Same thing," retorted Devro. "Both of 'em's 'cross the pond."

Kiesner slipped a hand into a briefcases, found the file folder he was looking for and passed it back to McKnight. Once again he was having trouble. Trying to concentrate on what Devro had said, he hadn't heard Kiesner's correction.

"That is the case file, Captain. It's coded "Queen.""

"Should'a been called *"horse*," Devro said. "That's what th' old-timers used to call dope. 'Cause they used to get on them ponies and *ride*."

Kiesner went back to the folder. "Some of the information in the file came from me, and some from Devro's 'follow-up' when I went back to Germany."

"Yeah, but go easy on th' way you say that 'follow-up,' my over-seas brother. I worked hard on puttin' some of that stuff together."

"Sure you did," Kiesner said, suspicious of the effort. "Captain, the rest of the information comes from the D.A.'s office."

"What you holdin' there, Cap'n Mac, tells about when she was gift-wrappin' the stuff and distributin' it to the poor, an' a little 'bout what she jabbed you with."

"It is not very good police work."

"I do good work. That's why Commander Ault put me on it."

"Sure," said Kiesner, doubtfully. "Oh, and Captain, you will notice that the coroner's report on the woman is missing."

McKnight spoke. He could hardly say the words. "Coroner's report? The woman is dead?"

"She is dead, sir," said Kiesner. "At least she is supposed to be."

Devro swung a full look to the back seat. "Why you look so sur-prised, Main Brother? Don't you remember wipin' her out?"

McKnight was too inwardly paralyzed to say anything.

"You took her right on outta here. Blam!" Devro continued. "Yeah, she's dead. An' she's been dead for a long time."

As he had been since returning to Whitehurst, Kiesner wasn't certain Devro had all the facts. The doubt occurred because in the rush to get the wounded cop to the hospital that night, the woman had been all but overlooked. Like McKnight, she ended up in the hospital. But she was taken to the Valley's Sherman Oaks Hospital. She was not seriously injured, and underwent a small operation the next morning. It dealt mostly with cleaning and stitching the temple wound, which stretched to the hairline. By evening she had checked herself out, and was never heard from again.

On the very same morning, McKnight, having been taken to County General Hospital, roughly twenty minutes away from Sherman Oaks, had undergone an interview. Lt. Eugene Richland, the big redhead from the officer-involved-shooting detail, had been told that throughout the night the lieutenant had been given medication to counteract the heroin in his system, and that it was all right to interview him.

While the counteracting drug might have had an effect, it didn't come close to restoring the lieutenant's faculties. No one knew it, least of all Richland, but McKnight's mind had been seared by pure heroin and sap from California's beautiful state flower. It also mixed with another agent. In time McKnight would pay the price. The fall from the wall didn't help. The mind would get worse. But in the interview, he had put up a front. He was articulate and believable. Then he ran out of gas. The interview was closed. His last words, said absently, were: The *woman*. Pause. *Shot*. Pause. *Killed*... He was hurt, and the very last word trailed off. In his report, Richland wrote: *Suspect, shot and killed*. Period. Case closed. Thus an arrest was never made.

Richland obviously was in serious error. To begin with, McKnight, even in that depleted state of mind, never used the term *suspect*. Secondly, he was not talking about something he had done. He was talking about something that the *woman* had done. He never finished the sentence. What he was trying to say was that it was the woman who had shot and had killed someone. He of course had meant *LeCoultre*.

There never was a follow-up. As was brought out time and again at the "trial of the century," it was a matter of sloppy police work.

Kiesner was still in thought. He knew how much McKnight had cared for the Spectrum 2010, and one of the more thoughtful things he did when he came back to the country was to find out what had happened to it. There was no reason to worry. Since the lieutenant was unable to take delivery, Lindencourt was good enough to cancel the order. The check was returned to the bank. Kiesner thought it was a nice gesture, but what bothered him was that McKnight no longer talked about it, and, figuring that it might trigger something disturbing, he was afraid to bring the subject up. Now he was beginning to wonder if the Captain even remembered making the purchase.

"Hey, Keezy-Key," Devro popped, "do some reporter from across the pond keep callin' you, askin' questions 'bout this case after all this time? "

"No."

"Come to think of it, it wouldn't a'done no good for her to call for you, anyway. You was still 'cross the pond."

"And she called you?"

"Still doin' it. She gives me a buzz every now 'n' then. An', honey, ev'ry time she calls, I can't stop talkin'. I just luuuv's them French accents."

McKnight was struggling hard, trying to recall some of the turns that had led to the house. Nothing was familiar.

Daylight was in full swing. The rain had eased somewhat when the car rounded the corner to the cul-de-sac and pulled to a stop in front of the long wet wall that hid a mystery.

It didn't appear that the place was in total disrepair, but it needed work and there was a foreclosure sign that was partially hidden by vegetation.

The gate was slightly open.

Devro switched the emergency light off and they sat for a moment as if waiting for McKnight to say something. Finally Kiesner said in a reminding sort of way: "Here we are, Captain, at what used to be Leslie Van Horn's residence."

McKnight, looking bewildered in the back seat, wiped a bit of perspiration from his forehead, leaned forward, and peered out the window.

"Are you okay, sir?" Kiesner asked.

Devro joined in. "You ain't still got all'a them bone aches, an' sore gums, an' things you used to complain about, is you?"

Without answering, McKnight looked at the file and placed it on the seat. He inhaled deeply, put his hand on the door handle and started to lift himself out. The two detectives started to move with him.

"No," he said. "You guys stay put."

"But, Captain…"

"Gentlemen, I'm cured. I'm just coming back here to remember. To get my mind in order."

"I don't think so, man," Devro said.

"Trying to remember what happened a year ago would be tough on anybody, sir," Kiesner added, sympathetically.

"Let alone what all you done been through," Devro added, unnecessarily.

"Why was I here?"

"That's it," said Devro, "we goin' in there with you."

"No, I said. All I want you to do is tell me why I was here. I know I was working on a case. I know I followed somebody here. I know something happened to me here. What I want to know is, what was the *real* reason I was here?"

Neither of them understood the full significance of the question.

"It can be analyzed to death," Devro said. "But the *real* reason, as you put it, was that you was in there because of that crazy woman, Leslie Van Horn. She was out of it, and she tried to do th' same to you.

The bottom line is, she was weird. Weird people do weird things. What we got to worry about is makin' sure you're on the right road to recovery. You done been out of it too long."

"You mean too much to all of us, Captain," Kiesner said. "We will go in there with you."

McKnight was out of the car now. He was studying the wall, and parts of that night started to come back. He lit another cigarette. "I have to go in alone. If I'm ever going to beat this thing, I have to retrace my steps. All I want to do is just see the place. Just to see where it all started. It'll be okay. Once I see what's in there, everything'll come back."

He left them and walked away in the light rain.

Inside the compound, except for neglect, the grounds hadn't changed much. Even if they had, he wouldn't have known the difference. Other than the revealing little light that came from the foot of the Buddha, he never got to see them that night. But he did see the Buddha and its slanted, almost all-knowing eyes. They had an effect, frightful at first, but he got over it. So, it could be said, seeing the form again helped. It was larger, but now he had a faint realization of why the Buddha across from the rehab center had significance.

Walking slowly, he looked around then went to the swing-bench and sat. He started tending to his nose, and freely rubbing his arms. He didn't know it, as he never got to see the clown that night, but it was the same place where the clown had once sat.

In the car, the two men tried to talk away their concerns.

Kiesner's eyes wandered over to the *foreclosure* sign. "In a case like this, where the deceased was involved in narcotics-related crimes, who takes over the property? The state?"

"I don't know. The place wasn't hers, and she wasn't into the stuff heavy enough to fall under the RICO Act," said Devro. "But somebody ought'a give this thing to the Mac. He's gonna need something nice and quiet to recuperate in for a short spell more."

"'A short spell more?' Devro, the captain has had it. Here's a man who's been in and out of rehabs and hospitals for a solid year.

He is almost worse off now than when he went in. He does not even talk the same."

"That's because his mouth's been hurtin' 'im. That's what he told me."

"To tell you the truth, I find it all quite strange."

"Hey, I don't see nothin' strange about it at all. Furthermore, the man's done beat it. All he needs now is that final jolt, an' just a little more time for recovery. The brain is something else, man. But he's on his way, now. He's ready to make the full comeback. The Mac is comin' back, Jack."

"I sure as hell would hope so. But I don't think so. Let me ask you this: Why do you think he wanted to return here, and then prevented us from going in there with him?"

"To prove to himself he's done beat it. An' you gotta r'member, dude, he's a loner. And he always did like comin' back to the scene of a crime. I know the man. He'd come back even when a case was closed. Check, check, double-check. Now, if you was to ask me what I'd say if he *stayed* back there, then I'd say we got a problem. But if he comes back within a few minutes, we got it made, Jack. Know what I'm sayin'?"

Devro dropped the subject in his typical manner, and studied the gate. "Man, I'd sure like to be livin' behind a wall like that. Can't you see me eatin' a coupla fatburgers in the teahouse?"

Kiesner's mind was on the captain. "Devro, it is bad enough the captain is addicted, but you have heard of the Stockholm Syndrome?"

"Yeah," laughed Devro. "It's about two blocks east of City Hall. No, man, that's where the *captee* falls in love with the *captor*. Everybody knows that. But what's that got to do with th' Mac?"

"Everything, I'm beginning to think."

"What is it you got in your mind, Homeboy? You soundin' mighty suspicious."

"I got in my mind, Devro, the concerns of a very good man who is in an awful lot of trouble. And it is a whole lot deeper than skin deep."

"Let it rest, my good brother. Let it rest. The Mac ain't got no problems he can't handle. He'll be back on his game."

McKnight was still sitting on the swing-bench in the light rain. He was searching his mind, pondering the question: *Why am I here?* He was not moving around; he was not searching for anything. In the car he had said he wanted to "get my mind in order." He did not appear to be doing that; it did not appear that he *wanted* to do that. For instance, he never moved from the one spot, he didn't even think about going over to the area where he had landed on the ground that night. Perhaps he couldn't remember, but even at that, he never even looked at the house, he never looked at the wall. He sat there smoking and feeling a deep and inexplicable hurt. Something was killing him. Every now and then he would rub his arms and press at the temples, trying to ward off certain impulses and giving clear evidence that something else was gnawing at him. The phrase *Please don't die* was trying to push through again. It was held up by something else.

He sat there a little longer, rubbing his arms, his eyes roaming. Nothing was coming forth, and so he stood. Where he was going, he didn't know. Without any reason he happened to look in back of the bench-swing. It was an idle look; there was no purpose behind it. But tossed in the corner of the small, sectioned-off place was a clown. He didn't know it at the time, but it belonged to Leslie.

The ugly thing was soggy, splotched, and caked with dirt. From the way it was positioned, it looked every bit like a discarded rag with a face. The head was sort of tilted, but the eyes were there. There was a kind of dead, dull look about them. The portion of the mouth that could be seen was fixed in a grin. The lips were faded red.

Something began seeping through McKnight's mind with a reminding clarity.

He quickly covered the clown with the soiled handkerchief.

The two waiting men saw the approaching captain at about the same time. He wasn't doing it well, but he was trying to walk briskly.

"Talk about makin' th' comeback," said Devro. "Dig it."

They gave each other a grin and topped it with opened-palm victory slaps.

"Good German bro, the main man *is* back. He's done beat the devil. Crank this thing up so's we can get on out of here."

"It is very good," Kiesner said, insecurely.

"Tol'ja. All he wanted to do was to come back to the scene of origin. All he needed was that jolt."

Kiesner cranked up, Devro opened the rear door to let McKnight in, the car U-turned, and they headed for home. Devro started to flip the switch, turning on the red light. Kiesner, not at all positive about anything but trying for optimism, said, "I don't think we have a need for that any more."

"You right, Homes," Devro grinned. "Th' emergency is over."

The red light was turned off and removed from the top of the car.

Not noticing the senior detective in pain in the back seat, the two detectives started happily chatting among themselves.

He thought it over several times before asking, but the question was killing him. He lit a cigarette, placed the file on his lap and thought some more. Full stress had returned. Finally the perspiring McKnight said, "....Guys, the woman, Leslie...?"

The slowness of the question dampened feelings. "Yeah. Leslie Van Horn."

"Leslie Van Horn. She was the woman who shot...?"

"She shot Detective Sergeant LeCoultre. — Go on."

"An' she was the same one who got me?"

"Yeah. She gave you somethin' that put a hurtin' on you," said Devro, not happy with the captain's faulty memory.

Kiesner wasn't happy either. "What is it that you want to know, Captain?"

McKnight gave a gentle rub to an arm. "Have I been back here since it happened?"

"Not that we know of."

"The woman...What happened to her?"

Now Devro was truly hurt. He swung a look to the back seat:

"You shot her, that's what happened to her. We just told you that a li'l earlier."

"....I sh-sh-shot her?"

"An' a damn good thing you did," Devro blasted.

"Oh, my God," said the senior detective. His head went back in pain. "Oh, my God."

"Hey, she was gonna do you in. She was stalkin' you. In checking her phone records for that day? Every place you called, she called," Devro said, now confusing even Kiesner. "She was tracking you."

"I was with him, Devro," the German said. "How could she have called every place we had been that day?"

"What difference do it make? She got to him, didn't she?"

The captain couldn't get over the notion that the woman had been shot.

"What's wrong with you, man?" Devro asked.

"She can't be dead. I couldn't have killed her." He was talking more to himself now. "I couldn't have done it. I just couldn't have."

"Hey, you had good reason. She was tryin' to do you in with the needle. The doctors up there said you was jabbed more times than a pin cushion. Marks were all over you," said Devro.

"You were missing for almost *twenty-four* hours, Captain. You and I were right in the middle of the case," Kiesner added.

"She got to you," Devro said, never having thoroughly checked any facts. "She musta been somethin' unreal to turn your head, cause you sho-nuff ain't into them kind'a legs. But she got to you. Had you all decked out in a tux, no less. You was cleaner than the board of health. Now, the way I see it, you must'a went to pick this broad up, an' y'all was gonna take off from there. Maybe after you showed up she tried to get you on the stuff an' you blasted her. But you sho'nuff pulled the plug on her, baby. BLAM! Right in th' head. Or was it in th' temple?...Whatever. She's dead. 'Bye."

"Devro, this woman reporter who called you, what paper is she from?"

"She never said. Only thing I know is that she's always calling from somethin' called the Savoy."

McKnight thought about it for a while. "Didn't this Leslie have...? Didn't she have a nightclub or something?"

"It was called the b.c." Kiesner answered.

"Take me to it."

Devro spun around and frowned, "Do *what*?"

"I want to go to the club."

"First of all, it's too early. It ain't even six in the morning yet. Next, the thing *ain't* there no more. An' next to that, goin' there don't make no kinda sense. It's probably done changed hands a hunnert an' one times since she's had it. Why you wanna go there?"

"Dammit, don't ask me *why*. Just go there. And go there *now*."

They couldn't fight it. Kiesner made the appropriate turns to head for the 101. On the freeway, they rode in a tight silence for a while, then the German, shifting a *watch this* eye on Devro, said, "Captain, you said you are cured now. We have taken you to the house; you have not had a chance to read the file you are holding. Something about this case still bothers me. I am due to go back home to Germany. I would like to have everything clear in my mind before I go, which will be Wednesday. In your own words, sir, tell us what happened."

It was a challenge, and the captain knew it. He would give it all he could. But he couldn't think.

Feeling that it might offer some relief, Kiesner again started to bring up the subject of the RV, but decided against it. Instead, he stuck with the case. "Are you able to tell us anything about that night, Captain?"

Struggling, finally McKnight said, "....I was working the streets a month ago."

"A *year*, sir."

"Detective Van Horn had killed Sergeant LeCoultre over some narcotics with a clown."

"Would you repeat what you've just said, Captain."

"Sergeant Van Horn had killed the clown over..."

Devro winked hopefully at Kiesner, and said under his breath:

He's puttin' us on, man. He's got to be puttin' us on. "You puttin' us on, ain't that right, Cap'n Mac?"

"Let him finish," Kiesner said to Devro, tautly under his breath. He then said aloud, "Go on, Captain — what happened next? Better yet, who assigned you to the case?"

"Lieutenant Ault…"

"No! Goddammit," a hurt Devro flared, unable to hold it in and now knowing the man was not even close to joking. *"You* was a lieutenant! *Ault* was a *captain.* He's now a commander."

"I'm sorry," said the veteran cop. "I'm sorry."

Kiesner, again recognizing the toll of stress, was gentle. "Do you still want to go to where the club was before we check you in, Captain?"

"I have to go to the club," McKnight said, afraid to voice what he was really thinking."

Devro was right. The b.c. was no more. The place had changed hands more than once. As it had been at the house, McKnight didn't allow the two detectives to come upstairs with him. They remained parked out front.

When the captain got out and went inside, Kiesner noticed how slowly he was moving. He bit his lip in thought for a long while, then said, "Devro, when I was away, did you spend any time with the captain?"

"'Course, I did."

"Did you spend as much time as we have spent this morning?"

"No. But I tried to spend more. I'd pick him up and take him for a drive a few times. He didn't like it, and he'd never talk. So we'd cut it short. Five or ten minutes out, and he'd want to go home. Check that. Most of the time, he'd want to go back to rehab. But he was down. Always down. He didn't even perk up when I brought his new captain's badge to him."

"Did you ever get the chance to talk with the police psychiatrist or any of the therapists about him?"

"No. But now I'm thinkin' I should've."

"While you guys were out, did he ever talk about Methadone or any of the medication he was taking?"

"He hated all'a that stuff he was s'posed to be takin'," Devro answered, which pushed him to something new. "Where's that file? I wanna check somethin'."

"He took it with him," Kiesner said suspiciously. "Devro, was he always at home or at the rehab place when you went to see him?"

"Not always. I missed him a few times. He was out."

"Do you have any idea where he was?"

"No. Why? What's botherin' you?"

"Do you remember I was saying he was worse off now than when he first went to the hospital?"

"I didn't get it then. But now I think I know what you're driving at," Devro said, with uncharacteristic sadness growing in his voice.

"So you would you agree with that now?"

Devro didn't want to admit it, but he had to. "He's worse, man. He's definitely worse. I don't know how'n the hell it happened. But he's definitely worse off."

"And we're talking about after a year of treatment. Nothing that lady could have given him that night could have affected him that long. It is not possible. First-time users' withdrawal symptoms generally only lasts for seventy-two hours. Do you know the first thing I noticed about him when I came back from Germany and saw him?"

"What?"

"His diction. I used to love listening to him talk."

"Something was wrong with his mouth, he told me one time. It's an on-and-off thing."

"Doesn't that tell you something?"

Devro was thoughtful. "I know where you're headed, homeboy; but since you brought it up, let me tell you what gets me."

"What?"

"He's been sweating more, an' rubbing both his arms. His legs ache, and his mouth is back botherin' him again. And did you notice how he's been dabbing at his nose?"

"Strange, isn't it?" Kiesner asked.

"Very."

"And, Devro, wouldn't you agree that the marks Leslie Van Horn were responsible for — *if* there were any marks in the first place — would've been long gone by now."

"Long gone, Homes," Devro said weakly. "Long gone. So you might as well go 'head an' say it: The man's been shooting-up all along."

"...So, since we are on the same page, if he was getting stuff through the rehab center, somebody had to be responsible. The counselors wouldn't have done it. Somebody outside had to arrange for it."

"It was somebody who wanted him down," said Devro. "Somebody who wanted to make sure he *stayed* down. An' I'll give you three guesses who it was."

"One will do," said Kiesner. "But do you think he knew who was having it done?"

"Of course. But I'm thinking Mr. Mac was too far gone to care."

When McKnight first came up the escalator, he remembered little or nothing about the hotel's lobby or the front of the club. He hadn't remembered the stores that were downstairs, either.

He stood looking at the place for a while, and as though something came back, he went inside and stopped momentarily in the tiny reception area where, after a period, he remembered someone had once sat there. He was trying to think of Gena, but the memory wouldn't take him back that far.

Moving into the main room, he vaguely remembered that the room configurations were the same. The decor was totally different. It was strictly French, and it had retained none of the old-world Van Horn elegance. What had confused him more was that, at that hour, the door was open, and there were one or two people inside.

There was activity, because an early-morning three-man janitorial crew was busy at work. When they saw him standing there eyeing the place, as unkempt as he was, they wanted to bounce him. He flashed his badge and they backed off.

The ailing detective wasn't satisfied with just coming in and taking a look around. He wanted to re-live a moment in time. He lit a cigarette and stood there, fighting to remember. In his favor, his tension had somewhat eased, and he was feeling better than he had in the car. It was easier on him here, because this was where he had first encountered the woman.

With the crew looking at him strangely, he moved to where the bar was. Gone were the moods, the etched and beveled glass, the textured tablecloths, the beautiful indirect lighting, and there was no massive painting of the chess set with the fallen knight.

He stood staring for a long time, certain thing coming back, his mind darted around fragments of the conversation he had had with the woman. He felt closer.

The phrase *Please don't die* came again.

As he looked around, trying to recapture the essence of that night, he believed that it was not a phrase that he had been hearing. It was a calling; a beckoning. In terms of what he had gone through — and was still going through — it had to be answered. He could do that, because the woman wasn't dead.

He knew it. He would find her, because he couldn't live without her.

Would he prowl the streets to take something with him? No.

Wherever she was, she had everything he needed.

11

The Los Angeles airport was busy as usual. McKnight greeted 11 a.m. by alighting from an old van loaded with mops, buffers, brooms, fluids, and all manner of cleaning gear. It was disturbing to see him. His luggage consisted of one suitcase and a carry-on. He was moving as swiftly as he could.

What he had done wasn't very complicated. He had ditched Devro and Kiesner, and, using his badge, he had pressed Ike Urrutia, one of the men from the clean-up crew, into service. He did hope that the man wouldn't be treated roughly once the two found out what had happened.

The captain made good use of the time, and he was considerate enough to pay Urrutia for his effort. Before dropping him off at LAX, the man had driven him to his apartment, waited in the van while he quickly cleaned up and came back out with two bags, one of which had already been packed for his journey to the Delta. Urrutia then drove him all the way out to Leslie Van Horn's house in the Valley. The only trouble they encountered was finding Leslie's house. The address was in the files, but McKnight had difficulty remembering the streets and turns, and he wasn't certain why it was necessary to go back to the house in the first place. Once there, though, he did do something unusual. He bagged the clown and took it with him.

For a time McKnight did keep Kiesner and Devro in mind, and he had enough concern to ask Urrutia to give the two waiting policemen his regards, along with the message that he would be in touch with them soon. If they weren't out front when he returned, he was instructed to call the Whitehurst station.

In time the two would figure out what he had done. They would, of course, worry, and would be obliged to report to Ault or someone in the department. But there was really nothing anyone in the department could do about it. He was a grown man, he had committed no crime. He was free to do as he pleased. Well, maybe he wasn't free, he thought, but he was still grown and he had the right to do as he chose.

Checking in and getting set for international travel was rough. McKnight's mind was taxed. To relax, he tried grabbing at anything. Perhaps, because he was traveling, the Big Bad Boy, sneaked back into his mind. He hadn't thought about it in a long while, and it came back like a long-lost friend. But the friendship was not to last. Something else that bumped his mind took precedence. Maybe if that "something else" hadn't taken precedence he would have been more pragmatic, devoted more thought to what he was doing, concentrated more on the files and the conversations he had had in the car with Devro and Kiesner, and would have chosen the right destination.

Right or wrong, though, the man who was mentally in and out of it, and gave telling evidence of suffering emotional turmoil and confusion, a man whom a police psychiatrist had described as a casualty of a type of schizophrenia called Brief Psychotic Disorder caused by heroin and perpetuated by stress, was on his way.

The psychiatrist had also said an episode of the illness typically lasted a day; the longest on record was a month. But the captain from the Los Angeles Police Department had been ailing for over a year.

He had also come close to having a complete mental breakdown.

The flight from LAX to Paris' Charles de Gaulle Airport was un-eventful, and took ten hours and twenty minutes.

Before blanking out on certain things, the troubled captain spent most of the time devouring the files he had taken with him, studying every dot, comma and hyphen attached to the case. He knew he wouldn't be able to retain much, but at least he wanted to become familiar with it enough so that in case the need arose, he would be able to talk about it intelligently — or at least to start off intelligibly, and then find some way to get back to the reports for support. That was all well and good, but going back to what he had initially done, had it not been so pathetic it could have been laughable.

Leslie Van Horn was located in England, but McKnight wound up in Paris. The blunder wasn't totally his fault. Going back to where the club — now French — had been, Devro's mentioning of France and then reinforcing it by mentioning the woman's French accent and the place where she was *supposed* to have been calling him from, had been cemented in his mind. Even as he stood absently at the Bradley terminal counter to purchase his ticket, he thought little or nothing about the destination he was choosing.

On the flight he was no different. His mind, for the most part, was glued to one thing and one thing only. It had everything to do with his needs and Leslie's involvement with heroin. It was only after re-peatedly going over the files and when the plane had approached touchdown at De Gaulle that he begin to fully confront his mistake: Leslie Van Horn was from England. And that was where he should have been going. He hadn't been thinking. And *that* was the key. *Not thinking.* It was understandable. It was a trait of anyone coming out from under a psychological disorder such as he had experienced.

Fighting physical weariness, yet fixed on using the error to his advantage, he put his mind through a series of calisthenics, and com-ing through the terminal, he tried to memorize every sign he saw. And while he was not sparkling, the exercise did have an effect, and he was feeling good because of it. He was feeling good, too, because he was in Europe. He hadn't broken down, and he was getting close to the woman. He needed needed a cigarette.

Lighting up, he calmly followed the rest of the passengers to the baggage-claim area, where he retrieved his luggage, and went to customs. While waiting in line, and after overhearing a couple talk about it, he decided to take the Chunnel train to England.

It was shortly after 3 p.m. and McKnight was dead tired when he arrived in London's Waterloo station after a three hour trip from Paris' Gare du Nord. The train station was jammed and he was beginning to get confused again. He was sweaty and anxious, his eyes were hollow and he had begun to shake just a bit. He tried exercising the mind again, but got tired of the technique and decided to steal another smoke. Feeling the need for outside air, he left the terminal and stood out front for about ten or twelve minutes. He then came back in, retrieved his luggage and followed directions to the taxi stand out front.

The driver, a dark-skinned man who wore a turban, pulled out, drove a few yards and said in a heavy English accent, "Where to, mate?"

The thought of race came to him again. It hadn't been with him for a long time, and so it was interesting to hear a dark-complexioned man speaking with an English accent.

He was in the process of trying to think of some of the other things he used to think about when his arms, like his legs, started tingling more. And again, his mouth wasn't feeling up to par. Pulling out a pack of cigarettes, he asked the driver, "Mind if I smoke?"

"If you're careful, it's okay." The driver traveled on, then eventually popped the "where to?" question again.

Maybe it had been planted in his subconscious, as Rusty, the desk sergeant, had included the name in her report, and the woman had twice mentioned the name at the club, but he depended on something the talkative Devro had said.

"The Savoy," he finally voiced.

The Savoy was positioned at the end of a short, but active street. It was an exquisite hotel, something all London could have been proud of. And upon checking in, he was as surprised as a person in his condition could get. All he had to do was say his name and everything was set. He didn't have to do anything. There was no *sign-in*, no *"how long are you going to be here?"* Nothing. Even being escorted upstairs to his room was filled with courteous mystery. The bellman wouldn't accept the tip.

The visitor from Los Angeles couldn't even begin to understand it. He tried, but he was too exhausted and pained to give it more than a cursory effort. To ward off what felt like a pulsating feeling attacking various parts of the body, he slumped into the big-backed chair. He was in it for only a few minutes when he started napping. Catching himself, he was about go over and plunge into a deep sleep on top of the bed covers when the phone rang. For an American, it was an odd ring. It took time to recognize and find the source. When he did, he picked up the receiver and held onto it, almost afraid to say anything. For a moment there was no *Hello* from the other end, either.

When the words finally came, they were smooth and calm. The woman's voice sounded as though it could gift-wrap honey.

"Welcome to England, Mr. McKnight."

It was *her* voice. It was *the* voice. No matter what anyone said or did, he knew — he *knew* — he would hear it again.

Instantly a thousand thoughts were snared in a cobwebbed mind. He was both apprehensive and exhilarated. He didn't know what to do. He knew what he had to be, though. He reminded himself that, at all times, he had to be strong; he had to be on his game.

Quickly he dug into his carry-on for a new pack of cigarettes and sent his trembling hands in search of a better lighter. It was not significant. He was simply confused for the moment. He found what he was looking for under the files and the first layer of handkerchiefs and other items, which protected three cartons of cigarettes. Under them was microcassette recorder. A gun was nearby.

"Well, aren't you going to say something?"

Although friendly and inviting, it was so unreal it was paralyzing. Trying to be helpful, the voice said something else.

McKnight didn't trust his own judgment. Anxiety was giving way to rolling clouds of doubt.

"Are you still there, Wyatt?"

Coming back, he said, "Yes. Yes. Yes, I'm still here."

"Good, because I'm still here as well."

"Where are you?"

"Twelve floors beneath you."

"*Here?* Twel…?"

"That's right," said the voice, brightening. "Twelve floors beneath you."

"You're *here*? At this hotel?"

"Same as you. You're in the Savoy. I'm in the Savoy."

"But where…?"

"In the lobby," she said. "I can't wait to see you."

He doused one cigarette and lit another. At the same time he asked the woman if he could call her back.

"Of course," she replied, "but why call if we can see each other in person?"

Again he was stuck. And he didn't like the way he was handling things. His responses were too confused and insecure. But there was a reason.

"Wouldn't you be glad to see me?" she asked.

"I'd give everything I've ever owned in my life to see you," he said.

The words *Please don't die* sprang to mind again.

Thank God, she hadn't.

All the tiredness had been laid aside. Everything that hampered movement — all the questions that had plagued him were gone. Within seconds he was on the elevator heading down.

He didn't fully know what he was doing; he didn't fully believe what was happening. In the lobby, he had forgotten where he was supposed to meet the lady. And so he stood in the center, scanning faces and drawing quizzical looks.

Then from behind him came the voice.

"Hello, Wyatt."

It was simple, direct, welcoming.

He turned. There stood the woman. He was speechless. He couldn't even begin to talk to her. Tiny beads of perspiration had begun to line the upper portion of his forehead, but he did nothing to remove them. He was too busy swallowing her with his eyes, devouring her with silent thoughts and questions. Almost as if to make an all-embracing move to her, he held out his arms. Suddenly he dropped them. He couldn't go through with the embrace, because something had tripped his mind. He took a step back, then another, and another. Then he turned and moved away swiftly. It was not in the direction of the elevators.

She didn't know what to think or do. Perhaps she would also have left had he turned for the door or the elevator. But he hadn't. From where she stood, it appeared he had gone to the bell captain. It looked as though he was seeking help of some sort. Now she was worried.

He felt sick, queasy, unstable, and it was not that he wanted to throw up when he entered the restroom. What bothered him most of all now was that he had brought his gun down with him.

Please don't die.

The phrase had reseated itself. Now he was positive of what his mind was trying to tell him. Despite what anyone had said, despite the police reports, the erroneous coroner reports and everything else, she wasn't dead. She couldn't have been dead, and the words *Please don't die* that had been circulating in his mind were only part of a state-

ment. In full, it should have been: *Please don't die, because I want to see*
you die. For killing me, I am going to kill you.

Please don't die before I get to you.

He didn't know it, but it had always been in the back of his mind
that he had to kill this woman on sight. There should be no waiting.
The moment you lay eyes on her, pull the gun and blast away. And feel good
about it. Watch her as she falls; see her as she goes down; pray that she
writhes in pain. This is the woman who has done worse than killing you.
She has turned you into an addict; a hophead; a stone junkie.

Kill her. Dead.

He had backed all the way into the men's room, but he wasn't in
there to relieve himself in the regular way. Fortunately that was no
longer a problem. He was throwing up. Wyatt McKnight, the man
who had come all the way to London to kill Leslie Van Horn, was at a
commode, throwing up. He had a hard time believing it.

As he leaned over a sink, clearing his mouth and nose in the busy
washroom, he was beginning to face the fact that none of those old
thoughts were valid. He had found strength, but he was feeling terrible, ashamed, senseless. How could he ever have had thoughts of
killing her? Had he sunk that low in his life? And even if he had, how
could he ever have had thoughts of killing *her?* From all that he could
remember — and it was growing by leaps and bounds now — she
had changed so very, very much, but even if she had not, he *needed*
her. He couldn't kill her even if he wanted to. She was his lifeline.

He went into a stall and stayed there.

Patiently Leslie stood in the center of the lobby, cutting a refined
figure in the historically grand place.

There was absolute nothing about her that was the same. She appeared taller, more statuesque. Her hair was brunette and bobbed;
her large eyes had a twinkling sharpness to them. And not that she
wasn't physically attractive before, but now she appeared to be the
very essence of woman. She was clear; poised. Beautiful.

Leslie Van Horn's metamorphosis had been so complete that it was impossible to even think that she could have murdered anyone, let alone be the sick and bizarre specimen that she had once been. Here, she was collected; serene; outwardly arresting and inwardly together. She was classy; a study in middle-years elegance.

In the bathroom, his mind brimming with thoughts, the sweating detective completed doing something he knew he had to do. He got rid of the gun by wrapping it with a bunch of paper towels and stuffing it into the trash receptacle. After that was done, he washed his face, lit a cigarette and remained at the sink, working on his nerves. When he felt composed, he came back out and stood for a minute, silently watching her from across the lobby. Seeing her standing there helped a great deal. Even more thoughts were coming back — including the fact that, fighting inner conflicts, she had lashed out and had been dangerously over the edge. It meant little or nothing to him. The only thing that seemed to have concerned him at the moment was that he knew this woman could not die by his hands.

Again he thought about the decision he had made with the gun as he moved across the lobby to face her for the second time. He was friendly and warm, and following her suggestion, they decided to spend a few minutes in the café that was close to the hotel's main entrance before going anyplace else.

Getting reacquainted was, for the most part, stiffly quiet. She was comfortable, he was not. She didn't know what he had done when he moved away in the lobby, but she knew he had done something. He was looking at her with different eyes. He was even trying to manage an occasional smile.

The two sat for a long while before anything was said. That was left to the waiter. He had come over to the booth and had taken the orders for the drinks. While waiting, she took note of how he had started to perspire, and how he was lighting one cigarette after another. She thought she saw him shaking a bit, too. She was about to say something when the waiter returned, bringing the two drinks they had ordered to the table.

The waiter put the drinks down. "Here we are. Your martini, Madam. And your order, sir. Diet soda....and salt?"

She waited for the waiter to withdraw and elevated her glass for a bemused toast. "To us."

He smiled and raised his glass. "To us. And thou?" Feeling somewhat sheepish, he asked, "Did I say that right?"

She laughed and generously said, "It sounded right to me."

He was successful in being low-key, and keeping his questions and amazement close to the vest. He didn't know where to take the conversation, and so she helped him. "Welcome."

"Thank you," he said, relieved, and then fought for something else to say. "Well, fancy this. *You; here.* Us."

"*Us* is right," she smiled, after he had trailed off.

"You look great for a corpse."

"Thank you," she said, not having the slightest idea what he meant.

Again he was stuck. He played with the salt shaker for a bit and purposely spilled a tiny bit of salt on the table.

She watched as he dipped a dampened finger in the salt and placed a few grains on the tip of his tongue. Since he did it with playfulness and casualness, she didn't make an issue of it. Nor would she mention the oddity of his drinking diet soda and tasting salt.

"You've changed a great deal." He was not at all positive, but he needed something to say.

"I would imagine we've both changed a great deal."

Again he fished for something to say. "Do you live here?"

"In the hotel? Heavens, no. I came here to see you."

He didn't understand it. Of course, there were a thousand things he didn't understand, and his memory wasn't helping.

She knew it. "I'm told my parents used to come here when travelling. But I live in the Cotswolds, which is a lovely two-hour drive from here."

"That was one of the names I had been trying to think of. What do you do there? Occupation-wise."

"I own a small antique shop. But I spend most of my time thinking about you."

"I hope the thoughts were favorable."

"They were. And are."

"S'nice. You don't have to think about me any more. I'm here."

"I'm glad," she said. "For how long are you here?"

"You mean that hasn't been figured out yet?"

"Not really."

"Well, how long I'll be here all depends."

"On?"

He wanted to say, *on you.* Instead he said, "It all depends on what turns up. I mean, I'm free now. I can do what I want."

"No job to go back to?"

"No. My department promoted me to captain, then hung me out to dry."

"Really?"

"Yeah," he said, lightly dipping another finger into the salt and not exactly telling the truth. "Yeah. They hung me out to dry. But departments do that to burned-out narcotics detectives. But the good news is, I'm now free to swim in any direction."

"Now, you aren't going to tell me you swam all the way over here, looking for work?"

"That's funny," he said, almost with laughter, "considering how confused I was in getting…getting to…"

"Yes?"

"Getting to wherever the hell I am," he said, trying make light of his inability to come up with the name of England. He lit another cigarette. "Wanna hear something crazy?"

"I'd love to."

"Would you believe I went to Paris first?"

"Paris, France?!" said a surprised Leslie. "I wondered why you were late getting here, but *Paris?*"

Later getting here? He thought about it. "I came here on a train."

"Oh, my," said the woman, "are we in trouble. Do you know how you got here to the Savoy?"

"I got your message."

She smiled. "Have you eaten? Would you care for some tea and scones? You can't be in England without having tea and scones."

"No thanks. I haven't had much of an appetite lately." He gave her a smile and stirred the diet soda with the swizzle stick. "Y'know, if you had told someone you were a reporter from China, I still would've come. I had to find you."

He said it, and started feeling uncomfortable again. Part of the problem was that she was not at all what he had expected, but there was a deeper truth nibbling at him and it was not because of the radical change.

"And you're alive," he finally said.

"You were expecting the alternative?"

"Well…no. The alternative wouldn't have been acceptable." He dropped it and was trying to think of her name. To get around it, he asked, "Is it Miss or Mrs.?"

"It's Miss," she said, knowing he was having problems. "Now, I don't see a ring on your finger, so I take it you're still 'eligible'?"

"I'm free, if that's what you mean."

"Well, if you are, and you're not here looking for work, and you're not here to arrest me, and I assume you aren't, then I'll assume you're here to court Miss Van Horn."

For the tiniest fraction of a second, he didn't know who she was talking about. He recovered. Handkerchief out, he said, "Miss Van Horn has covered everything but a shot in the arm."

She laughed. "Great. My heart's been aching for you. I think you're here to court me, and you're talking about a shot in the arm."

"It might not sound very suitable, but that's the way it appears."

He was smiling when he said it. But he was smiling merely to be courteous. Leslie, in time, caught the strange silence that followed, and came to a realization. She became disturbed. "Weren't you on drugs?"

"Of all the people to ask that," he said, looking at her seriously. "Aren't you?"

"Me??" she said. "On *drugs*?"

"Yes."

"No, I'm not on drugs."

"But you are still involved?" he said hopefully. "You still know how to make it?"

"Me? Involved in narcotics? You can't be serious. I don't know anything about narcotics. I would never be involved with such a thing."

"*Never*?"

"Of course not."

He lost control. "Don't you dare sit there and tell me that!"

"*Wyatt!*"

He sent a fist pounding on the table and almost exploded. "You *have* to be! You gotta be involved. Woman, you made the best of...!"

"Stop it, Wyatt."

"I didn't come all the way over here for you to tell me...!!"

"*Wyatt. Please*," she said, grabbing his arm. She was shocked and feeling embarrassed by the down-the-nose-glares the table was receiving from others in the room.

Realizing what he had done, he became as embarrassed as she. Why did he do it? It was stupid, idiotic, and he was straying. *Think, Mac, think. Stay on your game. Don't break down.*

Patting and wiping his brow, he composed himself and reached a hand out for her, which she accepted. "I'm sorry," he said. "I didn't mean to do that. I don't know what came over me. Maybe it was the strain of getting here. It won't happen again. I promise. What I was trying to say...I mean, what I was trying to get you to tell me was...back in the States...what accounted for your...no; your *reported* 'erratic' behavior; why a report — a police report, says that you were involved with narcotics. Why it would say you killed a cop over narcotics, and wouldn't settle for anything less than my being strungout on narcotics."

"I don't know what you're talking about."

"You *have* to know."

"Why do I *have* to know?"

"This is unbelievable. Incredible. Do you think I'm making these things up?"

She wouldn't add to that part of the conversation, feeling that he would explode again. She would only say a chilled, "So where do we go from here?"

Not trusting himself, he thumped another cigarette from the pack and lit it. "It's kind of hard to go anywhere from here. I know I've got the right person. But you say you were never involved, and that's good. Amazing, but good. Very, very good. Narcotics is the ultimate sign of human weakness. I've seen it turn grown men — women, too — into weak, schizophrenic idiots." He trailed off and returned with her words, *"Where do we go from here...*Oh, I know. Back in the States I did something to you. What was it?"

Quietly she said, "You shot me."

"Oh, my God," he said, seriously disturbed and as if he had never had the conversation with Devro and Kiesner, or had never read the report. "Where were you hit?"

She put a quiet finger angling up around her forehead.

"The temple?"

"It glanced the temple and the beginning of the scalp."

"I'm sorry. I'm really sorry," he said. He tried to remember the incident. Failing, he tried to lift the conversation. "Maybe we should look on the bright side. No scars. Not a hair out of place. You're incredibly poised. Maybe you should be shot more often."

"Maybe you should check your aim."

"But that's just the point. If you're not involved with narcotics and all of that...that...that weakness, there won't be a next time. You'd have no reason to wipe out one cop and try to destroy still another."

"Why do you keep saying that?"

"I say it because I'm still..." He didn't want to say. He made a change. "I'm saying it simply because one cop is still dead and you're responsible for it, that is, according to all the reports I've heard and read."

"And what else do the reports say?"

"They say a lot of things. The bottom line is, you're listed as dead."

"So when you said something about a corpse earlier, that's what you were referring to?"

"Yes."

"Well, considering that I'm sitting here at the table with you, it goes to show just how accurate your police reports are, doesn't it?"

"I don't know about that. I didn't take the reports. They say I never made any. But I will say this: I think you sustained injury, were probably hospitalized, and you fled the country without the blessings of the Los Angeles authorities."

"I thought you said you were no longer a policeman?"

"I'm not."

"Then, if I did do something wrong, of what concern is it to you?"

"Lady, via heroin and something you concocted, I was the other policeman you tried to destroy. And you came pretty damned close to doing it."

"None of this can be true."

"It's all true. So true, in fact, that I had thoughts of doing you in. And for me to think about killing anybody, I had to be sick."

"So you're admitting illness?"

"I said *had* to be sick. Past tense. I'm one of the few who's beaten a full-blown heroin addiction."

His sweatiness and edginess started growing again. He leaned over to the waiter who was servicing the next table over. "Sir, is it possible for you to turn that air-conditioning down? Or off? I'm burning up in here."

Leslie indicated to the waiter that it was a joke. After he moved away, she said, "Wyatt, you said you were burning up and you wanted the air-conditiong turned down. Think about what you said. And it's not at all warm in here. Next, you're in England. I'd be very much surprised if they had air-conditioning in here."

He touched the salt and dug for another cigarette. "Speaking of surprises, how did you know…? What I'm trying to say is, nobody knew I was coming here. I get here; I got no reservation, I get to the desk, I'm escorted to a room. I don't know how long I'm in there, then suddenly the phone rings."

"And?"

"And guess who was on the other end of the phone? How could you have possibly known I'd be in...in..."

"London."

"Right. How could you have known?"

"If you'd think about what we talked about you'd know the answer. It's really very simple. But if told you, do you think your condition would allow you to understand?"

"Well, then," he said defensively, "why don't we talk about how I got in this condition? Are you still lashing out? Are you still leading people to walled-off prisons and jabbing them with something that, if it didn't take your life, it'd take your brain?"

"That's not fair, Wyatt."

"'Not fair? Lady, there's something you don't understand."

"I don't understand it because I don't know what you're talking about. And you're not exactly making things clear."

"That's because, thanks to you, I've been too screwed up to know myself. All I know and all I care about is that there was some kind of deadly narcotic in my system, and it didn't exactly make for a happy camper. I've had some severe problems."

"I know that; I can see it. I don't want to sound cruel, but you're not the only one to undergo problems."

"You're saying that because you were hit by a glancing bullet and went to the hospital? How long did you stay? A day or two? Not even a fraction of the time I spent. Love, you're out; you're here; and from what I see, looking great, and doing better."

"I'm talking about something that went deeper than that," she responded. "But I don't choose to go into it."

"Why not?"

"I just don't, Wyatt. But whatever state I was in, and whatever I did, or *might* have done, is behind me."

"That sounds awfully convenient."

"It was because of your bullet."

He didn't like hearing it. "I said I was sorry. But you were shot, as I've been told, for a legitimate reason. Best of all, you're still alive."

"In that regard, I can say, so are you. But whatever happened to me was the result of your bullet. And I'm grateful for it. I really am. Call it a shock to the system, call it the right cerebral artery being hit and/or the ensuing operations; call it what you will, but it *saved* me. Whatever else happened in the past is over. Wherever or whoever I was as a person in the past is over. Finished. Done. Gone."

"Just a minute. Via heroin, a police lieutenant; no, a captain…*me*… incapacitated because of your special brand of heroin, which you and you alone administered, was *addicted*. Do you have any idea of the significance of that? What it means to come even close to saying that a police *captain* was on narcotics? Whoever heard of such a thing? Now, since it was me, I probably could have dealt with normal heroin. I might have been able to deal with what it's derived from: A sweet, innocent-looking poppy. Even morphine. But a special concoction of heroin? No dice. Me, or a ton of people like me, couldn't do it. And you administered it for a twenty-four-hour period, I'm told. That's deadly. Doesn't that bother you in the slightest?"

"Of course it bothers me. And it would bother me even more *if* I did all the things you and some reports say I did."

"You're using the word 'if.' That implies I'm wrong; it implies that the files from the L.A. Police Department are wrong; that the records from the Los Angeles district attorney's office are wrong. Everything; *everybody* all wrong. I have the files."

She was suffering. In the spirit of wanting to call a truce, she stirred at a drink she had barely touched. "I'd like to ask for your forgiveness."

"For what? You didn't do anything."

"You *think* I did something. That's almost sufficient."

"*Almost sufficient?*"

"I've obviously caused you harm in some way. I don't believe you would say I've done all of these terrible and wicked things unless something happened. Exactly what, I'm unable to say. I can't say, because from virtually day one of my life, until the shooting, until you shot me, I couldn't remember anything."

"You couldn't remember anything until I shot you? Boy, talk about outpatient care."

"Wyatt, please believe me; my life, my entire past was nothing but a maze of shadows and blurs. There are a million things I can't remember. I couldn't remember before. I can't remember them now. So please don't make light of it."

"It's not to make light of it. You said a bullet hit you. You said it cured you. I didn't doubt it, and I don't question it. I don't do it, because it falls within the realm of possibility. Easily. If a bullet hits you, it shocks the body. It's called blunt trauma. *Anything* can happen; stranger things *have* happened. Blunt trauma to the head has caused the blind to see; it's been known to cause the deaf to hear. It's inexplicable. Yell in somebody's ear, see how the brain reacts. Another way of looking at it: People have awakened after being in a coma for years, and medical science still can't explain it. There's a case where a woman had been using scissors and razor blades to mutilate herself for over thirty years, then suddenly stopped. I'm sure....just a minute," he stopped. "Did you ever say what the name of this illness was?"

"No."

"Oh, well; then what are we talking about?"

She wouldn't say.

"Under the circumstances, I think it's only fair for me to know."

She waited; she was ever so reluctant. "It was an illness suffered at birth."

"So this illness, as destructive as it led you to be, is something your parents or a doctor must've told you about."

"No, they didn't."

"Then how would you know about it?"

"It's what I figured out," she said. "But what difference does it make? It's over."

"It's wonderful that it is, love. But we're talking about a period of totally irrational and bizarre behavior, starting from what point in your life I don't know. I care, but I don't know. I find myself caring more and more. But I don't *know*. I'm told there are seven different types of schizoid behavior. You could've embraced all seven and qualified for an eighth. I don't know. Neither does anyone else, fully. We're talking about the brain. Save for religion, it's the greatest mystery known to man. There are things about it we'll *never* know. All I know is that I'm a victim of your strange narcotics and your off-the-wall behavior, and I'd be hard pressed to grant forgiveness for some illness in exile, or, judging from the way you say you were cured, what some might call a phantom illness. But not me. I won't be like your everyday skeptic. I'll just roll with the punches and go along with whatever you say."

She evaluated what he had to say, felt even more guilt, and said slowly, "I wish I could trust you."

"Trust works both ways."

She became even more hesitant.

"I'm waiting."

She tried to be brave. "It was not my mother's fault."

"I never said anything about your mother. I don't even know the lady."

"I know that, Wyatt. I'm merely trying to tell you something."

"I'm listening."

"I don't believe it was my father's fault, either. Do you understand?"

"You haven't told me anything. How can I understand?"

She braced herself and summoned more courage. "My problems stemmed from a prenatal condition."

At first he started to respond with a quip. He thought better of it and tried for understanding. "May I ask, if neither of your parents told you anything, how would you know your problems stemmed from a prenatal condition?"

"As I tried to say before, it was something I figured out."

12

Outside, she suggested a walk. He was glad to oblige. He needed air. It was a clear night in London, and there was much to see. But neither of them commented on anything.

Later, Leslie reached for his hand and they found themselves on a casual stroll all the way over to near Charing Cross station. McKnight saw a sidewalk facility, which, like a lot of things, was a strange sight for him. After Leslie explained what it was, he went inside.

He was sweating, and the abdominal cramps had him bending over in pain. The reminders of the addiction were back in full, and he was strongly in need of a shot. He would have given his life for one. He moved to the sink, fought the urge to throw up, cleared his nose, and doused his face in water. He dried off, waited a bit more and came back out.

He didn't know if he was successful in hiding his ailment, but he was fighting valiantly.

He was pulling on a cigarette when they came down the steps from the landing.

"Are you all right?"

"Never felt better."

She didn't believe him.

He knew she didn't believe him, but to get her off the subject he went back to what they were discussing in the hotel café, and something that was not at all clear to him.

"So," he said carefully, "there are a million things you can't remember."

"I'd say so."

"I know you don't want to talk about certain aspects of this thing, and I respect your wishes. I don't want to be persistent, but you said *fetal addiction* back there. I didn't know a fetal addiction could have such an effect on a person. I certainly didn't know it could last for so long."

"Well, it did."

"You also said something about *'shadows and blurs.'* What did you mean by that?"

"That was all I knew. That was all I could see of my past. Shadows and blurs. But, to repeat: It's over."

"Terrific," he said offhandedly, getting away from the subject. "It'd be nice if the gods of relief would swing down and give me a helping hand."

"That," she said, dryly, "would take about a ton of narcotics."

"How could you say a thing like that?"

"I'm not exactly blind."

"Listen, babe, I'm a bit frazzled, I'll admit. I get that way after long flights. Or when I'm pressured."

"When were you last under pressure, Wyatt?"

"Finding you was not exactly a cakewalk. Then, before I left the States, I was trying to find myself. Like when I went back to your house...?"

"I had a house in the States?"

"Leased with the option to purchase," he said. "What've you been thinking? That you just went over for a short visit, turned around and came back? Honey, you were part of the landscape. You were living high on the hog. The place you had came close to being the Imperial Palace. The only thing missing was the moat."

"So it was a Japanese house?"

"Yep. It's still there. Waitin'. That's where I got my first clue you were alive. ...No, I went to your club first."

"I had a house and a club?"

"Umhuh," he said, the pain and symptoms having eased during the walk. But his mind started wavering again. "Oh, and get this. Talking about going back to your place: It was raining, and I made the mistake of hitching a ride in this cab with a couple of guys to get to your house from the club. What a combo those two bozos were, a German and a black guy. They knew everything, even about you. And with me? Damn near my life's history. They even knew I had made captain. I'd never seen these two drips before in all my life, but they give me the news that I'd been promoted! Can you imagine? So I say to myself, I gotta get out of here, these guys are nuts. Clowns. A few minutes later, the cab pulls up in front of your place, I say goodbye and good riddance to them. I get out, go inside your gate. What do I see sitting there? A clown!"

"Wyatt, you're not making sense. What on earth are you talking about?"

"Los Angeles. Your quaint little Japanese villa where I spent time, drugged out; spaced. In fact, so spaced that even back in that last re-hab room I was in, I was haunted by this big Japanese image; like a Buddha. And his eyes; those cold and slanted stone eyes really had me going."

"A *Japanese Buddha?* You're still not making sense, Wyatt."

"There was one on the grounds of your villa. Don't you even re-member that?

"I remember an explosion, and tending to you in a fuzzy place."

"Well, you sure had one. Smaller. It was the last thing I saw be-fore blacking out at your place. So, every time I'd see the Buddha across from the rehab place, I'd think dope. Like I said, I'm clean now.

But if you ever want me to fall back and think about getting on the horse again, show me a Japanese Buddha. And make sure he's got those cold, hard eyes. That'll do it. Now, you're probably wondering if I've ever thought about getting even with you for getting me on the stuff. To be perfectly honest with you, yes. Yeah, I did. I waltzed my service revolver through Customs. No, I brought it through *two* Customs with that in mind. One here, and the other was in...? where'd I say I landed before I came here?"

"Paris, France," she said. "Wyatt, are you sure you're okay?"

"Positive."

"About that service revolver. Are you planning on using it on me? Again?"

"Are you kidding? I couldn't do that."

"I'm glad to hear it," Leslie said with more than a modicum of concern. "Not that you would, but I can understand if you'd want to."

"I couldn't do anything like that to you. I simply couldn't do it. Anyhow, I'd never shot a woman before."

"Until me," she said. "Incidentally, where is the gun now?"

"I turned it over to hotel security shortly after I called you."

"*I* called *you.*"

He gave it a thought; concluded that she was right, and moved on. "Anyhow, I happen to believe killing is wrong. Killing you would be worse." He added offhandedly, "Besides, what self-respecting addict would want to kill his supplier?"

"You're not being funny, Wyatt."

"It was a joke."

"It didn't sound like it."

"Well, it was. I can joke about it, babe..." He stopped. His eyes widened. "My God; *Oh, my God!*"

"Wyatt, what is it?"

"My God!!"

"*What...??*"

"The gun I just tossed wasn't my gun. It never belonged to me."

"So?"

"It was the one you used. It was the one LeCoultre gave you. I've never owned a Walther. I had a Magnum. A .44."

"What difference does it make? Though I still contend I didn't shoot anyone."

"No. Now that I think about it, it doesn't make a difference. But it seems so strange. I mean, all along I've been thinking it was my gun."

"Well, if it doesn't make any difference, why talk about it?"

He dropped it for the time being.

"Tell me what was it you started to say?"

"Can't remember," he said. "I do know I wanted to say that it had to have been my stupidity to have allowed you to get me started on narcotics in the first place. But I don't fault you. Sick people should never be faulted no matter what they do, or who they are. Do you agree with that?"

"Yes. But I have my own reasons."

They were crossing to Cleopatra's Landing. With Big Ben looming up in the background, McKnight looked up at the two beautiful black lion statues that looked as though they served as sentries to the river Thames. In a rare burst of energy, he thought about mounting one. A question had him moving away from the attempt.

He watched a boat slowly slip by and melt under the landing and asked, "Sweets, how much of this thing do you remember?"

"You've asked me that, " she said. "A few insignificant things have come back to me. I do remember some godawful splitting headaches. The last one was particularly rough. Then things started clearing up. I don't know when it happened; I don't know how — all I am certain of is that you came into my life. I never want that to change."

"Do you remember where you were when things started clearing up?"

"I have a notion it began when I was tending to you. Where we were, I don't know. As I said, it was all fuzzy. I remember being sad. You were being taken away. But I remember, clearly, being in an American hospital. I had already had surgery. But I couldn't remember anything specifically. I couldn't remember who I was, or where I was. I knew something had happened, then I found out I was in trouble."

"That's when you skipped?"

"I was afraid."

He thought about it, then lit a cigarette. "So you're all cured. You're not bothered with anything now?"

"Nothing. But I still can't remember the past."

"Well, I still think this is going to be great," he quipped. "You can't remember, and I'm unable to recall. We ought to go into the business of scheduling airline flights."

"You seem to know a lot, considering."

"Yeah, but I misappropriated the files," he said. "Would it interest you to know your case-file is coded *Queen*?"

"Why would a queen live in a Japanese villa?"

"Beats living in a Honda."

"With humor like that, you should've stayed in rehabilitation."

"Which brings up another interesting question," he said, as they moved down the one or two steps to the platform, close to the water's edge. "If I hadn't been in rehab…no. Lemme be more direct: If I had that old craving, could you find some way to provide me with the goods?"

She looked him straight in the eye: "Under NO circumstances."

"Just testing. Don't get salty."

"No, you weren't 'just testing,' Wyatt. You're not well."

"'Says who?'"

"Anybody can see it."

"Listen, sweets, I just left Los Angeles…"

"En route to London, and landed in Paris."

"No. France."

"Where is Paris located, Wyatt?"

"You know what you're doing? You're letting the fact that I'm tired and sleepy mislead you. We're talking Los Angeles. Drug City. In Drug City, I carried a badge. That badge could've been my entree into more drugs than you can stash in Big Bob, or whatever the name of that thing is over there."

"Big *Ben*. The clock is called *Big Ben*."

"Whatever," he said dismissively. "Now, I'm going to let you in on a little secret: I have been in rehabilitation."

"I know that."

"Lemme finish, because this is important. The record will show that because of the severity of my 'previous' condition — and that's the operative word: *'Previous'* condition — I'd been alternating between a lot of hospitals and rehab centers, but I was discharged months ago."

"No, you weren't."

"Yes, I was."

"You couldn't have been."

"Oh, yeah, I was. Now, granted, our rehabs and hospitals don't do a damn thing. They're a waste of time. You do a little detoxing, you go to therapy, take a Valium, maybe you're offered acupuncture, you come back, go sit in a hot tub, listen to some music tapes that are supposed to relax you, and maybe take some…some…Methadone, which I hated. I was doing better listening to music. Not my speed, but I think it was gospel."

"Did a psychiatrist ever talk to you while you were in the hospital, or during your stay in one of the rehabilitation places?"

"No; no need to."

"Wyatt, please be honest."

"Okay," he said, finally making up his mind. "At some point I did talk with a psyc for a few minutes. That's how I found out about the seven different types of schizos. He told me I had BPD."

"Meaning?"

"Brief Psychotic Disorder. Accent on *brief.* Nothing more serious than that. A lot of stuff I can't remember, but the deal can last for a day, the longest is thirty. You go through periods of delusions and disorganized behavior. You're in and out, says the psyc. You experience emotional turmoil and overwhelming confusion. After that, you're back on track. Like I am now. If I'd been a normal addict, I could've graduated to the upper levels. Then I would've had a problem."

"Did the psychiatrist say what caused this BPD?"

"Obviously, it was the special dose of narcotics you gave me. The way I figure it, combine it with stress and you've got some serious problems."

"And you haven't had any narcotics since that time?"

"Are you kidding? No way. But I could've had some. When I was first got in rehab, many, many times heroin was right there waiting for me. Someone saw to it that I wouldn't be without. It wasn't good stuff, but it was there for me."

"Do you have any idea who that somebody was?"

"The only thing that's important, Sweets," he said without conviction, "is that I never touched it."

"But you still get terribly confused. And you have other symptoms; something has to be wrong."

"What's wrong is that the whole detoxing and rehabbing thing is a joke. Somebody ought to wise up, pump some dollars into those programs and get serious about this nonsense. I told 'em that months ago, when I was getting discharged."

"Wyatt," she said, wearily, "to begin with, you weren't discharged 'months' ago. I know better. How do you think I knew you would be here? Now, listen to me. Please. I'm with you all the way. But you've got to stop deluding yourself. You've got a problem. A very serious problem. The psychiatrist might have told you this BPD thing is temporary, but from what I see, don't you believe it. Something is wrong. If your addiction was the cause, we can deal with it. Together we can beat it."

He tossed the cigarette away. "Save your breath, sweetheart. There's nothing wrong with me. Absolutely nothing. See how energetic I am, see how I've been thinking? I'm the last person on Earth who would become a drug addict. I hate 'em. Even when I was on the job, I'd spend my vacations chasing druggies. That's why it was all so strange when you did the thing, and this…this…euphoria;

this…this cloud-nine orgasm freed mind, body and soul, and my insides floated beyond the moon and soared all the way to the heavens with a feeling I had never known before. It was mellow, fantastic…and…oh, God; God, Lord Jesus, if I could get just one more hit. If I could have just one more tiny…"

Clutching himself, caught in his own emotions, he stopped and looked over to Leslie.

She knew he wasn't just talking to hear himself talk. On the verge of tears, she said, "I've ruined you."

He rushed to hold her, "Oh, babe, no. You're taking this to heart. Don't do that. Don't worry."

"I have to worry, Wyatt."

"No, you don't, sweetheart. You don't ever have to worry about me and narcotics. *Ever.* All I was saying is that I had to put up a hell of a fight. If not, then I'm hooked. And when you're truly hooked, there's not a power on Earth that can ease the pain. It's pure hell. But that little thing I had is over. I feared a mental breakdown, but I didn't have one. I'm a survivor. I came from a race of survivors." He dug for his pack of cigarettes and held them before her eyes. "See these rotten little monsters? What can be more addicting that these? Watch."

He tossed the cigarettes into the river. They watched the pack as it danced on a ripple under the light and then went away.

"I'm through with them," he said in earnest. "I'm making the resolve right here and now, I want the world to know: *Wyatt McKnight is finished with cigarettes forever.* I have had my last one. And this will show you, I can beat anything — *if* there is anything to beat. And remember, my love, back in that scones-and-tea bar in the hotel…"

"It's *tea and scones.* And it was not a bar. It was a café."

"Whatever. Remember, I was bothered by the heat. Not by the chill of an addict, not by cramps, not by a craving of sweets, not by…"

"All right, all right, all right," she interrupted again. "I'm trying to believe you, Wyatt. I want to believe you. With all my heart, I want to believe you."

"Then do it."

She searched his face. "Tell me this: If I told you I know where there are cabinets full of narcotics, could you tell me you wouldn't be interested?"

He was slow; very slow. "Yes."

"Say them. Say the words, Wyatt."

"If I saw morphine, I would *not* be interested."

"And if you saw the needles and everything else that went along with the needles, you still wouldn't be tempted?"

"I might be tempted, but I wouldn't weaken."

"It's morphine we're talking about, Wyatt."

He didn't say anything.

"Morphine, Wyatt. It's all around you. It's there; yours for the taking. There's no one to stop you. Tell me, what would you do?"

"We should be talking about you; your transformation. Not me."

"Answer the question, Wyatt. If you saw the morphine, tell me what you'd do?"

"I'd walk away."

"If you saw cabinets full of morphine, you'd still walk away?"

"Cabinets, closets — name it. I'd walk away."

"Would you, really?"

"I might be tempted, but I wouldn't weaken."

She was joyful; terribly relieved. "Oh, darling, darling, darling, Wyatt, I'm so glad. You've made me so happy. I'm so proud of you; so very, very proud of you," she said, kissing and embracing him. Then hopefully she said, "Now, tell me why you came to England? Why are you here?"

He tried to recall the title of the Otis Redding oldie, but couldn't.

She breathlessly waited.

To the woman who once made the *best of the best,* and choosing his words carefully, he said, "…I guess I'd have to say, I'm here because more and more it's like that old song says: *'You made me love you.'"*

It wasn't the right song. For her sake he felt that it would suffice.

She was pleased. They walked a bit more, then went back to the hotel and retired for the evening.

13

June 24 sleepwalked over London. An unwholesome-looking grayness settled over the chief city of the Commonwealth of Nations, a city that had stood so stirringly courageous during war.

The morning grayness was backed by the threat of rain. An already depressed McKnight stood at the window looking down from the twelfth floor of a hotel that was steeped in tradition.

The two had been up for a while, he longer than she. He had not slept well. He was cramped by pain and was thrown into the deeper throes of a swirling concavity by the hard want of a cigarette, another shower, and by the nagging, bottom-line question: *Why am I here?* The question of revenge came up. But it wasn't revenge. The question of revenge was a falsity; a coverup.

Nothing looked promising, and last night's love-making had provided no answers.

From a height that came close to miniaturizing cars and people, and rendered a sort of paltriness to all things human, he didn't like what he was thinking. He was twelve floors up. Wisely, he withdrew from the window and sat glumly on the corner of the bed. Inner demons, weakness, and disability were on his mind. Even in England they were a loathsome lot. And so were the probing questions.

He wasn't happy with himself. He wasn't happy about his visit. He thought about how he had dropped his guard and had revealed the BPD symptoms, was sorry that he had done it, and promised himself he wouldn't talk about it again. Nor would he ever bring up the subject he had had with another psychiatrist some months later: UTS, the Undifferentiated Type of Schizophrenia.

The police captain from California had almost forgotten, and now he wasn't proud that he had done it, but he had brought the clown with him from L.A. — not that it had been the sole purpose of going back to her house before taking off from LAX. But exactly why he had to bring the filthy wet thing with him wasn't easy to understand. Could it have been that he thought he was still working on the case? No. That much he knew. More likely it was to be a reminder to her. If she was as sick as he thought he remembered, he faintly recalled while getting his things together and driving out to the villa, there was the possibility she would not remember the encounter with him. But she would remember the clown. It should have been far too indelible in her mind to have been forgotten. So the clown, in a sense, was to be the bridge. He made a second trip to the closet.

He had to be careful. This was a changed woman, an entirely different woman. And he believed her. Still, he had to try one more thing.

From the other room, she called out to him. "You know the song you referred to last night? 'You Made Me Love You'?"

He had almost forgotten it. Glumly he said, "Yes."

"What follows 'You made me love you' is: *I didn't want to do it.*"

Her comment didn't elicit a reaction.

She was in the bathroom mirror, taking her time applying the last few touches of lipstick to a finely curved mouth. On the bureau in the room where he was, sat the salt shaker from the downstairs café. He had already used it.

He had not been saddled with the chore of repacking very much, and so whatever he had to do was done — including secreting something in the closet. There was nothing to do but wait for her. He was anxious; she was slow.

"I'm not sure going with you is the right thing to do," he said.

She didn't like the sound of it. "I thought you were bothered. Would you rather remain here in the hotel during your stay?"

"I don't know," he sighed, and wandered around the room as though looking for answers. He came back to the window and stared out with gnawing uncertainty. He was looking but not seeing. "Don't you think all this is a bit too improbable to be believed?"

"What?"

"The whole thing. All of it. Me having trouble remembering; coming all the way over here, looking for you; finding you. You, lost in so many ways. And after spinning out of control, a totally different person than anyone would ever believe."

"I believe it."

"Correct me if I'm wrong, but we couldn't have gotten to know each other that well. How can it be? I mean, the whole thing is illogical. It's inconceivable. What I went through; what you went through. Now, here. Us. Together. It's unreal."

"Wyatt, in your musing, you're making the mistake of so many, many people. You're underestimating the affairs of the heart. Time, bullets nor narcotics can't change that. We met; we clicked."

He thought about it a for long moment. Still doubtful and questioning, he yielded. "Maybe you're right, sweetheart. Maybe you're right."

She emerged from the bathroom and settled at the bureau. The salt shaker caught her eye. She picked it up. "Isn't this from the café downstairs?"

"It's a souvenir."

"But why a salt shaker?"

"I like hard-boiled eggs."

There was no way she was going to believe that. Into the wastebasket the little round thing went.

He casually went back to the empty closet, opened the door and stared into the corner. He knew what he was doing.

"I wonder why somebody left this thing here," he said.

"What?"

"Come, take a look."

Fluffing at her hair, she came over and took a look. She was not fazed in the slightest.

They were looking at the soiled clown he had placed in the corner earlier. Here was the clown she had had since childhood; the clown that had been so very much a part of her distorted life, and she didn't even recognize it. The ugly little thing sprawled in the corner meant absolutely nothing to her.

Withdrawing, she said, disinterestedly, "It's so dirty, probably the kid who owned it didn't want it any more. Doesn't say much for the maid service here, does it?"

She returned to the bathroom for her case.

He felt bad that he had done it, and he really hadn't needed the reassurance, but it worked. Never, ever would he have any doubts again about Leslie Van Horn. And, he thought, she should never have any doubts about herself. He wanted her to know how pleased he was for her, but at that moment he felt it would have been too obvious.

He moved on, thinking about what could possibly lie ahead.

She called from the bathroom, "How long had you planned on staying in England, Wyatt?"

"Until I get a few things in my mind cleared up, maybe," he said, picking up his luggage and waiting for her overnight bag.

"And last night didn't help?"

"Last night might have added to it."

"I hope that was a joke," she said, emerging from the bathroom and not appreciating what he had said. "Let's go."

He was glad to hear the words. He needed air.

Checking out was swift, and soon Leslie was aiming her bottle-green Jag convertible out from the underground parking. Uncharacteristically quiet for the circumstances, she nosed into the heavy street traffic and got set for the long top-down drive. She was quiet, because she was still perturbed over the *Last night might have added to it* comment he had made. She stopped thinking about it and tried to be upbeat.

"All set?" she said, buckling up while weaving over to a circle that led them to London's most famous bridge.

He gave an almost inaudible "Uh-huh," and lapsed back into silence.

Deciding to amiably chat, she said, "Would you care to know what else I've been doing with my time? It's something I've always wanted to do. Can you guess what it is? — Okay, I'll tell you: I've been studying law," she said happily. Still not getting a response, she changed the subject. "You're going to love my mother. She's such a kind and gentle soul, though I must tell you from the start, you've got to overlook anything she says. The poor dear has been ill forever. I try to stay with her at least a couple of days out of each month. Now, Father, bless him, he'll no doubt try to pump some things out of you, since I've never given any answers to anything he's asked about my being in the States. I figure the less said, the better. Got me?"

McKnight's sagging spirits wouldn't allow him to say anything. A fast driver, Leslie added more pedal power and threw him another quick glance. "Come on, Wyatt. Lighten up."

"Why?" he said. "I'm a long way from home, sailing on the wrong side of the road with the woman who tried to destroy me, and I'm going to her home, no less."

"This is England, Wyatt. We do drive on the left side of the road. And for a two-night stay, we're going to my parents' home, just outside the beautiful city of Bath. After that, we're going to my place in the Cotswolds. It's a beautiful little place. You're going to love it."

"I'm not so sure about this whole idea."

"You've indicated that before. You don't seem to be sure of anything, Wyatt. Yet you say you need me. Are you sure you need me, or do you need what you *think* I can provide?"

"What is that you can provide, Leslie?"

"You talk as though last night didn't exist."

"There are times when life can provide more than just a toss in the hay."

"I know what you're getting at, Wyatt, and let me set you straight. Last night was supposed to be a thing of beauty and joy. It was on my part. And I can't begin tell you what stark, rock-bottom fear it erased."

McKnight was thrown. "What 'stark, rock-bottom fear?' What are you talking about?"

"I don't choose to go into it," she said. "Now, I hate to sound harsh, but you didn't have to go through anything, so if you're sitting there sulking because of something else you didn't get, that's just tough."

"Oh, I'm sitting here sulking?"

"For the same reason you spent the better part of the night sweating and tossing, and clawing at your arms and legs, which, I might add, didn't occur because of an over-usage of energy on your part."

"Then what caused it, Leslie?"

Without saying anything, she gently steered the sporty vehicle to the side of the road and stopped. She applied the hand brake, and said, very calmly, "What caused it? Plain and simple, your addiction. Understand this: I cannot — and will not — provide you with any narcotic. I am not involved in it. I am thoroughly against it, and I will *not* approve of your partaking of it, in any shape, form, or fashion."

"Now hold on. You just said you knew where there were baskets full of narcotics..."

"I said *cabinets*. And I didn't 'just' say it. I said it last night."

"It doesn't matter when you said it, or how. It doesn't matter simply because I'm not interested. I am not in need."

"Yes, you are."

"You're wrong, Leslie," he said. "Listen. I'm going to make you a deal, right here and now. And you can take it to the bank: From this moment on, if ever I, at any time, show the slightest hint of wanting

— or taking — any narcotic, drug, or stimulant, I want you to take my gun and shoot me."

"You don't have a gun. Remember?"

The rain that had threatened in London wasn't encountered on the road. The countryside was beautiful, and the deep-green scenery leading into the city of Bath outdid itself. Adding to it was the Van Horn residence. It was a study in understated loveliness. It was aloof; idyllic; country. It had every charm one could ever want in a home. The windows were stone-mullioned, but the house, Neo-Georgian, was nursed by three restful acres that were backed by rows of stately trees. From them, a rolling lawn eased its way past an ivy-laced gazebo and permitted a gravel path to lead to a welcoming door.

Inside, the rooms were notably proportioned, with fine fireplaces and unaffected cornices running throughout. Except for a few George III, Louis XV, Linke, and Queen Anne pieces, most of the furniture was of the Sheraton or Regency period. Commanding the living room, next to the piano, was a carved Georgian chimney piece. The frieze and jambs were inlaid in Tinos. Carved in the center tablet was Leda and the Swan. Centered on top of it was a figurine. It was inappropriate and decidedly misplaced. On a first look it was innocuous; on a second, odious. It was called *The Porcelain Principe: Enfant en Femme.*

There had been a change in attitudes, and Wyatt and Leslie were laughing when the car pulled to a stop in front of the mansion. They had to laugh. At one point McKnight's erratic memory had gotten so bad that they couldn't do anything but laugh. They had gone back over certain points of the initial conversation, attempting to discuss a few things. The subject of the gun came up again. It was like pulling teeth, but the conclusion was made, correctly, that he had gotten rid of it in the washroom. That triggered other things in his memory.

As strange as it seemed, the laughter, combined with the long top-down drive in the dull but fresh air, also seemed to have worked wonders for him. He wasn't well, but he was doing a hell of a lot better. He was still aching for a cigarette, though. Before getting out of the car, they gave each other a make-up kiss and an embrace.

"Keep your pecker up," she said, using an English expression that would raise not only his, but any American's eyebrows because of misinterpretation.

Getting out, she called out with a spirited, "I'mmm hoooommme!"

Kent, the nose-in-the-air butler, who was already by the door, came out, delivering a "Welcome home, ma'am." He immediately went for the luggage.

Inside, the frail but warm Mrs. Van Horn was wheeled into the doorway by Chauncey, a short-skirted, gum-popping, bubble-headed nurse. Descending the stairs was the man who had hired her, Dr. Bernard Van Horn. He was the man of the house.

The doctor was an interesting man, deceptively engaging, charismatically old, inwardly energetic, bespectacled and bearded, and although the name Van Horn was Dutch, he was thoroughly British.

"Mummy, Daddy," Leslie beamed as everyone collected at the door," I'd like you to meet Mr. Wyatt McKnight. Mr. Wyatt McKnight, my parents, Dr. and Mrs. Bernard Van Horn."

There were all-around "pleased to meet you" handshakes, and Leslie added, just for fun, "And stay clear of Dad, Wyatt. He's a retired surgeon, itching to get back in the saddle."

The doctor guffawed.

"I know how you are, Dad. I know."

"Ah, but my little queen, who doesn't know everything, I would gladly give it all up to have one dazzling, final fling with you as a hoofer." He turned to McKnight and lied, "A pleasure to meet you, sir."

"Lovely," added Mrs. Van Horn. "Our Phyllis has told us so much about you. Haven't you, dear?"

McKnight knitted his brow. *Phyllis?* Leslie relieved him by slyly tugging at his sleeve and leading everyone into the living room.

Martha, the maid, was summoned, and in short order everyone

was being served tea and crumpets. It was an elegant setting. Leslie was beaming. McKnight had gone back to fidgeting a little, but his movements didn't appear to be serious. He was not aware of anything but the object on the mantelpiece. His eyes were deciphering the carnally graphic aspects of *The Porcelain Principe: Enfant en Femme.*

Dr. Van Horn reclaimed his attention. "Mr. McKnight, I can't tell you the depths of my thanks for the care and concern shown my daughter while she was in America."

Said a confused McKnight, "Thank you, sir, but…"

Leslie quickly jumped in. "I told Daddy how you got me to hospital and looked out for me."

"You were her 'savior,'" said the doctor. "Better yet, perhaps I should fine-tune that and say, I *understand* you were her savior."

It was a double-edged meaning, which Leslie quickly got. Following her lead, McKnight didn't say anything.

In a sweet voice, Mrs. Van Horn asked, "Were you the doctor of record, Mr. Night?"

"Mummy, dear, it's Mr. *'Mac'* Knight," Leslie corrected. "And the other day I told you he was a policeman. Remember?"

"Why would you have needed the services of a fireman, dear?"

The doctor chimed in. "He is a *policeman* from the United States, Mother. That wonderful country that provides the world with moral leadership. And on top of that, Mr. McKnight is a Californian. A true-blue Californian. I think it's time for your nap, dear. Chauncey?"

The nurse, who was already standing by, asked the doctor, "Shall I prepare her for a shot, sir?" The question caught McKnight's attention.

"She needs a *nap*, Chauncey," Leslie said firmly.

"But a shot if she gets worse," advised the doctor. "And on the way out, send Kent in, will you?"

"Yes, sir," responded Chauncey. She prepared to take the mother upstairs.

An agitated Leslie stood. "Leave her be, Chauncey. I will see Mother upstairs." She went to McKnight and gave him a peck on the cheek. "I'll be back shortly."

Dr. Van Horn watched as his daughter wheeled the mother away. He looked familiarly at the trailing Chauncey, then his attention returned to McKnight, who had stood for the departure.

"Please be seated, Mr. McKnight."

McKnight did as requested and directed his attention back to the piece sitting atop the Georgian mantelpiece.

The doctor reclaimed his attention. "Mother hasn't been well for years. I'm sure my daughter has spoken of it."

"She didn't dwell on it. We more or less concerned ourselves with her own illness while she was in America."

"And so she did talk about her malady? Interesting. Leslie actually talked about something that personal with you." He was trying for casualness. "Tell me what was said, Mr. McKnight."

"Actually, she didn't have much to say, Doctor."

"She must have said something. You said you two talked."

"It was very brief, sir. She said nothing worthwhile going into."

"Well, let me ask you this: How did she fare there in America?"

McKnight was about to give another evasive answer when, from the rear of the house, he could hear an exuberant Mrs. Van Horn. Her voice was followed by Leslie's. "On your mark, get ready, set: *GO!*" It was followed by disappearing giggling.

McKnight couldn't imagine what was taking place, but the doctor knew. And he was not pleased. He knew that they were in the rear, and that the mother was in the chair-lift and they were racing up to the second floor. It was something they always did, and Leslie would always let her win. And once up, they would laugh themselves silly.

It was one of the few occasions the two enjoyed a good laugh.

Dr. Van Horn had never appreciated the frolicking that took place between the mother and daughter. He thought it was puerile and undignified.

There were a number of things that displeased the doctor. Despite the welcoming door, having visitors in his home was one of them.

When they came, he wouldn't be contrary or do anything to make them feel ill at ease. He was pleasant. But he was also guarded. And when one left, one never got the feeling they should return any time soon.

It didn't take long for McKnight to feel as if he were trapped in a time warp. With Leslie gone, he also felt a certain tautness in the room. He thought that a lot of it, though, was due to his condition and the fact that he had never been in an English home before, certainly not one that felt as rigidly English as this. As a policeman he had been in homes of all types, meeting and investigating people of every stripe. But that was back home, home in the US of A. More important, in those homes, generally he was there because somebody had done something wrong, and, as a policeman, he was in charge. Here he was a visitor, a sick visitor who still hadn't come to terms with why he was there.

He had done his best to mentally prepare himself for the visit, and he was, he thought, holding himself admirably in check. Both habits, both addictions, narcotic and cigarette, were clawing at his innards with teeth so fierce that it felt like at any minute something was going to burst the brain, rupture the gut and send the blood spewing from the mouth and on to the hand-woven Pakistani rug. Still he held on and he was doing so with commendable calm, if he had to say so himself. Only once or twice did he noticeably rub an arm or leg. But he was not fidgeting too much, didn't touch his nose, and he was careful when he wiped his brow. He knew the doctor was eyeing his every move, and though having centered his attention on the piece that was sitting atop the Georgian mantelpiece, he clung to the phrase: *On your game, Mac. Stay on your game.*

The only thing that was throwing him off kilter at the moment was that, back at her club, he believed Leslie had alluded to her father, and in those allusions, she had said — or was *trying* to say — something terribly indicting about the man.

He thought he had it, became uncomfortable, then dismissed it.

Forgoing the question he had asked earlier, the doctor spent a few more moments studying the detective, then asked, "Are you well, Mr. McKnight?"

"Who, me?"

"You are Mr. McKnight, are you not?"

"Yes, yes. I'm fine, Doctor."

"I notice you're perspiring a bit, and you were rubbing your arms earlier. And you were scratching at your legs a time or two. Are you sure you're all right?"

"Positive."

"You seem to a have fixation with the figurine on the mantelpiece there. I take it you have an interest in art?"

"Er...no. Not an uncommon one. But what is that piece called, Doctor?"

"It is entitled: *The Porcelain Principe: Enfant en Femme*. I picked it up from a collector while I was practicing in India. Why do you ask?"

"There is a very disturbing companion piece that goes with it. Terribly graphic. Some would say gross."

"The more knowledgeable would say it is an interesting work of art that's very difficult to find," the doctor said, defensively. "Why would you be familiar with the accompanying piece, Mr. McKnight?"

McKnight was stuck for a moment. Wanting a cigarette, he shifted uneasily. "In Beverly Hills; no, in Bel-Air..." He lost it. *Stay on your game, Mac. Think.* He came back. "In a Los Angeles suburb, I had the occasion to arrest a dentist...no; it was a physician. Anyway, this gentleman had a large number of blow-ups of both pieces in his home."

"And for that you arrested him?"

"No."

"Then what was he arrested for, sir?"

"If you must know, Doctor, I arrested him because he was into...pedophilia. And if I recall correctly, there was a trial....I remember there was a child...no...I'm sorry, yes, there was. A father and son. The son was supposed to testify against the father. But we couldn't get a conviction for what the father had done, because on the stand, the son said, *'There are a million things I can't remember.'"*

"You seem a trifle disconnected, Mr. McKnight. But that's it?"

"No. What distresses me, Doctor, is that Leslie used those very same words. *There are a million things I can't remember.* The reason I remember them so well is that I was struck by the way she made the statement. And she said it more than once, I believe."

"Do you know when and where she made the statement?"

"Not at the moment, but it'll come back to me." McKnight struggled briefly. "Oh, I remember. It was last night."

The doctor tried moving away from the subject by dismissively saying, "Well, as I said, it is a very difficult piece to come by."

In came the butler.

"You wanted me, sir?"

"Er, yes, Kent…" he turned to the visitor. "Would you care for a drink, Mr. McKnight?"

"No, thank you, Doctor."

"Well, don't just stand there, Kent," the doctor ordered. "Get the man a Scotch and water. I'll have the usual."

Kent departed. The doctor returned to a puzzled McKnight, who had directed his attention back to the figurine.

"I'm glad you're here, Mr. McKnight," said the doctor, clasping his hands as though studying a patient's reactions. "Leslie thinks very highly of you. She's made that clear. Many times. Now that you're here, since you know of her illness — and the many pills she's had to take — I have a concern: When Leslie returned from America and, incidentally I fully supported her whilst she was over there, requiring great sums of money, I might add; but as much as she tried to disguise them, I saw fresh stitch marks, indeed, *stitches* in and around the temple area, and she was never seen without a head covering of some sort when she returned here. Interestingly, Leslie could hardly live alone before going abroad. She was into horticulture and chemistry and all that sort of twaddle and didn't know it. And to this day, doesn't even remember it. She lived in a fog. Now she's back; no more pills, her behavior is unassailable; she has her own little antique shop in the Cotswolds; she's dabbling in law, and her present-day memory is intact, and here I must add that I am relieved because she hasn't, as yet, resorted to 'manufacturing' a past. But interestingly, Mr. McKnight; here I have a daughter who is perfectly transformed, and is doing miraculously well, and she has steadfastly refused to discuss what it was that caused the recovery. Frightfully amazing, wouldn't you say?"

He waited for an answer. Seeing that he wasn't going to get one, he added, "And not *once* has she complained about her customary headaches. It's remarkable. Did something happen to Leslie in America that I should know about?"

"Not that I know of, Doctor."

"Come, come, Mr. McKnight. You can do better than that. And you aren't being as protective as you think."

McKnight sweated some, wiped his forehead, and was prepared to answer, all the while wondering why he was about to be so revealing. More than likely it was because he was trying to concentrate on some of the things Leslie had said during their long talk back in London, or wherever they were. Lots of things bothered him, such as the fetal-addiction question. But having seen the mother and having heard the doctor's instructions to the nurse, that part was becoming clear. What was not becoming clear was Leslie's inability to remember anything from childhood but shadows and blurs. He, of course, was not a doctor. He was a policeman, but, as he said to himself, someone he was growing fonder of by the minute had been robbed of something precious. To his way of thinking, it was an act as serious and as grossly wrong as anything he had handled in his career. He had no choice but to try to get to the bottom of it.

The detective sent an involuntary arm rubbing his arms and legs in deeper thought, and directed his attention back to the figurine.

"Mr. McKnight? You were responding to my question about what happened to my daughter?"

"Doctor, your daughter was stabbed....She was stabbed...and..." *On your game, Mac. Stay on your game,* he admonished himself. "No, I'm sorry. Leslie was shot."

"Did you say *shot*?"

"Yes, sir."

"With a firearm?"

"Yes, sir."

"My word, this is alarming," blurted the doctor. "She was *shot* by whom?"

"They never found out."

"*They?*"

"The police. But she was…shot…and, in fact, erroneously listed as dead. I'm told that it was the shooting that restored her ability to remember things."

"And you expect me to believe that?"

"I had my doubts, too, Doctor. But those are the facts. As far as I know them."

"You need rest," advised the doctor. "We'll just let the subject drop until you're clear-headed."

"I'm more clear-headed than you think, Doctor. And at the moment, rest is not my concern."

"I'm inclined to ask what *is* your concern, but I don't imagine the answer will be entirely straightforward, so I shan't pursue it. But I would like to know something: Are you people that barbaric, to think *everything* can be handled through gunfire, then just dismiss it by saying a person was *shot?*"

"Which *you people* are you referring to, sir?"

"Let's just say you Americans. For the time being."

"And after that?" McKnight asked, his racial concerns having grown.

"Who knows? But be assured it won't be as nonsensical as your earlier assertion." The doctor leaned back in the chair, and continued to study the visitor, whose eyes didn't want to leave the figurine. Bugged by the uncomfortable thought that he had dismissed earlier, McKnight turned to the doctor. "I have a question for you, sir. It's a medical one."

"Ask. But first, my question. Have you people always sought to solve your problems by way of gunfire?"

"I believe our history is a lot less violent than yours, sir. Didn't you people chop heads off for sport?"

"Your question, Mr. McKnight."

"You know about blunt trauma, don't you, sir?"

"Any surgeon would. But what is your question, Mr. McKnight?"

"In medicine, if a memory, or the mind, is renewed because of blunt trauma, is it possible that that same mind — younger, vulnerable, and chemically altered — could that mind have been lost the same way? Because of something it *accepted* as blunt trauma?"

"If so, I wouldn't recommend going to America for the cure. No, to be serious, that is a very interesting question, Mr. McKnight. But you've just attempted a hypothetical scenario dealing with the mind. That hypothesis alone should tell you there is nothing about the mind that is certain; no theory about it is absolute."

"And that, of course, would apply to a child's mind."

"*Any* mind," emphasized the doctor. "Does that answer your question?"

"I'm not really sure, Doctor."

"Well, give it some thought," Dr. Van Horn said with professional polish. "Now, being a surgeon and not a detective, or a devotee of fiction, if you will, as a matter of curiosity, let me ask you: What would have been the circumstances regarding this…this…'*shooting*'? A shooting, I might add, that left a poor, defenseless white woman with a rather oddly angled head wound. I say oddly because, standing, as most victims are, the trajectory would have been more or less straight. It would not have been angled in an upward direction, as if it had been created on an operating table."

"First, sir, does it make a difference that it was a white woman who was shot?"

"You tell me."

It was going to be a momentary stand-off. Kent, returning with the drinks, interrupted the quiet that followed. "You have a call from St. James Hospital, sir."

"Have them call back in the morning."

"Yes, sir," said the departing butler.

McKnight was still edgy. The doctor was back on him.

"The question was, Mr. McKnight: Your apparent racial sensitivities aside, what would be the story behind the stabbing…no; excuse me. It was a *shooting*, I believe you said. Did you not?"

"It was a shooting, doctor. I was in error when I said stabbing."

"Now that we have that straight, what would be the story behind the shooting? Humor me."

"Nothing I say is to humor you, Doctor."

"Proceed."

"Leslie was shot. What happened at the time was a police matter. I'm not at liberty to say anything else."

"I keep forgetting you are…*were*?…a policeman? Which is it, sir?"

"I'm a cop."

"A *cop*. Saying it that way makes it more American. It gives it bite. Very good."

The doctor, noticing that McKnight had not touched the drink, stood and moved it closer to him. He returned to his seat.

"To continue, Mr. McKnight, if Leslie had not been 'shot' or 'stabbed,' which I understand is an equally common occurrence in certain areas of America, she could have opted for, or perhaps she could have been *talked* into having one of those horrid corrective operations by a close friend. Or if she had been shot in the temple area, and the doctors were told of an existing mental condition…"

"Hold it right there, Doctor," said a nettled McKnight. "Leslie was shot. She was operated on for that shooting. In criminal matters, American doctors are not allowed exploratory surgery whether it involves the skull, suggestions, or anything else. In line with that shooting, it is reported that your daughter took a man's life, and I can tell you first-hand, she almost destroyed another."

"Oh, so now Leslie has taken a man's life."

"A policeman's."

"She must have been extraordinarily busy in the relatively short period she was over there."

"Make light of it if you wish, Doctor. But that's what happened."

"If she took a man's life, Mr. McKnight, why is she here? Why isn't she incarcerated? Is that not what happens to most offenders in your country? Or are they just taken out and shot?"

"If guilty, or, rather, if *proven* guilty, incarceration is what is *supposed* to happen. But it doesn't always work that way. We have people walking the streets who've done far worse than she has. But I'm not here to excuse anything Leslie did. She doesn't need to be excused anyway. Certainly not by me. She doesn't need it by me, because I seriously doubt she could or can be held responsible for anything that happened."

"And why is that, sir?"

"Because, and I'm sure most doctors will agree, what she did happened all during that fog she mentioned, that period of *'shadows and blurs'* that you spoke of. *Shadows and blurs* she now remembers."

"And so, despite what she says you've done for her, and all that she's told us about you, you really are a policeman, and you really are here in some sort of an official capacity?"

"If it eases your mind, Doctor, I am no longer a policeman. I'm here thinking I was going to enjoy the first leg of a permanent retirement."

The conversation ended for a moment. Neither man pressed for anything. McKnight was obviously feeling better, because his memory was serving him reasonably well and his conversation had not been as disjointed as it could have been. He didn't know what had caused it. He didn't question it.

Dr. Van Horn had digested all that was said, but he still had bothersome concerns. He was going to ask what he thought was a serious question when Leslie made a brief stop back into the room.

She started with McKnight. "Darling, I don't want to appear rude, but I'm upstairs, starting to read a little something to Mother. She loves that. Would it be all right with you if I go back up and finish? It'll only be a moment."

"Sure."

"And, Dad, is it all right with you?"

"I believe so, my dear."

"Tarara," she said, giving McKnight another peck and leaving.

While she was leaving the doctor looked at her for a long moment, then came up with another question. "Are you married, Mr. McKnight?"

"I'm not sir."

"By the by, I understand you were to arrive yesterday. Where did you spend the night?"

"Under a blanket."

"Oh?"

"Under a blanket on the plane, Doctor."

Doctor Van Horn stroked his beard, "I'm relieved to hear that. May I ask, sir, what is your current relationship with my daughter?"

"I don't think our relationship should involve a third-party interest, Doctor. After all, Leslie and I are well into the serious side of adulthood."

"I deem it important to know the relationship you have with my daughter."

"Why, sir? She's a grown woman. This is not some underage teenager we're talking about."

"Damn it, man, just answer the question and stop fiddling. It could be for your benefit as well as mine. It is no secret that Mother is ailing. And I don't mind saying she has been 'chronically,' if not conveniently, ailing all her life. And I've had to deal with it. Now there is virtual dementia. You've just seen her. Put two and two together. Since Leslie's childhood was affected, there could be a parallel there. They're of the same cloth; so close that when Leslie was a child and Mother spoke of our time in India, Leslie would wear a turban. When Mother spoke of the Orient, Leslie had to have a kimono. Mention America, and she would really go over the edge. And I can't tell you how many times she's been a runaway."

"Leslie admits she was over the edge, Doctor. My concern is what drove her there."

"She was not 'driven' anywhere."

McKnight gave the defensive man a look, stood, scanned the room, and returned to the figurine. He absently patted his pockets for his cigarettes, realized he was in the wrong for wanting to smoke in the house, and moved from the mantel to the piano. It then occurred to him that he had promised Leslie he was no longer a smoker.

"Doctor, earlier I had asked you a medical question dealing with the mind. I have another one, sir. Let's say that I were here doing research."

"For?"

"A book. Let's say a medical journal. And let's say that there is this young girl who was ill as a child. It is the father's view that this illness was expected, and indeed had all the reasons to manifest itself more readily in adulthood than it had in childhood, and... "

"And therefore the father is never really surprised by anything the daughter does, or with whom. Come, come, Mr. McKnight, I know where you're going."

"Would it not, Doctor," McKnight continued, "would it not be far better to say that the cause of that illness stemmed from the mother's pregnancy, rather than something else?"

"Aside from being rudely presumptuous, you're headed in the absolute wrong direction; a direction you're making quite personal, sir. It is also a direction, if I read you correctly, in which I could be held at fault, since I took full care of Mother, and prescribed her medication during pregnancy. And still do. Make no mistake: I do not believe a defective baby belongs on this Earth. If — *if* a pre-born baby of mine was likely to suffer a defect, I would have personally aborted it. And I would have done it in a heartbeat, as you Americans like to say. As to your immediate concern, Leslie has had problems since the cradle. Who was to blame? No one. What was the cause? Nothing. Did she manifest schizophrenic traits in the later years? Yes. Embarrassingly so. Neuroleptics, and in recent years lithium, Prozac, Clozapine, and anything else I can name didn't work, and, in fact, may have created a tardive dyskinesia effect, for which Leslie has only herself to blame. Now your question could very well be: Did she suffer something called *fugue syndrome*, a pathological amnesiac condition wherein one is conscious of one's actions but has no recollection of them later on? I don't know. She's stable now, but I can tell you she was always running off somewhere, and I strongly suspect that while she was away she developed a radically different personality. Upon returning, she certainly acted like it."

"Let's talk about a different set of specifics, sir. Give me the hows and whys of an infant illness that is still, after all these years, devastating your daughter."

"She was always withdrawn and emotionally flat. There are no 'different set' of specifics; no 'hows or whys.'"

"Then give me something, sir — in terms that I can understand," McKnight pressed. "Give me a *when* or a *what*. *What* was Leslie like as a child? *When* was her illness first observed? *Why* was she lashing out?"

"Everything I've said, Mr. McKnight, is a family matter, which *should* preclude your interest. I gather it does not. I therefore feel it necessary to say, or necessary to repeat: Because of Mother's condition, do not dare think that Leslie was — at any time — nurtured on narcotics. Be assured: There was no in-utero exposure that was — or could have been — the cause of Leslie's undeveloped cognivity or neurological breakdown."

McKnight didn't say anything.

The two men sat in silence for a short while, then tired of being in the man's presence, the doctor got up, and went to the library. Moments later, he returned with several books and journals.

"These are medical books. They are not works of fiction. The others are referred to as medical journals. If you are going to write anything in future, sir, I suggest you use them as your guide."

He dropped the collection in the man's lap, looked him in the eye, and left the room.

14

When night came at the Van Horn residence, McKnight was hurting again. Badly. Leslie had escorted him upstairs earlier, but the stress he had undergone with the doctor seemed to have unleashed every hurt he had in him. Later, he had started running a tub of hot water. While waiting, he fished around a bit, then found himself leaving the upstairs bathroom, dumping a couple of pills into a glass of water as he made his way across the hall to the room Leslie had prepared for him.

It won't work, he said to himself. The little white, round things couldn't give relief. The long white ones could, and he hadn't had one since last night. Last night he had thrown the pack of cigarettes into the river with such conviction and his words to Leslie had been so strong, that he was certain he would never light up again.

I can beat anything, if there's anything to beat.

Weakening more, he sat, got up, roamed around the room, sat, got up again, then sat again. Promises-be-damned. He sprang to his feet and went to his carry-on, removed a fresh pack of cigarettes from one of the three cartons he had brought with him, and lit up. The first puff worked. The brain felt it first, and it felt good. When the nicotine journeyed through the rest of the body, he felt even better. The pain was not gone, but now he could cope.

McKnight's room upstairs was three doors down and across from Leslie's. It had a nice feeling to it. It was fairly spacious, and Leslie had done a wonderful job of making it comfortable. The shared bathroom was directly across from it, and he heard Leslie when she came upstairs. He quickly doused the cigarette and frantically fanned at the air, trying to clear the smoke.

"Darling, I'm placing some extra towels in the bath, just in case," she said.

With one of the doctor's books in hand, he was casually lying down, waiting for her to come into the room. She headed for the bathroom across from his room. Before going through the door, she could be heard saying, "Oh, that Chauncey."

She was perturbed because Chauncey, the nurse, whom she had her suspicions about, had left a cloth on the sink that belonged to the mother. Removing it, she looked at the bathtub, saw that the water was running and cut it off.

"Another bath already?" she called to McKnight.

Inner conflict bubbling, he rose from the corner of the bed and went into the bathroom.

"Hi'ya feelin'?" she asked, trying to relieve him by sounding brightly American.

"Okay."

"Well, you've been hanging in there wonderfully."

He mumbled something.

"Like your room? I've had it ready for you for the longest."

"You really knew I was coming, huh?"

"I never had any doubt. I don't know where it came from, but I knew there was a bond between us. It was like it was something magical, you know? But let's not question it. You're here; I'm happy. And guess what I did? Before going off to meet you in London, and while I was up with Mother earlier, I came in here and gave the room a few extra touches. See how I look out for you?"

She was on her knees folding the towels to slide into the sink-cabinets. To be close to her, he sat on the side of the tub. He watched her for a moment, and tried to be as delicate as possible.

He took a deep breath and asked, "You trust..." He broke it off and tried again. "You really like your father, don't you?"

She laughed. "I love my dad. Old age has gotten to him, as it will with us all, but I do love him. With some of the things he used to say when I first got back, I sometimes got the impression he thought I should be in nursery."

"Why do you say that?"

"Well, sometimes we'd be talking and he'd slip a baby phrase into the conversation."

"I don't follow."

"You know, talk in a kind of babyish way. And then there was a time or two that he'd act as though I were helpless."

"And being a grown woman, you didn't find that odd?"

"No. Don't forget, I was just coming back to ground zero."

"Meaning when you first came back from the States and before he knew you had a memory."

"Correct."

"He thought you were still lost in this 'maze of shadows and blurs'?"

"Apparently so. Why are you asking? "

"Oh, nothing. Just curious, I guess," he said, trying not to be alarming. "Now, when he learned your memory had been restored..."

"Not restored. I never had a memory in the first place."

"Did it ever occur to you that you have one, but it's in regression?"

"I never had a memory, Wyatt."

"Okay. Have it your way. For the moment. But when your father found out you were like everyone else, that you had been perfectly transformed and now had a memory, was he excited for you?"

"Not really."

"You didn't find his lack of excitement strange?"

"Dad's thoroughly English. He's not an excitable person. He's controlled…"

"And would you say *controlling*?"

"Sort of."

"And he never knew about your injury?"

"He saw the scar, but I wouldn't talk about it."

"Was he afraid when he learned you had acquired a memory?"

"No. What was there to be afraid of?"

He didn't answer. Tactically, he slipped to another question. "After your return…incidentally, where were you staying when you first came back?"

"Here for a couple of weeks. I needed to be somewhere while recuperating. I also wanted to be close to Mother."

"Whom you could remember."

"Yes. Almost as it had been with you. There are certain instinctual things, procedural things that pull you through. I don't understand it; don't ask me about it. But because you don't know what you're doing doesn't mean that you are unable to do them. It's the same with people. Because you don't know who they are, or even who *you* are, doesn't mean that you don't intuitively know you are a part of them and they are a part of you. That's what happened to you, that's what happened to me. It was all instinctive; intuitive. It only means that if you are in a tunnel, such as I was, and, if you don't mind my saying it, such as you are, you go for the light."

McKnight took a moment to sift through what she had said, and still not certain that he understood, he wanted to go back to talking about her father. "So, after your return, your father, in a sense, was talking to you and treating you childlike. Did you get the impression that's the way it had been before you took off for the States?"

"Could have been."

"And since, you say, your father wasn't exactly excited by this facility of yours to recall, would it be safe to say that after he learned you now have it, he became somewhat distant?"

"Sort of. I mean we're chummy and all, and it's not enough to set off any bells, but there is a little something between us. But how would you know that?"

"Just guessing."

She gave him a look and went back to working with the towels. "But Dad's an okay guy. Did he tell you he used to practice in India?"

"He mentioned something about it."

"Well he did. He's very knowledgeable. And he has a great sense of humor. Maybe that was what all the baby talk was about. You two should get along famously. What were you talking about down there?"

"Nothin'."

"That was a long time to be talking about *nuttin'*," she said facetiously.

He picked up a towel, dabbed at his face. "I told him about you bumping somebody off."

"Oh, Wyatt, you didn't."

"It was okay. It came up casually."

"This is terrible. We agreed not to say anything about what happened in the States. What did he say? What does he think?"

"He doesn't think anything. I'm telling you, sweets, it's okay."

"He isn't angry?"

"No. Not in the slightest. We went on to other things."

"Such as what?"

"That porcelain piece on the mantel downstairs…"

"You mean the *Principe Enfant en Femme?*"

"Whatever it's called. Have you ever taken a close look at it?"

"Not really. I know Dad loves it. Personally, I've never cared for it. Maybe that's why I've never really looked at it. What brought the subject up?"

"It reminded me of a case I worked on a few months ago."

"Couldn't have been months ago, love."

"Months, years…the results were the same."

He stood, and thought for a second or two. He was trying for the right approach to an extremely sensitive subject. He leaned on the sink. "Is it possible you could be wrong about this fetal-addiction thing?"

"I doubt it," she said, having no trouble with the question. Nor did she realize what was behind the question. "I've thought about it too much. And, sweets, let me correct you about something I've been studying up on. For obvious reasons. Fetal addiction is not a 'thing.' In the U.S. alone, I believe there are something like 350,000 addicted babies born each and every year. There are thousands more born in England, and untold numbers around the world. Fetal addiction, my lover, is never a 'thing.'"

"I stand corrected."

She pecked him on the cheek and went across the hall to his bedroom. His inner need having risen again, he rubbed his arms and went into the bedroom to join her. Spotting the doctor's books and journals that he had placed on the bureau, she asked, "What does my dad want you to do, become a doctor?"

"I would seriously doubt that," McKnight said. He still had a question on his mind. "Babe, going back to what we were just talking about: What if a...what if, let's say, an *attempt* at something even more repugnant than what you think happened? What if it could have been a factor in your loss of memory?"

"Well, it wasn't exactly a loss of memory. As I've said before, I don't think I ever had one to lose. But I don't know of anything that could be worse than what I told you."

"Would you say..." Haltingly, he was trying for a new and more direct approach. "Would you say your father had a hand in your problem?"

"If he did, he wouldn't deny it. My father is a very honest man. And, as I told you in the hotel, he was not in any way at fault."

"But if you had no memory, how could you know that?"

"Actually, I don't. I know my father. And if you're referring to when Mother's injections first started, Dad had to have been doing what he thought was best for her. He is, after all, a doctor. A surgeon. And I believe a damn good one, at that. He hasn't practiced in years, but he still had to know something in order to become a doctor. Especially a surgeon. Unfortunately, the time we're talking about, my birth, a fetus suffered. Me. Or mine. Mother, as you have seen, is still suffering. Needles will do that."

"But what if your problems had little or nothing to do with your mother's addiction?"

"Condition."

"All right, *condition*. But what if they didn't?"

"But they did," she said, remaining staunchly oblivious.

He didn't want to take it further. His arms beginning to tingle with a heaviness, he was about to return to the bathroom when he said, as though pushing a cause, "I notice your mother is still on the needle."

"A treatment, I'm quick to add, that I am not in the slightest way in agreement with."

"But you've just said you believe your father is a damn good doctor. Doesn't that put you in disagreement with a damn good doctor?"

She'd never thought about it before. And now she wouldn't comment.

McKnight delayed the next question. Trying for an opening, he asked: "Would your mother be on morphine? Which is stronger than heroin, and therefore offers more relief?"

"Yes, she is, Wyatt," she said, now fully aware of where he was taking the conversation. "And morphine is here in the house. And Mother is on it. And she has been on it for as long as anyone can remember. And she looks twice her age. And you can let it drop right there."

"I was merely asking from the standpoint of what would happen if she were taken off the needle. She would probably die, wouldn't she?"

"There is that possibility."

"We certainly wouldn't want anyone to die, would we, Leslie?"

"No, we wouldn't, Wyatt," she said, with awareness. "Nor would we want a strong man to weaken."

A 4 a.m. quiet enveloped the residence. The house was beautiful in the moonlight. Leslie could see a portion of the moon from her bedroom window. She hadn't slept a wink. The earlier conversation with McKnight deeply bothered her; it sounded as if he were trying to tell her something about her father. She was bothered, too, by the last part of the conversation, not because they had talked about the mother's need for morphine, but because he had been quietly rubbing his arms while doing the questioning. Now, as she lay there, her mind roamed back to something else he had said in London. *"Brief Psychotic Disorder. Accent on 'brief.' Nothing more serious than that. It lasts for a day, the longest is thirty days. You go through periods of delusions and disorganized behavior. You're in and out. The psyc's words. You experience emotional turmoil and overwhelming confusion. After that, you're back on track. Like I am now. If I'd been a normal addict, I could've graduated to the upper levels. Then I would've had a problem."*

"It lasts for a day, the longest is thirty." That was the key.

His withdrawals, common sense kept telling her, should have been over by now. Common sense kept telling her, too, that Wyatt was in more trouble than either of them had realized.

Quietly she rose, put on her bathrobe and went out of the room that had been hers since the day she was born.

There was a small sliver of light escaping from under his door. She leaned an ear against it; she heard a muffled sound.

She quickly entered, and was horrified at the sight. It was something she had never dreamed she would see.

McKnight had tried reading for an hour or more, but he couldn't continue. The books and journals were on the floor, and he was hunched on the side of the bed, sweating and heaving. His withdrawal symptoms were pumping; his teeth were clenched on a towel.

Racing to his side and cradling him, Leslie was so hurt she could only sob. "Oh, Wyatt, Wyatt, Wyatt. My darling, darling Wyatt. I'm so sorry, so very, very sorry..."

Sorry, too, was Dr. Van Horn. From the mother's room near the end of the hall, and from a place he normally would not have been at that hour, he had seen Leslie when she went in. After waiting to see if she were coming back out, the doctor quietly went up to his room and sat in the dark for a long while. He then reached for the telephone, got the operator, and asked for assistance in calling Los Angeles.

After the call, he summoned Chauncey to his room.

15

"But, Wyatt you can't say that. You can't tell me you were all right last night. I was there. I was in the room. I *saw* you. I *held* you."

"Wrong. And the deal still holds, sweetheart."

It was morning. The man in denial was energetically leading Leslie down the stairs for breakfast. He was upbeat and making an attempt at bounciness.

"Wyatt, you can't deny what happened. And you've got to stop lying to yourself."

"Why is it so hard for you to believe I'm over my little problem? You got over yours, I'm over mine. And from what I'm led to believe, yours was a whole lot worse than mine. Blunt trauma cured you. R&R cured me. The deal we made in the car still holds, love. Shoot me if I'm wrong."

"I'm not interested in 'deals.' I'm worried about you. I have good reason to worry. Last night you were out of it, Wyatt."

"My behavior last night was strictly because of Paris jet lag. Nothing was out of the ordinary. I remember everything that happened while you were there; I remember everything after you left. And when you left, sweets, I spent the first part of the night reading books and going over the files again. Then I got myself some sleep. Plenty of it. Now my concentration is in order, and I feel just about the way you look: *wunderbar*."

"Wyatt, get real," she said, stopping before making the swing to go onto the veranda, where breakfast was being served. "You couldn't have suffered Paris jet lag."

"Why couldn't I, my lovely?"

"You arrived in England on a train."

"Good morning, Mummy...Martha," Leslie said to her mother, and to the maid. Pointedly, the greeting did not include Chauncey, the nurse, who was standing behind the mother at the table.

The Van Horns loved breakfasting on the veranda. The grounds were lovely, and it made a wonderfully tranquil setting. The weather was calm, and from the way they were seated, the view was endless.

"Will the doctor be breakfasting?" inquired Martha, not seeing the master of the house, who was never late.

"Yes, where is Daddy?" asked Leslie.

At that moment the doctor appeared. "Good morning, all," he said brightly. He sat, and, to McKnight's surprise, closed his eyes for a quick table blessing. Imperiously done, he said, "Don't forget church on Sunday." He nodded for the table to be served.

"And how are you, Daddy?" Leslie asked.

"Feeling more chipper than ever, dear. And please overlook my lateness. It's rude. I find rudeness of any sort intolerable."

McKnight felt the jab, but didn't say anything.

Mrs. Van Horn asked, "Forgive me, darling, but what are you feeling so cheap about?"

"He said '*Chipper*', Mummy," Leslie said. "And, Daddy, you are late because of...?"

"A call from the 'colleagues of the board.' They want the old warhorse to come back to the fold. They desire me to come back and serve in some sort of an advisory capacity. And maybe get involved with an operation or two."

"Will you do it?" Leslie asked.

"Hah! What a question."

"But are you going to do it, Dad?"

"I've given the matter due consideration, I think it is a most wise decision on their part, and I shall breakfast with them tomorrow morning. Now, then, as to answer your question, Mother, I am especially..."

Leslie interrupted. "Dad, you recently told me it's been years and years since you've practiced. At your age are you sure it's...?"

"It's rude to interrupt, dear. But to answer you, going back to hospital still has that ring of challenge to me. Age has nothing to do with one's expertise. And we'll let it go at that," he said, ending the subject. "Getting back to your question, Mother, I am in the pink because of the newfound health of our lovely daughter, who, knock-knock, didn't have to undergo any of the 'operational' horrors there in America. And I am in the pink, my dear, because of the presence of one Mr. Wyatt William McKnight, a lacerating mind from the wilds of America."

"Hear, hear," smiled Leslie, not realizing the undercurrent.

"He sounds like a fascinating chap," said the mother. "When is he arriving?"

"Mother, Mr. McKnight is sitting to your left. Do you remember you were introduced yesterday afternoon?"

She was unable to remember. At Leslie's urging McKnight said, "Good morning, Mrs. Van Horn. It's nice to see you again."

Not waiting for the mother to respond, the doctor said to his daughter, "So, what are you two up to today?"

"I'm taking Wyatt for a sightseeing drive. And maybe we'll do a little shopping."

"Mr. McKnight seems to have a most peculiar interest in fiction," the doctor said with a sharpened edge. "Maybe you can stop by the library and pick up something to quench his thirst."

Leslie laughed it off.

To deflect the doctor, McKnight asked Leslie, "Is it possible we can see the White Cliffs of Dover? Or maybe see the S.S. Great Britain?"

"The cliffs are an enormous distance from here, but we'll see," she said, and was aware that he was not eating. "Now, eat your food. And don't put too much salt on it."

"Oh, I think this is so blessedly wonderful," said Mrs. Van Horn. "It's something I've always wanted."

"What is that, Mother?" Leslie asked.

"To breakfast out here on a warm summer night. And to have the help sit at the table is divine."

"Mother, Wyatt is my guest."

"And it isn't night at all, Mother," Dr. Van Horn corrected, but not with the gentleness Leslie had used. "It's morning."

Pathetically, the kind old lady realized something was amiss, and lapsed into another silence. Dr. Van Horn motioned for Chauncey to come and wheel her away.

"I'm sorry," the mother said. "Please excuse me. And, my darling daughter, I'm sorry if I have offended you." She turned to the visitor. "And to you, sir, my very deep apologies."

With the tiny beads of sweat returning to his forehead, McKnight stood respectfully for the departure.

The doctor said to Chauncey, "I'll be up shortly for the injection."

"Do be very careful with her, Chauncey," Leslie said, and not with her kindest voice.

Leslie waited until they were completely gone, and, trying to suppress an irritation that was now full-grown, said, "Dad, if you do go back to hospital after all these years, would…"

"Not *if*, dear. *When*," confirmed the doctor. "It's a certainty."

"It's a 'certainty,'" repeated Leslie, unsettled. There was no question about it, she was bothered by her mother's condition, and it was as if it had been her first time thinking about the injections. But it was

not the first. Even in her troubled state, she had questions. But because of her talk with Wyatt, she thought harder about everything
that was taking place. She put her fork down and stared at the plate
thoughtfully. She braced herself. "In Mother's case, Dad, if you had
it to do all over again, you wouldn't make the same medical decisions, would you?"

"Regarding what, dear?"

"Regarding the shots you've been giving Mother all these years."

"Of course I would. The shots have worked wonders for her."

Leslie's thoughts had developed into anger.

She was angry when she left the table, she was angry when she
left the house and drove the car through the polite streets of Bath; she
was angry when she arrived at the efficient-looking hospital, and she
was even more angry when she asked the trailing McKnight to wait
outside while she went in to discuss something with the hospital administrator.

As he sat outside the office, being reminded of his stay back in Los
Angeles' Queen of Angels Hospital, McKnight knew that scheduling
a stop at Bath Medical was a long way from what Leslie had planned
for the day. Being in *any* hospital was certainly the last place he wanted
to be; it was the last place he thought *she* would want to be. But he
knew she had been stung by what her father had said at the table, and
he could tell that the anger went beyond the norm. It was understandable.

At the table, Leslie had given her father the benefit of the doubt.

There wasn't much activity in the corridor. As the visitor from
America sat there thinking about how different the English hospital
was from the hospitals he had seen, he was busy reassessing Leslie's
question to her father. He realized that she had asked the question
regarding her mother's shots in a way that allowed the father to say,
"No, dear, I would not have done the same. Never would I have started

her on this rot called morphine. It is a narcotic, and it has destroyed this lovely woman. It has taken away a wonderful mind and has made her a vegetable, and it was all because of gross stupidity on my part. And I would do anything in the world to have her back."

But the doctor hadn't said anything like that. He had said: *"Of course I would. The shots have worked wonders for her."*

McKnight was still thinking along those lines when a tray of syringes on a cart was being pushed his way. It was coming from the opposite end of the corridor from where Leslie had gone. Noticing his sweaty condition and trembling knee when she neared him, the nurse made a momentary stop.

"Are you all right?" she inquired.

"I'm okay, thanks."

The nurse moved on with the cart and stopped at a room a few feet down the corridor. She was only in the room for a minute or so before Leslie emerged from the office. When she came out, McKnight was standing. His hands were in his pockets.

Leslie looked dissatisfied. Obviously the visit hadn't gone well.

Outside, as they descended the stairs to the car, he was trying to be tactful.

"Why were we here?"

She was in no mood for discussion. "Mother needs more medication."

"And in England you get it from an administrator's office?"

She didn't respond, and nothing was said until they climbed into the car.

Before starting up, Leslie handed him a small bottle. "I got these for you."

He looked at her and at the small pill bottle, and sagged. "Aspirins? Wonderful."

The ride was not long, and they ended up parking the car and walking to an area that led to the little bridge at Bath's Stourhead Gardens. It had not been a planned route.

The city of Bath was Georgian, and owed its name and existence to the country's only hot springs. In 1091 it had become a cathedral city, and for over two thousand years it had played host to visitors the world over. While Bath was the name, it very well could have been called Bathed. It was immersed in goodness, and, to this day, few cities could match it. It was just plain beautiful. It was the kind of city that made you think that even before the Romans, the miracle of nature humbled the aristocracy and ennobled the inferior.

Apparently bridges were on Leslie's and McKnight's minds, and from the little Stourhead bridge they made their way to the bridge in Stourton, near Mere. From there they could see landscaped gardens, lakes, and temples.

On the Stourhead bridge they stopped midway. A desultory Leslie, wanting to be alone with her thoughts, had moved to the other side. McKnight was glad that she did.

The visitor from America had stolen two needles from the nurse's cart, and now he was feeling pain. He was also feeling guilty. Deciding to split the difference, he reached into his pocket and dropped one of the needles into the water.

He watched it sink. Feeling a little better about what he had done, he moved across to Leslie, who, with her back turned, naturally hadn't seen the drop, and was immersed in another set of problems.

The conversation was low-key.

"How are you doing, love?"

"I don't know, Wyatt. I just don't know," she said disconsolately.

"It's going to get better," he said.

"Do you mind if we didn't get to Dover today? We'll get an early start in the morning."

"That's okay. Making the request wasn't really for my benefit."

"I know. You were saying it to get back at Dad."

"Didn't know you were aware of what was going on."

"I'm beginning to realize a lot that's going on. Finally."

"I sure hope so," he said, and tried to steer away from the subject. "Hey, but I remembered the cliffs, didn't I?"

"Yes. Why did you pick them?"

"I liked the song. I remember seeing them in an old war movie. When the world was going crazy, those ol' White Cliffs of Dover just hung in there. Kinda like you have to do."

She knew he was trying to deliver a message. It worked. She was comforted by the words — and the fact that he could remember.

"Anyway," he continued, "if I got too close to those ol' cliffs, I might think they were big piles of coke an' I'd try to smoke 'em."

There was relieving laughter.

She wanted to show him something she thought special.

Leslie didn't know why, but the Wookey Hole Caves, at Wells, Somerset, were something she wanted him to see, and so she took him there.

The city had done a nice job of lighting the place and the guide was most efficient in pointing out the stalactites and stalagmites. To McKnight, the caves, with their half-mile of brooding chambers and their lazy, unmoving bed of slime-colored water, looked like the interior of a giant dead brain. It brought back thoughts of the Los Angeles morgue.

The Wookey Hole Caves were forbidding, the echo carried for a long way.

"Mighty spooky in the holes of Wookey," he said, lightly.

Leslie's mind was on something else. Finally she slowly asked, "Wyatt, who was LeCoultre?"

He was taken aback by the question, and didn't answer until they were making their way out of the cave. He was glad when he saw the first beam of daylight.

"LeCoultre was a cop," he said, having pushed the name far back in his mind. "He was the detective you shot."

"Why do they say I did that?"

"Because when you pull a trigger and fire at someone, and that someone is hit by the projectile from the gun you fired, that is considered shooting someone."

"Thank you," she said. "Not that I am going to believe it, but why would I have done that?"

"Because you were involved in narcotics. And LeCoultre was a cop who had become addicted to heroin."

"I was never involved with narcotics. It's repulsive."

"My love, you continue to say that. You were involved. I'm not saying it, the LAPD is. But I can tell you, the way I figured it, whatever you were doing could have been classified as an overgrown joke. LeCoultre, on the other hand, was serious. Now, I'm trying to remember how you two met."

"You said I had a club. Maybe he was…what do they call it? A regular?"

"It wasn't that kind of club. Furthermore, it was much too sophisticated for Mr. LeCoultre. This guy was a *total* loser."

"He could've been involved with one of the waitresses. I couldn't have known him, especially if he was that kind of person. What kind of club was it?"

"A toy. The kind that was destined to fail. You kept the doors locked."

"Oh, you! Stop clowning. I need to know these things."

"If you do, then don't ask me to fill you in on everything. I can only quote from the records and certain things that bounce back to mind. The records says Detective Sergeant LeCoultre burglarized your home, taking narcotics and paraphernalia. I say you sicked a dog on him. I say when you found out the dog didn't do the job, you hopped in your car, caught up with the fleeing cop, shot him, came back to your house and got rid of the gun by tossing it over the wall, which, I now recall, was not the cleverest thing to do."

"I simply couldn't have done *any* of that. I've never even seen a gun, let alone known how to use one."

"You used a gun. That I'm sure of. Assuming the gun was mine when I went to the hospital, they put it with my personal things. There it stayed. It wasn't something I looked at every day. When I saw it, I thought it was mine, too. I must have. I brought it over here with me."

"How did you get the gun in the first place?"

"I obviously found it that night, put it in my pocket, and stayed on the case."

"So, then, what happened to the gun you used to shoot me?"

"That would've been my gun. Apparently it was never found. I'm thinking you ditched it."

"Ridiculous. And the idea of my using narcotics is totally out of the question."

"You may not have been a user, but you were an 'entrepreneur.' That's on record."

"This whole thing is so silly and ludicrous, I'm going to forget all about it. That's it. No more talk about it."

"You committed murder. That's not exactly a thing I would call silly. Granted, the man was a snake. But he was also a cop. You don't think the LAPD is going to say 'that's it.'"

She planted her eyes skyward and started idly humming.

"I just thought of something," he said, reclaiming her attention. "Even though you're still listed as dead, dead or alive, killing a cop is not exactly a thing to have on a lawyer's resume."

"Oh, you didn't forget." She brightened with sudden interest. "Think I'd make a good lawyer?"

"I hope so. You might have to defend me."

"Why?"

"I shot you, remember?"

For the next stop Leslie could have chosen the Roman Baths' gilt bronze head of Minerva, or the Georgian Gardens, or they could have wandered over to Parade Gardens; she could have shown him the incredibly serene Abbey and its monuments; or the Guildhall, or, since he had spoken to Kiesner about them, perhaps he could have gotten a kick out of seeing Scallywag, home of the jeans museum. She could have taken him to any number of interesting places. She chose the

Royal Crescent. It was nice that she did. The long, crescent-shaped building was an architectural wonder.

Her mind was on something else.

From the Crescent, talking little, they took a quick 14-mile trip to the Cloisters, Lacock Abbey. There they recalled the dignity of silence and said little. Heading back out, McKnight asked a question that had been brewing since yesterday's arrival at the house.

"I hope you don't mind the question, Leslie, but I've got to ask it. How long has your mother been suffering with Alzheimer's?"

"Her condition has not been medically determined, and I'd rather not talk about it."

"As if not talking about whatever it is will make it go away after all these years?"

"Where's there's love there's hope," she said, quietly. "And besides, us knowing more about it, and her being put away, isn't going to change anything. There is still no cure; she can't be treated any better."

"Or kept any higher."

"I'll choose to overlook that, my darling."

"Sorry," he said apologetically. Moving on, he asked, "You went to the hospital to check up on your father. Why?"

Now she was hurt all over again, and she was not willing to talk.

He said with patience, "You might as well let it out. Whatever drove you there and whatever you learned there is hurting you inside."

After more persuasion, she slowly released, "Father lied to me."

"By…?"

"I'd rather not go into it."

"Why not?"

"Because sometimes he can make me so mad."

"How?" he asked.

"Well, like now. Don't get me wrong, I love my dad…but…poor Mother. With him, it's always something. It always *was* something."

"Like what?" he urged. "You're trying to say he was always on her. What was he on her about?"

"Everything. Her age, her illness, the way she speaks. He doesn't like her being Irish, he doesn't like the fact that she was raised a Catholic..."

"What *does* he like?"

"I don't know. Like the other day, I left the Cotswolds to come and prepare your room. Mother was in pain again. He started harping about how she was never able to withstand pain, and that she's always had some illness or another, more than likely imagined, he says. More than likely *imagined*!? Mother almost didn't survive delivering me. And before you ask again, I have a friend at St. James. Actually, he's an old friend of Mother's who still practices there. He's told me a lot. Now that I think about it, I was told he was a close friend of Dad's first. Then something went wrong. I don't know what it was."

"When you were a child, this doctor was the one who examined you?"

"I would suppose so."

"And took care of you all your life?"

"I would imagine so. He's certainly told me about the pills he's had me on forever. But he explained they were harmless. They didn't do anything."

"Well, if he was giving you pills that did nothing, there had to be a reason. It seems to me it had to have meant he thought your condition was psychosomatic. Or maybe, more seriously, it was because..." He broke it off. Something went deep into the mind.

Troubled by what he was thinking, they walked a bit more. "All right, tell me this, since he is a friend, does the doctor ever visit your mother?"

"No."

"Does he ever telephone?"

"As I understand it, he used to come to the house quite a bit. But he hasn't been there in years," she said. "And Mother isn't allowed access to the telephone."

"Why not?"

"She's too erratic to be on the phone. She hardly knows what it is, anyway."

"Has this doctor ever told you anything about your father, and why he doesn't visit?"

"Mother suffered terribly. She…"

"And this doctor friend has said nothing about your father, Leslie?"

"Mother suffered terribly, and she…"

"Leslie, *stop*," McKnight said. "We've got to talk about your father. Maybe this doctor at St. James didn't know, or maybe didn't want to tell you — which is more likely — but I believe, many years ago, that in the most disgusting way your father hurt you."

Leslie's mind simply refused to register what he had said. She continued walking, almost babbling. "Wyatt, Mother almost died."

"Leslie, you've got to stop it. We should be talking about your father, and you choose to hide. You don't have to do that any more. Look, knowing your father now, and realizing you grew up around this man as a little girl...Sweetheart, listen to me. Your mother's doctor friend doesn't come to the house any more because he can't take what has happened to her, and because of something that happened to you. He supplied you with placebos for all those years because if he gave you anything else he'd have to tell you, or somebody, why. And if he told that somebody *why;* if he told them the full story, your mother would end up helpless and alone. In her condition she'd have to be put away."

"Put my mother away?"

"Somebody would have to, because your father would be in prison. Love, even back in Los Angeles, I believe it was at the club, you tried to tell me something about him. I've been trying my damnedest to remember what you said ever since I've been here, but I can't do it. But I do know you were trying to let something out that was buried deep inside you. Now, all I'm asking you to do is *think.* Start with the figurine on the mantelpiece, the *Enfant* thing; take any and everything; take his innuendoes, take everything he's ever said or done, and what your father is becomes as clear as daylight. Let me give you an example. You used to have a clown, the same clown I showed you in the hotel closet. Your father used to scare the hell out of you with that very same clown. I brought that clown with me from Los Angeles. I took it from *your* house. It was *your* clown — the *very same* clown your father used to manipulate your mind."

"What are you talking about, Wyatt? It's nonsense."

"I'm talking about your father."

"And you're not making a damn bit of sense doing it."

"Maybe I'm not. All I'm asking you to do is *think*."

"You're talking about my mother being alone; my father in prison. Are you sick? What innuendoes? What pills? And you're talking about a clown from Los Angeles? What clown? What are you talking about? And I don't see what my father and my being a little girl and some art piece...s-s-some art piece on the mantel..."

"Go on."

"S-s-s-some piece..."

It was a slow dawning. She couldn't take it further. She stood there, her face as immovable as stone. McKnight gave her time and room; room and time. Then he tried to get through again.

"Babe, prenatal addiction might have contributed to your behavior, but something else robbed you of your memory. Despite what you say, you *had* a memory. You think not, because of a pre-born condition. Fetal addiction. Not so. You remember shadows and blurs. How can that be? It *can't* be, because before birth there is nothing to remember."

He still wasn't getting through. "Leslie. Think. Listen to the words. *'Enfant en Femme.'* 'Child into woman.' That's *not* art. That's a sick man's fantasy. When we get back to the house, look at that piece in the proper light. You'll see how revolting it really is. And it *means* something. Ask your doctor friend at St. James. He'll tell you. He knows the full story. Why do you think he stopped visiting your house? He was an old family friend. But no more. *Why?* And go back to something I believe you said about having 'rock-bottom fear' that night in the hotel. Why did you say it? You're a grown woman. Why terror because of a natural act?"

She had to move away from him.

He waited until she had settled and moved to her. He reached into his pocket. "Love, there's one other thing. In trying to understand why and what you went through, I've been leafing through a book and some of the journals your father gave me. I stumbled across something called Shared Psychotic Disorder. Like my BPD case, it's a form of schizophrenia. Its main feature is a delusion that develops in an individual who is involved in a close relationship with another person who has a psychotic disorder with delusions. Your father talked about something called the *fugue syndrome* — as if that was the cause of your problems. I don't know anything about that, but I do know that the book says that the primary cause of Shared Psychotic Disorder is the controlling person in the relationship imposing the delusion onto the weaker person. It's more common in women than men. If that's so, I'd bet it would be even more so in the case of children. Especially where 'shadows and blurs' are concerned."

Her mind was numb; her face ghostlike, she turned her back to him. He allowed her all the time in the world.

Feeling for something, he reached into his pocket and withdrew the remaining syringe. He walked a few feet in the other direction and got rid of it. If she could face what she had to face, so could he.

Thinking she needed him, he moved slowly back to her. Although her back was to him, he wanted to put his arms around her, but he held off. She felt his presence and turned slowly. "I remember," she said softly.

"What do you remember?"

She took more time, much more time. *"Mother."*

It was not at all what she was supposed to say; it was not what he had expected her to say. His frustration was showing, but he didn't say anything.

When she finally said something, she was vacant. "I remember there were times when Mother wasn't so erratic. Don't forget, I was ill also, and I'd do the strangest things, like I was in school, and I'd imagine she would come to school for me. I'd simply leave. I don't know where I would go, or what I would do. That was all a part of the problem. I do recall, now, when…when…when *Father*…when *Father* said I could no longer attend school because of my condition…"

She had to drop the rest. She came to him, sadly. "Wyatt — help me. — *Please help me.*"

He embraced her. "Let it go, babe. Let it go. It's going to be all right."

"And Doctor Nieves knew?"

"Is he the doctor friend at St. James?"

She nodded weakly.

"He said nothing because he was trying to protect your mother. But you've overcome, sweets. Let it go for a while," he said, paining inside and tightening his embrace. "Let it go."

In the hour that followed, they both tried to put the matter on hold. To help them, Leslie thought it would be a good idea to see the Roman figures at the Guildhall. It was an idle stroll.

Staying away from the other subject, Leslie asked, "How are you holding up?"

"Great. For the moment," he lied. His legs and groin were feeling as bad as his arms.

"You haven't had a cigarette today. I'm proud of you. You're overcoming all the urges."

"Yeah," he said, without strength. "All the urges. And that one I've had for about a century. It started when I was a kid going to school; we used to sneak down to the boiler room to do it."

"Was it a good school?"

"I don't think so. It was segregated; another promise denied. What about yours?"

"Isn't that interesting? In all the years, I've never been able to think about school. And now to remember," she reflected. "I remember Miss Emmett's room. I remember that special time of day when I would see this car's window reflecting in the sunlight. I knew that would be Mother and Kent coming for me in the convertible. Mother would be wearing white gloves. And she'd bring a pair for me. We'd sit in the back seat, very proper and ladylike, and we'd be driving along, seeing and commenting on the wonderful scenery. She would talk about her favorite place: the Cotswolds. And she'd talk about the quaint countryside, and the beautiful little Elizabethan towns. It's a pity she never got there. I suppose that's why I ended up there. And have my antique shop there."

"You said the Cotswolds aren't that far away."

"Two hours."

"Couldn't you come and get her and let her see the place she's always wanted to go?"

"I've not been allowed to do that."

"Why not?"

"Father still doesn't trust my driving."

"Couldn't Kent do it?"

"Let's move on, Wyatt."

Taking the advice, McKnight changed subjects. "Well, as far as houses go, there can't be many places better than where she is now."

"I've been redecorating it. Trying to bring a few of the rooms up to speed. I've done a lot. Except for Father's room, of course. He doesn't allow anyone in there. Now I'm kind of terrified thinking about it."

"I don't presume you would remember, but just in case, do you know if you used to run away a lot when you were a kid?"

"I wouldn't think so. But I'm not sure."

"All right, let me ask you this. Has your father ever visited you since you started living in the Cotswolds?"

"No."

She said it coldly. He asked her about college. She didn't remember anything about it, and she said nothing else until they reached

Walcot Street. There, and all the way down to London Road, they went in and out of a few stores, where Leslie picked up some gifts for her mother. McKnight settled for getting her a huge bouquet of roses.

In Bath's Upper Town, there was a brasserie called Woods on Alfred Street that was a crowd favorite. Leslie had talked him into going in for a bite. Standing there, she was doing well until she mentioned that the house specialty included lamb and pigeon. McKnight couldn't see himself munching on anything that had spent a lifetime decorating statues, buildings, and whitewashing car tops. He had also fought the idea of eating something as cute and innocent as a lamb.

They ended up at the Star on the Paragon.

With its scrubbed floors and dark paneling, it was a traditional place with a lively bar.

Sliding into a booth, Leslie looked at the packages and bouquet. "Mom's going to love these. And the flowers for her are lovely. Thank you, my darling."

"My pleasure," he answered, glad to be sitting.

The waiter came over and they ordered.

"So," she said, after that was done, "from the way you sounded when you were talking about your school, America didn't live up to its promise."

"Didn't then. Ain't now. Hasn't done it in over two hundred years."

"Why not?"

"Problems."

"Well, I think there is enough time left for all problems to be solved."

"I don't know. Hurt by bigotry, crippled with indifference, I think the old girl could very well be running out of time. She might be maxed out. Asleep at the wheel. But if we hurry, we might manage to kill each other off. Two hundred and twenty million guns in the country, shootings in schools, playgrounds, even in the Capitol building itself. But maybe you're right. Maybe there is still time. We're only averaging — what? A hundred and thirty murders a day."

"A great memory, but now you're sounding like an expatriate."

"Better than being a fugitive."

"That brings me to something else I've wanted to ask. "Do you think someone is still going to come after me, even though I haven't done anything."

"Li'l darlin', you did something. Believe it. And don't you dare think you've made a clean getaway. Thanks to people like my former captain, a thoroughly reprehensible and incompetent man, if there ever was one....what th' hell was his name? Anyway, thanks to him and a bogged-down system, you fell through the cracks. But the arm of American law is long, sweetheart. And, personally, I happen to believe people who violate the law should face the music. And, my dear, you can be extradited."

"If I went back to the States to 'face the music,' would you face it with me?"

"Not to be exclusively racial about this thing, but my standing up in court with you wouldn't serve to your best advantage. But don't let going to court faze you. When you go, take your purse and learn theater."

"Why?"

"In America, you don't go to court. You go to a performance."

"Then why face the music?"

"Because it's the honorable thing to do. In theory."

"Good. Let them convict theory, not me."

He laughed. The meal was served, of which he ate little. They had a few drinks, and were back home before evening.

Entering the house from the pantry, Leslie asked, "Do you really like it here?"

"Oh, this city. Beautiful. England, great."

"I meant here at the house."

"It's.... okay. Kinda like being a part of Masterpiece Theater."

She laughed.

"Why'd you ask?"

"Mother seemed a bit more shaky than usual this morning. I think I should spend an extra day with her. And then...and then...it's off to my place for a little R&R."

Leaving from the kitchen to the hall, she whispered: "I'm glad you had enough in you to listen to your policeman friend."

McKnight smiled. With a thick tongue, he started sounding like Devro: *"Hey, Hey, Keezy-Key, do some reporter from across th' pond keep callin' you 'bout this case after all this time? ...Oh, no? Well, she stays in touch with me. An', honey, ev'ry time she calls, I can't stop talkin'."*

They playfully joined together: *"I just luuuv's them French accents."*

Laughing, and moving past a room that was just off the pantry, Leslie noticed the door was slightly ajar. She closed it and continued moving through the house.

"What was that?"

"Dad's medicine room."

From the foyer, she called, "Hiiiii, where are you?"

"We're in here, dear," Dr. Van Horn's voice responded. "In the sitting room. I'm reading to Mother. Rudyard Kipling. He wrote a wonderful piece on taking up the white man's burden."

It was as if she had buried him so far in the back of her mind that she had forgotten. It all came back. By the time the doctor's voice had finished, she was in the living room. Leaving McKnight in the foyer, she had made a beeline to the *Principe Enfant en Femme.* Everything McKnight had said concerning the figurine and the doctor was swirling through her mind. She stood there staring hard at it, as thought it harbored some deep, dark secret.

Her face was still frozen when she arrived in the sitting room. She had the more than difficult task of being kind to an ailing mother in a small room with a man she now despised without limit.

McKnight was lingering by the door.

Reacting to the packages and flowers, the doctor said, brightly, "Well, what do we have here?"

Leslie ignored him and said to the mother in a voice that did not fit the occasion, "The flowers are from Wyatt."

"Ooooh, look. Aren't they grand, Daddy?"

"Wonderful," said the doctor. "What's the occasion, Leslie?"

She would not respond to him in any fashion, and busied herself assisting the mother in opening the packages.

"And, Mother, as your are about to see, Wyatt and I decided you should have some new…frillies and a bathrobe."

"Aren't they lovely? And pink! My favorite color."

Neither the undergarments nor the bathrobe were pink. They were white, but Leslie didn't correct her. "Here, let me help you try the bathrobe on for size."

Mrs. Van Horn shyly nodded, indicating a stranger was at the door.

"It's only Wyatt, Mother. And he did buy you flowers."

McKnight gave Leslie an understanding look and discreetly stepped away.

Mrs. Van Horn came back to her daughter. "But I knew someone was here, didn't I?"

"Yes, you did. And I'm very proud of you."

Having gotten rid of the two syringes earlier, and with his need strongly on the surface again, McKnight eased back to the room Leslie had described as *"Dad's medicine room."*

He slipped inside; his eyes were on the prowl.

The medicine room was like an old-fashioned doctor's office, the kind he thought he remembered seeing years and years ago, except that the dark paneled walls were lined with leather-bound books. The roll-top desk was made of oak, and on top of it were stacks of periodicals and pamphlets. In the corner was a coat-tree, and from it hung an off-white lab coat. There were many cabinets. Most of them were glass-encased. Instruments could be seen behind the glass. To the left was a refrigerated unit, which attracted the detective's attention. Next to it was a sink.

He checked the cabinets quickly, then opened the refrigerated unit. There he saw what he was looking for. On the bottom shelf was the morphine. The syringes had been filled and were waiting. Obviously they had been prepared for Mrs. Van Horn. After hesitating a moment, McKnight sent a hand out to reach for one, then painfully decided not to. Having made a mental note of everything, he quietly left.

When he returned to the sitting-room door, Leslie was standing in the doorway, waiting. She had her suspicions but was not thoroughly certain as to where he had been. There was tension, and without being asked, he nervously explained, "I was looking for the bathroom."

"The downstairs guest bathroom is in the other direction," Leslie said. She didn't fully fault him, because possibly he didn't know. But the seeds of mistrust had been planted. They would remain with her all through the night.

They went upstairs and sat in his room.

Since they had eaten late while touring the city, they didn't have dinner. Deciding that they both should retire early, Leslie engaged him in a small conversation, told him she loved him, and expressed the hope that he would have a good and full night's sleep.

16

McKnight had already gotten undressed for bed, but he lay on top of the covers. It was shortly after 10 p.m.

He was having a hard time; the night was aiming to be his worst. He was sweating and clutching himself, and the only way he thought he could help himself was to spend a few minutes in the bathroom. He didn't throw up and he didn't run the bath water, but he did remain in the bathroom for more than a few minutes.

When he returned across the hall to his room, on his dresser was a syringe. It was neatly placed on a cloth napkin. He didn't remember seeing it there before, and it was certain Leslie hadn't placed it there. With the old saying *Never look a gift horse in the mouth* swirling in his mind, he started sweating again. He immediately went for the pack of cigarettes he had hidden away. He lit up. It didn't work. He was in trouble. Serious trouble. Slowly he went to the dresser and picked up the syringe. It was fully loaded, and he could almost taste the relieving sensation. He thought about Leslie; he thought about the hard time she was having, and he thought about his promise. He stared at the syringe, and at his arms. He felt his groin and his legs. The pain grew.

Prayerfully he fell to his knees, and shot the syringe forward. With the syringe thrust forward in his hand, holding it like a Catholic would hold the crucifix, he started shaking. It developed into a fight; like the devil trying to wrest the crucifix from the hands of the fiercely devoted, he struggled and the syringe fell to the floor. That was a sign. He had won. He had beaten the devil; he had beaten the demon. He had beaten them both, and at that moment he was convinced — he was *positively* convinced — he wouldn't fall back again.

Pleased, and breathing hard, he stood. He put on a shoe, lifted his foot and brought it down as hard as he could, stamping on the syringe, smashing it to pieces.

I can beat anything, he said to himself.

Sweating and claiming internal victory, he lit a cigarette and sat on the corner of the bed. He was sitting for only a moment when there was a rap on the door.

With that odd mixture of feeling tremendous over an achievement while nursing biting pain, the man of strength didn't feel like moving. The knocking forced him to. He put the cigarette out, stood, and tried to clear the air of smoke. He sat again and leaned back against the headboard, pretending to be casual. He was determined to not let her see him going downhill on any level. He tried to have a smile in his voice when he answered. After all, there was great news he could share with her. He had beaten the devil.

"Come in, hon."

"Is everything all right, Mr. McKnight?" asked the doctor.

17

It was 3 a.m. The exterior of the Van Horn residence was foggy and quiet.

It should have been quiet inside as well, but the heavy breathing accompanied by the occasional squeaks from the staircase steps overrode all silence. McKnight had been on the steps. The victory that came with the smashing of the syringe did not hold, and he was now rounding the turn to the medicine room. Once there, he tried the doorknob. It turned but it wouldn't give. He yanked at it angrily several times, then started pulling and cursing.

Surprisingly, a calming hand was placed on top of his. "I told him to lock it and keep it locked, Wyatt."

He couldn't look at her. He slumped down. "I'm, sorry, babe. I'm sorry. I'm terribly, terribly sorry."

She knelt down beside him, keeping her hurt inside. "I understand."

"You're not angry with me?"

"Of course I am," said Leslie. "But I understand."

"I remember saying one time: 'After you take that first hit, you don't care what you're doing. If you take a second and third, God Himself doesn't care. After that, both will and mind are gone. The monkey's on your back and nobody but nobody knows what an addict will do.' Whoever thought a thing like that would apply to me? But I promise you something, sweets. I swear, it won't happen again. I won't let it happen again. I'm going to beat this thing," he said, trying to show strength. "Does the deal still hold?"

She nodded quietly.

"I'm really in that tunnel, aren't I?"

"Yes, you are," she said quietly. "But I believe you'll find the light. I have faith in you."

"You know something? I'm glad we met, and I'm glad we clicked."

"So am I," she said. "And you no longer question or underestimate the affairs of the heart?"

"Never again," he said. "Not as long as you're around. Because, babe, you're some kind of a woman. Time, bullets, narcotics — nothing will ever change that."

He remembered. She was pleased.

"Does it bother you that I've never said the words before?"

"In a way. But I understand. You didn't want to fully commit, because you were trying to protect me. But I'm a grown woman, Wyatt."

"...And a terrific one."

They embraced, and went back upstairs to his room. They spent the night there. She was on top of the covers, he was underneath.

Nothing sexual was consummated, and nothing sexual would have been consummated as long as they were in her parents' house. But their respect for the house didn't stop the man of the house from thinking differently.

Quietly from the cracked door down the hall, Dr. Van Horn saw the two going into the room again. He closed the door and sat in the darkened room with a rock-hard imagination. Not that she was needed at the time, but on a night when he could have been spending more hidden moments upstairs on the third floor with Chauncey, he was occupied with something that shouldn't have been.

It was not his sole thought, and he undoubtedly would have been equally disturbed had it been any other man, but it vibrated through the doctor's mind that he hadn't been close to a dark-skinned man since he left his practice in India those many years ago, and now one was not only in his home, but in a room with his daughter. Not that he had ever included Mrs. Van Horn in anything, but at that moment, suppressing a destroying urge, he felt like going to the next room, shaking her out of sleep, dragging her down to the visitor's room, kicking the door open, pointing to the two entwined bodies, and saying, *See, see, see!*

If it had happened, Mrs. Van Horn probably would have said, as she often had said when romance registered, *How lovely.*

18

Dawn was foggy.

Leslie was up and was downstairs before anyone. She hadn't slept a wink. She was sitting in the parlor, quietly overlooking the tranquil grounds. Finally she rose in exhaustion and went to the intercom.

"Kent, Mr. McKnight and I will be leaving for the Cotswolds shortly. See to it that the car is ready."

She went upstairs and spent the better part of an hour doing nothing but looking at the sleeping McKnight. Having had enough of that, and because she could hear the faint, discordant sounds of "Chopsticks" coming from the piano downstairs, she went to the closet and started to remove her suitcases. Quietly bringing the first one down, she swung an idle look out the window. Below she saw an overturned wheelchair. It was her mother's. Leslie was horrified. She raced out of the room and down the stairs. In passing the piano where Chauncey was crucifying notes, she angrily said, "Chauncey, your termination check will be delivered to you in a matter of minutes."

"But I was hired by the master of the house, ma'am."

"Pack your bags and leave! *Now!*"

Outside, the overturned chair created all sorts of visions in her mind. Suddenly she spotted her mother. She was a little dirty, but she had managed to crawl to the seat in the little flower-laced alcove in the garden. Leslie was so relieved she could have fainted.

"Mother, she said, breathlessly coming over to her, and brushing her off. "What are you doing out here. I've told you, you must never, *ever* be alone."

"But I'm not alone. My nurse is with me."

"No, she isn't, darling. Chauncey is inside," Leslie said. "What are you doing out here?"

"Waiting for the children. They're coming to the Cotswolds from America."

"Sweetheart, there are no other children. And America is thousands and thousands of miles away. But we will get to the Cotswolds. I'm going to get you there if it is the last thing I do."

"Will you take the whole family?"

"If you wish."

"All of your brothers and sisters?"

"Would you like for me to have brothers and sisters, Mother?"

"You already have them. You're too wonderful to be alone."

"Okay, if you want me to have brothers and sisters, then I have brothers and sisters."

"That's nice. Now I'm happy. Because that way we will all be here in the house, and we can all do something I've always wanted to do but have never been able to do."

"What is that, Mother?"

"Protect you, my darling, darling girl."

Leslie knew what her mother was trying to say.

She cried.

19

Although the fog had not lifted, breakfast found the foursome around the breakfast table on the veranda. It was strained. Martha was in and out, and so, for that matter, was Mrs. Van Horn. But only she was dozing in and out. With the last dozing, Leslie gave her a gentle nudge. She awoke for a moment.

Trying to be conversational, she asked of anyone who was listening, "Thousands and thousands of miles. That's a frightfully long way, isn't it?"

"What are you talking about, Mother?" the doctor responded.

"The Cotswolds in America," Mrs. Van Horn said.

Dr. Van Horn withdrew his attention from her and directed it to the visitor.

"The squeaking stairs probably kept her up last night. Did they bother you at all, Mr. McKnight?"

"Not really, Doctor."

"Well, they certainly aroused me. I could have sworn I heard you up and about."

"As a matter of fact, you could have, Doctor. I was up for a bit. An old injury from the job acted up. It does that sometimes." He looked at Leslie, "But only for a little while."

"What sort of injury is it? Maybe I can take a look at it."

"I don't think so," responded Leslie, marking the first time she had faced her father or said anything to him since returning from yesterday's touring. The doctor was fully aware of it.

"Well, now, darling, is it your injury or his?"

"It's mine, Doctor," McKnight said, cutting him off from Leslie. "But Leslie has a point. As I told her, it's an old back injury that acts up whenever I don't sleep in a certain position."

"And you did *sleep* without being unduly aroused by anything?"

"*Father!*"

The doctor gave her a long look and moved on. "How did you get the injury?"

"Transporting a prisoner," McKnight said. "He didn't want to cooperate, a scuffle ensued, and he was subdued."

The doctor tossed a look at the dozing mother. "Mother, would you like to go up to your room for an injection?"

Leslie threw her napkin down. "The shots are over."

The statement was surprising. The firmness with which it was said was even more surprising.

"What did you say, dear?"

"I said the *shots* are over. Mother will *not* be taking them any more."

"Are you now studying medicine, my love?"

"No, Father, I am not. I'm looking out for my mother."

"It's a little late for that now, isn't it?"

"No, it isn't," Leslie said, unmoving. "As long as she has breath in her body, it is not too late. And her new nurse will be so informed."

"A new nurse?" He looked around. "What happened to Chauncey? Where is she?"

"She's been discharged."

"Might I ask why?"

"She shouldn't have been here in the first place. And, I might add, I've always wondered why you would have hired such a trollop."

"She was hired because she was good."

"At what?"

There was strong eye-to-eye contact. More like challenges, the eyes were. The hot moments would have continued had Kent not entered and bent to say something into the doctor's ear. Leslie didn't like that, either. It was not polite to whisper in the company of others. With his eyes even more firmly on Leslie, the doctor said to the butler, "Wheel Mother to the lift and back up to her room. That is, if I am permitted to give such an order in my own house."

"Which has been supported by my inheritance," said Leslie, as though preparing for a fight.

The doctor stood, burning with anger. He laid his napkin on the table with firmness and departed the veranda.

In the foyer stood two men. One was an intellectual sort, tall, with a heavy mustache that extended beyond tight lips. The other man was distinguished by a deep cleft in his chin and an out-of-date, tight-fitting, gray twill suit.

"Sorry to trouble you, sir," said the tall man. "But are you Dr. Bernard Van Horn?"

"Yes, of course I am."

"You have a daughter by the name of Leslie Van Horn?"

The doctor didn't respond to the question.

The tall man did the introduction. "Doctor, this is Inspector Yarborough. I am Chief Inspector Malcolm Benchley, Scotland Yard."

Without saying anything, the doctor turned and moved back to the veranda, leaving the two detectives standing there. Having heard Leslie's name, and having some idea as to what they wanted, one would have thought the doctor would have moved with more concern. He was moving leisurely when he arrived back on the veranda,

which could not be seen from the foyer. On his move, Kent was rolling Mrs. Van Horn's wheelchair out.

On the veranda, the doctor waited for a moment and casually
braced his arms on the chair he had been seated in. "Leslie, if you
don't mind, there are two policemen here, looking for you."

She sprang up from the chair: "*What??*"

"I said there are two policemen from Scotland Yard in the foyer of
the house inquiring about you."

"*Oh, my God.*" She tossed a terrified look at McKnight, who pushed
his chair back to stand, but waited to see if the doctor had anything
else to say.

Leisurely, the doctor continued. "I took the liberty of telling them
that you were not here, nor could you be reached in the Cotswolds.
Feeling that it would be of further help, I also told them that we have
a visitor from America looking for you as well. I hope I haven't over-
stepped my authority in that regard, as I have apparently been doing
in other matters."

Leslie, ignoring the dig, breathlessly said to McKnight, "Wyatt,
what do we do?"

McKnight, edgy, knew he had to come up with something. He
sat looking at the sugar bowl and tapped his pockets for a pack of
cigarettes that he didn't have with him.

"I forgot to mention, Mr. McKnight, I did not tell them you were a
policeman."

Both a frightened Leslie and a hard-thinking McKnight were concerned with the doctor's casualness. At the same time, they had to be
asking themselves why the police would be showing up at this time.
McKnight tossed away whatever he had been thinking, and sprang
up. Hurrying out, he said, "I'll meet with them, but I've got to run
upstairs for a second. Be right back."

Using the back way, he ran up to his room. He took a few puffs
from a cigarette, got the files he had been dissecting off and on, went
into Mrs. Van Horn's room for an instant, and was studying hard when
he returned downstairs. He was so engrossed that he almost returned

to the veranda with the cigarette hanging from his lips.

McKnight didn't know why the detectives would show up at this time, but he certainly knew that if they were from Scotland Yard they were going to be damnably tough. So tough, in fact, that they might even have him sliding back in the direction of the dreaded BPD syndrome. He had to find a way to gain the upper hand. He came back and sat at the table, speed-reading certain sections of the files and mumbling to himself. A couple of minutes later he said to the doctor, "I'm ready. And, Doctor, if I may ask you to go one step further; introduce me to them as *Captain* McKnight, Los Angeles police. And no matter what I say, please don't you say anything. Not a word."

He and the doctor started to go out. Leslie stopped him for a worried embrace, again to Dr. Van Horn's extreme displeasure.

"It's going to be okay," McKnight said, comforting her.

"Are you going to be all right?"

"Sure," he said. "I've got your case history here, and I've got..." He dug into his pocket and displayed the aspirins she had given him earlier at St. James. "Remember giving me these? Valium."

It was a joke, but Leslie didn't get it. She could have died.

In the foyer, Mrs. Van Horn was at her charming best.

"Oh, I tell you, she is the best daughter a mother could have. And thank you again for inquiring about her. But, between you and me, I'm going to give her a good spanking if she goes abroad again without taking Father and me. Kent, be kind enough to go and get my lovely daughter."

Kent and Mrs. Van Horn had not gotten far. Both McKnight and the doctor were surprised to find her in the foyer, exuberantly conversing, or rather, having a one-way conversation with the two detectives. Quickly, McKnight took a deep breath, tucked the file under his arm and rushed to her side. He knelt down, and held up two fingers. "Mrs. Van Horn, how many fingers am I holding up?"

The cutely excited lady said, "Four!"

"And today's date is?"

"A holiday!"

"You have a visitor from America. He likes you. And his name is?"

"Why at night!"

He looked at her with sympathy, and said to himself, "'Why at night.' Why us?" he said, referring to both sets of troubles. "You dear, precious darling, what can I say? *Erin go bragh.*"

She was wonderfully joyful. "Oh, dear, how lovely," she said. She hadn't heard the Irish phrase in years. In fact, Irish phrases weren't allowed in the Van Horn residence.

"I think she'd be better off back on the veranda," McKnight said suggestively to the butler.

The doctor watched Kent roll her away, shot another hard glance at McKnight, and said to the detectives, "Inspectors Benchley and Yarborough, this is Captain Wyatt William McKnight of the Los Angeles police."

The visitor from the States had been right. The well-known English stiff upper-lip was working. They were unsmiling, and they were going to be tough. Now he knew for sure that he had to be at the top of his game.

McKnight flashed his I.D. "Homicide."

"'Homicide'," repeated Benchley. "Quite impressive. With the murder and crime rate being what it is in Los Angeles, you must be quite the experienced one, Captain."

McKnight knew the man was trying to disarm him. The English had a way of cutting, of asking one question while meaning another. With anyone else, he could have faked it. But not with these guys. Thinking fast, he said, "We're not quite as crime-free as you, Inspector. In the first half of this year, we've already seen 237 homicides, 413 rapes, 5,864 robberies and 9,168 aggravated assaults."

"Then nationwide, your statistics must be truly frightful," said Yarborough.

"Pathetic. Two percent of all adult Americans are convicted criminals. That's living with the theory that nothing has changed: The rich get richer and the poor go to prison. And the beat goes on. You can understand why I'm retiring."

"You're going out?" asked Benchley, the taller of the two men and the man who was obviously in charge.

"As soon as I've closed the books on a fairly heavy caseload. As you can see by my files here, I've even brought some of my work with me."

"What brings you to England, Captain?"

"The alleged murderess, Leslie Van Horn."

"Gentlemen," said Dr. Van Horn, stunned and not having the slightest idea what McKnight was up to. "I think it would be best to handle this in the sitting room."

Once they went inside the smallish room with the connecting door which the doctor had gone through, and sat, Benchley, the tall one with the mustache, asked, "Captain McKnight, are we to understand you are familiar with the Van Horn case?"

"Very much so. It's one of several I'm working on. Before announcing my retirement, I was the detective of record. To date, my replacement has not been announced."

"The case history?" Benchley asked.

"May I first inquire why you're here? I mean, you were no doubt contacted by Interpol at the behest of the Los Angeles police," said McKnight.

"We're here to ascertain the whereabouts of Miss Van Horn for the Los Angeles police."

"You, of course, have no warrant or extradition papers."

"It's a letter of inquiry. Sent by fax."

"Merely inquiring. Good. I didn't think anyone back there would be jumping the gun before my return. As to the case: At approximately 21:15 on the night of July…"

"You couldn't possibly mean the month of July," Dr. Van Horn interrupted. He was seated next to the ancient Victrola in the library just off from the sitting room. "In July, Leslie was back in England, recovering from a head wound that — to this day — remains mysteriously unexplained."

McKnight was thrown off stride by the voice. His momentum slowed, he took a quick look at the file and corrected himself. "On the night of *"June* 24, last year, one detective Sergeant Verneau B. LeCoultre was shot and killed on the outskirts of Los Angeles while operating a stolen car. His death was drug-related. The gun used to kill Mr. LeCoultre was a 9-millimeter .380 PPKS Walther, a gun Mr. LeCoultre no doubt came by illegally, and, either under the influence or showing off, he taught Miss Van Horn how to use. She did. On him."

"So there's no doubt as to her involvement," confirmed Benchley.

"None whatsoever," McKnight said, continuing to surprise. "But if I were you, I wouldn't waste my time making it a matter of paramount concern."

"I'd be interested in hearing why, as a captain of police, you would take that position, sir."

McKnight started to answer, but knew he was heading for trouble. He reached for the bottle of pills. They weren't going to be of any help. Holding them in his hands, he started patting for a cigarette. Finding them, he lit up.

When the smoke carried into the other room, Dr. Van Horn called from the library, "Please do not smoke in my home."

McKnight took a final puff, and put the cigarette out.

Benchley pushed. "You used the term 'under the influence,' and then you say the policeman's death was drug-related. Who was using the drugs?"

"Good question," contributed Dr. Van Horn. "And who was it that shot and wounded Leslie? And why?"

"Doctor," responded Benchley, "if you don't mind."

"Miss Van Horn was shot by the policeman, Detective Sergeant LeCoultre." McKnight said, refusing to be caught. "The one who was using the narcotics."

"Oh, really?" exclaimed Yarborough.

Benchley frowned. "A detective sergeant was using narcotics?"

"Heroin, in fact. It was pure and uncut. And before that, the gentleman was an alcoholic. And burglar. Mr. LeCoultre was the epitomy of the walking wounded, which is why I harbored no sympathies for him."

"But he wasn't the only policeman who was on drugs, was he, Mr. McKnight?"

"I wouldn't know, Doctor," McKnight said, trying for deflection. "I wouldn't know because I'm in homicide, not narcotics."

"And, Doctor, if you don't mind, please let us conduct the inquiries," Yarborough said.

"Now, Captain, you said you are here because of — your term — the 'murderess' Leslie Van Horn. Yet you imply you are not here working on the case."

"I'm not. As I said, or as I had intended to say, I'm here because of the parents of the 'alleged' murderess. I did not say I was here working on the case. If I were here working on the case, Scotland Yard would have been duly notified by me or my department. I'm an old family friend..."

"Of whose?" the doctor asked from the library room.

"Of Mrs. Van Horn's," McKnight said with deep irritation. He turned back to the detectives. "Because of Mrs. Van Horn's worsening condition, I thought it best to come over here and give reassurance that there was nothing to worry about, as far as her daughter was concerned."

"That could be considered a conflict of interest."

"Not if my interest as a policeman is on the wane."

"Because you are retiring?"

"More because of my interest in the cause of justice. Less because, despite what any warrant or extradition papers may indicate in the future, as an LAPD captain I'd say Leslie Van Horn cannot, and indeed should not, be convicted."

"My word, man," pronounced Yarborough, "for a policeman you're taking a rather extraordinary position."

"And, really," supported Benchley, "if Miss Van Horn is duly charged with the crime of murder, isn't the matter of conviction up to your courts? And not some police captain."

"Not 'some' police captain, Inspector; the police captain of record. And what you are implying hinges on the word: *If*. And that is, gentlemen, *if* the case ever gets to court. But even at that — at the time of trial, I would be considered the policeman of record. Without me, the Los Angeles district attorney would have no case."

Startled, Benchley asked, "Are you implying, Captain, there is a possibility you would not testify?"

"What I am saying, sir, is that if the prosecution depended on my testimony, and/or the evidence obtained via my efforts, the prosecution would lose. The district attorney is mindful of the fact that I've never presented a case to them that they did not win. We're talking one hundred percent."

"I dare say, Captain, it must not have been easy for you, working your way up the ranks. America is not known for being charitable to members of your race to begin with. If your actions appear less than…"

"Excuse me…" McKnight interrupted. "Henshaw, is it?"

"Chief Inspector *Benchley*."

"Excuse me, Chief Inspector Benchley, but race is not an issue in this matter. If America has a problem, it is merely a reflection of the world's problems. And I say that being fully cognizant of England's troubles and the Yard's questionable record. As to the case, if my actions are to be indicative of anything, let it be my passion for the cause of justice."

"I presume," said the chief inspector, "you would inform the prosecution of your 'passion for justice' at some point before trial?"

"As discussed with my immediate supervisor, a Captain…a Captain…???" He was stopped. He was doing well, but the mind stopped delivering. The roll was over. Dr. Van Horn, who could not see him from the other room but missed the voice, virtually skipped to the doorway.

McKnight started sweating. It appeared he was relapsing and would not be able to continue. For some reason he was in fear of breaking down. He patted his pockets for a cigarette, lit it, took three or four quick puffs and put it out. Recovering, he said, "Please excuse me, gentlemen. As a Californian, I'm not accustomed to your climate."

"Mr. McKnight," said the doctor, "in summer our climate cannot be very much different than yours."

"Apparently my flu bugs haven't gotten the message. As a doctor you should know they are independent little bastards, who are constantly sticking their noses in places where they don't belong. They are a lot like people."

The doctor returned to his seat.

Benchley, in a voice loaded with suspicion, and wondering why the man had been so cutting with his host, asked, "Are you saying you have the flu, Captain?"

"*Had* the flu. Past tense. I'm in recovery, but as you can see, I've retained some of the symptoms. Chills, sweats, shakes, nose irritation, et cetera," McKnight answered. "Now, where were we?"

"We were discussing your immediate supervisor, a Captain…?"

"Devro," McKnight bluffed. "Captain Roland T. Devro, whom I urge you to call, or perhaps I can call for you."

Benchley declined the offer.

"Whatever," McKnight continued, "my position regarding the Van Horn case has been, and will continue to be, made indisputably clear to any and all parties."

"Then, sir," Benchley said, "wouldn't it be advisable for your district attorney to consult with your commander, seek a delay, and assign another team of investigators to the case?"

"You may advise them of that, if you wish."

Yarborough supported Benchley by saying, "I dare say, sir, if the team is at all worth its salt, it seems they can come up with sufficient evidence that would warrant Miss Van Horn's extradition. They could have already done it. As you've indicated, the case is already a year old. They've certainly had enough time."

"But they *haven't* done it, which clearly indicates my departments lack of interest. But, gentlemen, let me caution you: If Leslie Van Horn were not innocent, innocent by reason of a troubled childhood, caused by a weakened mother and the happenstance of birth…"

"I'd be careful, Mr. McKnight," Dr. Van Horn said, feeling he had been silent too long.

McKnight overlooked him. "If Leslie Van Horn were not inno-cent, innocent by reason of momentary insanity, traumatized by a crazed and drugged-out detective — a *law* officer — who invaded the sanctity of her home, then my course of action, and the actions taken prior to my flight here, would have been quite different."

"And what course of action was that, Captain? Benchley asked.

"Come, come, Inspector," McKnight said, indicating he wasn't going to reveal anything. It was a bluff. He couldn't remember.

"Captain," Benchley said, trying it another way, "both you and the letter of inquiry state that Mr. LeCoultre was shot to death. May I inquire as to the whereabouts of the gun?"

"Interesting," blurted Dr. Van Horn.

"*Doctor!*" Yarborough exclaimed.

"You've done your homework, Inspector," McKnight said.

"I'm wondering if you were in any shape to do yours," Dr. Van Horn said, refusing to be quiet.

"*Doctor, please,*" Yarborough said. This time it was more of a plea.

Benchley picked up: "Captain McKnight, as captain of record you would have had access to the evidence from day one, and as late as your flight to London."

"You can assume as much, sir."

"Well, in having had that, and since you are such a staunch de-fender of Miss Van Horn…"

"Excuse me," McKnight cut in. "I am not so much of a defender of Miss Van Horn as I am a defender of justice. The LAPD's code is to *protect and serve.*"

"Thank you for informing me," Benchley said. "But it seems to me that if you had access, you could have taken the evidence and done anything with it that you wished."

"You're referring to the murder weapon, of course. If you are, you are quite correct. I could have done anything with it."

"Captain, I must tell you, sir, as a professional man sworn to uphold the law, I have difficulty in accepting your position."

Said McKnight: "If I were a professional man devoid of compassion, Inspector, I would have difficulty in *taking* that position."

Yarborough got back into the act. "What the chief inspector is saying, sir, is that if you've done something with the evidence, or something to obstruct..."

"Listen," McKnight interrupted, "I don't need either of you to tell me anything about evidence and/or American law. And I certainly don't appreciate what you are implying. Now, I don't wish to be rude about this thing, but I've probably handled more murder cases on my lunch breaks than either of you have handled in a lifetime. Cutting to the chase on this particular case, even my commander, a very studious and highly respected officer of the law, recognizes the fallibility of the Van Horn case, and while he does not condone my every action, he nonetheless applauds my view and would be hard pressed to recommend anything beyond mild censure. My commander will also tell you, and I'm certain your individual commanders will agree, that the withholding of evidence — as you wrongly suspect, is not an extraditable offense. Should there be a change in Miss Van Horn's status, meaning if she is duly charged, listed as a fugitive, and a warrant is issued, she still would have little or nothing to worry about. As the lead detective, I might not be able to testify. Miss Van Horn is attractive, intelligent, and eligible. In fact, we both are eligible. And we do very much like each other, which means marriage is not out of the question. That being the case, it is well to remember that a man cannot be compelled to testify against his wife."

A long, uneasy quiet ensued. The American would remain unyielding. With nothing to be gained, departing words were said, and the two men left.

At the parked car in front of the house. Benchley withdrew the faxed letter of inquiry from his pocket. Had it not been for laws against littering, he might have torn it up and thrown it away.

Yarborough saw the terminating look on his face. "She's in there, you know."

"I know she is. But it's an American problem," Benchley said succinctly. "No cop, no gun, no evidence. They'll never be able to extradite her, let alone convict her. I'm through with it."

Dr. Van Horn was very unsettled over hearing McKnight say that a man could not testify against his wife. It of course meant that, if he understood him correctly, he was thinking about marrying his daughter. What saved him, for the moment, was that McKnight had said some other things that were not true, and more than likely the statement was made simply to protect Leslie. He momentarily buoyed himself and stepped from the library.

"A splendid piece of work, old chap. Remarkable," he said to the perspiring McKnight, who had slumped down in a chair one of the policemen had used. He was looking as though he had just been through a major prizefight. "I must say you've earned a 'shot.'"

A cramped McKnight looked up at him, wordlessly.

"I'm speaking of brandy, of course."

"Doctor, you tried your damnedest to sabotage me. Why?"

"Oh, come, now. We're all entitled to a little joshing every now and then."

"Call it what you want, but you were trying to hang me — or Leslie," McKnight said. "Let me tell you something, sir, I don't know what your game is, but get this in your mind: No matter what you do; no matter what you try, you are *not* going to sink this ship. Leslie's nor mine. If time, bullets or narcotics couldn't do it, you can't either."

Dr. Van Horn looked at him dismissively and returned to the veranda. He wasn't fully inside before Leslie was on her feet.

"What happened? Where's Wyatt?"

"Wherever he is, he's no doubt thinking he can pilfer something from the medicine room. Since cursing me and threatening the police, there's no telling what he's up to. And he said something about narcotics. Leslie, I have something extremely serious I want to…"

It was too late. She was gone. Dr. Van Horn looked at Mrs. Van

Horn and said, "Mother, did it ever occur to you, your daughter is in love with a Negro?"

"How lovely," she said.

The medicine room was locked, but that was the first place Leslie looked. Frantically she bounded upstairs. She looked in his room, her room and the bathroom. Worried stiff, she hastened back down again and was drawn to the billiard room, which was in the basement.

McKnight was smoking freely and hiding pain when she at last found him.

"You had me worried," she said, showing relief by tightly hugging him. "I'm so glad you're all right. You are you all right, aren't you?"

"I'm fine."

"Am I on my way to the chain gang yet?"

"Not yet."

Timidly she asked, "So, how did it go?"

"Okay."

"Just *okay?*"

"It went fine."

"You don't look it."

"Just tired, I guess," he said. "I've been sitting here thinking about what I used to be, when character, and principle, and standards counted; thinking about when I was young, and filled with hope and promise, and not the sorry disappointment I am today."

With care, she removed the cigarette from his hand and put it out. "You're smoking, but you're not a disappointment. And you will always have principle. Even in your worst state, you will always be a good policeman — and a better man." She quickly added warmly, "But you're not leaving here."

He was wired to another thought. "This man. Up, down, in, out. One minute you're the greatest thing that ever walked the Earth, and the next, he's trying to sink you with me. *Why?* What's he up to?"

"Who? What are you talking about?"

"Your father." He dropped it and said, "Where's the john? I gotta go to the john."

"The *restroom* or *bathroom* is right there where I just tossed the cigarette."

He acknowledged the lack of thought, stood and walked over to the door. He again said, *"What could the man be up to?"* He was talking to himself as he went in and closed the door.

Strangely, McKnight had a strong change of attitude once he was behind the bathroom door. His voice was light and relieved. Even fun. Talking over the running faucet, he called out, "Hey, babe, you know what I haven't had since being here in London?"

"'London.' Great. You remember," she said, feeling better and picking a ball on the table to playfully roll it around.

"I haven't had tea and scones."

"And not scones and tea?" she joked.

"Nope. Tea and scones."

"If you keep that up you'll be a full-fledged Englishman."

"Never. England or the English is not the stuff of legend."

"So now that you're doing that well, tell me what happened upstairs," she said anxiously. "And what was this about Father?"

"Oh, with the Scotland Yard guys? Talk about winging it. Boy, did I do a number on them," he chuckled. "But it worked. You're safe."

"Really???"

"Yep."

"Honest to God??"

"The posse is gone, and I seriously doubt they'll ever return. Or anybody else, for that matter. There'll be noooo extradition for you, my lovely."

"Oh, Wyatt, that's wonderful! *Fabulous!* Come on out so I can give you a hug."

"In a minute."

"I want to hear all about it. Did they find out I didn't do anything?"

"Not exactly."

"Oh, this is wonderful-wonderful news. *Smashing.*" She gave it a thought. "Why do you think they showed up at this time?"

"Cops usually come when they're called."

"What? What are you saying?"

"Nothing."

As he had, she dropped it. She was still upbeat. "I'm so happy. Now, all we have to do is work on your problem."

That did it as far as he was concerned. She had no way of knowing what he had been up to, but behind the door, and probably much to his own shock and amazement, and certainly to his disappointment, a syringe was ready. Using a towel, he had made a tourniquet by tying off a thigh and was all set for a patting fix. Needle at a 45-degree angle, rotated to avoid scarring, and ready to go in the same direction as the blood was flowing, he was doing it by the book. It was the closest he had come since leaving Los Angeles, but when he heard the word *problem* and the concern that went along with it, he couldn't do it. He sighed heavily. He couldn't remember who he said it to, but something he had said not too long ago crept back into his mind. *"After you take that first hit, you don't care what you're doing. You take a second and God himself doesn't care. After that, both your will and your mind are gone. The monkey is on your back, and nobody but nobody knows what an addict will do."*

Slowly the troubled man untied the towel, pulled his pants up, placed the syringe back into the little black encasement and put it back into his pocket. He stayed looking in the mirror for a long time, shook his head in disgust, and said to himself, "How low are you gonna go, Mac? *How low are you gonna go?*"

For a purposeful sound effect, he flushed the toilet. As he watched the swirling water in the bowl, over the noise he said, "I don't have a problem."

"Darling, yes, yes, yes, you do. You're constantly sweating. One minute you're hot, the next you're cold. You cramp, you crave sweets. You want salt. You never complete a meal. Let's face it, love, you can't even beat the cigarette habit."

He tossed her words around in his mind, thought about what he had done and came out of the bathroom, full of renewed resolve. "You know what I've got to do? Get someplace where I can rid myself of all temptations. That's what I've got to do. *I've got to do it. I simply have to do it.*"

"What temptations are you speaking of, love?"

"Nothing."

"But you must be talking about something."

He didn't want to go into it. "When did you say we were going to your place?"

"I was thinking tomorrow. But now I have to stay long enough to interview a new nurse for Mother. A competent one. But what temptations were you speaking of, Wyatt?"

"Can't your father hire a nurse?"

"Father will never bring another nurse into this house to attend to my mother as long as I am alive. Male or female."

McKnight noticed the look behind the statement. She was angry. "But it's his house, love."

"It's *my* mother."

The implications were clear. Not necessarily wanting to get away from the subject, he asked, "Let me ask you something: The people in the hospital said I had this poison in my system. And another thing that made my case so rough was my age, blood type, the uncut heroin, which was mixed with a poisonous poppy and something called pheno...cyclohexel...piperidine? Somebody told me what it was, but I forgot. Got any idea what it was?"

He had the name wrong. It was phenylcyclohexylamine, but it didn't make any difference. She couldn't go back that far.

"I wish I could help, but I can't."

"Do you remember how you learned to do all those things?"

"No, I don't. The knowledge just came. Genetics, maybe; maybe from books. I don't know. I was told I was once strongly into horticulture and chemistry. Wyatt, last night won't be repeated, will it?"

"Last night won't be repeated, counselor. That's a promise."

He gave it serious thought and extended his hand, indicating they should leave.

"Why, Mr. Rhett Butler," she joked in a Southern accent, "I do hope your intentions are honorable."

"They are. But we're going up to see your mother."

He hadn't been as light as she had been.

Mrs. Van Horn was in bed when the two came up. Her room had an Oriental flavor to it. She was awake, and Leslie could hardly believe how beautifully lucid she was. She sat on the bed with tears in her eyes as her mother spoke from the heart.

"Darling, you and you alone have held this family together. It has not been easy. It is very difficult for you to fully understand, but you have been marvelously courageous. Despite the many horrors you have suffered because I have not been there for you, I have longed to tell you: I love you. I beg for your forgiveness, and I hope the blessed joy you now know will last forever."

Leslie was too choked for words. McKnight, who had been standing by the dresser, came over and sat with her. Mrs. Van Horn gave him a smile.

"She's fortunate to have you."

McKnight held her hand. "I'm fortunate to have her."

It was embarrassing. It was going to hurt Leslie terribly, but he had to do it. Honesty and the will to keep fighting forced his hand. He reached inside his pocket and extracted the encased syringe. Leslie's eyes widened in sorrowful disappointment.

"Mrs. Van Horn," he said, placing the encasement into her feeble hands, "this belongs to you. When I came up to prepare myself for those two gentlemen, I came in here and took it. I apologize. I was dishonest. I was weak. And I was terribly, terribly stupid. I promise you I won't give in to temptation ever again."

Leslie was near tears; Mrs. Van Horn was touched.

"I understand," said the mother. She looked at it for a long while, touching and studying the velvet. Sadly, she didn't know what it was.

Leslie was still damp-eyed when night came. Earlier McKnight had been in her room with her. He didn't remain, because he felt his presence was contributing to her disappointment. And his hands were shaking. He kissed her on the cheek, quietly said "I'm sorry," and went to his room. She didn't respond. She remained downcast, unable even to think about the victory that had been achieved with the police.

If he had resorted to stealing her mother's syringe, it was bad. Truly, truly bad. He couldn't last much longer. She knew it.

At midnight Leslie was still dispirited, and had only moved from her high-backed chair to the corner of the bed. Later, unable to sleep, she checked his room and came downstairs for a cup of coffee. She thought he was asleep, but he wasn't. Passing through the dining room and heading for the kitchen, she happened to notice the medicine-room door was open. It should have been locked; Wyatt couldn't have opened it. He didn't have a key.

Thoughtfully, she closed the door and went into the kitchen to prepare a pot of coffee. When she came back out, she went to the telephone. Getting the Whitehurst station, she asked for the black detective whom she had spoken with in the past. Devro was out for the day. She had his home number, but it was in her telephone book at home in the Cotswolds. Too exhausted to think, she asked to speak with anyone who could give her some information regarding medication for Captain Wyatt McKnight. It was a long shot, and from the man's tone she knew she was not going to get much information, if at all. She got no information.

She concluded that she would have done better by calling the rehabilitation center again, but she was fearful of doing that because she thought someone might have recognized her voice, or might have traced the call back to England. The same could have been done with the police, but she didn't think about it.

The depressed woman spent the rest of the night at the dining-room table, sipping coffee and worrying.

McKnight, on the other hand, spent the night on the floor in the bathroom. He had had a rough time of it and had wanted to soak himself in a tub of hot water after she had checked up on him. He didn't do it, because he thought the running water would awaken the household.

He was also trying to stay away from Mrs. Van Horn's needle.

Full morning found Dr. Van Horn coming downstairs. He went directly to the library. Humming a merry tune, he cranked up the Victrola and sent Mozart swirling around the room. The doctor mounted the ladder and began his search. Moving up a little higher, he instinctively turned and looked down. Leslie was standing there.

"Aha," he said, brightly, and as though nothing had happened, "the little breath of sunshine is here to check up on her pater, to see how prepared he's going to be for his 'colleagues of the board' this morning. Rest assured, my love, I will dazzle them."

She turned the Victrola off, and paced a bit. Taking her own time, she was summoning courage.

"You're frightfully quiet, my love. And I've never seen you looking quite so tired and haggard. Surely you can't still be bothered by that little tiff we had at the table yesterday morning. We must have an understanding, Leslie. Mother gets what Mother needs. Are you with me on that?"

She wasn't listening.

"Oh, and there was another curious little item I wanted to make you aware of. It is about Mr. McKnight. He said a rather strange thing to those two policeman that were here. He said a man couldn't testify against his wife. He told those bloakes that, and he isn't even married. Don't you find that interesting?"

Whatever she had in mind couldn't wait any longer. Under any other circumstances she would have questioned him about the medicine-room door being invitingly unlocked. This was more pressing.

She decided she would form the question in a way that would allow him easy access to the road of denial. She was direct.

"Deny what you did to me as a child, Father."

He said nothing.

20

It was minutes later, but it felt like hours. Upstairs in the bathroom, the cassette recorder McKnight had brought with him was pumping out gospel music. It was hard-driving. He was partially dressed in a sweatsuit, but he was on his knees in the prayer position. Something was definitely wrong with this man, a man who had long feared wallowing in a narcotic-starved mental breakdown.

He was holding a straight razor in his hand, his eyes were glassy, and when he stood he didn't know whether to first use the razor on the soap or on his chin. Confused, he placed it on the sink. He checked his arms; his legs. They were pumping for a shot. Should he put soap on them, cut them? He picked up the razor again, held it for a second or two, and placed it back down. Then, for no reason at all, he screamed in silent agony. Now he was cold, very cold. He was shivering. There was a knock on the door, which he heard, but he didn't know which way to turn. Over the music, the knocking continued. He decided to stop looking. He sat on the side of the tub and lit a cigarette.

It was Dr. Van Horn on the other side of the door. Getting no response to his taps, he entered.

McKnight continued smoking. He was staring blankly at the wall. The doctor moved in to cut the cassette recorder off.

He was terse. "I have something to say to you. I suggest you remove your clothing, take a cold shower and re-dress yourself. I shall be waiting in the guest bedroom. And put that cigarette out."

McKnight didn't move. The doctor took it upon himself to remove the cigarette from his fingers. He turned the shower on, and pointed. "Get in there."

The doctor had been waiting eighteen minutes when McKnight appeared in his room. He had changed into a sweatsuit, he was quiet and there was something about his look that said he was close to being normal.

"I will be brief and direct," Dr. Van Horn said. He was seated in the chair across from the bed. "I have known of your addiction since your arrival. You are too far gone to last much longer. At the moment, I don't know if you are into your game-playing mode or not. I can assure you that I am not. I insist that you leave my home immediately. If you leave quietly and alone, and I stress the word *alone,* I will supply you with enough morphine to last you for one year. Additionally, I will see to it that, in some way, you are supplied with a pad of prescriptions — American prescriptions — in an amount that will last you for another year. In addition, I will allow you as many Transatlantic calls as you'd care to make. Have I made myself clear?"

McKnight looked at him thoughtfully.

"Have I made myself clear, Mr. McKnight?"

"Yes, you have, Doctor," McKnight said soberly.

"I'm glad I have, because I want you to be sane enough to understand."

"You know, that's quite an offer to make to an addict. When you called the Los Angeles police the other night, what was the official quote? *'The captain's recovery is in serious doubt'?"*

There was no response.

"You did call them, Doctor. I know you did. And I can tell you how I know. But if that's what they told you, they're right. Any minute now, I'm going down for the count. We both know it. I've seen enough hardcore addicts to know when it's over. But enough about the highlife. Now, the situation at hand. She's gone, sir. Leslie killed a cop, but *you* killed *her*. And now you want to bury her by trying to get me to sneak out of here, so you can tell her that I left crawling and whining, just to hurt her even more, for some rot you did. Maybe you'll tell her that I was going to do myself in. I feel like it. Oh, God, do I feel like it. It's worse now than ever. But I'm not gonna do it. I've still got some fight in me. I may not win, but as long as I'm sane, as long as I'm breathing, I'll be fighting. You'll go out before me. On your way, re-member I said it. And let me tell you why I said it, Mister: In all my years of dealing with people, you take the cake. You're sick; sicker than the three of us you've been trying to take advantage of. You thrive on weakness. Today mine, yesterday Leslie's, the day before the mother's. I'm tempted to ask how that makes you feel. But that would be a dumb question on my part, because you don't even know the meaning of the word. Now, I've got a choice. I could, right here and now, end that miserable thing you call a life, and, so help me, I'd take full and absolute responsibility for it. Or I...or I could....I could...."

"Or you could *what*, Mr. McKnight?" Dr. Van Horn asked after waiting a moment or two.

McKnight's mind was on the way out again. He tried and tried, but there was nothing there. He was not shaking or sweating, but his eyes were growing ever more glassy.

The doctor leaned forward in the chair. "I can't hear you, Mr. McKnight. You'll have to speak up."

"Sssssh. They're here. Somebody's listening."

"Are they really?"

"Yes."

"It's the bitch. Leslie," said the doctor.

He shouldn't have said it. McKnight's hand shot inside his sweatsuit pocket and came out wielding the straight razor. In a flash, he leaped over the bed and landed at the foot of the chair the doctor was sitting in, almost knocking him over. With the razor at the frozen man's throat, he rattled, *"Say it again and you won't live to see tomorrow."*

And just as rapidly he withdrew. He landed on the other side of the room and made another change. It was as if nothing had happened, and as if he were talking to a long-lost friend.

"Hey, remember in the hospital? Remember what you and I used to talk about? The degree of mental illness? You'll appreciate this: The other night I'm in the lobby of this bar, with a broad. English. Right off the bat, she starts talking about guns, and telling me about this history-making recovery she's made, all because I shot her up here in the...the...what do you call this thing up here?"

"The head."

"The other one."

"The kidneys."

"The kidneys. Right. She's saying I shot her in the kidneys while I was strung out on drugs."

"Imagine. You on drugs."

"Can you beat that? You want to talk about an addict? Talk about Sherlock Holmes. Stone junkie. But there was another broad, English, who almost did the number on me. I got so wiped out that when I woke up in the hospital I was scraping the paint off anything I could find, and eating it! Even off the bed! The people in there said I got mercury or lead in the system. Memory is affected. My memory? Affected? What a joke. Pal, they told me that and I snuck out and got some China White, some bleached crystals, got some ICE, mixed it with crack, and went for the tar. Yes, baby, that's what I did. And over the weekend? 'Member that long, hot, dry, wet, weekend? I got me some Pheno... cyclo... hexel-something. And I was cool. Floating. You hear me, Jack? I was up there! Why'd I do it? Because I *remembered* where. I knew *where* and *how* to get it. I mean she's sick, and they think I'm addicted. Ah, but she's smart. She knows an addict likes to return to the source; the giver."

"Which is why you're here."

"Right! You got it." The detective stopped. "Hey, what happened to the other guy?"

"He went back to hospital."

"Stockholm Syndrome got him, huh?"

"Yeah."

"Y'know what that is?"

"Lover's quarrel."

"You got it. Say, who are you?"

"The other guy."

"You a doctor?"

"Sort of."

"Great. Means you know what I'm talkin' about. Anyhow, we know the body needs salt. The body minerals are depleted and they go wacko. But not this cookie. In all my years of being on this sorry excuse called a police department, I've never even had nose candy. How many of these apes walking around with badges can say that? You called 'em, you talked to 'em. But lemme tell you what gets me. You got these legalization-talkin' sonsabitiches calling the queen mother of narcotics a chemical substance. A *chemical substance*? A chemical *wha-a-a-t-tt*!? *Va fata la gamma nata!* It's *HORSE*! And for years, decades upon decades, when the horse was stampeding the minds of the underclass, when it was relegated to the junkyards, and barrios, and ghettoes of these good and precious United States, no-body gave a good goddamn. But the moment — the *very instant* it started slaughtering and conquering the minds of Mr. and Mrs. Snow White, the genetically pure…the nation…the nation declares…the nation…. de…"

The ranting slowed to a stop. A new thought entered his mind. The words had a familiarity to them. He started repeating them. "…The nation declares *war* on it. Just a minute. Horse? War? Conquering? No. What is it!? *Conquest.* Conquest, slaughter. Famine. Death. ….What's that from? I've heard it before….. *Conquest. Slaughter. Famine. Death*? It's the four something…. the four *what*?!!"

"The Four Horsemen of the Apocalypse, Mr. McKnight."

"*Yes*, but it means something. C'mon! What's it mean?!"

"The end."

"The end. The end of *what*??? C'mon. Nations don't end. You can't kill land."

"Right again."

"C'mon! *What do you kill?!*"

"People."

"*People!*" The detective reeled away from the doctor and landed on the other side of the room, holding his head. He was like an erupting volcano. "Oh, my Godddddd! *Oh, my Godddddddd!!!*"

He came back to the doctor. He was on his knees, tears welling the eyes. "Doctor, please don't think I'm paranoid, but listen to this. Please, just listen. Listen. You gotta listen for a second: Nation's black males: Number one cause of death? Homicide. *Homicide* at the hands of his brother, <u>but</u> spurred by the needle. Young black female, *nine times* more likely to die of this virus thing, started in Africa, *spurred* by the needle. Doctor, please, talk to me. Tell me what I'm thinking is too preposterous. Tell me I'm insane! Crazy! Wrong! Tell me anything! Tell me I'm wrong, wrong, wrong, wrong-wrong!!! Tell me I'm out of my mind! Tell me I'm nuts; that I'm a basket case! I mean, the homicides, the virus, the mortality rate — even the black prison population! Out of control! C-c-could there be any truth to...? Oh, God. Oh, God-d-d-ddd!!! Ooooh, my Lorddd, no!!! *No, no, no, no, NO! It can't be! It can't be!!!*"

"Any truth to what, Mr. McKnight?"

"Talk to me!! You know what I'm saying!!!"

"Yes, but I want you to say it."

"This...this...this...thing about black people...This thing about..."

"Go ahead. Say it, Mr. McKnight. This thing about...?"

"...About b-b-blacks and genocide? C-c-c-could there be any truth to it?"

"You tell me."

He was back on his feet, shouting over the man. "No! Goddammit!

You have to tell me! You represent the power! You *are* the power structure! And you're a doctor! You're the expert in damaging fetuses! *You're an expert in killing!"*

"You're a sick man, sir. Sick and racially dangerous."

"My race is in danger because of their race-ending stupidity, aided and abetted by people like you, the goddamned criminal elite, and you're telling me *I'm* sick?!"

He was back with the razor. The doctor pushed back in his chair, eased to his feet and went to the door. He wasn't as outwardly fearful as one might have expected.

"I want my daughter to witness this."

"Get her! Get her!!! And if she's the same somebody who's been trying to get me to go home with her, tell her it's time to hit the road! I wanna ride the queen's horse one more time! Me! Wyatt McKnight! On the horse! Ridin' with Harry."

The doctor slipped out. The sick man watched the door as it closed, then looked at the razor he had been holding onto tightly. Suddenly he dropped it like it was electrified. Terrified, he jumped back.

The razor had almost attacked him.

In her room, Leslie had packed her suitcase and had gotten some boxes and was removing things that had been in the room long, long before she knew she even had a room. She was thoughtful and quiet.

The doctor knocked on the door. Without waiting to be asked in, he entered.

"You'd better come with me."

She refused to lower her dignity by even looking his way.

"It's about your friend. Captain Wyatt W."

The woman was out of her room and into his room in a flash.

"Wyatt...???" she said, moving to the bed to be with him.

He had undergone another rapid change. He was low, downcast, and he was sitting on the side of the bed, sweating and shaking profusely.

"I'm fine, babe. I'm all right." His voice was hoarse and thin.

"In your earlier moments of lucidity, Mr. McKnight," said the doctor, who was standing in the doorway, "your bursts of irrationality and death-threatening violence aside, you were saying some very odd and provocative things, so I find it difficult to know what it means when you say you are fine and when you are not. I am most loath to repeat the term you used, but given your low opinion of Leslie and myself..."

"Stop it, Father! Just stop it!"

McKnight spoke through his pain. "S-s-s-sweets, w-w-we gotta get out of here. W-w-we gotta get out of here, but I...but...I...I'm too sick to leave. I'm hurtin', babe. I want to die." He curled down on the bed.

"You're going to be all right, baby; you're going to be all right." She was patting and consoling.

He started rocking. "Every bone in my body aches. In between my toes. My groin, my gums. My gums, they're killing me. I'm freezing. Just let me die...I wanna die..."

"Father, help me! Help me!"

Dr. Van Horn came over, motioning for the man to open his mouth. He took a very brief look inside, withdrew, and led the reluctant Leslie to the connecting room for a low-toned, doctor-like consultation.

"The problem, as I see it, is that your friend is beyond addiction, and maybe beyond help, as least as far as getting help here in England. Without question, he'd be better off back in the States. But that's your decision. Being a policeman, he naturally didn't want anyone to know he had been injecting himself, nor how much. No matter what he tells you, he has had narcotics in extraordinary amounts. And I'd say he's had some within the past three or four days, certainly within the week."

"Oh, my God!" said a hurt Leslie. *"Oh, my God."*

"He eventually switched to injecting himself in the mouth. It is a phantom ache now, but he did experience prolonged oral pain from before. He has traces of tears and lacerations in the mouth. In addition to his gums, I'd say he has been shooting himself between the toes, and I would not be surprised if he hasn't been shooting himself directly into a certain appendage as well. The penis. He's complained of groin pain. At the moment he is undergoing difficulty because his bone marrow is narcotized. As to treatment, I believe Methadone was out. Or very limited, at best. His case is far too severe. He could have been on Busoco or on Corbomazaphine, two drugs they were trying out in the States not too long ago. Perhaps he could have had Naltrexone or Buprenorphine. I can tell you this as far as his addiction goes: In addition to heroin, he's had some sort of synthetic drugs, causing neurochemical and molecular changes in the brain. If it happens again, he could go into MPTP — Parkinson's. In that case the only thing that could possibly save him would be an eventual transplant, from a fetus. Which I would recommend."

Leslie was too stunned to speak. She was on the verge of collapse.

"Miss Van Horn!"

Martha was screaming from the bottom of the stairs. *"Miss Van Horn!!! Come quick! Come quick!! He's broken down the door!!!*

Dazed, Leslie left the room to see what the hollering was about.

Martha was still screaming. *"The medicine room, Ma'am! He's trying to get in there! Your gentleman friend has broken down the door!!!*

She was not in shape, but she fired off a *"Get Kent!"* and fled down the stairs.

When she got close to the medicine room she could see that McKnight had already broken down the door and was fighting with the cabinets. Not finding what he was looking for, he went to the refrigerated units and began clearing them out. He saw the needles and went for them on a tear. Leslie screamed and pounced on his back.

Kent, arriving seconds later, joined the melee. Restraining the man was no easy task. With Leslie begging and fighting, McKnight finally went down, but he was still holding onto a syringe. At the height of the scuffle, and without using the syringe, suddenly his eyes took on a dreamlike quality. His mouth curled upward, then went straight. Soon the body surrendered itself in absolute relaxation. All the tensions were gone. Euphoria replaced pain.

He felt good. *Lord, God-Jesus, did he feel good.*

From his hand, the syringe rolled free.

Leslie thought he was dead. She was petrified. In panic, she began talking to him, slapping his face and rolling his head from side to side. She felt for a pulse and a heartbeat. Both were still there. It was an irregular beat at first, then it moved with a certain predictable beat. Still straddling him, she turned to check the rest of the body. At his feet, she saw the doctor.

Then she knew.

It was either in the foot, ankle or leg. But Dr. Van Horn had sent the needle point home, and was still astride the man. Leslie was devastated. She almost fainted. She leaned down to check the unconscious man's pulse. His cardiac functions had slowed, but not to the point of death. She caressed his face and, over and over again, she said something loving.

She kissed him, then looked back at her father. She spoke quietly, simply, and pointedly. Her large elegant eyes didn't move.

"If he dies, you die."

21

Late afternoon surrounded the beautiful house in the city of Bath. It had a funereal quality about it. Everything seemed slowed, as though even the light of day had abandoned responsibility. The day had grayed.

The only thing lively around the Van Horn residence was the lady of the house. Her voice was laced with romanticism.

"It is a wonderful drive, isn't it, Kent?"

"It's lovely, ma'am."

From the tree-lined serenity outside, the voices invited attention to inside the garage. There Mrs. Van Horn, her pale, delicate features framed by a bonnet made of lace, was perched in the driver's seat of the old Bentley. She was lovingly negotiating through imagined streets and picturesque lanes in a sturdy, motionless vehicle that had been elevated on blocks for years.

Kent, his slender, nose-pinched face topped by a beret, sat dutifully in the rear seat, making like the perfect passenger. As he had done many times before, he was listening without interruption.

"These afternoon drives so remind me of the young years, when Father and I were courting," said Mrs. Van Horn as her gloved hands made a gentle turn on Nowhere Street to No Place Lane, her story never really varying.

"Father was such a handsome young swain. But my father, a stern and Victorian man, never liked him because he was Japanese. And so I wouldn't allow him to take my hand in marriage until after he had graduated university. He did. And we were married in the Cotswolds, my favorite place in all the world. What a glorious event that was. You have never seen so many flowers; so many beautiful gowns, and lovely faces. It was all so enchanting. And our honeymoon was divine. Since then, my life has been a dream. Up, up, and away. He became a pilot, and we agreed we wouldn't have children. And it's wonderful that we didn't. And did you know, Kent, in all the years, Daddy and I have had only one failing. Between you and I, I still harbor regret. Maybe he'll get around to it one day. I pray that he does. But he has never flown me back to Ireland. Ireland should have been the king of England. Like our beloved daughter. The queen."

22

Leslie had made a quick trip into town. When she returned, having purchased some packing boxes and materials rather than ask her father for anything, she and Martha carried the boxes upstairs to her room and she quickly went to see about the sleeping McKnight. It had been her fourth or fifth visit to the room since the incident. She carefully checked him over and departed. Going back to her room, she saw the doctor climbing the stairs.

They said nothing to each other.

In her room, she resumed packing. She wasn't in there long before the doctor cracked the door open.

Apologetically, he said, "Your mother and I really don't want you to leave."

Leslie continued circling the room, saying nothing.

Coming fully in, the doctor said, "Dear, there are times when, using my best judgment as a surgeon, I must make drastic decisions. They are not always easily understood."

Wanting him out of her presence, she said, "*Don't* overlook what I said downstairs, Father."

"It was so reprehensible, how could I?"

"Quite easily. Coming in here with your artificial sympathies and telling me what Mother doesn't want when she is totally incapable of having a single clear thought of her own is reprehensible. What you did to Wyatt McKnight, who you knew had an addiction to narcotics, was reprehensible. *You* are reprehensible."

"What I did for your friend was strictly for his benefit."

She was so fired up by that statement that she could have exploded. Instead, she expressed anger by uncharacteristically throwing an armload of clothes into the packing box without folding them.

"Understand something, Leslie. Mr. McKnight was in pain. I've managed to ease that pain. I should have your gratitude."

"My *what*?"

"Your gratitude. Can't you understand easing *pain*?"

"I understand it a lot more now, Doctor. A hell of a lot more," she said, referring to something else. "As to Wyatt, he could have been helped *without* morphine."

"He was out of control, Leslie. He was paranoid. Schizophrenic. In that state of mind, he very easily could have taken a life. You saw the state he was in."

"We could have used a restraint until the danger passed. We could have tied him up. We could have done anything, *anything* but give him morphine. Giving an addict morphine has got to be one of the most sinister and idiotic things I have ever heard of. Next time, find a rope!"

"Using a rope to restrain a man is not appropriate behavior."

"And giving him morphine *is*?! You're a surgeon, for heaven's sake!"

"Yes, I am. And for your information, giving him morphine is no worse than the heroin he's had. Heroin converts to morphine and binds to opioid receptors."

"Whatever the hell that means," she fired. "But I'm sure its all the more reason you had no right to give him anything! You knew he had an addiction from the moment he walked through the door!"

"I knew no such thing!"

"YES, YOU DID!" she exploded. "And you purposely unlocked and opened that medicine-room door last night, hoping he would come down and find the syringes. From the moment he walked into this house, you were hoping he would fall back to his old ways, and maybe kill himself while doing it! Do you think I'm stupid?"

"I think you're irrational!"

She was too angry to respond.

The doctor looked around the room, as though going back through the years. "Something has happened to us."

Leslie was incredulous. "What _us_?! And how *dare* you!!"

"Again, you're going back to that one issue you brought up downstairs. You're totally ignoring the fact that I've spent a virtual lifetime providing you with a good and loving life."

That did it. She threw the lid of one of her suitcases down. "You call what I had a *'good and loving'* life?! You must be mad! I never had a life! Think about it! From the start, I never *knew* a life. I never knew the *meaning* of the word! I never knew the joy of childhood because you almost destroyed me. That *'act'* — your *art*, that *'issue'* aside, which I _will_ get to, but you almost destroyed me by addicting mother, who couldn't help but pass it along to her child. *You* did it, Father. You did it with your quick-to-jab, dope-'em-up mentality. And because of you, I killed a man! *I destroyed a human being!* I took a *life*. And I was all set to take another one. Will you ever wake up?! Think of the lost years, Father! *The lost years!* They are *gone,* and the bells are still ringing because of what *you* did. And, Father, two doors down the hall there's a guinea pig in there. That's my mother! Look at her and tell me about a *good and loving life.* Look at her and tell me about the pain you've eased! And before you pass your 'medicine' room on the way to meet with your 'colleagues of the board,' go across the hall and look at that shell lying there — that shell that's supposed to house a man; and then, *Doctor,* come back and tell me what you've done for his benefit."

"Dear..."

"*Shut up, Father!*" she fired. "Because your work is not done. Your benefits are not over. You want him to have a transplant! *A transplant?!* You are hideous! Ghastly! You are disgusting! You are abominable! You are gruesome, and you are a *degenerate!* Get out! *OUT!*"

He turned to leave. But he stopped to say something.

"I was wrong."

"You're damned right you were wrong!"

"....I was wrong because I should have aborted you when I had the chance."

23

Had it not been for her ailing guest, Leslie would have been long gone from the house that even at night bespoke the charm of England, the house in which she grew up. She would have been gone, and somehow, some way, she would have taken care of her mother. But neither the mother nor the past were the issues at the moment. Wyatt was.

She had closed out her room and her bags and boxes were packed. Kent had already placed them in her car. Everything that couldn't fit in the car was in the garage. She would send movers for them. She wanted nothing of hers to remain in the house.

She was in McKnight's room, fully clothed on the bed with him, reading and occasionally nodding, while waiting for him to awaken. She had been waiting for hours.

It was a strange tap on the door. It had no force behind it. Leslie thought it was her father, and she would not have responded had the second set of taps not been accompanied by Kent's voice. He was told to come in.

"Ma'am, your father just rang from his room. He would like to see you. He says he has found the rope." He withdrew.

Leslie became angry all over again. She tried to submerge it by going back to the book. It couldn't be done.

A few minutes later she heard her mother's voice coming from the next room.

"Oh, excuse me," said Mrs. Van Horn. "I was looking for Father."

Leslie got up. She was seriously puzzled, because no one should have been in the other room, least of all her mother.

The voice continued, "It's been quite some time since my last injection, and I am seriously in need. Perhaps the children would like some, too. But me first. I am really hurting."

When Leslie opened the door and saw her mother in the wheelchair, she was crushed again. The mother was not talking to a person. She was the only one in the room.

The elegant lady with the fortitude of a lion would be crushed yet again.

Her mother looked up at her, pleading with unknowing eyes.

"Chauncey, dear," she said. "Can you help me?"

Leslie was so hurt that she couldn't cry. With a determination she had never used before, she found herself charging out of the room, going down the hall and almost running up the stairs.

Dr. Van Horn's bedroom was on the third floor, and at that time of night it was dark and brooding. It was unusual for the man of the house to have separated himself as he had done. In a way, though, it was understandable. Mrs. Van Horn was terribly erratic, and he had not slept with her since leaving India those many years ago.

As accommodating as the home was, there was ample room on the second floor for him to have had practically any kind of room he desired. He preferred the third floor. He said it was because it was spacious and that even though there was a library in the house, it allowed room for his many personal books and medical journals. He also said he liked being out of the way, which, admittedly, was odd for a controlling man.

On the way up, Leslie didn't think of that peculiarity. Prior to

McKnight, she had never thought much about any of the doctor's peculiarities. Mostly, though, it was because she had no memory.

As she rounded the landing, a thought did filter through that, in all the years, she had never been in her father's room.

Leslie was wrong. She had been up there before.

She had been carried up there.

She did not remember now, nor would she ever remember that she had been carried up those very same stairs many years ago, and that many years ago, up there, in the very same room where she was headed, had been the start of those *shadows and blurs* she had spoken of; that they had been created there; that those long-ago, memory-destroying shadows and blurs were those of the movements of a man, creating blunt trauma. Repressing a mind.

They were the movements of a man on top of her.

On top of a child.

She was moving swiftly for the door now. First and foremost would be the matter of her mother. Next would be that *"issue,"* that *"act"* she said she would be getting to.

When she placed her hand on the doorknob there was a sort of stiffness to it. She never noticed. She was too fixed on entering to have it out once and for all with her father.

The door gave, and in the dark, the rope that was attached to it snapped the door all the way open. *Whack, whack, whack,* went the rope as it spanked at the air. In a millionth of a second it tightened around the doctor's neck, buldged his eyes, and yanked his feet straight up from the stool he had been standing on.

Had she not fainted, and had there been light in the room, she would have seen that her father was naked, and that his face had been painted black.

Leslie would have seen, too, that there was a look-alike clown in the farthest corner. He was sitting amid pictures of her. There were pictures of her all over the room.

The pictures were from her childhood on.

24

The investigative activity broke a hardened quiet, and it seemed that they stayed longer than necessary, but the police had a job to do. They were thorough.

If Kent or Martha hadn't called the police, McKnight aroused earlier, would have. About an hour after they were called, he was still on his feet, not functioning well, but functioning enough to have been of assistance to Leslie.

He was having a hard time of it, but he remained at Leslie's side, and thanks to him, she was able to ward off niggling questions from the police. Leslie, obviously, had nothing to hide, but she was terribly exhausted. She was also still in shock. McKnight, though unstable, did his best to protect her. The police were understanding, and the body was removed without incident.

The period that followed the body's removal was long and somber. Leslie was drowning in an angered misery. She did her best not to let it show. It was only with the return of the police the next day with their series of routine questions that it appeared she would not make it through with any strength.

Of all the questions that were asked by the police, it was the question *Was he ill?* that had gotten to her. Not to mention his interest in his wife's young nurse, but here was a man who, with pictures of her all around, had hanged himself. He was nude, with a painted black face, and he had been responsible for ruining every life that was in the house, and they had asked her: *Was he ill?*

And to the question, she had answered, *Not that I know of.*

Even in death she was protecting him. She hated — she *despised* — herself for having answered the way she did.

She could have killed herself for saying it.

To fight what she had done, the very next day she made the funeral arrangements. She wanted her father buried as far away from the house as she could manage.

The day had already been rough, because McKnight was not feeling well and he was forced to spend most of it in bed. After looking after him and completing the funeral arrangements, she tried to forget all about her father and busied herself with getting help for her mother, who, it was decided, would not be told of her husband's passing. That was suggested by Dr. Nieves, the friend of hers at St. James Hospital. It was reasoned that the doctor's death probably wouldn't have registered, but with the mind being what it was, one never knew.

Leslie also agreed, reluctantly, that the mother would, for a time, remain on morphine. How long she didn't know.

With Wyatt, of course, it was an altogether different matter. She managed to get medication for him. It was Methadone.

She got a case of it.

It came late, maybe because as a policeman he had an immunity about death, but McKnight eventually became so shocked over the doctor's death — and at his own behavior that had preceded the event — that even he agreed it was time to put his addiction away forever.

The words were said with all the conviction he could muster. Leslie believed him; he believed himself. They knew it was going to be a hard and bitter fight. They knew it was going to be far harder and far more bitter now, since certain feelings had come back to the surface. Addiction was a monster, and if the monster ever resurfaced, hell and all its dominions could not keep it under control. But they were a fighting pair, strong and full of resolve. They both felt — they both *knew* — it was a fight worth fighting, and a fight they would eventually win. It was not impossible. They had come close before, and they should have won. They believed they would have won except for the misdeeds of one man.

He was being buried in the morning.

All that day, though, Leslie was still being haunted by the question, *Was he sick?*

All that night she was still dogged by the answer she had given to the police.

It struck her again. *Not that I know of.*

She would never forgive herself for saying it.

25

The day came. The arrangements were being carried out as per Leslie's instructions. The service was being held miles away from the city of Bath.

The doctor's remains would not be close to the house.

The church stood there mist-like. It made no pretense of being anything but a church. It was small, and it was surrounded by ancient gravestones that were being devoured by the hunger of weeds. Cobble-stones led to a chipped door.

Reverence was inside.

The service was Protestant, and it was not well attended. The doctor had not been a very popular man. Leslie had not notified many people. She had invited Dr. Nieves, but he had declined.

It was understandable.

As he sat there looking around, and feeling strange about being in an English church and, in a way, wondering about the value of soul-stirring moments found in a black church, McKnight recalled that the doctor had said grace at the table that morning after his arrival. He wondered just how religious the doctor had been. Not much, he learned after overhearing two old former patients talking about him as they entered the church.

Several people talked about Dr. Van Horn, and McKnight managed to learn quite a bit about him before deciding to go back outside to see what was delaying Leslie. He also had begun sweating a bit and he needed air.

The wondrous *Panis Angelicus* was being sung when he left. By agreement, he had gone inside without her. It was only proper that she be left alone to think.

Dressed in sober black, she was still sitting in the back seat of the limousine when McKnight came out.

The driver, Fran Rogan, a deserving man with a kind face, had moved away from his vehicle and found a tree to stand under.

McKnight didn't say anything. He stood at the door, which was already open. After a period of silence, and knowing he was there to escort her inside, she said, "I can't go in there."

He took his time asking, "Why not?"

"It's too hypocritical."

"He was not the man you'd want a father to be, but since your mother can't be here, and with no other family member around, I don't think attending his funeral would be hypocritical."

"You never had him as a father," she said. "And you weren't responsible for his death."

"I don't wish to be morbid about this, but I'm sure the death certificate is going to read something like: *'Death by hanging. Self-inflicted.'*"

"Father died because of what I said. And it was me who opened that door."

Now she was angry with herself all over again. Listening to her own words, once again she was protecting him.

McKnight didn't say it to admonish her. It was to help her. "Your father died because of what he was, and what he and he alone had done. And if it's at all important to you, love, his death certainly stunned me into a new reality."

There was no comment. McKnight gave an inward sigh and signaled for Rogan to come and drive them away.

On the start of the fifty-plus miles back to Bath, and breaking a heavily reflective mood, Leslie said, "Even with his name-calling, his petty jealousies, his brutal spite, his gutter thoughts, you didn't hate him. Why?"

"*Why*," McKnight repeated to himself, then thoughtfully said, "I think that at one time I was trying to settle on his childhood; the controlled and controlling little English country boy. The English don't change much, and so I began to think that he was no different than his father. And his father's father. I came back to thinking of who he was. I thought about the very first time we talked. You were upstairs with your mother. We played a little mind game, that's how I got to know him. I learned that he wanted to laugh, but couldn't; he wanted to play but didn't know how. Then suddenly he was old. An old sick man.

"Why did he do what he did?" McKnight continued. "No one will ever know. But I'd bet being loved and incapable of loving in return had something to do with it. Being loveless can make you angry, and striking out can be a lifelong occupation. No, I didn't hate him. I pitied him." He thought about it some more, then said, "Which reminds me: That St. James Hospital. They weren't seriously thinking about letting him come back to do any surgeries, were they? I mean, what was he — in his late 70s?"

"They only called because they wanted to know where to send his old records. They were housecleaning."

"Is that what you found out the day we went there?"

"Yes," she said. "Wyatt, you think Dr. Nieves knew all along? What Father had done?"

"Yes."

"And do you think he knew who, and what, Father was?"

"He had to have known. But you've got to give him credit. He was faced with a horrible, horrible dilemma."

"And by not telling me what my father had done to me, do you think he made the right choice?"

"In a way I think he did; in a way I think he didn't. And you have to consider something else. Maybe he told you and it never registered. Had I been in his shoes, I think that's what I would have done. Maybe he tried to tell you any number of times. Seeing that it wasn't working, maybe he decided never to bring the subject up again."

"Okay, if he hadn't told me, why wouldn't he?"

"I don't know, sweets. Maybe the thought of scandal was on his mind, but I'm sure he didn't report it to the authorities because it was out of concern for your mother. You were not well, and if anything had happened to your father, your mother would've had to have been put away. Forever. Would you have wanted that?"

"I can't bear to think of my mother being put away. Even in the state I was in I don't think I could have borne it. With her incontinence, the loss of body control, and other personal ailments, I don't think she could've made it."

"I think your Dr. Nieves knew that."

She studied the anonymity of the passing scenery for a while and returned with a thought. "Taking one's own life is such a selfish thing to do. What self-serving cruelty. Now he's gone; wandering off some-place—*free*. Mother is still here, still unable to cope. But you mustn't worry, Mother. I will take care of you. *We* will take care of you." She patted him on the knee. "We're coming home to do that, aren't we, Wyatt?"

"After lunch. Tea and scones, maybe."

"And not scones and tea?"

"Nope."

"Good. You still remember."

"Yep."

"There are some cigarettes in the compartment there. Would you like one?"

"No. No, thank you," he said.

"And you're still taking your medication?"

"In double doses."

"I called Dr. Nieves about it. He advised me not to take Mother off medication. But I think I'm going to do it anyway. What do you think?"

"Don't do it. It'd kill her. Her dosage isn't as strong as a person's in the streets, but stopping her now would kill her. It's too late to even try to wean her off."

She digested the advice, and sighed. "Father, I'll get over you; I'll get over what you were. I'll get over your being a liar, a degenerate, cruel; inept. A sonofabitch. But as far as taking your own life and leaving my mother in the condition she's in, never will I get over it. Never will I forgive you. That was a rotten thing to do."

The ride continued in silence. They took in the quiet countryside until they spotted a deep road that led to a virtually hidden restaurant. It was a good thing there was a sign on the road, otherwise they would have missed it.

It was a cozy place. The menu was mediocre, but the view from the patio more than made up for it. The panorama included rolling hills dotted with distant cows, and although it could not be seen from where they were sitting, the very thought of a long, chauffer-driven Rolls Royce parked out front seemed out of place.

Leslie watched as McKnight brought his wine glass down from his lips.

"You have to start all over again. Are you up to it?"

"I would do anything to restore some integrity to my life." He stared out at the peacefulness, relaxed a bit more, and said, "I think I'm going to write a book. It'll be about the life and times of a denying addict."

"Do you have a title for it?"

"'High Today, Gone Tomorrow.' Subtitle: There's No Hero in Heroin."

"I'd like to add a few chapters."

They laughed.

Leslie came up with a thought. She was slow in asking the question. "Wyatt, you said that while you were in rehabilitation someone saw to it that you were supplied with heroin — which I think is outrageous. But isn't that a bit hard to do?"

"Not if you're a bigwig with the police department. It's easy. Find a weak counselor, maybe one on probation from jail — as many of them are — tell him what the deal is, and you're all set."

"Are you saying that someone from the police was responsible?"

"Partly responsible. The rest I could get on my own."

"But why would anyone do that?"

"I was down. I had a commander who wanted me to stay down. What better way to do it than that? Ply me with some cheap Harry, and I'm gone."

"That's contemptible."

"You never knew Ault. He was worse than LeCoultre, the guy you bumped off. He was a lot like your father. Evil. And there's no quitting in evil people." He took a sip of wine. "You know, in thinking about the department, something just occurred to me. I was in such a hurry to get to you, I don't think I handed in my resignation."

"Drop 'em a note. Because you're here to stay — for more reasons than one."

He smiled agreeably. "No offense, it's lovely here, and I will be getting a pretty good pension, but this is not exactly the kind of place I had in mind. And if I stayed active, did you ever stop to think of what I'd do here?"

"Sure. You'd make a great private detective."

He laughed, and they chatted a bit more. Then breezily he sighed, "Aaahhh, the heroin factor. ...What tales of woe it weaves."

Then, much to her surprise, he pushed his chair comfortably back from the table and pulled an encased syringe from his pocket. He had been so casual she couldn't respond normally.

"Wyatt, where on earth did you get that?"

The focus of attention remained on the syringe as he held it up and allowed the contents to ooze out of the needle's point and drip aimlessly down the barrel, and on down to the plunger. A late morning sun peeked from behind a cloud and caused the syrup to sparkle.

"When I woke up after my ordeal, I went to shave. There it was in my kit. Now, whether your father wanted me to think it was from you, I don't know. I seriously doubt it, though. But I do know he intended to kill two birds with one stone. You and me."

"He *what?*"

"He wanted to destroy us both. Interestingly, your father, after he realized we were serious about each other, and after his initial confusion about me, thought everything I did was an act. That is, until he called the police in Los Angeles."

"He called the Los Angeles police?"

"On you. And me."

"How would you know he did that?"

Despite the question, she was still thinking about the little instrument that was oozing the syrup-like substance down its sides. She was thinking, too, about the repercussions without end; the hard fight of an addict, and what on God's earth would she do if he should slip again. She kept an eye on his every move.

"How do you know what he did, Wyatt?"

"Your father introduced me to the guys from Scotland Yard as Captain Wyatt *William* McKnight. There's only one other person alive who has ever used that name. My former commander. He knew I never liked it. Your father had to've talked with him. When you introduced me to him, you never said Wyatt *William*."

"How could I say it? I never knew you had a middle name."

"Neither did your father."

"You have some police files with you, you said. He could have sneaked a look at them."

"Wouldn't have done any good. I never use my middle name. I hardly use the initial. Even at that, I spent a lot of time on the plane blanking out your name and mine. Of course, I don't imagine anyone knowing either of us would've been fooled."

"So why did you do it?"

"I'm the guy who ended up in Paris, remember? I didn't know where I was going, what I was doing, or who I was going to run into.

All I remember is that I was having trouble, and I wanted to be as anonymous as possible. For both our sakes. And if you remember, when we first sat down in that place in the hotel, I even had trouble remembering your name. I was in and out. Confused as all hell. Were all the BPD symptoms taking over again? I don't know."

"Interesting. So, why did Father call the police in Los Angeles?"

"Several reasons. Thinking racially, at first he thought I had shot you or, more likely, I had stabbed you, since knifing had been in the news of late, and black crime makes news the world over. Then he didn't want to believe I was a policeman, let alone a police captain. Next, as a doctor, he knew I was addicted. He wanted to make sure my department knew it and would do something about it, such as calling me back home. Anything to get me away from you. Lastly, and most important, because of me, he wanted to let them know where you could be located."

"To turn me in?"

"To turn you in."

"He would have done that to me?"

"He tried to. But he didn't know procedure. He thought the LAPD would send someone over here. Instead, Scotland Yard showed up."

"And they can still come back?" she asked timidly.

"They could, but they won't. You're set. No need to worry. Nobody's going to approve a budget for the LAPD to come all the way over here on a fishing expedition. What good would it do? Where's the evidence? The gun? I blew that by tossing it back in London. Motive? None. Who's going to testify against you? Who's pushing for case closure, his grieving ex-wife? I don't think so. Even at that, you didn't know what you were doing. You were a sick puppy. I never believed you killed a man. You were getting rid of a symbol."

She put a relieved and gentle hand over his free hand. "Thank you."

"Anyway," he continued, "on the dope angle, your father put me through the test. Again and again. I was addicted. No doubt about it. But the good thing is, I never fell for one of his syringes."

"But he left the medicine-room door open for you, didn't he?"

"And before that, he left one on the dresser. I smashed it to bits."

"I'm proud of you."

"He definitely wanted me on it," he said facilely. "And that night when I lost it, I fell right into his hands."

"But you couldn't help it. You were really sick."

"Boy, was I ever. And I really, *really* needed something to ease the pain. Here we are, days later. The pressure valve has been released. Notice how the memory has improved? And the shakes are gone. It really is relieving; soothing. But I'm not kidding myself. There is a price to pay. That's one of the things that makes it all so goddamned beguiling. That false sense takes you there, then dumps you right at the door. But there's no question, your father knew I was addicted. And he probably knew I would've gone anywhere on the planet to satisfy the need."

"To include coming here to England?"

"Particularly to England. You're here." He touched her hand to reassure her. "Maybe that's why I came, but it's certainly not why I stayed."

"And you're staying because…?"

"Love conquers all. You said it best. We met; we clicked." He diverted his attention from the syringe. "And we're going to keep on clicking. But you want to know something? I wouldn't be surprised if even at this very moment, your father were somewhere waiting for me to take one more hit. And then, solidly re-hooked, frustrated, down-in-the-dumps, and, if I didn't die of an overdose…"

"For which I would be blamed?"

"For which you would be blamed. And if I didn't die, I'd do something like call Scotland Yard, tell them all I know and that I would go back to the States to testify against you, and maybe I'd go so far as to plant this on you or in your purse — and tell them you're holding."

"Good Lord."

"Good Lord is right," he said, lowering the syringe and looking grimly at the remaining contents. "But whatever you had in mind, good Doctor, it is not to be. I am over this. And *we* are over *you*."

With a seldom-seen satisfaction on his face, he wrapped the syringe in a napkin, got up from the table and carefully dropped it into a trash receptacle.

Leslie was terribly relieved that he did. Even though he was calm, logical, and articulate — which may or may not have been because of what her father had done — just seeing the needle in his hand sent cold shivers up her spine

It also kept a disturbing thought alive.

26

They were in Keynsham. It was peaceful. The weather was noble and they couldn't resist taking time out for a brief walk down a country lane. They held hands but didn't talk much. Nature did it for them. Perhaps because he had discharged the contents of the needle without perspiring or dying from want, he felt victorious and as they walked along he wanted to share the feeling with her. He didn't want it to be in a serious way, he wanted it to be light. He wanted to speak through humor. He thought and thought, but there was nothing to draw upon. Maybe he could come up with something later.

When the limousine rolled away from Shaftesbury's, the cute little restaurant that was off the beaten track and struggling to survive because it was, McKnight's mind had shifted back to the syringe. He thought he should have broken it. He didn't know why.

As the car left the lane and slipped onto the main road, he was still wondering why he hadn't crushed the syringe into little pieces. It would be a pity if anyone found it and tried to use it, he thought. The walk had told him that Keynsham, like Bath, Bristol, Kingsmead,

Gloucester and any number of quiet and removed places, didn't deserve the kind of destruction this kind of needle could bring. It could kill a way of life.

Despite her look, and the fact that she was overjoyed by the strength he had shown and by what he had done with the needle, Leslie didn't enjoy lunch as much as she could have. After the initial sip, she never touched the wine. Now, inside the car, she sat with a ruminating look that had started faintly and grew more pronounced by the minute. She, too, had been thinking of the needle.

The key came back: *It lasts for a day, the longest is thirty days.*

She was quiet for a long while. Then, as if having thought it all out, she spoke calmly. "Wyatt, I know that most of what Father said about your condition in the end should be discounted. But I'm thinking. When we were at Cleopatra's Landing that evening in London, you described taking narcotics as euphoric; an *'orgasm that freed, mind body, and soul,'* you said. Do you remember saying it?"

"Something like that."

"And you said every time you took it, your insides soared with a feeling you had never known before. Is that true?"

"Except for loving you," he said. He leaned over and pecked her on the cheek. "But absolutely. There's no other feeling like it. Period. That's why people become addicted. Harry is a world beyond. And morphine is the granddaddy."

"And you got this euphoric and orgasmic feeling each time you used narcotics?"

"I *got* that feeling each time. Past tense. I'm over it."

"To go back to Father, and I can say this because when Kent and I put you to bed the other night, I saw what were obviously needle marks. They were quite numerous. *Frightfully* numerous."

"So?"

"It's a horrid and dreadful thought, but Father said you had been injecting yourself in the groin, in the mouth, between the toes and in other places. Could any of that possibly have been true?"

"It's all true, I'm sorry to say. I'd shoot up any place to avoid detection. I'm lucky I'm not dead. Damn lucky."

"So when you said you were hurting all over, the pain was a direct result of the body needing narcotics?"

"Which, again, I'm sorry to say, started because of being at your house back in Los Angeles. You got me on it, love."

"And when you arrived at the L.A. hospital they checked all over your body and they said you had a number of punctures on various parts of the body."

"Yeah, you really did a number on me."

"And that police report, how long does it say you were at my house?"

"Almost twenty-four hours."

"Talk to me, Wyatt."

It was just that abrupt. In light of what she was saying, she had every right to be that abrupt. She had trapped him, and he knew it. He was trapped by his own admission and the phrase *stay on your game,* and all the phrases in the world wasn't going to change anything. Wyatt W. McKnight had been a user — a hard user — before he had even heard of Leslie Van Horn.

He had to have been.

According to established facts, when he had arrived at the house that night, she had administered a shot or shots that kept him in a coma-like state for something like twenty-four hours. Actually, it was less. But except for firing the gun, he couldn't move. With the type of heroin she was using, *"pure and uncut,"* and mixed with traces of phenylcyclohexylamine along with the California poppy, the genus Eschscholtzia californica, she had administered only two shots, three at most. With the dosage she was using, anything more could have killed him. Mixing it, no matter how slight, according to most chemists, could sear the brain. One shot had been in the ankle, the other in the left leg. Yet it was his arms, groin and legs that he was constantly rubbing. And, according to him and to the reports, punctures were found on other parts of his body. As Devro had observed back in Los

Angeles, the doctors reported that he had been *"jabbed more times than a pin cushion."*

So, then, that night in his apartment before going to the b.c. to meet her; that night when he craved something else, but poured a drink, that night which followed a late afternoon when, under the guise of furthering the investigation in his office, he had looked at the two syringes strangely and carefully and placed them in his desk drawer; that day that followed a night where, at the scene where LeCoultre had met his death, he had retrieved another loaded syringe and still had not turned it over to the property room, the question to him, then, should not have been *Have you ever been tempted?*

The question, always, should have been *How many times have you used?* Moreover, *when did you start?*

"Talk to me, Wyatt," Leslie said again.

Nowhere in her mind was she trying to absolve her guilt. She had been a part of the late stages of his downfall; she acknowledged it, and she was feeling terrible because of it. And she would always be there, fighting for and with him every step of the way. But she had not been the prime source of his suffering. Now what she wanted to know was, what it was they had to fight? How deep was the problem?

"Talk to me, Wyatt," she repeated.

Wyatt W. McKnight wanted to talk to Leslie Van Horn on the ride back. He wanted to say a thousand things to her, but he didn't know if he should — or could. He wanted to say, as best as he could remember, that he had been in and out of hospitals, had had counseling, had been in and out of rehabilitation, and had sought help on his own. He wanted to say that he had purchased this vehicle — he no longer remembered that it was the Spectrum 2010, or, as he had dubbed it, the Big Bad Boy. It was to take him home; back to the simple life, back to the cleanness of his yesteryears, where he didn't have to *know* anything, where he didn't have to *be* anything, where he would be away from temptation; away from junkies, dealers, runners, and people of ill-will; where his only hope was to sit on a crumbling old front porch and rock away his remaining years.

He wanted to say, too, that for a sick man — an addicted man — leaving the bright lights of Los Angeles was fraught with danger; that in leaving, the ease with which that body-seizing, gut-soothing syrup came would be no more; and that as the lights behind him dimmed, the need that was within him would not. Could he tell her that?

Could he say to her that, in trying to escape the hold of narcotics, he knew that on the road he would not always remember where the simple life was, and that there was the fear of becoming ditched in some Godforsaken place and going crazy by not being able to satisfy a need that only God himself could understand?

Could he tell her that he could not remember the details — times, dates, nor places — but he knew that many, many times over the years he had arrested addicts for burglary, for robbery, for holdups; for breaking into pharmacies, medical warehouses, doctors' offices, hospitals, pawnshops, and what-have-you, all because they were answering the call of the monster; that in the morgues of Los Angeles he had seen vacant eyes, darkened teeth, collapsed veins, scabs, scars, boils, abscesses, and punctures so numerous they defied counting?

Was it right to say to her that one night — when the supply Ault had provided had run dry — he lost it, and that he was actually *on the streets* with the dregs of society; that he was *with* the bowel-loose, skeletal-looking addicts; that he actually saw the needle going into the old and worn, and into young muscles that flagged, and into young female bodies that should have been ripe in nubility but had long since kissed firmness goodbye?

Was it the time to say that even among the new he had seen sickness in the faces and hope on the wane — victims of contaminated needles that had oozed black heroin, spread AIDS, occasioned Hepatitis A, B, and C, and gave strength to a flesh-eating bacteria that didn't know when to stop; that old and new, every addict he had ever seen was swearing off the stuff while ready to kill for an euphoria that only the horse could bring; that as a cop, an addicted cop, he could do nothing but arrest them for violating the law — a law that was, at best, ill served? Should he tell her that?

And, lastly, should he say that on the very night he was meeting her he knew full well that the drinks he had had at his apartment would not work, but that just a hint of the contents in the syringes he had left back in his desk drawer at Whitehurst would? — And did?

Got is infinite in his mercy. But it takes two to tango.

"Wyatt, talk to me."
"What do you want me to say, love?"

27

It was a deep and thoughtful ride, heading the rest of the way home.

Allowing Wyatt McKnight the clear benefit of the doubt because when he was young he would sometimes resort to a humor rarely displayed as an adult, and allowing him the benefit of the doubt, too, because perhaps the pain of need commingled with traces of a BPD that bamboozled the imagination should not have come at that time, but rolling past the scenic countryside there was a giant Buddha that loomed up over a pagoda-like building. It was deep in the fields. The question was, was it real? Or was it something deep in the fields of his mind that took him back to the days when he was in the rehab facility in Los Angeles?

With both of them thinking about the ramifications of the earlier conversation, the ride continued in quiet.

It started slowly, from deep inside. His knee started shaking. He dug for his handkerchief and wiped his nose. Soon he started wiping his forehead, as if he had begun to feel a chilly sweat.

"Sweets," he said, sending the free hand into his pocket for a cigarette. "I've got an idea. Remember when you said something like: *If you're in the tunnel, go for the light'?*"

"I remember it well."

"Let's go for the light."

"Meaning?"

"Well, now that I know that a shot won't kill me, and with your father gone, and you're kinda down, let's turn this thing around and go back to that restaurant and get that syringe. Let's go get Harry."

"Turn the limousine around and 'go back and get the *syringe'?*" There was incredulity in her voice. "For what reason?"

"So the both of us could fire it up."

Leslie could hardly believe what she was hearing. "Let me get this straight: You want us to go back and get the syringe so that you *and* me — the *two* of us — could be...*on narcotics?*"

"There is logic to what I'm thinking. And that dose did stabilize my memory. But the only way to truly beat something, is to be close to it. Clicking. Together; one helping the other. Going out on a limb, proving that love conquers all. Even narcotics. *Especially* narcotics. It's supposed to be unbeatable. Let's put it to the test."

She didn't hesitate a second. She pressed the button to roll the limousine's glass partition down.

"Mr. Rogan?"

"Yes, Ma'am?"

"How far are we from the nearest hospital?"

McKnight sputtered, "The *hos*...?"

"How far, Mr. Rogan?"

"At the fork in the road just up ahead, ma'am. It's south to Combe Road. Home is north."

She sat looking at her man searchingly, her arms folded. *At the fork in the road.* Moments passed, and with her eyes still on him, she called up front to the driver again.

"Home north? Hospital south, Mr. Rogan?"

"Yes, ma'am," reaffirmed the driver.

McKnight interjected: "Love, I mean, you *do* know I was kidding?"

"Just as I'm about to kid you?" she said. "Mr. Rogan, head south."

She again locked eyes with the man for whom she cared so very, very much.

The question was: Was she serious? The better question was: Was he?

If she were serious and he did go to the hospital, it would mean little or nothing as far as a cure was concerned. There were narcotics at the hospital, and if he felt so disposed, he would find a way to get them. And, true enough, the cabinets at the house were fully loaded. The doctor had seen to it. And Wyatt McKnight knew it. He knew that the mentally corrupt man could not have departed Earth without that final gesture.

He toyed with the cigarette at eye-level, thought about the unmerciful struggle of quitting, and lowered it to his lap. Easing his head back restfully on the seat, he refocused on the word *habit*. That sent his mind all the way back to that night in his apartment when he was being drawn to her for the first time. Thoughts of music and the Mississippi Delta tried placating the mind, but the call of dope was in the heart. Then, as now, he thought about the awesome power of heroin. Then, as now, he thought about the love of a woman. That, too, was power. But now he no longer wondered which was stronger. As he had said to himself then, he didn't have a choice. Now he did.

It was only a few days ago when his troubled body absorbed that long-awaited hit, and it felt good. *God, Lord-Jesus, did it feel good.* It brought back that first-time sensation of some years ago. He didn't know why he had started on heroin; why he — of all people — would stoop to do such a base, mind-destroying, body-corrupting thing. Curiosity, perhaps? Alternative recreation? Working around it too long? A test of strength, maybe? Stupidity, surely. It didn't matter. It was vile and evil; it was provided by vile and evil people. But the feeling one got then — and each time thereafter, was supreme. It was orgasmic; the summit of all highs. But it did not deserve to be repeated. Plummeting down from that cloud-reaching ladder was pure hell, and

Earth's ground was without mercy. It was ruthless and relentless, offering nothing but stabbing agony and gut-wrenching torment. One minute you fear you're going to die, the next you're praying that you will.

The former Los Angeles police captain toyed with the cigarette longer and allowed his mind to roll with something else he had said to himself in his apartment on that fateful night: *In a life devoid of romance, the question could never be who do you love and when did you start; rather, it has to be what do you love and when did you start loving it?*

With renewed resolve, he ignored the cigarette and looked at the woman beside him. He did it slowly. It had been ever so thought-filled and slow, but his eyes were filled with love and admiration. In his mind, it was ever so clear why he had come to England. The words of the song said it all: *I've Been Loving You Too Long to Stop Now.*

And so a question that had long plagued him did not have to be repeated. The answer was at hand. Or so it seemed. Still there was a fork in the road; and, beyond it, a far more troubling fork. Cursed and brutal; cruel and conflicting, it stretched with a Sisyphean heaviness that only an addict could understand.

In his favor, though, Wyatt William McKnight was a fighting addict.

The limo rolled on. Black and graceful, it appeared benevolent under a midday sun.